I opened my mouth and screamed...

at the top of my voice. A hand was clasped across my mouth for a moment and then some rough cloth was forced between my lips. Someone seized a handful of my hair and, by this means, pulled me painfully out of the chair. Someone ripped the bodice of my dress, exposing my breasts. Two hands grabbed my waist and I was lifted, carried a few steps and thrown onto a bed. Two large hands held me helpless.

I tried to spit the cloth from my mouth, but it was impossible. I found it difficult even to breathe. I raised myself, only to be forced flat again by the man with the hoarse voice. I only hoped it would be quick and not brutal. Fighting was instinctive, but it wasn't going to do any good. What would happen after I was violated, I didn't know. Perhaps I would be killed. But I told myself fiercely that *I must live and find my father and mother so that they'd be warned against beasts such as these!*

The
Magic
Ring

Dorothy Daniels

WARNER BOOKS

A Warner Communications Company

WARNER BOOKS EDITION

Copyright © 1978 by Dorothy Daniels
All rights reserved

ISBN 0-446-82789-4

Cover art by Melissa Duillo

Warner Books, Inc., 75 Rockefeller Plaza, New York, N.Y. 10019

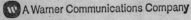 A Warner Communications Company

Printed in the United States of America

Not associated with Warner Press, Inc., of Anderson, Indiana

First Printing: October, 1978

10 9 8 7 6 5 4 3 2 **1**

ONE

I walked slowly down the dark paneled corridor to
Mrs. Gardner's office. I had asked for this emergency interview, but still I dreaded it. A renowned artist, Mrs.
Gardner did not run this school solely for profit. She was
a dedicated woman and resented the slightest interrup-
tion in her teaching plans for any student. I was not one
of the best, though I felt I was improving, but now I was
going to ask for a leave of absence of no definite length.
She would not be pleased.

She answered my knock on the door with a crisp
command to enter. I walked into the room to face the
austere woman behind the spindly but lovely Louis XIV
desk. She was a large woman and when students drew
caricatures of her, they always drew her at this desk, for
the difference in proportions made her appear elephan-
tine.

She was, and not just in my opinion, one of the best
art teachers in the world. She was a noted portrait artist
in her own right, and had paintings of famous people
hanging in many museums over the world.

She watched my approach and, through that uncanny
ability which often enabled her to predict what her pupils
were about to ask, began the interview.

"I am not inclined to grant you any time off, Angela.
I presume that is what you are about to suggest."

"It's my parents, Mrs. Gardner," I explained. "I received a letter this morning. . . ."

"I'm aware of that. Letters and packages from Italy
are not so routine in this small school that they are not
brought to my attention. Is there some trouble?"

"I don't know," I said. "I'm afraid there is. I have a

5

feeling something is wrong and I should go back to find out."

"In that event, I will grant you whatever time off you require." She motioned to a chair beside her desk. "Sit down. I've some comments to make on your work. After you've heard them, it may be you won't even care to return."

I sat down abruptly, both apprehensive and startled. "Oh, Mrs. Gardner, I wouldn't want to leave here now. I feel I'm just coming along."

"You've been with us a year and a half. You're eighteen now . . . plenty of time for you. However, very few leave this school as accomplished artists. I can only start you off. More often than not, I give my students the kind of advice and criticism that frees them from wasting their time trying to paint like Raphael."

"You mean, then," I asked in dismay, "I'll not ever become a good artist?"

"Oh no. You will, no doubt, be quite adequate in most respects. Yet in your work you show a talent that should lead you elsewhere."

I leaned forward. "I don't understand."

"I refer to the way you dress the subjects you paint. I took one of your recent paintings to my dressmaker and had her make up an evening gown matching the one you created for that full-length portrait you did a month ago. The gown was pink. Do you recall?"

"Yes," I said, still mystified. "I will confess I liked it."

"The gown was eminently successful. My dear, we're nearing the end of the nineteenth century and the twentieth is going to be one in which young people like you are going to discard all previous styles, fashions and mores. There is bound to be an important place for someone who can design clothes as you do—in your paintings. We're already moving away from the slow process of making gowns and casual dresses to order. There's a ready-to-wear market growing larger every day and someone has to create styles and fashions for it. Have you followed me, Angela Gambrell?"

"Yes. Yes, indeed," I said quickly. "The idea, though

6

strange, is exciting. However, at this particular time I cannot . . . well . . . act upon what you suggest. This morning I received a letter and package from Florence where my father and mother live. It's a strange letter. The package contained a small gift. I have to read between the lines and I'm frightened. I have a feeling something has happened to my father and mother—or is about to happen. I must go back at once. I only wish it didn't take so long to make the journey."

"Your father is a prominent person, isn't he? Some connection with the Italian government?"

"He is a member of the House of Deputies, Mrs. Gardner. And a banker."

"When you go back, do you think you will still be able to speak Italian? You've been in the United States so many years."

"I live with my aunt—my mother's sister—and we often speak Italian. I still have a good command of the language."

"Go then, Angela, and write me about what you find. I pray your fears are all unfounded."

I rose. "Thank you, Mrs. Gardner. I'm very grateful for your advice. I shall try to follow it."

"Good. Keep in touch with me and come by when you get back. I can put you in contact with people who may be quite useful to you."

I returned to my room and reread for the tenth time the letter that Papa had sent:

My darling Angel:
This will be brief because I am pressed for time. I hope this finds you in good health and you are coming along well in your studies. I am sending you, separately, a little token which you may one day find useful. It is a ring, a unique one. I do believe it is a good-luck ring, a ring that can virtually work magic. Wear it always, but never, under any circumstances, call attention to the ring, even casually. I remark that it has magic qualities. Whatever happens as a result of wearing this ring must be

7

your secret alone. I mean that no one, no matter what the circumstances, must be aware of the nature of the ring.

Now I must reluctantly inform you that your mother and I will be totally occupied with important business that requires constant travel. If you do not hear from us for a considerable time, do not be concerned. I cannot give you an address where you might reach us because we don't know where we will be. Please understand that it is of the utmost importance that we do this.

One final request. Burn this letter promptly after reading it. This is important.

Mama sends her love, as I do.

> Stay well and happy,
> Your loving father

I laid aside the letter which presumably told so much and actually told little, and that which it did tell was full of mystery. I opened the small plush box containing the ring, a cameo set in gold, and removed it. Truly it was a strange ring, rather large and heavy for a girl, but the workmanship was exquisite. The cameo, a woman's profile, was surrounded by beautifully intricate gold filigree. My own experience as an artist told me how difficult this would be to duplicate.

And yet I certainly saw nothing magic about it. Did they still think of me as a child to be told fairytales? I slipped it on the middle finger of my right hand and admired it for a moment, until my thoughts went back to that strange letter. It seemed unfair of my parents to tell me so little, and then not even let me keep the letter. But Papa had said to destroy it, so I would.

I folded the letter, closed my hand around the small bulk it made and went down to the school kitchen. A tin box contained matches and I helped myself to one. I stepped outside into the alley, took time to read the letter once more and commit as much as possible to my memory. Then I struck the match and held it to the edge of the letter. The flames had nearly reached my fingers before

I let the remnant flutter to the ground where it continued to burn until it was entirely consumed. I ground the ash into the earth, then went back to my room. I began packing my clothes and possessions which I would carry home in a carriage.

I slipped out of the building without saying good-bye to any of my schoolmates because I could offer no explanation as to why I was leaving in the midst of the school year. Outside, I hailed a carriage and gave the address where I lived with my aunt, Miss Celestine Guillermo. For the first time, I didn't enjoy the people on the streets, the buildings, or the congested traffic caused by drays, wagons, buggies and the new electric trolley cars which made their noisy, fast and sometimes dangerous way along the middle of the street.

We lived in a fashionable section of Philadelphia. It was an eight-room flat, much too spacious for two people, but Aunt Celestine insisted she required this much room to maintain appearances.

Aunt Celestine was a tall, slim, handsome woman with an aristocratic bearing. She possessed a rather long nose which she considered distinctly Roman and of which she was quite proud. Since mine was identical she frequently reminded me I should be also. My reply was always the same: I would greatly prefer a straight one. She would then go into a lecture about my heritage to which I listened patiently, but I never changed my mind. Her face was lean, her eyes were large and very dark. She had long, raven hair, center-parted and worn in a thick braid intricately coiled at the base of her neck. Like many Italian women she wore black almost exclusively, but her clothes were as fashionable and chic as she.

I loved her as much as I did my own parents. Perhaps more, for I saw her every day and she gave me the love and guidance my parents would have, had I been raised in their care. However, I had not seen them in seven years. I was four when they placed me in her care. For fourteen years I had been away from home and the city of Florence was as strange to me now as Lisbon or Calcutta where I'd never been.

When I let myself into the flat, Aunt Celestine came

imperiously out of the kitchen. She did not like surprises.

"You have been expelled," she said sharply. "What else would bring you home without warning?"

"I have not been expelled," I told her, "and you very well know that. There is going to be a change in my plans, however, but we won't go into that now. This morning I received a letter from Papa. A very strange letter. . . ."

"Indeed. What was strange about it? I too received a letter from him. He is well, my sister Rosa is well. They are going to be busy for some time and unable to write while they are traveling. This is not unusual."

"You don't believe that," I challenged her.

"And why should I not? Your papa is a public official, also a man of finance. His civic duties, his banking position require him to travel. He is never separated from your mama if he can help it, so she travels with him. There will be no time for letters, and he says so frankly."

"Aunt Celestine," I said patiently, "I am now eighteen years old. I was sent to the United States when I was four, to live with you. I have been here ever since. During that time Papa and Mama came here to see me only once briefly. They are kind and loving people, yet they sent me into exile at a time when they should have enjoyed their only child. Why did they do that? Have you an answer?"

"Of course I have. Your father is an ambitious man, your mother no less so. She did not have time to bring you up properly and she turned to me. They didn't want you to have to travel as they did. I was a lonely woman, never having married, so I was happy to have a child to love and care for. Does that satisfy you?"

"No, because I don't believe it," I said calmly. "No loving parents would consider their only child as being underfoot and a deterrent to their own ambitions. They are not selfish people and you know it. There is another reason and it frightens me, because I do not know what it is. I think you do."

She lapsed into Italian. "I swear by my soul and my heart, I swear there is no other reason. You, little one, are suspicious by the nature of your few years. You daydream and not always pleasantly. Now have done with this foolishness."

"I'm going home," I said softly.

"You *are* home." Her brows raised slightly as a sudden thought occurred to her. "*Caro Dio,* surely you are not thinking of going back to Italy?"

"Yes, Aunt Celestine. I am leaving as soon as I can make the arrangements."

"Why? What makes you take such a drastic—and expensive—trip?" My decision had upset her as much as Papa's letter had upset me.

"Because I feel there is something wrong and I must satisfy myself one way or the other. As for expenses, Papa sends me more money than I can use. He is a wealthy man, is he not?"

She eyed me impatiently. "He is not a poor one."

"Our home in Florence is a *palazzo,* is it not?"

"*Si,* a *palazzo.* Not the biggest, but not the smallest either."

"Then the expense will not count. I'm not asking you to go with me, but this is something I must do."

"My child, have you thought this all through? You are not a citizen of the United States. There are quotas now, not too liberal for Italians. Not as free as when you came fourteen years ago. They might not let you back."

"I will risk that."

"But your studies. You have the talent to become a great artist."

"Aunt Celestine, where in all the world do the greatest artists in history come from? Where, except perhaps Paris, is art so well practiced as in Italy? I am going. Nothing you can say will dissuade me."

Celestine, who had moved to the edge of her chair, now leaned back in surrender and resignation, reverting to English. "There may be important reasons why you should not go back."

"What?" I asked bluntly.

She shrugged. "Now, how do I know? I say that because of the way I feel about your father's letter. If he

11

wanted you back, he would have said so. In plain words, he told you *not* to come back and *not* to worry about him."

"Which is precisely why I do worry and why I will go back. I repeat, you can't talk me out of it, Auntie."

She was not giving up. "It is a long journey. Not a pleasant one."

"Today's steamships are comfortable."

"But you are very young and very desirable. There will be men who will annoy you. . . ."

I laughed aloud. "I can manage such men. I will be on a ship and the captain and crew will see that I am not troubled."

"In Italy you will meet young men who are the most ardent lovers in all creation. Italian men are skilled in the art of love. An innocent girl like you will have no chance. . . ."

I laughed again. "Auntie, you make Italy sound most interesting."

She eyed me with feigned impatience. "You are incorrigible," she said brusquely. "I disown you."

I went to her quickly, bent and kissed her. "I'm flattered, darling Aunt Celestine. You used to say I was placid and unromantic."

She smiled and her arms went around me. I knelt and placed my head on her lap, as I used to do when I was a child. "I do love you, Auntie, and I respect you for being wise in all things. No doubt your advice is also wise, but I cannot accept it. I must go and see for myself."

"*Si*, I know this. I have never been in full approval of . . . no matter." She waved her arms as if to dismiss an unpleasantness. "I send you with my love and my prayers. It may be you will need them, especially the prayers. There is a ship leaving New York in two days. I reserved for you a first-class cabin, with instructions that you are to be closely guarded every moment and any who might try to molest you should be thrown overboard."

I stood up accusingly. "You knew all along that I was going."

"*Si*. I know you. Perhaps your father will have my

12

head for this, but I feel you should go. To tell you the truth, I'm worried myself. May I see your letter?"

"I burned it, Auntie. The letter instructed me to."

"Mystery on mystery," she said. "I too burned mine, for I was also instructed to do this. Well, we must get you ready. There is packing to do. I shall send a coach to verify your passage. And pay for it. If you need clothes, there is not much time. I will go to New York and wave as the ship sails."

"You will not come with me?"

"I cannot. Your father instructed me long ago not to return under any circumstances. Come back to me, angel. I will be a lonely woman until you do."

"I will. I could never forget the love and kindness you gave me when my own Papa and Mama were unable to do so. If there is a quota that refuses me entrance, I will swim."

With Auntie's help, I was packed before supper and late that night we left for New York by train. There we checked into the Waldorf-Astoria and after a few hours of rest we visited department stores, particularly B. Altman's where it was possible to buy stylish, ready-to-wear traveling dresses. While I watched the models parade before me, I became more than ever aware that Mrs. Gardner was probably right and my field lay, not in brush and canvas, but in the exciting and creative field of fashion design.

I sailed at midday, with Aunt Celestine tearfully waving good-bye from the pier. I waved back until I could no longer see her. Then, sadly, I made my way back to my cabin. This was a fast ship, but it would take days and I was young and eager—and worried.

While the ship maneuvered out of the harbor, I sat in my cabin, slowly turning the ring on my right hand around and around. I'd followed Papa's instructions and I'd not even told Aunt Celestine about it. I wished the ring was magic enough to whisk me to Florence and to provide me with all the answers I sought.

Still restless, I stood up and walked over to the mirror. I removed my hat and set it on the dresser while I regarded my reflection. My cheeks were flushed with excitement, or was it fear? I wished I were tall like my aunt, but I was a mere five feet three. However, I was careful to choose clothes that gave the illusion of height. My best feature was my eyes, which were deep-set and a dark brown. And while my smile was pleasant, I would never be tempted to paint a self-portrait, for my face was round, with no bone structure visible. I realized my aunt spoke the truth when she said I would never be the ravishing beauty my mother was. I smiled at the thought of my reunion with her and Papa.

TWO

Florence was a lovely city, ancient and beautiful. Thanks to Aunt Celestine, my Italian was sufficiently fluent to let me understand and to speak well enough. At the dock I summoned a vehicle from the line of carriages, had my luggage placed aboard it and gave the driver the address of the Gambrelli *palazzo*. I doubted that my parents would be there, but it was the place to begin my search for them.

Passing through the streets, I became lost in the loveliness of the city, despite its crowded, noisy streets. Certainly this was not like Philadelphia, but then I never thought it would be. My carriage driver, in the belief I was a rich American tourist, gave me a running history of the buildings we passed, augmented by comments on the city government which, he was sure, was lacking in consideration of the citizens, especially the carriage drivers.

When we pulled up before the large, marble-fronted structure set back from the street, there was no flash of recognition in me. I'd completely forgotten the place where I was born.

I asked the driver to wait. If Papa and Mama were away, the house might be locked up and I'd be unable to get in. I climbed the four wide granite steps, crossed the marble veranda and yanked the heavy pull beside the great double doors. The clamor of the loud bell was evident even out here on the veranda. For a moment there was only a discouraging silence. Then I heard footsteps and I braced myself for the meeting with my father, or mother, for the first time in seven long years.

The door opened and a maid in a trim uniform waited for me to identify myself.

15

"I am Angela Gambrell."

"*Che?*" The name made no impression.

"My father and mother live here," I said, trying not to sound impatient. "This is my home."

Her eyebrows arched. "*Che cosa?*"

"Signore and Signora Gambrell." I spoke slowly and even managed a smile, though I was puzzled and beginning to feel a faint irritation.

"*Niente,* Signorina. This is the *palazzo* of Signora Perriti. You have made a mistake."

I said, "I was born in this house. My parents live here. What are you trying to tell me?"

She shrugged. "Signore and Signora Gambrell do not live here."

I decided to waste no more time. "Then I would like to speak with Signora Perriti."

The girl stepped aside dutifully. "Come in, Signorina. I think, perhaps, that you have the wrong address. I will ask Signora to see you."

I walked into the *palazzo*. It was a lovely home, very spacious, furnished with good taste, and completely unfamiliar. I left the reception hall and entered the drawing room. Over the white tiled fireplace where I expected Papa's portrait would hang, there was the painting of a buxom woman. I had no idea who she might be.

When I heard footsteps, I turned and found myself facing the woman in the painting. Her smile was gracious, though puzzled.

"Good afternoon, Signorina," she said. "My maid tells me you believe your parents live here. Are you sure you have the right address? Though you speak our language, your costume identifies you as an American. Sometimes our addresses are confusing to foreigners."

In fluent Italian I said, "Signora, I am Italian. I have lived for years in the United States, true, but I am still an Italian. I did live here—in this *palazzo*. Many years ago, with my parents."

"But you say your papa and mama live here now. How can that be? Did your parents not emigrate to America with you?"

"It's not easy to explain," I said, "but I'll do my best.

16

You are right. I am confused, though not about the address."

"Please sit down. I will be of assistance to you if I can."

"Thank you," I said gratefully. After I was seated, she took a chair opposite me.

"My husband and I have lived here for twelve years or more," she informed me. "How many years ago since you were here?"

"Fourteen," I said. "I was sent to live with my aunt in America. Always I sent letters to this address. I never heard that my parents had moved."

"It must be confusing for you, my dear. As for the letters, I have no recollection of them being delivered here. But then, neither do I remember who owned this house before we did, but I'm sure if I looked among my husband's papers, I might find out. Will you excuse me for a few moments while I try to solve your problem for you?"

"Of course. I am sorry to put you to such trouble. . . ."

"My dear, if I can solve this mystery for you, it will certainly be no trouble. Now . . . the name again? Your father's name."

"Gambrell. Luigi Gambrell."

"I will not be long, I'm sure."

She walked quickly from the room and I heard her going up the grand staircase at the end of the reception hall. I looked about once more. It came to me then that a room is just a room and its identity and character are created by the furnishings and decorations. My eyes vainly sought out something that could stir my memory. Nothing did. Perhaps I never had lived here. After all, fourteen years is a long time and I was only four when I left for America. I would have liked to inspect the rest of the house, but I was straining the hospitality of my hostess now, putting her to all this trouble.

She returned with a legal-looking document that she handed to me. "You are correct. Once this house was owned by a family named Gambrelli. That is a slightly different spelling from. . . ."

"Forgive me," I said. "My aunt insisted I drop the

17

last letter to make it sound more American. I've always used the name Gambrell." I scanned the document. It was a bill of sale dated thirteen years ago and it was signed by my father as the seller. I handed the document back.

"I'm most grateful, Signora. I cannot explain this. Forgive my intrusion and again, please accept my thanks."

"It was nothing," she said. "I wish I could have been of more help. Perhaps my husband could be, but unfortunately he is in Rome and not due back for some time."

"I shall go to the police," I said. "They must have a record of my parents."

"Truly I am sad for you, my dear. It may be they are dead and no one ever notified you or your aunt. You should be prepared for this."

"No," I said confidently. "I've heard form Papa and Mama many times since."

"That is well. No doubt the police will find them for you. If you are in need of more help from me, you have only to call again. I'll be happy to see you . . . and to learn what did happen."

I left the house thoroughly confused and frightened.

The headquarters of the local *Carabinieri* was a large white granite building with imposing wide steps and entrance. Once again I instructed my driver to wait and, as he seemed slightly doubtful, I gave him a substantial sum of money. He settled down contentedly and I entered the building to be confronted by a young policeman at the information desk.

"I wish to speak to someone about my parents, who seem to be missing."

"Signorina has lost her papa and mama?" He chuckled at the idea. "We look for lost children, not parents. Why don't you go home and wait until they come back?"

"You don't understand," I said patiently. "I've come from America, but my home here has been sold and nobody knows where my parents are. There must be some kind of record."

The officer picked up a pencil. "Your father's name, then."

"Luigi Gambrell. I mean Gambrelli."

"You seem uncertain. . . ."

"I can explain that. Please send me to someone who can help."

"You can file a report with me and we'll do what we can."

"That's not enough. I need information. From records, perhaps . . ."

"Signorina will file a report." He grew stolid and cold. "We will then look into it."

"Please," I implored him. "I want to talk to someone in authority."

"I have authority enough! Now do as I say. I will provide you with a blank. . . ."

Someone moved up beside me. The young officer promptly drew himself up and paid the utmost attention.

"What is wrong here?" the man at my side asked.

I glanced at him, hoping against hope that I would find someone sympathetic to my needs. The man was perhaps twenty-eight, tall, slim and handsome. His dark eyes regarded me with interest. His ample mouth was one great smile, his teeth were even and beautifully white, his manners excellent. He bowed slightly.

"May I be of assistance, Signorina?" he asked.

"Thank you," I answered. "I'm trying to find my parents."

"It is a missing persons case, sir," the young officer tried to explain.

"Let the Signorina speak for herself," the tall man said authoritatively.

"*Si. Scusa,* please." The young man lowered his gaze.

"I am Vito Cardona. Of the *Carabinieri.* An inspector, if you please."

"Thank heavens," I said. "Now perhaps I can be understood. I have lived in the United States for fourteen years, ever since I was four. My parents sent me there. My father is Luigi Gambrelli. Once, seven years ago, he and my mama came to visit me, the only time I saw them in all those years."

"There was trouble between you, perhaps?"

"No. No, not at all. I loved them and they loved me.

19

I don't know why they sent me to America except that Papa was such a busy man. Oh yes . . . he was once a member of the House of Deputies and spent much time in Rome."

"A deputy? Gambrelli . . . yes, the name strikes a note. Please go on. Or better yet, let me take you to the local chief. We can talk there."

"Thank you. I am grateful for your kindness."

"We are here to do what we can, Signorina," he said in flawless English. He was so amused at my gasp of surprise that he smiled, then laughed aloud. It was pleasant laughter, very masculine and very kind. As quickly, he sobered and spoke.

"Oh yes, I speak English with ease. I went to college in the United States. In fact, I grew up there, just as you did. Perhaps I'll tell you the whole story some day, but first we must find your parents."

He escorted me to a large, nicely furnished office where a man in a somewhat gaudy uniform rose to greet me. Inspector Cardona made a quick, crisp explanation of my problem.

The chief seemed impressed. "Of course I have heard of Deputy Gambrelli. It is some years since he was an elected official, but I remember him as a quite famous man and a fine public official. Now tell me the rest of it, Signorina."

I gave him every detail, save the fact that I'd had a letter from Papa not ten days ago. I also refrained from saying anything about the ring, with its supposed magical powers.

"It seems strange they never told me they'd moved. Stranger still that for years I sent my letters to that address. I feel there is something terribly wrong."

"Now be calm, Signorina," the chief ordered. "A man as well known as your papa cannot simply have disappeared. Everything will be explained in due course. In the meantime, I suggest, Inspector Cardona, that you escort the Signorina to a fine hotel and see that she is made very comfortable."

"My pleasure." Vito Cardona smiled. "May I invite you to supper, Miss Gambrell?"

"I would like that," I said. "We can talk and perhaps come to some conclusion."

"We can hope. Even so, it would be my pleasure."

"You will hear from me in due time," the chief assured me. "*Arrivederci, Signorina.*"

The sleepy driver came to attention when he saw my escort. Apparently, Inspector Cardona was well known in Florence.

He directed the driver to take me to a small but luxurious hotel. That he had influence here too became quite apparent, for I was quickly installed in a beautiful suite of rooms while Inspector Cardona waited in the lobby.

I hastily changed from my traveling dress to a simple dinner gown, one that suited my figure and my complexion well. It was a nile green silk tarlatan over nile green taffeta. The decolleté blouse had large revers with insertings of fine lace. The folded belt was of mauve velvet. Other than long gloves, my only adornment was a string of pearls.

When I returned to the lobby, Inspector Cardona rose from the chair he'd occupied and I could see by the expression on his face that he approved of my gown.

"Truly you are beautiful," he told me. "I thought so before, but now . . ." he stepped back a pace to admire the gown, ". . . even more so. I shall be delighted to take you to supper. Right here, if that suits you. The restaurant is exceptional."

"I'd like that. I'm quite tired," I admitted.

"I promise not to keep you up late. Of course I shall see you again. In the line of duty," he added, his smile friendly.

"I will appreciate whatever help you give me, Inspector."

"Please . . . titles bore me. My name is Vito."

"I like it. I am Angela."

He took my arm lightly. "This will be a great opportunity to talk and I can perhaps learn things that may help us find your papa. Shall we speak English? This is a rare chance for me to see if my English has lasted as well as I believe it has."

We were led to a fine table, somewhat secluded, so

21

we could talk without being distracted. Vito ordered wine to be served at once. While we waited for it, we studied the menu and gave our supper order. I noticed Vito selected a main course that I knew would take time to prepare. I suppose this was what my aunt meant when she warned me about romantic Italians. A fact I enjoyed. I'd never had much opportunity to be with young men; Aunt Celestine was extremely strict. While we sipped our wine, he asked me about myself. His questions seemed more friendly than official, but at last he asked gently, "When did you hear from your papa last?"

I decided to be honest with him. "Ten days ago. The tenor of his letter led me to believe there was some kind of trouble, so I decided to come back and find out. I'm more convinced than ever that my suspicions were right."

"Ten days ago?" he said thoughtfully. "That does make it a strange situation. Before that, how often?"

"Once a month at least. I always answered and he received the letters too, because I recall he would comment on something I'd written about. Yet the Signora stated she had no recollection of my letters coming to that address."

"I cannot comprehend this yet," Vito admitted. "We will find the answers, never fear. He was, I think, a well-to-do man."

"I have always assumed he was."

"At least you do not have that problem then. I take it he provided for you."

"All my expenses and spending money were handled by my aunt. She was most generous and from time to time my father would send me a check. I presume he also reimbursed Aunt Celestine for what she spent on me."

"He and your mama were both well? No illness that might send them to a sanitorium. Perhaps one needed care and the other went along. Some sicknesses take years to cure."

"I'm sure Papa would have written me. At the very least he'd have let my aunt know if he didn't wish to worry me."

"Yes, of course he would have. I'm only examining

22

as many aspects of the case as I can. He and your mama were devoted?"

"Extremely so."

"That is good. I'm sure we shall get to the bottom of it and find them. Now I want you to enjoy the evening. At least, the food and the surroundings."

I smiled. "And my escort."

He gave me a look of feigned concern. "I hope so."

Our supper came and we enjoyed it over light conversation. I learned that Vito, like me, came from a prominent family who sent him abroad to study.

"They were disappointed at first," he told me. "I think they wanted me to study law, but I was more interested in catching criminals. The work fascinates me and before I came back, I saw to it that I was well instructed in police work. I joined the *Carabinieri* and I rose in rank swiftly because few of our officers have a great deal of training."

"I'm glad you're interested in your work, Vito, because I'm going to be too. As I told you, I've already given serious thought to going into fashion designing. Once my parents are found and the mystery is solved, I shall stop in Paris to learn what I can there."

"Why not in Rome as well? We have stylish women in Italy. Though you've probably not been here long enough to notice."

"Oh, but I have. I see some stunning gowns in the dining room."

"Yours is the loveliest," he said gallantly. "And you are the most beautiful woman here."

I felt color flood my face. "I have never received so many compliments in one evening."

"Then obviously you've spent little or no time in the company of the opposite sex."

"You're flirting with me, Vito," I said, sobering.

"Yes," he admitted. "Italian men have a weakness for that. However, I must confess you have made quite an impression on me."

"Not the wrong one, I hope," I said stiffly.

Again he laughed and I felt vaguely uneasy at the way it stirred me. "Please don't be offended. I admire your courage in traveling across the ocean alone, and your concern for your parents."

We said good night in the lobby and he held my hand a little longer than one would consider proper in the States. I slipped my hand free and walked the few steps to the elevator. I thought once again of my aunt's statement regarding the romantic nature of Italian men. I chided myself for responding to his flattery like a foolish schoolgirl.

Once I was in my suite, the enchantment of the evening was gone. I felt suddenly lonely and overwhelmed with concern for my parents. Nothing made any sense.

The next morning I checked directories at the library. I studied the activities of the House of Deputies in Rome and, sure enough, Papa's name was among the most illustrious of these politicians, but his term of office had expired years ago. Apparently he'd not sought re-election. From his record, it was obvious that he could easily have remained in his post.

These records, however, did nothing to reveal what his personal life had been like, or where he could possibly have gone after his term was over.

And so I turned to bank records. There I found his name as chairman of the board of a large banking enterprise. He was listed right up to the year when he'd dropped out of politics. It seemed he had abandoned his banking connections and his political career simultaneously. Something drastic had happened then. Was it so serious as to cause him to go into hiding?

Vito came in time to take me to supper, all part of his plan, I suspected. I had no objections. When I was with him, I forgot my loneliness and some of my worry. I felt if anyone could find my parents, it would be he.

But his news was neither enlightening nor promising.

"Your father and mother," Vito told me, "seem to have dropped out of sight years ago. For reasons nobody seems to know, your father did not choose to run for the House of Deputies again though his accomplishments there were exceptional and he could easily have been re-elected. Soon after his term expired, he resigned

24

from the bank. All we can discover after that is that he was seen about the city and observed a few times in Rome. Then he and your mama . . . vanished."

"What of the *palazzo* where I believed they were living? I addressed all my mail there. It seems unbelievable that the present occupants didn't receive it."

"They swear they know nothing. I have no reason to doubt their statements, for they are well respected and would have no reason to lie."

"What of the servants? Could they have intercepted it for Papa? I know he received my mail, for in his replies he frequently commented on things I'd told him in my letters."

"The servants have been checked carefully. I confess your parents' whereabouts is a complete mystery—one most difficult to explain. However, I can tell you this—the last time your parents were seen, they made several purchases in one of the big stores in Rome. We found the man who drove them there in a hired carriage. They told him not to wait. Oh yes . . . they maintained an address in Rome, as all the Deputies do."

"I didn't know that," I said petulantly. "Why would they have kept it from me? Did they leave any of their possessions in Rome?"

"Nothing," Vito said. "Your papa closed out his account in one of the banks. I learned that they believed he was going to return to Florence and resume his life there. The trail of your parents ends at the department store. That is the last place they were seen."

"Then is there nothing we can do to find them?" I asked in dismay.

"We have not given up. Rome authorities are working on it and will continue to do so. Your papa was an important man. No doubt you will be asked a thousand questions before this is over."

"The letters I received from them . . . saying nothing about this . . ."

"I cannot explain that, Angela. I wish to heaven I could, for your peace of mind. As for now, we're at an impasse, but sooner or later something will turn up.

Some small thing to give us a start. Once that happens, we'll find them."

"Vito, do you think they are dead?"

"If so, they were not buried under their own names. Nor were they admitted to any large hospital. We have begun to check this aspect, but nothing has come up so far. Of course, it does take time, but then the name was well known and important. People would have remembered. In my opinion, they are alive. After all, you received a letter from your papa. You may be assured we're working to solve the mystery of your parents' disappearance."

"I appreciate what you are doing. I suppose I am becoming more alarmed than I should because I am completely alone."

"Not completely." Vito spoke with quiet reassurance.

I managed a smile of appreciation. "You're very kind, Vito. I was thinking of my Aunt Celestine. I miss her terribly." A sob escaped me.

He reached across the table and covered my hand with his. He squeezed it gently. "Of course you do."

I swallowed hard, forcing back the tears that threatened.

Vito spoke softly. "When I told you I would see you often, I didn't mean it would be entirely business. I've never met anyone like you, Angela. I admire your courage, your tenacity and, of course, your beauty."

"I'm not beautiful," I said in all honesty, for my nose was distinctly Roman and, therefore, long and slightly humped.

"To me you are. There's a quiet beauty about you, a radiance that I sense each time I look at you." He paused. "You have that rare quality—an inner beauty—that draws people to you. Perhaps because you like people. You do, don't you?"

"Yes." I managed a smile, knowing he was trying to cheer me. "My Aunt Celestine used to say, look for the good in people. All of us have a little bad, but you can forget that when you learn the good points."

"I'd like to meet your Aunt Celestine."

"You may one day. If you went back to America. I doubt she would come here."

26

"Why not?" He seemed surprised at this revelation.

"She loves her adopted country. So do I. I hope one day to be a naturalized citizen of the United States."

He nodded and his smile was a little sad. "I was hoping you would never wish to return. I am serious, Angela. With each passing moment I find myself falling in love with you. I could put that in stronger language, but this is not the proper time for you."

"No, Vito. My parents' disappearance consumes my every thought."

"Then we shall get back to my reason for being with you. Do you have any other relatives here?"

"There is an uncle, Aunt Celestine's brother Carlo. I can't recall where he lives. His name would be Guillermo."

"Tomorrow I shall send your aunt a cable and ask her where to find him. Perhaps he would know something. It's well worth trying."

"Of course it is. I'll repay the expense of the cable."

"That is official business. It will be paid by my government."

"I must admit I'm once again grateful. You see, I have some money at home and I can send for it, but it is not a great amount. Naturally I thought I'd surprise Papa and Mama and money would not be of any importance. Now it seems it may be."

"There is no need to worry," he assured me.

"But this hotel is so expensive."

"*Si*, but I have arranged that it will also be paid for out of police funds. You are most important to our investigation and we cannot hope that you will be here to help us unless we undertake some of the expenses. You may be certain there will be no bill."

"Are you sure you're not paying for this?" I asked.

"Me? On my pay? Oh no, my dear Angela. Even our delightful suppers are paid for."

"I'm sure," I said, "that I would not be this well treated in Philadelphia. And I do appreciate your concern—and help."

"It's my duty," he said. "For once it happens to be pleasant. I refer, of course, only to you and not the circumstances which brought us together."

"I wish there was something to go on. It seems there is nothing I can do except wait. And yet the very thought angers me. They were highly respected. They led clean, decent lives. But something must have happened to cause them to vanish as they did. Everything is so unreal . . . as if it couldn't have happened. Yet it did, under circumstances that give us nothing to go on when we try to find them."

"I know, Angela. Tomorrow I'll go back to work on this. We'll soon have an answer."

Back in my room, I prepared for bed. I was tired, sick with apprehension, puzzled by the whole thing. The only person I had to help me or understand my problem was Vito, and his role was that of a police officer. Still, he had made it evident at supper that he was beginning to regard it as more than just another police case.

I enjoyed his attention and his charm, but I was scarcely in a mood to ponder the question of whether or not I could return the affection he felt for me and which he'd expressed so discreetly. Vito was handsome, nice to be with, attentive and gracious. If his attentions became too obvious, I would have to do something about it, but at the moment I was too dependent on him as a police officer of some stature to shy away from him.

I sat by the window overlooking the small, colorful and, by day, noisy square. Certainly this was not staid and formal Philadelphia, but I knew I loved both places.

I began thinking back, tracing everything from the moment I received Papa's letter, and the ring which he called magic. I moved the ring around my finger and wondered when it was going to show me its power, if there was any.

There was a sharp knock on my door. I hesitated before rising to answer it. No one here knew me except Vito and if it had been he, I knew him well enough to be sure the knock would have been accompanied by his voice.

It came again, followed by a man's voice.

"Signorina, it is a bellboy with an urgent message."

I sprang to my feet and reached the door in a few seconds. I had only taken time to throw a robe over my shoulders. When I opened the door, one of the hotel employees faced me, holding out an envelope.

"Signorina, this message came by hand a moment ago. It is marked important and deliver at once."

I told the boy to wait while I returned to the bureau. I opened my purse and took out some change. I gave him the tip, accepted the folded paper, closed the door and quickly carried the message to the lamp beside the bed. There were two lines neatly printed by hand on the paper.

. TO LOOK FOR YOUR FATHER, GO TO 1160 GIOVANNI STREET AT ONCE. IMPORTANT.

I dressed as rapidly as possible, consulted the note once more to memorize the address, then left it on the bureau. I hurried downstairs, mentally complaining about the slow lift, and made my way across the lobby to find a carriage at the door. This late at night there was no doorman and only a scant staff of sleepy hotel employees. It didn't matter. I had, at last, been given a clue. I felt my voyage across the ocean had not been in vain after all. In my mind, I was already conjuring up pictures of a joyous reunion with my parents.

THREE

I gave the driver the address I'd memorized, settled back in the carriage and drew up the collar of my lightweight coat for at this time of night, Florence was definitely cool. The streets were quiet, the city slept. I felt a great upsurge of hope and my heart pounded in anticipation.

Deep in my own thoughts and my hopes, I didn't pay attention to where the driver took me, though I realized the streets had narrowed and the business area had been passed by. So had most of the luxurious homes and we were now in a more modest part of the city.

The carriage pulled up to the curb and the driver jumped down from his seat to help me out. He indicated a private dwelling where all windows were dark except for a pale semblance of light which slipped through the small panes of glass set on either side of the front door. I asked the driver to wait. If, by some cruel quirk of fate, this turned out to be a false message, I would need him.

I ascended the three steps leading onto the porch while the driver got aboard the carriage. As I approached the door, it opened and a woman, all in black, with a thin, wrinkled face and dark, unfriendly eyes, let me in without a word.

She closed the door and motioned that I was to sit down in a chair she pointed out. Then she left me. I tried to look about and see what sort of place this was. Two candles in an inexpensive chandelier hanging from the ceiling dimly illuminated the room—there were more shadows than light.

I began to grow nervous, for the silence in this house was making me apprehensive. If Papa had sent for me, if he was in this house, he'd have come bounding down the stairs at the end of the short hall. Or Mama would have called to me and reached my side in a moment. Instead, there was nothing, only this eerie silence.

The chair on which I sat was close to a doorway that I imagined led into the parlor. It was from this room that a rush of feet preceded my being suddenly seized from one side and, before I could get even a glimpse of this rough-mannered individual, a blindfold was tied over my eyes.

I cried out in alarm. "Please . . . please, what's the meaning of this?"

A man spoke softly, his mouth close to my ear, for I could feel the warmth of his breath against my cheek.

"Signorina will not struggle or cry out. We do not wish to gag you, but if necessary we will. *Capisce?*"

"Where is my father?" I demanded. The man was holding my right hand and my right elbow in a tight grip indicating if I tried to get free, I would likely break my arm.

"We wish to ask you questions, Signorina, about your father. We do not wish to harm you in any way. I shall now help you up the stairs to a room where someone is waiting."

"My father?" I demanded. "Is he here? Answer me!"

"No, he is not here, but with your help we shall find him."

"Who are you?" I asked. I was being propelled along until we reached the stairs and I was warned to climb them with the man crowded at my side.

There was nothing I could do to resist. If I screamed, I sensed that I would be quickly and, perhaps, painfully silenced. I had no idea what was in store for me, but it concerned my father and therefore I'd be wisest to see it through. I stumbled up the stairs.

I heard a door open. My captor whispered something. I was led into a room and I felt the edge of a chair move against my legs. I was gently eased into it. A hard, straight-backed chair.

"Signorina," a new voice said quietly, "do not try to remove the blindfold. If you do, we shall be compelled to become quite harsh with you."

31

"Who are you?" I asked. "Do you know where my father is?"

"You know where he is. That is why you are here. We wish to talk to him."

"I do not know where he is. I've been trying to find him. The note you sent indicated my father would be here. . . ."

"It indicated nothing. It was only meant to get you here. If you are reasonable, this will be a not unpleasant interview. If not, we shall have to teach you that our questions are to be answered. Do I make myself clear?"

"If I answer these questions, will it help me find my father and mother?"

"I am sure of it."

"Why do you wish to find him?"

"That is our affair. We are asking the questions, not you. How long were you in America?"

I was frightened, I sensed these were evil men, but if I pretended to cooperate, perhaps I'd get some idea of what this was about and where Papa might be. So long as the questions were innocuous enough, I decided I would answer them.

"Since I was four years old."

"How long ago was that, if you please?"

"I am now eighteen."

"Fourteen years? Have you never seen your father and mother since then?"

"Once, seven years ago. They came to America on a visit."

The man asking the questions now directed one at someone else in the room. "How does that correspond?"

"It is correct," another man said.

"I am happy to know you are not lying, Signorina," the spokesman said to me. "How long did he remain?"

"It's not easy to remember. I was eleven years old. Not very long."

"Your mama was with him?"

"Yes."

"They always were together, *si?*"

"Always," I agreed.

"Have you heard from him since?"

32

"Of course."

"Many times?"

"More than once a month. Signore, I would be happier in answering your questions if I knew why you were asking them."

"We wish to find your father too."

"To harm him?" I asked quickly.

"Now what gave you such a silly idea? When did you hear from him last?"

"I will answer no more questions," I said. "I do not care to be questioned by men who insist I remain blindfolded. And I want assurance you do not mean to harm my father and mother before I tell you more."

"Signorina, I ask you once again, politely. When did you hear from him last?"

I remained mute, fearful of what was going to happen, but even more afraid that what I might tell this man would harm Papa and Mama.

"You are going to be stubborn?" he asked, in a voice slightly harsher.

"Tell me who you are, why you wish this information, remove the blindfold and I will answer anything you wish."

"It would be sad to mar the beauty you are blessed with, Signorina," he warned. There was no doubting the malevolence in his voice.

"Tell me why. . . ." I began to repeat.

A hand struck me violently across the face, cutting off my words. I cried out in pain and began to bring a hand up to touch my face. Someone seized the hand and held it roughly.

"Signorina, do not be foolish," my interrogator warned. "When did you last hear from your father?"

"I told you I will not answer. . . ."

I was struck again, harder this time. I set my lips firmly, made no outcry.

"I think I should handle this," another voice said. A deeper, hoarse voice. Whether the hoarseness was to disguise it or not, I didn't know, but it was a voice I'd recognize again.

"Signorina," my interrogator said, "my friend here

has a great liking for the process he uses to make an attractive young woman answer questions. It is not a pleasant way for you."

"I ask only that I be told why," I responded.

A hand closed around my breast. I screamed in pain as it was twisted cruelly and violently.

"Again?" the hoarse voice asked.

"Please," I said. "Please . . ."

My breast was enclosed in the man's large hand and once again I screamed in intense pain. I came very close to fainting. My body fell forward and I could no longer hold my head up.

"Wait for a few minutes," the interrogator said.

"Si," the harsh voice agreed. "But then if she does not answer, I shall throw her on the bed and take her. I hope she refuses to speak."

I opened my mouth and screamed at the top of my voice. A hand was clasped across my mouth for a moment and then some rough cloth was forced between my lips. Someone seized a handful of my hair and lifted me painfully out of the chair. Someone ripped the bodice of my dress, exposing my breasts. Two hands grabbed my waist and I was lifted, carried a few steps and thrown onto a bed. Before I could move, two large hands held me helpless. I tried to spit out the cloth in my mouth, but it was impossible. I found it difficult to breathe. I raised myself, only to be forced flat again by the man with the hoarse voice. I only hoped it would be quick and not brutal. Fighting was instinctive, but it wasn't going to do any good. What would happen after I was violated, I didn't know. Perhaps I would be killed—but I told myself fiercely that I must live and find my father and mother so they'd be warned against beasts such as these.

"That will be enough," my interrogator said sharply. "Let her up. Let her up, Atillio. You heard me."

"Si . . . si . . . but what is the harm in going through with this? She is worth having, this one."

"If she has not spoken by now, she is not going to do so."

The man on the bed slid off it. A kinder hand grasped my arm and pulled me into a sitting position. I automatically drew my torn gown about me as best I could. I did make one desperate attempt to pull off the blindfold for a look at these beasts. I didn't even know how many there were. Only two had spoken, but I guessed there were others.

My hand was seized, pulled around behind my back and the other hand also drawn back painfully. The bodice of my dress dropped to my waist. Something, it felt like a piece of cloth, was then used to tie my hands. I was pulled to my feet, marched out of the room, down the stairs again. The front door opened, but I was not led out. Apparently someone was making certain my exit would not be observed. There were whispers. Two men, one on each side of me, grasped my arms. I was lifted off the floor and, suspended between the pair, I was carried out of the house and placed in a carriage. It began to move immediately.

I tugged at the bonds tying my wrists, but it was impossible to free myself. After ten minutes or so, the carriage stopped. It must have been the driver who helped me out of the vehicle, then freed my hands. Suddenly I was pushed backward until I fell against some kind of bush which entangled me for a few moments.

When I removed the blindfold, the carriage was already far down the road, turning onto the street. I was in what seemed to be a public park, very dark and silent. I managed to get free of the bush and I staggered over to a concrete bench where I sat down to steady my nerves and quiet the urge to begin screaming for help.

I didn't need help now. In my state of disarray, my gown badly torn, my face probably bruised, I didn't want anyone to see me. I didn't know where I was, how far I might be from my hotel. No carriages or other vehicles came by. I sat there for some time, unaware of how many minutes did go by. Then I heard the peal of a bell announcing the hour of three. The sound was familiar. The belfry where that bell was hung happened to be not a block from my hotel.

The realization that I wasn't far from security and privacy helped to bring back some strength. My senses stopped whirling about and with the passing of terror, a slow anger began to turn into rage.

I arose, steadied myself, for I was still shaken by the ordeal. I covered myself with my torn bodice and then, keeping to back streets, I managed to make my way to the hotel. It wouldn't do to use the front entrance so I crept quietly down a side street to the service entrance. I entered, moved down a long, narrow corridor dimly illuminated, and entered the kitchen where the remaining warmth of the range was welcome. Everything was closed down for the night, which made it possible for me to reach the stairs, climb them to my floor and enter my hotel suite without being seen by anyone.

They'd not taken my purse. Surprisingly, my room keys and my wad of lire notes were intact. They'd not been interested in stealing from me. I locked my door and went at once to the bathroom, grateful that this hotel was modern enough that I could draw hot water even at this time of night.

I ran a tub, removed my completely ruined gown and examined my face and my breasts. I was going to show ample marks of that hideous attack by morning, and the application of cold washcloths to my face was not going to reduce the swelling. My lower lip was badly bruised. I felt dirty, soiled by the attack of those men. That I hadn't been violated was strange, they'd gone so far.

I bathed, felt somewhat better, especially after I'd splashed myself with cologne and put on a nightgown. I went to bed, but it was almost dawn before I fell asleep, with the lamp beside the bed burning because I was afraid of the darkness for the first time in my life.

The hours until dawn were a nightmare. I dozed and awoke with a cry of terror as the memory of that awful experience returned. Fortunately Vito didn't arrive until early afternoon and by then I had managed to get enough rest to calm my nerves.

"Please ask Signore Cardona to come to my suite," I told the bellboy who announced Vito's presence in the lobby. He came promptly and the relief I felt because of his mere presence helped more than the fitful sleep.

"Are you ill?" he asked as he entered. "The boy

36

said . . ." He regarded me more carefully and then came rapidly to face me at close range. "You have been hurt. What happened?"

"Last night, quite late," I explained, "one of the hotel bellboys brought me a message asking that I go to an address on Giovanni Street, number eleven sixty." Stumbling I described the terrible events of the night. Vito listened silently, his face dark with emotion.

"I didn't expect this," he said when I finished. "The note. You have it?"

"Yes." I went to the dresser. It was not there. "Vito, I know I left it right here."

"One of the bellboys brought it?"

"Yes, he was in uniform."

"You will please wait here," he said. "I will not be long."

He returned in about half an hour. "I'm sorry, this took more time than I expected. I have arranged that every man wearing a hotel uniform be lined up for your inspection. I'm looking for the one who brought you the message. All I've talked to deny they were involved. So will you come down with me now and look the men over?"

"Does anyone know . . . what happened? I mean . . . exactly what?"

"No. They have no idea why I insisted on the lineup."

He led me to the kitchen where sixteen uniformed men were assembled. I walked before the line of them, studying each face. Finally I shook my head.

"He is not among them," I said.

Vito waved his hand at the assembled men. *"Grazie,* you may all go."

Vito then asked me to accompany him and in a carriage he hired, we were driven to 1160 Giovanni Street. As the carriage approached the address, I saw that it was a stately building comprising several expensive flats.

"This is not the place," I said. "Not even the neighborhood, Vito."

"I didn't think it would be," he commented dryly. He ordered the driver to begin traversing all of the streets. "They gave you a false address, they had a carriage

37

waiting and the driver was one of them. Can you describe him?"

"No, Vito. I didn't look at him particularly and it was night, quite dark. Do you know why they're after my father? Why they are so interested in reaching him?"

"I have no idea, but it certainly accounts for the secrecy he displayed, going off as he did and leaving no trail of any kind. Was there anything unusual about the carriage? A torn seat, peeling paint . . . anything?"

"I noticed nothing. I was so excited at the prospect of finding Papa, I was only concerned with getting to the address."

"What of the men who questioned you . . . hurt you?"

"I didn't see them, of course. Only two of them spoke. One seemed quite polished. A cold, heartless man, no doubt, but at least sensible enough to know there are limits to torture and abuse. The other, the one who harmed me, had a hoarse kind of voice. Like someone with a cold, perhaps. Maybe it was his natural voice, for he didn't seem to have a cough or any thing resembling a cold. Oh yes, I remember now. The other man called him Atillio."

"Would you recognize the voice again?"

"Ten years from now. I feel it's going to haunt my sleep."

I kept watching the streets along which we drove, but I saw nothing resembling the house or the neighborhood where I'd been lured. I did locate the little park, which was of no help, for I had no idea of the route taken by the carriage which brought me there in the night. There was nothing we could do but give up.

"I'm going to change your address," Vito said. "We'll use another name for the register. You must remain indoors as much as possible. I shall take you to supper each night and to dinner each noon. There will be strange men outside your suite and it may be that men will follow you should you go out without me. They will be police, the best men I have. This is not going to happen again and I hope we can track down those responsible. Especially the one with the hoarse voice. I would very much like to meet him."

My fears now were for Vito. "I believe them to be dangerous men. Please don't go in search of them without help."

"You can be assured of it because I wouldn't want them to get past me. Now I'll get you to another hotel and arrange for your protection. I'm thinking of one that faces the *Palazzo Medici*. It is a more open area, a fine old place where it will be easy to guard you. And if you go abroad, for you cannot always remain locked in a suite—there is much to see. The Arno River bridges are worth seeing and you can cross them on your way to *Giardino di Boboli*. Such beautiful gardens. You will find enchantment in everything. With time, they will grow more beautiful."

"Vito," I said, "you speak as if you believe I will remain in Florence forever."

"I wish you would," he said frankly. "But of course you will not. However, I ask that you remain until we clear all this up."

"I will remain until I am sure it will be impossible for me to find my parents in Florence. However awful this experience has been, Vito, some good came from it. Those people are convinced Papa and Mama are alive and that means they must be."

"As you say, there is some comfort in it, but at a price I do not care for."

"What you are saying is that my parents are in hiding."

"*Si.*"

"But why?"

"I cannot answer that, Angela."

"Cannot or will not?" I studied him closely, wondering if he was keeping something from me. His eyes were serious and they looked directly into mine. I could detect nothing evasive in his manner, though I repeated my question.

"I cannot, Angela." He paused, then added, "I wonder why they let you go."

"What you are really saying it that you wonder why they didn't kill me."

"*Si.*"

"So do I. They had the opportunity."

39

"I must get you out of that hotel." He gave. instructions to the driver, then addressed me. "We'll remain there only long enough for you to pack. I will arrange at the hotel desk that nobody knows you have gone. Your name will remain on the register as a guest and your suite will be treated as if it were occupied. Hotel people are very cooperative with the police."

The carriage turned the next corner and we were on our way to the hotel. We were both silent now. Vito was in deep thought, his brow slightly furrowed.

He helped me out of the carriage and ordered the driver to go around to the side entrance and wait for the luggage he would send down. We entered the lobby. A bellboy, standing beside one of the red plush, high-backed lobby chairs, bent down to whisper something to the man in the chair. He arose quickly and came toward us.

Vito's hand went under his coat and stayed there. I saw two more men alerted to approach the stranger from behind, but not to take any action at the moment.

He was tall and slender, with a lean face. A small, trim mustache and a vandyke, so miniature in size it seemed to disappear depending on the way the light caught it. He was dressed in the very latest men's fashion. His pale gray trousers were narrow and perfectly tailored. His vest was white, and little could have been whiter or cleaner. His coat was long, resembling evening dress. He wore gray kid gloves, carried a slim cane of blond wood with a silver handle. Spats covered the upper part of his shoes.

He removed his gray fedora and bowed low. "Indeed there is a family resemblance, dear Angela. I am your uncle, Carlo Guillermo. I came at once upon receiving my sister's cable."

"Uncle Carlo," I said eagerly. "I am glad to see you."

I kissed him on both cheeks and he embraced me, the lightest, most delicate embrace a man had ever given me and yet it fulfilled its purpose of making me welcome.

"I insist on monopolizing you," he said gallantly. "I am retired, with sufficient income, so I can grant you all of my time."

"Oh, Uncle Carlo, that isn't necessary. This is Vito Cardona, a good friend."

Carlo shook hands with Vito, again very delicately. "I didn't realize you knew anyone in Florence, or all Italy, for that matter, Angela. I'm delighted to meet any friend of yours, of course. You know, Angela, you have grown to resemble your mama to a remarkable degree."

"Thank you, Uncle," I said.

"Signore," Vito said candidly, "do you happen to know where Angela's parents are?"

Carlo shrugged his shoulders, lifted his arms and created a look of intense dismay on his handsome face.

"I have searched for them for years, it seems. I cannot understand where they went or why. Have you heard, Angela?"

Vito had clasped my arm lightly. His fingers tightened slightly, warning me not to say too much, even to this man who professed to be my uncle. I was quite certain he was not an impostor, for I recalled Aunt Celestine talking about his gallantry and his addiction to dress.

"I have come to search for them myself," I told him.

"Then you've heard nothing? It's been years since I did. Do you think it possible that they are dead?"

"I refuse to even think such a thing," I said quickly.

"Well yes, you are likely quite right too," he said. "They were in fine health. Luigi was a famous man, you know. Thought well of in the House of Deputies at Rome. Being his brother-in-law gave me entree everywhere."

"Will I see you again, Uncle?" I asked.

"See me? You can't get rid of me. I wish to help you search for your father and mother because it is my family duty to be of assistance. Besides, if I do not, Celestine will send me a letter that will put me to bed for a week. She can write nasty letters, my dear sister. So I will be your escort."

"I'm sorry, Uncle," I said. "I'm going to leave town for a few days."

"Oh—that is bad news—for me. I wasn't prepared for your abrupt departure."

Vito said, "Signore Guillermo, it happens that Angela

will vacate her suite of rooms here in this hotel. Would it be possible for you to occupy them?"

Uncle Carlo's face lit with pleasure, but only momentarily. "Well of course, there are considerations one must . . ."

"The rooms are paid for," Vito repeated.

"In that case, I suppose I could stay. Are meals included?"

"Within reason," Vito said.

"Then I shall stay."

"Fine," Vito said. "If you'll excuse us now, Angela has to pack. Then you may arrange to move right in."

"I'll see you again soon, Uncle," I said. I kissed him lightly on the cheek. He smelled of fine cologne.

"I will be impatient for you to return, dear niece," he said. "Good day to you, Signore." He bowed slightly and stood back for us to pass.

Vito and I continued on to the ancient elevator with its equally ancient operator, trim in his dark blue uniform. Vito accepted my key and unlocked the suite door. Before I entered, he went in first to make a swift inspection of the premises.

"We can talk while you pack," he said. "The sooner we leave here, the better. Your uncle can stay in your place and report to us if anything happens."

"I hope we aren't placing him in danger by allowing him to move into this suite."

"I don't think so. He has no idea where your parents are. I'm sure those characters are aware of his relationship to you. I'm also certain they consider him of no help to them."

"I'm fast getting the impression you don't like Uncle Carlo."

"I didn't mean to be rude, Angela. I don't dislike him, but you must admit he is a bit of a fop."

"Aunt Celestine says he is a very kind man. And a very elegant one."

"I'm certain of the latter. What I am not so certain about is whether he is genuine. Fortunately, that is a matter I can check on easily enough."

"I doubt that's necessary. Aunt Celestine described

him perfectly. Even to his ridiculous little goatee which half the time is scarcely visible."

Vito laughed heartily. "I noticed—now it's there, now it isn't. Depending on the light."

I paused momentarily in my packing and joined him in laughter. "We're being unkind, Vito."

"Yes," he agreed, sobering. "I'll close those two pieces of baggage you've packed."

I started filling the third bag, then paused and gave my attention to Vito. "What are you doing about finding my parents?"

"Nothing just now. It could well be you are being watched and even this step will do little to fool them. So it would be wise to move cautiously. You could jeopardize their safety. They are the ones being sought—not you. You wouldn't want to be the means of their being killed."

"Oh no," I exclaimed. "But why should anyone want to kill them?"

"Someone may want to do just that. Else why are they in hiding?"

"Do you believe that?"

"Yes. The question is why? Why? Why?" Vito walked around the bed, grasped my arms and turned me to face him. "I don't like to frighten you, Angela, but I don't want your parents hurt and I don't want you hurt. We must move warily, not impetuously."

I smiled up at his serious face. A lock of his dark hair had fallen over his brow. Without a trace of self-consciousness, I brushed it back, combing it with my fingers until it was in place. Vito gathered me close and his lips covered mine in a kiss that began gently. I must confess I responded. At first I was too surprised to protest, but as his mouth became more demanding, I pressed my hands against his chest and tried to free myself. He let me go, but I could see the kiss had aroused his passion. His breath had quickened and he held me so close I'd felt his rapid heartbeat against my bosom. It had unsettled me also, but I did my best not to show it.

I said, "You shouldn't have done that, Vito."

"I couldn't help it and I'm sorry if you're angry."

43

"I'm not angry. I have grown fond of you, but I do not care for you in the way . . ." I didn't know how to finish the sentence, but he did.

". . . I kissed you. I will confess the touch of your lips set my blood on fire. I love you, Angela. However, I will do my best to keep my emotions under control."

"Please do." My voice was unsteady, just as his was. "I'm not a prude. Yet, even if I did love you, I'm too concerned at the present time about the whereabouts and safety of my parents. Besides, it would be selfish of me."

"I don't agree, but I'll keep it in mind. Now finish your packing. I'll go over by the window where I'll be a safe distance from you."

"I'm not afraid of you," I scoffed. "In fact, I like having you with me. I'm afraid of nothing when you are."

"When I'm not with you, be wary," he cautioned, walking over to the window.

I resumed my packing, talking as I did so. "Vito, one of the many things that trouble me is why nothing was ever done about actively searching for my parents."

"Why would any search be made when no one knew they were missing? Even you didn't know until you arrived in this country."

"Exactly. Except that my parents lived here—they were well known. Once they stopped being seen, certainly someone would have instigated an investigation."

He turned to face me. "Did your uncle think their absence constituted an investigation?"

I gave an impatient shake of my head. "You're asking as many questions as I."

He laughed softly from his place at the window. "It does seem as if I am parrying your questions. I don't mean to, Angela. I agree—it's not easy to understand. However, try to remember your father retired as a deputy. When he disappeared, along with your mother, people in Rome believed he had returned to his *palazzo* here in Florence. In Florence, we believed he had remained in Rome. No complaint about their absence was ever received by any police department. I have made a careful

44

check of that. Bear in mind that such complaints most always come from relatives. You made no request that we search for them. Nor did your uncle."

I tucked a glove case into my bag and walked over to where he stood. "I'd scarcely make a request for a search when I received Papa's letters."

"Well," Vito shrugged, "there you are." He rested his arm lightly on my shoulder. "Don't be discouraged, Angela. Try to keep your spirits up."

"I will," I said, managing a smile. "I've finished my packing."

"Good. I'll bring you to the carriage and come back with the driver for your baggage."

We left the hotel by the back stairway. The carriage was waiting and took us a distance of about two miles to the new hotel where Vito had seen to it that everything was in readiness for me.

It was a small hotel, not more than fifty rooms, I judged. It faced the delightful *Palazzo Medici* and the lovely grounds. There was ample space all around the hotel. No one could come or go and not be easily seen. I presumed any back exit would be also watched.

A flock of pigeons arose as the carriage rolled through the park-like area. As the carriage came to a stop, two men in business suits sauntered a little closer. Vito paid no heed to them so I realized they were also of the police.

A white-haired, very efficient *portinaio* emerged to supervise the handling of my luggage and direct me to the hotel desk. It was not necessary for me to sign a register and my approach was merely to identify myself.

Vito said, "Your rooms have already been inspected and you will be quite safe here, I'm sure. I have to leave, but I'll be back soon. Stay alert, Angela. At the first sign of anything suspicious, turn to the men I shall leave in the lobby and outside the hotel. If you display the slightest alarm, they'll come to you. Otherwise, disregard them."

"Thank you," I said. "I do feel safer now. Will you see Uncle Carlo?"

"I'm going to make certain he's who he says he is, and

45

what manner of man he happens to be. I won't talk to him, no. Not now. If he comes here, you must maintain a cautious attitude."

I regarded Vito's concern lightly. "I'm not afraid of Uncle Carlo. Nor do I doubt his identity. My aunt has pictures of him, though not recent ones, but they show a family resemblance and so does he. Also, from her I learned he is amiable and quite unambitious, except socially. Even when Papa referred to him, it was in a humorous vein."

"That may have been true some time age." Vito spoke with the customary dubiousness of a police officer. "And it may be still true. Nonetheless, I must check on the kind of man he is now. I'll do my best to return and take you to supper. If that is not possible, promise me you will have supper served in your suite. As with all other meals when I am not at hand."

I nodded acquiescence. "If it hadn't been for last night, I would say you are overprotecting me."

"Please, Angela," he urged, "don't for a moment, take this lightly."

"I shan't," I promised. "And I'm grateful for your concern." On impulse, I stood on tiptoe and kissed his cheek.

His laughter was deep yet soft. "I shall look forward to your next spell of gratitude. May it be soon. *Arrivederci,* Angela."

After he left, I took a few moments to look about the lobby. For such a small and relatively obscure hotel, it was certainly an elegant one. The gold of the wall decor, paper and ornamentation was not gilt paint, but pressed gold leaf. The mirrors, an ample quantity of them, were encased in ornamental frames inset with semi-precious stones, adding a further air of grandeur. The rug, neutral in color, was thick and sufficiently padded that one sank into it to a depth all but covering one's shoes. The elevator which took me to the tenth floor was capable of holding two people easily, and it rose and descended as smoothly as a piece of fine machinery.

The rug in the corridor leading to my suite was as

luxurious as that in the lobby. I did notice a man standing at the end of the corridor. He was holding a newspaper, which almost concealed his features, and seemed to be reading it. I hoped he was a detective assigned to guard me.

My suite, where a middle-aged maid was already at work unpacking my clothes, was large and airy, consisting of a bedroom and a parlor of ample size. The furniture was of the French Regency period. It caught my imagination to the point where I let my mind slip back in time and thought of myself as a member of the aristocracy of that period.

But the maid, unpacking my baggage, quickly brought me to my senses. When she completed her work, I provided her with a gratuity which brought forth a typical Italian torrent of *grazies*.

After the door closed behind her I sat down wearily, grateful for a few moments of quiet and relaxation. My expedition with Vito, plus his endless questions, had wearied me. Yet I had no time to give in to it. There were matters of concern which I must think about, such as what was I going to do now.

There was the very serious and important question of money. Papa was, to the best of my knowledge, a wealthy man. He had provided generously for my welfare, with money Aunt Celestine kept charge of. I wondered if he had placed a lump sum in an American bank years ago when I was sent to her, to be used for my support and education, or did he send sums periodically? I had no idea, though I could state affirmatively that while my aunt had raised me with discipline, I had not lacked for either worldly comforts or the proper clothes.

Being that wealthy, Papa must have left his money in some banking institution. Perhaps Vito could find the right one. I would ask him the next time he came. Of equal importance was how long I would be required to remain in Italy. Or how long did I wish to remain. If there was nothing I could do to find my parents, and Vito had exhausted every means at his command, there was little value in staying on. If I went back to live with

47

Aunt Celestine, the chances were better that I would, hopefully, receive some mail from Papa as I had in the past.

I would have to make up my mind fairly soon, for I was running out of cash. Aunt Celestine could cable me more, of course, but I had a strange feeling I belonged back with her. I was beginning to feel I had come on a fool's errand. Certainly, Papa preferred I be there.

I did wonder, as I sat by the window to rest, what this could be about. Papa and Mama were missing, but it seemed to me that everyone worried less about that fact than they did about the people who were trying to find them. Certainly the theory that Papa and Mama had gone into seclusion somewhere meant that it had been Papa's wish. The seriousness of his reasons was amply displayed by the undisputed fact that he and Mama had gone off some years ago. The men who sought them, however, were still committed to finding them and they were certainly undismayed by the necessary use of violence. They'd displayed that well enough in what they had done to me.

I also realized—and Vito knew it as well, though he'd not mentioned it—they had let me go for the time being because I was quite likely the only link they had in their hunt for Papa.

Perhaps they guessed he might come to me in a desperate effort to help me. Especially if he learned what had happened and what could be in store for me at the hands of these desperados. Possibly with the help of the police I might actually track down Papa. If that happened, these unidentified ruffians would be ready to pounce. I came to the conclusion that my presence here was not only a danger to myself, but to the welfare of Papa and Mama as well. I made up my mind that I would return as soon as possible.

At last I rose to begin changing my dress. As I studied my still somewhat swollen face in the mirror, I raised my hand to touch my now almost normal lower lip. The strange ring on my right hand glittered slightly in the mirror. I shook my head. If there was any magic to that ring, it hadn't manifested itself so far. Perhaps it had been a little joke of Papa's. I quickly discounted that. I realized he must be in a desperate position and not apt to indulge in silly little jokes at the expense of the daughter he hadn't seen in seven years.

I would continue to wear it as he had instructed.

FOUR

It was the following day before I heard from Vito and then it was a hand-delivered note. He had learned that Papa had banked through a man named Alberto Babani at one of the larger financial institutions. Vito suggested I pay him a visit for he'd be more apt to cooperate with me than through a routine police inquiry. I went off within an hour of having received the information.

"I wish to see *banchiere* Babani," I told the first bank employee I encountered. I was directed to a rear desk at which a man in a white-edged vest and a black suit was at work over a stack of papers. I sat down and regarded him. He paid me no heed until he had completed totaling a row of figures on a long page. Finally he laid down his fountain pen and settled back, displaying an ample paunch and an intelligent manner. His blue eyes were studying me carefully while not seeming to. A vandyke gave him added distinction.

"What can I do for you, Signorina?" he asked.

"I am Angela Gambrelli," I explained. "My father is Luigi Gambrelli and I have been told that he banked here and that he usually did business through you."

"Of course," he said affably. "You look somewhat like your mother. I thought, when I first saw you, that you seemed familiar. How is your honored father?"

"I don't know. He's been missing for several years. Both he and my mother."

"Missing? Doesn't he live in Rome now?"

"I wish I knew, Signore Babani. No one seems to know."

"But such a well-known man . . . how could he disappear? And what in the world would cause him to go away like that? Without informing his daughter? It's incredible!"

"I agree, Signore, but the fact remains, my parents are

50

still missing. I had wondered if you might have an idea or a suggestion as to where they might be."

Signore Babani eyed me with sympathy as he spoke. "I saw him last—oh, it was long ago. He arranged to sell his *palazzo* through the bank. The transaction was quickly completed, for it was a fine house and such places were then in demand. He gave us orders that the proceeds, and what he had on deposit here, be sent to his bank in Rome, which we did."

"Then he has no funds still on deposit here?"

"None, Signorina. Everything was closed out. I never doubted that he had chosen to live in Rome permanently."

"He gave you no reason for doing this?"

"None was necessary. A man sells his house and moves, it is customary that he close his accounts here if he intends to live elsewhere. I think he said something about buying real estate in Rome."

I arose. *"Grazie,* Signore."

"If there is more I can do, come back to see me. I liked and respected your father and I would do all I could for his daughter."

As I returned to my hotel, I was aware that my carriage was followed by another containing two men. I was certain they were bodyguards provided by Vito.

I asked my driver to take me to the nearest office where I could send a cable. There I composed a message to Aunt Celestine asking her to forward me sufficient money for my return and for the remainder of my stay in Florence. I told her I'd been unable to find my parents, that a search was being made for them and if she had any information to help us, to cable it at once.

I returned to my hotel then, feeling that I had done everything possible and all else must be left to Vito and the *Carabinieri.* I spent the rest of the day reading newspapers or looking out of the window. When Vito arrived late in the afternoon, I was delighted to see him.

"I realize you've been confined here much of the day, except for your visit to Signore Babani. Perhaps you'd like to sit in the park. It's a warm, pleasant afternoon," he said. "We can talk there."

51

"I'd love that," I told him. "Though I can't say I've very much to report."

"Well, neither have I, but as I said, it's a nice day."

At the park we found a vacant bench and sat down. The pigeons began to flock around us, looking for food. Vito had brought a small sack of seed which he gave me to toss out among the birds.

"I talked to the banker," I told him. "He said Papa sold our home and closed out his bank account here, ordering everything sent to Rome."

"We already learned that. However, I thought you should learn the news firsthand. In Rome he drew out large sums of money over a brief period of time. Nobody knows what he did with it, but so far as we can find out he has no banking connections anywhere. Not under his own name."

"I cabled Aunt Celestine asking her to send me some money and any information she may have about my parents. I don't think she has any, though, unless there's been another letter."

"Let me know if she sends any information. There's one thing that troubles me. Your Uncle Carlo also seems to have vanished."

The information shocked me. "Vito, is this some kind of conspiracy against my family?"

"I doubt that. Carlo had an expensive supper sent to his room last night. He finished it, along with a couple of bottles of wine. He signed the check with a good-sized tip for the waiter. Carlo seems to be a man of expensive tastes, especially when someone else is going to pay the bill. That's the last anyone heard of him. I had arranged that all *carabinieri* be on the lookout for him. I also received information from his home town. He gambles—quite successfully at times. He is a confirmed ladies' man, one *vigliacco,* it is agreed. The English would call him a cad, living by the sweat of others. But at least he harms no one. Oh, he breaks a few hearts—and pocketbooks, I suppose—but nothing illegal."

"I know he was once a problem for Celestine, when they were young and living here in Italy. Sometimes, when she spoke of him, it was not with the warmest affection, though I'm sure she would come to her brother's aid if he needed help."

"Carlo rarely needs help. He's self-sufficient. That's a good description of him. He looks out for himself first. Now, about finding your parents, we found not the slightest trail leading to them. We're keeping it all quiet for the time being. If there is nothing to this, if your parents had a good reason for going off as they did, we might harm their reputations by announcing that they have been missing for several years."

"Thank you, Vito. I won't be troubling you much longer. I can't do anything here and if I am back in the United States, Papa may reach me. I got his letters there and I have to presume that there will be more."

"I have been haunted by that ever since I've known you, Angela."

"It bothers you that Papa may write me?"

"Oh no! I hope he does. I'm concerned with the fact that you're going to leave Italy." He shooed off a too-inquisitive pigeon threatening to settle on my shoulder. "In my country," he went on, "we men are not bashful when it comes to flirting with a pretty girl and we whistle at all women, young or old, beautiful or not. I'm a devoted believer in this, but when it comes to being serious with one girl . . . it's another matter and I find myself fumbling for the right words."

"We discussed this before, Vito. My feelings toward you haven't changed."

"Nor mine toward you." He spoke softly and his eyes regarded me adoringly. "I've known you only a few brief days. Yet it seems as if I've been searching for you all my life. The thought of you leaving tears at my heart."

"I'm sorry, Vito."

"So am I. I feel a complete failure."

"If circumstances were different, perhaps . . ." I held up a warning finger at the look of hope in his eyes. "I said perhaps. I think of you as a dear friend. I have tremendous admiration and respect for you as a man. As for your being a failure, that isn't so. If anybody could have found my parents, you would have."

"Be assured, Angela, we shall continue our efforts here to locate them." Vito took one of my hands and held it between both of his. "Perhaps one day, when the mystery of the disappearance of your parents has been solved, you might think of me as more than just a friend."

"I can't give you an answer to that now, Vito. But I will say I am fond of you. I really wish I could say I loved you, because if ever I needed someone strong, it's now. And you are strong and brave and a very dear gentleman."

Vito smiled. "Thank you." He raised my hand to his lips and kissed my open palm. "Once again I must say it, I love you, Angela. I shall always love you. Remember that and if you ever need me, send word wherever you are and I will come at once."

I was so touched by his declaration of love and devotion, I raised my face to his. There was no need for words. He kissed me. It was not a momentary kiss, but neither was it one meant to arouse passion. There was both beauty and sadness. His hand rested lightly on my cheek and he spoke my name, calling me Angel, even while our lips still touched.

At last I broke the embrace, widening the distance between us.

"Thank you, Angel," he said. "I will cherish this precious memory the rest of my days."

I turned the subject back to my reason for being here. "How quickly will it take to get an answer to my cablegram?"

"Oh—perhaps by morning. Or late this evening. It depends on how quickly your aunt arranges for the answer to be sent."

"I am impatient to hear from her."

"And I am impatient because I cannot show you Rome and Venice and all the beautiful places in this country. One day when you come back, I hope you will grant me the privilege of doing so." His voice had trailed off and he was looking beyond me. His features expressed concern.

"What is it, Vito?"

"I don't know. One of my men is hurrying across the

54

park. By the look of him, something has happened." He rose quickly, meeting the policeman a few feet away from the bench where I sat. They spoke briefly in an undertone, then Vito dismissed him. The policeman moved with a speed that indicated there was an urgency to his mission.

Vito turned back to me. "He goes to bring us the carriage. Your Uncle Carlo has been hurt."

I was instantly on my feet. "What happened?"

"I don't know yet. I'll take you to him."

When we pulled up in front of a large hospital, an officer came from the doorway to advise Vito. They talked for a few minutes before Vito helped me down and while we walked briskly into the hospital, he told me what he had learned.

"Carlo must have gone out last night after supper. He was found in the middle of the night lying in a gutter some distance from his hotel. He was not drunk and he claims to have been run down by a large wagon. Apparently the driver was either afraid to stop and summon help, or he didn't know he'd struck Carlo. At any rate, Carlo had been lying there for some time, quite badly hurt. We'll find out the extent of his injuries from one of the doctors."

"Poor Carlo," I said, crossing myself. "My poor little uncle."

We were admitted to Carlo's room where a doctor had just completed an examination of his heart and was returning his stethoscope to the pocket of his white coat. While Vito drew him aside, I went to sit beside the bed on which Carlo lay.

His face was so bandaged it was difficult to recognize him. Both eyes had been severely blackened, his left arm was in a cast. From the way he lay I suspected one or both legs were also being kept rigid by casts.

"Carlo." I bent over him. "It's Angela."

"*Grazie.*" He spoke feebly. "I hoped you would come. See what has happened to your poor uncle. If my face has been damaged . . ." He groaned.

"You will be better soon," I told him. "Is the pain severe?"

"Very. I may die." He groaned again.

55

"No, Carlo. You will recover."

"You don't know how I am suffering."

Vito pulled over a chair and sat down beside me. "In case you've forgotten me," Vito said, "I am Inspector Cardona of the *Carabinieri*."

"I remember you," Carlo said. "Have you found the driver of that damn wagon? I'll never live through this." He groaned louder.

"First of all, the doctor has told me you will get well, but it's going to take some time. However, I want a better story from you. When did you leave the hotel last night?"

"I don't know. I was bored. I wanted to go for a walk."

"Nobody saw you leave. If you went through the lobby, you would surely have been noticed at that time of night. Did you leave by the service entrance?"

"I didn't want to be stopped by some bore who would wish to talk. To chatter about things of no interest to me. People recognize me everywhere."

"That may be so. Did you have a definite reason for leaving the hotel?"

"Only to get some exercise, as I told you."

"Very well. What happened?"

"I was walking about, thinking of Angela and her father and mother. I didn't pay much attention to where I walked. Suddenly this big wagon, or whatever it was, came out of the dark and struck me as I crossed the street. I went reeling. I tried to get up and go after the driver, but I was stunned and badly hurt and the pain was excruciating."

"Carlo," Vito said quietly, "you're a bad liar."

Carlo closed his eyes with a long sigh. It sounded like an admission of guilt.

"The fact is," Vito went on, "you left the hotel by the service exit at 11:10. There was a man with you. Both of you got into a waiting carriage and were driven off. You were found four miles away, at a few minutes after three o'clock. You were not struck down by a wagon. You were beaten up. One arm is broken midway between the hand and elbow. Your leg is broken too—the left one. The right one was kicked so badly it will take even longer to heal than the break. Now I want the truth. Who was the man

56

you left with and where did he take you? Why were you beaten?"

Carlo opened his eyes again. They seemed to be glistening with tears, though there was so much bandage it was hard to tell.

"I owe money. A great deal of money. A gambling debt."

"Is that why you were beaten?"

"Why else? I could not pay. I will get worse next time."

"More than one man beat you," Vito said. "Where did this happen?"

"I don't know. I was taken somewhere and blindfolded."

"Are you lying again?" Vito asked in anger.

"Vito," I reminded him, "I too was blindfolded and taken somewhere."

"You didn't lie about it," Vito said tersely. He resumed questioning Carlo. "Was there more than a gambling debt involved? A woman, perhaps?"

"Perhaps. They said it was gambling money. I am very sick. I cannot speak of this any longer. I am dying. I wish to speak to my niece alone, *per favore.*"

Vito shrugged as he rose. Clearly he was not impressed by Carlo's fear of dying. He moved to the foot of the bed, realizing the uselessness of questioning Carlo further.

"You should have told the truth, Carlo," I admonished. "Vito is here to help you."

"Are you going back to America soon?" he asked, making no apology for his behavior.

"Yes. I am wasting time here. In America, I might hear from Papa."

"Will you take me with you? I must get out of here. Next time they will surely kill me. You can see how bad off I am now. Angela, if you want to save my life, help me get away."

"Carlo, were you beaten for the same reason I was kidnapped? To be forced to tell what you know about my parents?"

His eyes assumed a blank stare. "Now what makes you think that, in heaven's name? This was a personal thing—a gambling debt—and . . . and the man to whom

57

I lost all that money . . . I went to see his wife about it and we became friendly. That is . . . well, her husband found out. I can't get together all the money I lost. Even if I did, I still think he'll kill me because of his wife."

"What am I going to do with you, Carlo?" I asked in dismay.

"All I'm asking is that you take me with you," he pleaded.

"I don't even have enough money to get home. I sent a cablegram to Aunt Celestine, asking that she send me money. If there is enough left over after I pay for my ticket back and my hotel bill, I will give it to you."

"It isn't just the money. It's his so-called honor he wishes to satisfy. I believe he is going to kill me."

"Why don't you tell Vito who he is?"

"Yes, Carlo," Vito said. "I will warn him that if anything else happens to you, we shall look for him immediately."

"You would never find my body," Carlo said sorrowfully. "I cannot accuse him when he wasn't there. But I believe he will be the one who will use some horrible means to put an end to my miserable life."

"I told you all I can do for you," I said. "I suggest you relax so you will regain your strength quickly."

"Who will pay my hospital bills? Also, there is the doctor."

"Carlo, please listen. I have no money. Whatever money Papa had vanished with him. I am completely dependent on your sister."

He gave a despairing sigh. "She will no longer lend me money. Please cable her again and tell her I met with a terrible accident and will die if I don't get prompt medical care."

"I will do no such thing, Carlo," I exclaimed in dismay. "What has happened to you you brought on yourself. I sympathize with your suffering. I do not sympathize with you when you are so consumed with self-pity that you will stop at nothing to get what you want." I didn't add that that included another man's wife, for he did look pitiful bandaged and certainly aching from head to toe. My voice softened as I added, "When I return to America, I will talk with Aunt Celestine about you. It may be she will take compassion on you and send you the money for a voyage to America. But I will not send her a cablegram regarding this dreadful situation you find yourself in."

"I'll be dead by the time you get back," he vowed. "I am far more seriously hurt than you think. I may never walk again. And if I get out of here, I will be killed anyway. There's nowhere I can hide, Angela. Have pity on me. I know I'm a wastrel and of no value to anyone, but I am alive and I want to stay that way."

"I told you what I will do," I said. "Now you stop thinking about dying or becoming a cripple. Vito will see to it that you are guarded. As for the expenses at the hospital, you must have some assets back where you live. Otherwise how did you exist? Be practical, Uncle. Do something for yourself and stop depending on others."

"You will let me know about Celestine and if she sends enough money . . ."

"I promise."

He reached for my hand. *"Bacio le mani.* I kiss your hand, Angela. I will do as you say. Command me! I will listen, I swear. Do not desert me. I am suffering enough."

I withdrew my hand and then, as one would do with a mischievous child, I bent and kissed his cheek. Vito escorted me from the room and out of the hospital.

"I think he's telling the truth now," I said. "About his gambling and his foolishness with the wife of the man he owed the money to. I also believe they will likely try to kill him after he recovers. Can you do something for him, Vito?"

"I can place him under guard, but not for very long. I'll take you back to the hotel now."

"I am concerned about Carlo. He is my uncle. But what can I do? I'm all but destitute. I came with the idea of meeting my parents. I never dreamed there would be financial worries."

"Perhaps it's not as serious as Carlo pretends. You know we Italians are a volatile people. We let more or less simple things grow all out of proportion. I will see that

Carlo tells me whom he owes the money to, and I will then see this man and warn him if anything happens to Carlo, we shall hold him responsible. Sometimes that works, but not always. Especially if Carlo owes money to someone high in the ranks of the Camara or the Mafia. They are not easy to deal with, though we did strike them a blow two or three years ago that they'll not forget in a hurry."

"I have heard they are quite influential," I said. "Celestine spoke of them, but I really didn't understand. Can they kill Carlo and not be punished for it?"

"They can. We'd punish them if we could, but it's impossible to prove anything against them. Just hope it is not those people Carlo has been mixed up with. For if it is, and they have determined to kill him, there is no place on earth where he can hide."

"Is he in danger now?"

"No. They'll let his wounds heal."

"Poor Carlo," I said. "Perhaps, after I get back to Philadelphia, I can do something for him. I'm sure my aunt will take pity on him once she hears the story."

We found the carriage waiting. During the drive back to the hotel, Vito was singularly quiet.

"What concerns you?" I asked.

"Oh, it is nothing," he replied. His tone was light, but his eyes held a hint of sadness. "Nothing except that my world is falling to pieces. You will go away soon. Who knows when you'll be back, if ever. My world will never be the same."

"Mine will be richer for having known you. I'll miss you, Vito. No one other than my aunt has been as kind to me."

"*Grazie.* But with me, it is different. I am in love with you. I find the thought of life without you unbearable. Will you be back? Will I ever see you again?"

"I can't answer that, except to say I am still seeking the whereabouts of my parents. If the trail should point in this direction, I'll be back."

He nodded. "I understand. I am as bad as Carlo. I cannot or will not accept the facts."

"You're not like Carlo. He is weak. You are strong.

60

I needed your strength. I still do. I will be lost without you."

"You are strong, Angela. You must continue to be. I should not have opened my heart to you." To my relief, he changed the subject. "Send me word when you get the money. I'll arrange for your stateroom. I have certain influence there."

The carriage pulled up before the hotel. Vito helped me out and held my hand as we walked up the stairs to the door. In Florence, this open display of affection was not frowned upon. In Philadelphia it would have been. I liked the Italian way.

I stood on the hotel steps watching until his carriage was swallowed up in the maze of vehicles on the streets beyond the park. The *carabinieri* stationed at the hotel were nowhere in sight. I wondered if Vito, feeling I was safe here, had withdrawn them.

I went directly to my suite, unlocked the door and stepped inside. Instantly, I knew something was wrong. The window shades had been drawn and the parlor was only dimly lighted. I was on the verge of turning to flee from the suite when a man rushed out of the bedroom and seized me before I could escape. I'd never seen him before. He was short, pudgy, a fat-faced, evil-looking individual who would have given me shudders if he accosted me alone on any street. Here, it was even worse.

There was no doubting what he wanted. My kicks and my struggles did nothing to stop him as he carried me into the bedroom. One fat hand was held tightly against my lips. He kicked the bedroom door shut, dropped me on the bed and tore open my shirtwaist. Suddenly I knew him, though he'd not spoken a word. His method of attack was the same as that of the man who had tried to violate me when I was kidnapped.

I tried to get free of him, but it was no use. And this time there was no one to stop him, no command he was bound to obey. I did manage to dig my fingernails deep into his cheek, which caused him to grunt in pain and, momentarily, lift the hand against my mouth. I screamed. The hand clapped down hard again, cutting off the sound. I doubted I'd been heard outside of this room.

"I will kill you if you fight," he warned, in that hoarse voice which I recognized immediately. "I have dreamed of you since the other time. They would not let me have you then, but now I will not be denied."

He finished tearing off the blouse and began tugging at my skirt. My arms were free enough for he couldn't hold them, keep a hand over my mouth, and disrobe me at the same time.

I fought him as best I could but my blows, kicks and scratches did nothing to slow him down, and I sensed he would carry out his threat to kill me if I continued to resist. The man was mad! My flailing right hand knocked over the lamp on the table beside the bed. I curled my hand around the base of it. With one final burst of strength I managed to partially sit up and before he knew what I was about to do, I threw the lamp base through the bedroom window.

He jumped from the bed and moved to the window to look out. I was off the bed too, but not in time. He hurled me back onto it in a rage.

"I could not forget you," he growled in that awful voice. "Always you came back and now I have found you, there is no way you can escape me. If you scream, I'll strangle you. If you fight, I'll break your pretty face. Do you hear me?"

I let myself go limp in surrender. His fingers tore at my skirt, his face closed down on mine and his mouth found my lips and fastened there. I prayed for someone to come to my rescue, and for a fleeting moment dared hope I'd been heard. He raised his head as if to catch some alien sound, but apparently nothing else disturbed him for his face came down again, his lips crawled over my face. I closed my eyes in revulsion. There was no way I could get clear of this beast . . . would he kill me when his passion was satisfied? That thought gave me one last surge of strength and I tore my nails into the back of his neck.

He raised himself slightly and cursed me. It was horrible and terrifying. I was sure he'd kill me now. One hand reached for my throat. I continued to struggle. Suddenly I heard a loud noise, and the man flung himself off the bed.

Two men of the *Carabinieri* burst into the room and rushed at my assailant. He bowled one of them over with a headlong rush of his own. He darted out of the bedroom, crossed the parlor and was in the corridor running madly toward the stairs. The other officer followed him. I got to my feet and staggered to a closet for a robe to cover my partial nakedness. I went to my open door. I saw the officer level his gun and fire once. Then he disappeared from view. The second officer, having regained his feet, glanced at me to assure himself I was all right and then he rushed out of the suite too.

I stepped into the corridor to see for myself what had happened. Both officers were kneeling beside the intruder. They rose and shrugged. Even from where I stood, I could see the bloodstains on the carpet. I turned back to my suite and sat down, so shaken I was on the verge of tears, but fighting to retain my wits.

The two men came in. "Signorina, we are very sorry. We were outside the hotel. Only by night do we guard the corridor."

"The man?" I asked.

"He died instantly, Signorina. One of us will remain just outside your door, the other will get word to Inspector Cardona to come at once. Were you harmed . . . injured . . . ?"

"You came in time and I thank you with all my heart. I am not harmed because you came so promptly."

They looked relieved. I suppose they would have been reprimanded had the beast Atillio succeeded in defiling me. They bowed as they backed away and I closed the door and went directly to the bath. There I bathed myself carefully and dressed, choosing a pale blue afternoon gown. I was still trembling with nervousness and kept looking about me to make certain I was alone.

There was a knock on the door of my suite and I heard Vito speak my name. I unlocked and opened the door. Relief flooded through me at sight of him and I made no protest when he gathered me in his arms. Then the tears came. I was ashamed, but I couldn't control them. Vito bent, swooped me up in his arms and carried me to the

63

sofa in the parlor. He placed me gently on it and knelt beside me. He held one of my hands. His other hand lightly stroked my brow in a soothing gesture. His eyes, filled with compassion, never left my face.

He placed his handkerchief in my hand and I used it to dry my copious tears. I turned away from him to blow my nose, then I slipped the handkerchief into my skirt pocket. I would have it laundered before returning it to him. I noticed him restrain a smile.

"I'm all right now, Vito." I sat up and motioned him to sit alongside me on the settee.

He did so and once again reached for one of my hands which he held between his.

"Did you identify the beast?" I asked, managing a calm I was still far from feeling.

"Not yet. Do you know if he was one of the men who kidnapped and held you in that house?"

"He was." I answered without a moment's hesitation. "I recognized his gruff voice. He is the one called Atillio."

"Did he try to pry information from you? Or was his reason for coming here solely to satisfy his lust?"

I shuddered. "It was . . . lust. He said they would not let him have me before, but this time no one would call him off."

"I've been trying to figure out how he found you. I think I know."

"How?" Such a thought hadn't occurred to me.

"Carlo, your uncle. Atillio may even have been hired to beat him. Or, if not, he was watching Carlo, knowing of your relationship to him."

"He must have had some identification on him."

"His pockets were empty. He may have done that himself, so if he was caught, there would be no information concerning his background. He'd have done that to protect himself from the wrath of his cohorts."

"Why should they care?"

"Because debasing you did not fit in with their plans."

"They didn't mind Atillio torturing me in that house."

"That was necessary to make you talk. Raping you was not. I should have assigned more men to protect you."

"They were there when I needed them and they came promptly."

"Thank God you were able to throw that lamp out of the window."

"I thought I was strong," I said glumly. "I'm not. I had hoped I was brave. I'm not that either. I want to go home. I'm frightened."

"Of course you are," Vito consoled. "You have reason to be. And don't belittle yourself. You did nobly."

"Vito, I want to go home. By now Aunt Celestine must have sent the money I asked for. Would you mind going down to the desk and asking if there is a cablegram?"

"At once," he said. "I have a man outside your door so you need have no fear."

While he was gone, I assembled my luggage. Anything to keep from thinking about what had happened. Vito was back in five or ten minutes.

"There is no answer," he said. "I sent one of my men to the cable office to inquire there. If they have no word, he will send another cablegram to your aunt. They have her address at the cable office so we will lose no time."

"Thank you, Vito. If you were not here to guide me and help me, I'm sure I would have gone mad by now. What will I do if Celestine doesn't answer? Though it's beyond me why she won't."

"You will have to wait it out for this night," Vito explained. "The cable company will report if the message cannot be delivered. By morning you will know. In the meanwhile, will you have supper with me?"

"Here in this suite," I said. "I don't care to go out of it after what happened."

"I'll go down and wait for the man I sent to the cable office and with your permission I'll order supper to be served at seven."

"Thank you. I can do some packing in the meantime."

I managed to complete the packing, except for the necessities I'd need before I left. Vito returned, his manner apologetic as he reported that no reply had as yet been received.

I forced this new mystery not to interfere with an otherwise pleasant supper. When he left, I kissed him. It was an impulsive gesture and Vito thanked me with a smile. I wished I could have responded to his declaration of love. Certainly I'd never find a better man, or a more considerate one.

There was no reply cable next morning and I gave up waiting for one. I took a carriage to the bank of Signore Babani and I was quickly admitted to his office. I sat down and removed my gloves.

"I'm delighted." Taking my hand, he once again bent over and kissed it. "It's not often a pretty girl visits an old man like me twice in only a few days. You have found your father and mother, I hope."

"No, Signore. Not a trace of them, but I'm not giving up. I came to ask that you extend a loan to me. Enough that I may return to my aunt's home in the United States."

"A loan?" he asked with raised eyebrows. "But I thought . . ."

"I know." I spoke with a trace of nervousness, fearful he was going to refuse. "We are a wealthy family. But I came here depending on meeting my parents, so I did not carry a great deal of money. I have sufficient in a Philadelphia bank, but I can't get it out in time. I wish to return to the United States to see if I can discover a trace of my parents there."

"It is unusual," he said.

"I'm aware of that, but the sum need not be large."

"I can see your problem, *si*," Signore Babani admitted. "But as a banker I am governed by rules which could get me into trouble if I broke them."

As my nervousness increased, I began turning the ring Papa had sent round and round my finger.

I said, "I know, but I hoped there might be exceptions."

"Yes . . . yes, exceptions." He noticed my nervousness. Or was he looking at the strange ring Papa had sent me? "Sit down, Angela. I don't know what came over me. Of course we'll grant you a loan and a substantial one. I shall personally guarantee it myself. Now how many lire would you need? And add a few thousand for good measure."

I gave him the amount I required, too amazed at his

sudden change of heart to ask any questions. The transaction was made in five minutes' time and I was handed a thick sheaf of currency, lire in large notes.

"Thank you, Signore," I said. "You have relieved my mind. As soon as I can reach my bank, I'll cable you this sum at once."

He stood up as I was ready to depart. "Dear Angela, your father was a friend of mine. I admired your mother. Who am I to deny you a trifling loan of money? I hesitated only because the banker in me was temporarily stronger than the common sense I usually display. I beg your pardon for not realizing that from the first."

I left the bank in a considerably better frame of mind than when I'd entered. Now I would let Vito know and he would take care of my steamship accommodations.

But there was Uncle Carlo to consider before I sailed. Poor Carlo, such a frightened man with all his terror brought about by his careless way of living. Yet I couldn't help but like the man. He was part of my family; I couldn't turn my back on him.

I had my driver take me first to the hospital. When I stepped into Carlo's room, he sat up abruptly, his face filled with trepidation which subsided only when he recognized me.

"Uncle Carlo," I remonstrated mildly, "you must not be so afraid."

"That's for you to say." He settled back, but still looked uneasy. "You are not in my position. I may be murdered at any moment. Each time the door opens, I expect to be killed."

"There are *Carabinieri* to guard you," I told him. "I had to identify myself before they'd let me in. Nothing is going to happen to you."

"Perhaps not in the hospital," he grumbled. "Though if these people wanted to kill me now, no police guard would stop them. I speak the truth, Angela. And there is the question of money. How can I pay my bills? I am not able to work."

"You've rarely worked in your life," I told him bluntly.

67

"However, I'll see what's to be done about that after I talk to Aunt Celestine."

"She'd let me fry in hell," Carlo exclaimed. He gasped, as if suddenly struck by an idea that could be catastrophic. "You are going back then?"

"Yes. With luck, I shall sail tomorrow."

He extended his free arm. "Take me with you. Please, Angela, take me or this will be the last time you'll ever see me, for I shall be killed. I know that. Take me to the United States where I can hide. Where they can't reach me. I beg of you, save my life."

"Carlo," I said severely, "I can't take you. I'm not even sure they'll let me back in. I'm an Italian, not a citizen of the United States. There's a quota in effect now. Only so many Italians are allowed to emigrate. At least I have an Italian passport and I grew up in the United States, but you have nothing. They'd make you wait until your turn on the quota came, and heaven knows when that would be."

"Half of Italy is emigrating," he said disconsolately. "Surely you must have some influence. You could get me in."

"I told you, I may not be able to get in, let alone trying to persuade them to let you through. Besides, you're certainly in no condition to travel on such a long journey. I'm sorry, Carlo. I'll do what I can, but only after I get back."

He sighed and slid down in the bed. For a moment I thought he'd pull the sheet over his face in an infantile gesture of dismissal or despair, but he didn't go as far as that.

"I have to abide by whatever you say, Angela. I will let you know as soon as I feel able to travel."

I bent down and kissed him *"Arrivederci,"* I said. "May you be well soon."

He didn't answer me, but settled back on his pillows, his manner that of a sulky child. I gave him a chiding look and left him to return to my waiting carriage for the rest of the trip back to the hotel.

As always, another carriage followed mine, stopped when I did, then waited until I resumed my journey and took up the vigil again. And there were two men stationed outside the hotel as well. While I knew Vito was providing me with the very best protection the *Carabinieri* could furnish, I would feel safer in Philadelphia.

I wrote a hasty message to Vito and gave it to the driver to deliver. It informed him I was ready to depart for my voyage to America.

An hour later, Vito was seated beside me in my suite.

"I'm filled with sorrow," he said quietly. "But in all honesty, I feel a sense of relief that you are going to leave."

"I thought you didn't want me to go," I teased.

"You will be safer there, I think," he said simply.

"If there are no letters from Papa awaiting me, or no evidence that he has been in America, I will be back fairly soon. I hope you will be here, Vito."

"You may be assured of that, Angela."

"Please—be kind to Carlo. He is weak. And frightened."

"His kind never learns," Vito said. "And I don't like you worrying about him when you have your own problems."

I rested my hand lightly on his shoulder. "I promise I shan't worry about him if you will give me your word that you will look after him."

Vito smiled, despite himself. "I promise, my dear. But let's forget Carlo for the time being. If you are ready, I shall put you aboard the train to Genoa. You will arrive about two hours before your ship sails. It is a good ship. The stateroom is reserved. You have but to present the money for your ticket. You do have the money?"

"Oh, yes," I said brightly, eager now to depart. "Signore Babani was hesitant at first. But he changed his mind once he . . ."

I stopped for a second. I was about to tell Vito about the ring which had finally exhibited its magic qualities—if getting a loan from a banker was magic. But Papa had told me never to say anything about the ring to anyone.

"Once he realized how important it was and how secure the loan would be," Vito finished for me. "Are you packed?"

"I can leave at a moment's notice."

"Then we shall be off. I'll send up for your luggage."

Twenty minutes later, we were on our way to the railroad station. We arrived there just as the train to Genoa pulled in, so we had little time for a farewell. Once my luggage was aboard and I had the seat assigned to me, I stepped off the train for a few moments. I wanted to be with Vito until the last possible moment. I suddenly realized I had no one to help me.

"I am so deeply in your debt, I don't know how I can ever repay you."

"I don't want repayment," he replied seriously. "I do want to know if you uncover any clue as to your parents' whereabouts. Will you write me?"

"I will send you a cablegram," I said, "should I have any word from them."

"And if you sense any further danger, will you inform me?"

"I promise."

"Good. I can do a certain amount, even from here. The police in America cooperate with us. Don't hesitate to go to them if you feel imperiled."

"I shan't," I promised. "Though it won't be the same. I will miss you, Vito."

His arms closed around my waist in a gentle embrace and he smiled down at me. "I hope not. One day you will come back—when your troubles are over. And I pray that day will be soon."

"I hope so," I said.

"Perhaps you will miss me more than you think." He kept his tone light, but his eyes were serious. "We have less than a minute left. May I have a farewell kiss?"

"I would like you to kiss me."

I stood on tiptoe and placed my arms about his neck. Though I didn't love him, I was fond of him and could think of no other way to express my feelings, especially since I might never see him again. It was a lingering kiss, but Vito kept his emotions under control. The train's whistle blew a warning signal. Vito released me reluctantly and, just as reluctantly, guided me to the platform steps and stood there until I found my seat. I sat beside a window and smiled at him, standing motionless just beyond it.

He waved as the train started and even walked beside the window, his face soft with the glow of love. As the train quickened its speed, so did he and he ran alongside until the train outdistanced him. I waved back and pressed my face against the window until he disappeared from view as the train rounded a curve.

I settled back for the journey, trying to force myself to study the country. But I was too aware of the failure of my mission. My berth was already made up and I undressed and drew the covers over me. In my loneliness the crude features of that horrible man named Atillio came to me. Once again I saw the horrible lust on his face and the defiance in his eyes. I could feel his hand at my throat as he tore away my clothes, exposing my body. I closed my eyes tightly and held the covers more tightly against my neck.

I had to stop thinking of the past. There was too much for me to do. There had to be some way I could contact Papa. I hoped there would be at least one letter for me when I returned.

By late afternoon I was aboard the great ship, one of Italy's best ocean liners. I had a modest sum left over, sufficient for my needs, after I'd paid for my transportation. I made a decision to remain in my cabin during the voyage.

I was still fearful I might encounter my abductors on board this ship. They had made threats and I had little doubt but they would carry them out if they found it necessary. They had not believed me when I told them I did not know the whereabouts of my parents. And so long as they did not, I felt my life reasonably secure. It also gave me cause to believe my parents were alive.

Yet what could have caused them to disappear?

The voyage was boring and seemingly endless, but it did provide me with a lot of rest. I took my exercise in the early morning, just after dawn, where I met only the employees going about their duties, though giving me a cheerful greeting as we passed.

At long last the ship docked at the pier in New York. I stood at the rail, searching the crowd for some sign of Aunt Celestine. Her height should have made her conspicuous enough in the crowd on the pier, but before I went down the gangplank, I knew she had not come to meet me. She could not have received Vito's cable.

For me, it was not simply a matter of leaving the ship, finding a carriage to the railroad station and making my way directly home. I was an alien. I was not an Italian who'd gone abroad with a United States passport. I should be entering as part of a quota. Customarily I should have gone to Rome or the nearest United States consulate and applied for permission to re-enter, but there'd been no time. I'd not thought of it and if Vito had, he'd not mentioned it. In any case, my situation was not an ordinary one and, I thought, deserved special attention.

But I was marked for treatment not usually offered a first-class passenger. Someone pinned a numbered tag to my coat and a uniformed official herded me over to a group from steerage, all headed for Ellis Island. It was a new experience for me and I didn't especially enjoy it. I wanted only to reach Philadelphia as quickly as possible.

A curtain of wire, strung from one wall of a large room to the opposite wall, made the place where I was sent look like a cage. None of my fellow travelers seemed upset over this. They were patient, quiet, likely more frightened than I, but I sensed they were part of a quota and would be allowed to enter after the usual examination and a study of their papers. About myself I wasn't so sure. After what seemed hours of sitting on a hard bench, I decided to force the issue.

"Please," I called to a uniformed man, "it is of extreme importance that I see whoever is in charge."

"Wait your turn," he said. "Who do you think you are? You don't have permission to enter." Much later I learned he knew this by the color of my tag. "So sit down and be quiet."

I tried pleading with him. "Sir, I have lived in Philadelphia for fourteen years. My aunt has a home there. I went back to Italy because of an emergency. Now there is

72

even a greater one. Please take me to someone in authority."

"You got any kind of passport?" he asked.

I took my Italian passport from my handbag and he studied it to verify that what I'd told him was the truth. The dates of my departure were on the document.

"I'll see what I can do," he said. "Don't get up your hopes too much. Maybe they'll believe you and maybe not. Sit down and wait. That's the most popular saying here. Sit down and wait."

He was correct. I waited almost three hours, growing more and more nervous while my worry increased tenfold. I missed Vito's comforting presence.

I felt the ring Papa had sent me. I'd thought for a few seconds that its magic was working when I asked for a loan, and I wondered why it wasn't working now.

The same guard came back, carrying the passport in his hand. My hopes dropped, even though he was smiling.

"One of the supervisors will talk to you, only because I told him that you spoke English like a native and maybe your story is true. This man hasn't much authority, but if he believes you, he'll do what he can. I have to warn you, however, that he likes to make people uncomfortable. Best I could do. Come along. I'll take you there."

He let me out of the cage and we walked for what seemed to be a mile before we reached a row of offices. He opened the door to a large room, in which there were at least thirty desks, all manned by people in shirtsleeves, engulfed in either a mound of paper or families trying to make themselves understood. He motioned me to the proper desk, then left. I sat down on a hard chair. The man who would decide my fate looked at me coldly. He was a tall, angular, austere-looking individual.

"Now what do we have here?" he asked. "Let's see . . . your papers state you traveled first-class. True?"

"Yes, sir."

"Also, you have an aunt in Philadelphia and make your home with her. Right?"

"Since I was four years old."

"Why did you not become a citizen?"

73

"I'm nineteen. I understood you must be older unless your parents become citizens."

"Or you marry an American," he said. "You understand we have quotas. You left, an Italian citizen. You return, still an Italian citizen. You are granted no more rights than any immigrant. In fact, you're not even in the quota. I can't help you."

"But what must I do, sir? It's imperative for me to get home quickly."

"I'll guarantee you won't, Miss. There will have to be a hearing."

"But it is imperative . . ."

"I told you, we cannot make exceptions."

I was by now too desperate to give up. "May I speak to someone else? Someone with authority to make an exception. Or at least give me a chance to find out if my aunt is ill. You see, she didn't answer my urgent cablegrams and she didn't meet me. That isn't like her. I'm afraid something has happened to her."

"You're not asking to override the quota?" He didn't seem moved by what I'd said, though his growing impatience subsided.

"I only wish to know about my aunt. The rest of it can be straightened out, according to your rules and regulations, but please let me try to contact my aunt."

"Come with me," he said. "I promise nothing, but you can talk to the Commissioner. He's the only one who can break the rules."

The Commissioner had a more spacious office, though there was nothing luxurious about the furniture. However, there was more room than in the cubicle I'd just left. The examiner who'd brought me here motioned me to a row of chairs situated quite far from the Commissioner's desk. I obeyed while he stepped behind the Commissioner's desk and spoke softly, close to his ear. The Commissioner, a portly man, balding, with a round, cherubic face, looked over at me and shook his head. My hopes began to vanish, but the examiner was persistent. He placed my passport on the desk and the Commissioner studied it a moment. Then he raised a hand and signaled me to come before his desk. The examiner, his role completed, favored me with a nod, not one inclined to induce hope. I thanked him in a whisper as we passed. Then I stood before the large desk and the Commissioner looked up at me.

"I know you practically grew up in this country, Miss, but you are not a citizen. It's most essential that we have rules and they cannot be broken for one person who asks for such a favor."

"I know that, sir," I said. "However, my case is different."

"I'm sorry, Miss. No case is different."

"I can prove there is a need for me to contact my aunt. Isn't there some way I could send her a message? At least grant me that privilege."

He nodded. "I suppose I can do that much. You may sit down and write her a note."

"Thank you." My smile was one of gratitude and relief.

To my amazement, he smiled back, then said, "After all, we're not here to persecute people."

He placed a fountain pen and paper before me. I drew off my gloves and began to compose the message. I paused in thought because I really didn't know what to say. If I asked her to come and rescue me, that would be like asking for special treatment and might only delay my getting free if the message was delivered at all.

Suddenly the Commissioner pulled the paper from under the pen and held out his hand for the pen as well. I surrendered it with a sinking heart, wondering what I'd done wrong.

"I've reconsidered," he said. "Just a moment, Miss." He first stamped my passport, with what kind of stamp I had no idea. Then he picked up the telephone on his desk.

"I want this done instantly," he said. "Locate Miss Angela Gambrell's luggage and have it sent to . . ." he studied the passport again before he looked up at me. "Is this your aunt's address?"

"Yes, sir," I replied.

"Good." Into the phone he continued to give orders after reading off the address. "I'll want a carriage waiting

75

in fifteen minutes for the young lady and her passage through immigration is to be done with dispatch."

He hung up, pushed the telephone over to my side of the desk. "If your aunt has a telephone installed, you may call her if you like."

I shook my head. "She didn't have when I left. Do you mean, sir, that I'm free to go?"

"You are indeed. I'll arrange all the paperwork so you won't be inconvenienced. I hope you find things normal when you get home. I'm sorry you had to be delayed this way, but there was no help for it."

"There is no need to apologize. I'm most grateful and deeply in your debt, sir."

"Good luck," he said, and stood up as he offered me his hand. I felt his forefinger very gently brush the strange ring on my hand. It could have been just an accidental gesture, but somehow I thought it had a meaning. As if he was telling me the ring had performed its magical powers. Or was the ring itself trying to tell me this and the Commissioner's touch merely accidental?

I didn't know. I was too excited to concentrate on it though in my mind was the now-firm conviction that the ring did possess some strange influence. It seemed to have worked with the banker in Florence. This time there was little doubt that something had abruptly changed the mind of the Commissioner and I could attribute it only to the ring.

"I shall have you escorted to a ferry which will leave the island the moment you are aboard," he said. "A carriage will be waiting for you at the dock. I wish you well, Miss Gambrell."

"I thank you, sir," I said.

A minor official was summoned. He escorted me straight to the ferry which cast off within two minutes after I was aboard. Clearly this was not a scheduled run, for there appeared to be no passengers aboard except me. At the dock, I was escorted to a waiting carriage. There was no need to give the driver any orders. He already had them. My escort spoke to the driver after he helped me into the vehicle. The driver nodded and began the trip to the railroad station through the maze of afternoon traffic, traveling at a good speed, skillfully avoiding the horse cars, vans, carts and lumbering wagons. There were a few motor cars. More than Philadelphia had, I thought. Certainly this was not Florence, Italy.

At the station, my driver left the carriage and brought me straight to the ticket window. There was some conversation before I was asked to pay for my ticket, which proved to be a Pullman reservation. When I boarded my train, an hour later, my luggage was already aboard and I was handed the claim tickets for it.

Obviously, something had worked wonders for me and eased every mile of the way with a remarkable, efficient dispatch. I studied the ring as the train pulled out of the station. If it was responsible for what had happened, truly it was a magic ring.

I was tired from the ocean trip and the ordeal which had followed it. I was considerably worried about Aunt Celestine too, but at least I could now relax and rest.

Soon I'd be with her. I'd surely surprise her, for it seemed evident that, for some reason, she'd never received my cablegrams or those Vito had sent. I wondered if she had heard from Papa, and if there would be one of his cherished letters waiting for me. I began to doze and the rest of the journey passed without incident or much awareness on my part.

In Philadelphia, a porter handled my baggage and placed it aboard a carriage. I gave my address to the driver and settled back, completely relaxed. I felt that I was home again. I loved this city. I would go back to school and eventually, I would arrange to find work with a fashion designer. For the duration of the drive, I felt as if my worries were over. I told myself everything would be right once my aunt's arms enclosed me. I even assured myself there would be a letter from Papa.

When the carriage drew up in front of our apartment building, I instructed the driver to place the baggage in the lobby. I would have a doorman carry it to our flat. I paid the man, adding a gratuity, and then walked into the building. There was no one in the lobby. I stepped into the elevator and operated it myself. Quite the usual thing, for the operator had other work to do as well and everyone cooperated.

I walked down the familiar corridor with a light step. I would ring the bell, wait for the door to open and see Aunt Celestine's face light up in surprise. Before I could do so, I saw that the door was secured by a massive padlock. Also, there was a strip of paper pasted across the door. I read it with growing apprehension: NO ADMITTANCE BY ORDER OF THE JUDGE OF PROBATE.

I read it again, wondering. Was my aunt ill? But illness wouldn't cause this . . .

Judge of Probate! The very term sent a shudder through me. I took the elevator to the lobby. I scarcely noticed my baggage was placed alongside it.

Peter, one of the employees, was walking toward it. He gave me no smile of welcome when he saw me and he was a warm, friendly person.

"What has happened, Peter?" I asked, even before he reached me. "The door to my aunt's apartment is sealed. Where is my aunt?"

"I'm sorry, Miss Angela," he replied softly. "Sorry I got to be the one to tell you the bad news."

"What bad news?" I asked needlessly, knowing my worst fears were realized.

"It's your aunt, Miss Angela," he said, his manner sympathetic. "She's dead."

"What happened? She was in fine health when I left."

"Wasn't nothing wrong with her health, Miss. She was murdered. By a thief I guess she surprised while he was robbing the apartment. The police know all about it. I don't know any more than what I just told you. You better see them if you want the details."

I walked over to one of the chairs decorating the lobby and sat down. I should have known nothing would have kept her from answering my cablegrams. *Murdered,* Peter had said.

I took a handkerchief from my handbag to wipe away the tears that were already running down my cheeks. I had made a horrible error in going to Italy. Aunt Celestine would still be alive, had I been here. I was young and strong and I could have fought off the burglar.

I was barely aware of Peter talking to someone in the lobby. Later, I learned he had rung the bell of an occupant who had a telephone and requested that he contact the police.

FIVE

My tears ended, but I still sat in the lobby, so staggered by the turn of events I couldn't think.

A gray-haired, fatherly-looking policeman touched my shoulder. "I am Sergeant Warren, Miss Gambrell. We've been waiting for you to return. I'm sorry it had to be under these circumstances."

"It's horrible," I said faintly. "What . . . who . . . ?"

"I know. Look, I have permission to unseal your flat. We can talk there."

It required but a few moments to unseal and unlock the door. My own key opened the regular lock, but the detective barred my entrance with an arm held across the doorway.

"We haven't touched anything. It's gruesome in there and after the shock of learning about what happened to your aunt . . ."

"I can face it," I assured him.

But when I stepped into the parlor, I wondered if I could. Everything in the room was ruined. Pictures had been taken down and their backs ripped off. Padded chairs had been slit open, tables overturned, every drawer pulled out and the contents dumped on the floor.

The other rooms were no different. It was like the work of vandals bent upon complete destruction. But it was Aunt Celestine's bedroom that made me turn away with the feeling I was going to be sick. The bed was unmade; apparently Aunt Celestine had been asleep when the intruders entered and she'd been murdered there. The sheets and pillowcases were covered with dried blood. I backed out of that room and sat down in the parlor. The sergeant righted another chair and carried it over to place it so he'd be facing me as we talked.

"I'll give you the few details we have been able to assemble," he said. "First of all, we've no idea who did this. Professional burglars do not usually ransack a place as thoroughly as this and if they do kill, it's done quickly."

"What do you mean by that?" I asked.

His lips compressed and he turned his head away from me.

"Please tell me," I urged. "I have to know."

"Your aunt was apparently tortured before she was killed," he said quietly.

I covered my mouth to hold back a cry of anguish. "Why? In heaven's name, why?"

"They must have thought she had money or jewelry hidden here. Did she?"

"No. She was far too sensible for that. She kept only small amounts of cash. She used a checking account to pay her bills and she never did have any large amount of jewelry. What she did have wasn't valuable."

"Sometimes," Sergeant Warren said, "they come to believe an intended victim is wealthier than it's ordinarily believed. In this case, they were wrong."

"When did it happen?" I asked.

"About three weeks after you left. For Italy, wasn't it? The building employees told us."

"Don't you have any clues to the murderer?"

"None. I'm sorry. I wish I could tell you that we had these murderers locked up."

"There was more than one?"

"Oh yes. We figure at least two, perhaps three. No one man could do this thorough a job."

"The mail," I said. "Was there any?"

"We found some in the mailbox in the lobby."

"Were there any cablegrams?"

"I don't recall there were."

"There were at least three, perhaps four sent to her from Italy. I was surprised when she didn't answer any of them or meet me at the pier in New York. May I see what mail there is?"

"I'll fetch it. Won't be a moment. I'd appreciate the key to the box. We had to have the mailman unlock it for us."

I gave him the key and while he was gone, I went to examine the wreckage in my room. I didn't go near Aunt Celestine's. Not yet. Eventually I'd have to, but for the moment my sorrow and horror were just too much.

I returned to the parlor and waited for Sergeant Warren to return. I moved restlessly about the room and went over to the window overlooking the street. Directly across from the building I noticed a man. He had coarse features, was poorly dressed and certainly not a resident of this fashionable neighborhood. He seemed to be looking up, straight at me. Or at the window. I stepped back.

Sergeant Warren returned with a considerable amount of mail.

I turned away from the window to address him. "There's a man across the street staring up here."

Warren came to my side and looked down. "I don't see anyone."

I looked to find the man gone. "It is probably nothing to be alarmed about," I said. "It's just that he seemed unsavory. May I examine the mail?"

He nodded. I stepped to a table lying on its side, and set it upright. I placed the mail on it and stood there, examining the envelopes. There was nothing from Papa and certainly no cablegrams. Most of the mail was personal in nature and addressed to Aunt Celestine. The rest were bills.

"Anything," Warren asked, "that could help us?"

"Nothing." I motioned to it. "You may examine it if you wish."

"While I was downstairs, I took the liberty of using a tenant's telephone to call the cable office. I was told that several came from Florence, Italy, and were hand-delivered. Perhaps slipped under the door. I don't know what happened to them. There was no trace of a cablegram when we searched the flat. Do you attach any significance to the fact that someone else got them?"

I felt there was a great deal of significance, but I was reluctant to tell the Sergeant about Papa and Mama and the mystery I'd unearthed in Florence. The sinister aspects of their disappearance seemed to call for keeping it all a strict secret until I knew what it was about.

"I wish I knew who did," I said.

"Perhaps the burglars got them. The crime wasn't discovered until two days after the murder."

"Those cables would not all have reached here in the space of two days. But then, what significance could they have? I don't know. I'm too mixed up to think about it."

"We're doing our best, Miss Gambrell. These are difficult cases to solve. What I'd like you to do is go over everything, as you straighten out the flat. If you find anything is missing, please give us a description of it. Often these burglars try to sell their loot, or pawn it, and sometimes we can trace it back. An inventory of all articles stolen would be of great help to us."

I looked about the room. "I don't know what they could have taken from drawers and cupboards, but I can't see anything missing otherwise. There's a lot of damage, some things likely beyond repair, but as for anything missing, I can't tell yet."

"Well, when you get around to it. Though the quicker you check your aunt's possessions, the better our chances of finding anything that's missing. Are you afraid to be alone? You've had a severe shock."

"I have my emotions under control now." I spoke with far more conviction than I felt. "I have to face up to this tragedy. After I bathe, I'll begin putting the apartment back in order. Thank you for your kindness and patience."

"Send for me, or come to my office if you need help. If you find anything missing, I would like to know about it at once. It could be it was sold to a pawnbroker. Once we have the description of the article from you, we'll check the pawnshops. We might not only find the item, but the pawnbroker might be able to give us a description of the robber. Pawnbrokers are very observant. They've helped us often."

"I know every piece of furniture in this apartment. I'm just as familiar with the silver, crystal and the few pieces of jewelry my aunt possessed."

"Good," Sergeant Warren replied. His mouth opened to speak, then his lips compressed tightly. I knew the reason, so I saved him the trouble.

"Where is my aunt's body?" I asked.

He looked relieved. "Since we couldn't get in touch with you, the Probate Court ordered your aunt's body held until you returned. You will have to take charge of her funeral. Not a pleasant prospect, but it has to be done." He took a card from his pocket. "This has the name and address of the mortician."

"I'll take care of everything tomorrow."

"You handled yourself well, Miss. You'll make out."

"I'll have to, Sergeant. But thanks for your praise."

He set the card on the mantel, started for the door, then turned abruptly. "Oh, I almost forgot. Don't touch anything in your aunt's bedroom. Someone from the force will be here to take the sheets and pillowcases and other blood-stained objects. When the murderers are caught, they will be used as evidence against them."

"I won't even open her door, Sergeant," I said.

He nodded, knowing full well the shock I'd endured from my brief glimpse of the room. We said our farewells and he left.

I hated the sound of the door closing behind him, for I dreaded being alone in the large flat where I'd spent my growing years. I knew for the first time what it was like to have no one. Nor did I have a soul to turn to. If my parents were ever to return to me, this was the time.

My room was in a terrible state of disorder. I had quite a job ahead of me. Nonetheless, I took the time to draw a tub of hot water, undress and immerse my body right up to my neck in the water. I felt the stiffness leave me as my muscles relaxed. I didn't waste any more time than necessary. Once out of the bath, I toweled and put on a wrapper. I went to my bedroom, took the empty drawers from the floor and slipped them into their proper niches in my writing secretary. I picked up writing paper and envelopes strewn over the floor. A quilled pen and sterling silver inkwell had been tossed onto the floor and blue ink stained the rose rug. There was no sign of Papa's letters which I kept tied with a pink ribbon. I replaced the drawers in the bureau and picked up my sweaters, shawls and scarves, folding them and depositing them in the proper drawers. There was also a lingerie chest which had been emptied. The drawers were tossed onto my bed, my lingerie, hosiery, fans, gloves and artificial silk flowers were all in disarray on the floor. I put the drawers back and placed what hadn't been destroyed in them. Some of the gloves had been stepped on and their buttons broken; some of the flowers were crushed from having been walked on. It even appeared that some of them were touched with blood. As if the murderers had walked in it and tracked it in here. Even a few pieces of my lingerie had touches of it. I threw them into the wastebasket beside my desk. If the police desired them as evidence, they were welcome to them.

Once my room was in order, I returned to the parlor and went to work on that. I made many trips to the kitchen, for most of the bric-a-brac was broken; the paintings, torn from their frames, had been ruined.

Strangely, the dining room was untouched. I checked the crystal, china and silver, along with the table linens, and found them intact. The mere sight of the orderly room sent a shudder of fear through me. Everything was intact. So far, all I'd discovered missing were Papa's letters. Which meant it wasn't an ordinary robbery. It seemed to me the murder of my aunt was, in some way, connected to the disappearance of my parents. Had she died because she couldn't tell the killers where to find them? My kidnappers had been brutal with me, but they had let me live. Could it be I was more valuable to them alive than dead?

There was no answer to that puzzle, so I turned my attention back to the flat. I worked diligently, never stopping once to rest. Exhaustion finally claimed me. I gave a final look at the living room—not a piece of upholstered furniture was intact. Stuffing protruded from backs, arms and cushions. The walls were bare, for the paintings and prints had been torn from their frames. Most of the frames had been smashed. I wondered if no one in the building had been aware that something horrible was going on at the time my aunt was being tortured. Didn't she cry out? Or did they blindfold her and hold a hand over her mouth while they questioned her, raising the hand only long enough for her to answer? If she had screamed, even once, the torture would probably have

85

been more severe. I dared not think of what she had been forced to go through.

A light knock on the door made me break out in goose-pimples. I quickly got hold of myself. I could not panic at the slightest sound, or even a knock on the door. Then memory swiftly returned and I moved briskly to open it, for I recognized the knock.

Peter was standing there, holding a paper sack. "I know you didn't have anything to eat, Miss Angela, 'cause I know there was no food in the ice box. I asked the detective if I could clean it out so it wouldn't smell. You'll have ice tomorrow."

"That was thoughtful of you, Peter, and so is this." I reached for the paper sack he held out. "I will pay you for it."

"Oh no, Miss Angela," he protested. "Your aunt did lots of nice things for me and my wife. We said it's our turn to do something nice for you. It's milk, chicken salad and some cookies."

"How can I thank you? I didn't realize I was hungry until you spoke of food. I haven't eaten since breakfast."

His lean features broke into a smile. "I'm sure glad I brought this."

"So am I," I said. "And I won't ever forget. Suddenly I'm starved."

"I got your baggage too. I didn't want to bother you before. It was an awful thing for you to come back to. Your aunt took real pride in her flat. It was the most beautiful in the building."

"I didn't know that, but thanks for saying it, Peter. Will you carry my bags into my bedroom, please?"

"Sure will, Miss Angela. Anything else you want me to do?"

"I have some cartons of various things which were broken. They're in the kitchen. But they can wait until tomorrow morning."

"I'll take them out now." He was already on his way to the bedroom with the baggage. "No need for you to look at what happened to all those beautiful things. You shouldn't have had to clean up the mess. I wanted to, but the police said no one can touch anything until you get

86

home. Guess they wanted to see if you could make any sense out of it. Doesn't make sense to destroy things."

"No, Peter, it doesn't."

He talked as he worked. The bags deposited in my bedroom, he headed for the kitchen. I followed him and opened the back door.

"No sense making more steps for you, Peter," I said. "I think you'll have to drag those cartoons out. They're heavy."

He tried lifting them, but to no avail. "Guess you're right, Miss Angela,"

He dragged one out the door, then stood erect. "Close this door and lock it, Miss Angela, after I finish. And do the same to the front door. You left that wide open."

I set the sack on the table. "I'll do something nice for you and Sarah one day. I won't ever forget this."

"Wasn't much," Peter said. "Sarah told me to tell you if you're scared, she'll come sit here all night."

"That's dear of her. But I can't be a coward," I said.

"After what happened here, no one would say you were. It's got all the tenants scared."

I was also, though I didn't voice the thought. However, I did ask a question which came to mind. "Did anyone hear my aunt cry out?

"No one, Miss Angela. The police questioned everyone in the building."

"Certainly it would seem they would have heard drawers being pulled out and thrown to the floor. The way they were scattered about, it must have made noise."

"Might have, Miss Angela. The apartment below is empty. Has been for three months. The one above is empty now. People are staying with relatives till they find another place. Wouldn't live here after what happened."

"That's understandable," I said.

Peter pulled the third carton into the hall. "You lock the door now, Miss Angela. I'll stand right here till you do. I'd have made you do it before, but I can see it from here and no one got in."

"I'll be careful."

"Better be after what happened."

87

I closed the door, turned the key in the lock and slid the bolt, then I walked through the apartment to the front door. Peter was already there, waiting for me.

I said, "Good night, Peter. Please thank Sarah."

"I will," he replied. "And when you finish eating, you get your rest. Just one thing more, Miss Angela."

"Yes, Peter?"

"Sarah and I would like to attend your aunt's funeral."

"That's very kind of you. It will be tomorrow afternoon,"

"That's what we figured. The owner gave me the day off. Sarah and I will be here. Your aunt was good to us. We want to pay our respects."

"I'm grateful and she would be too. I'm also pleased you will be with me. You've made me feel a little more easy. Good night."

He nodded, but didn't move until I closed the door and turned the key in the lock. I went back to the kitchen, got a glass, plate and a fork, washed and dried them and emptied the sack.

I devoured the food gratefully, washed the few dishes, put out the light and went to my bedroom. I shuddered as I passed my aunt's bedroom.

I closed the door to my bedroom, put on a nightdress and got into bed. I had to use my arm as a pillow, for the pillows had been slashed and emptied. The vandalism had been complete.

I doubted I would be able to sleep, but the food settled well in my stomach and my exhaustion was complete. I fell into a deep sleep.

I awoke, hearing the sound of my own voice crying out in terror. I'd been dreaming. Not a pleasant one. I was reliving the terror of that night I'd been kidnapped. I tried breathing deeply and slowly to calm my nerves, but it was no use.

I got up, put on my robe, went to the kitchen for a glass of water and moved through the darkness into the parlor. I was restless and frightened and wished terribly there was someone in this city I could confide in. But I knew that if I did, I would surely endanger my parents.

I went over to the window and stood there looking

down at the street. It was easily visible through the lace curtain. My attention was immediately drawn to someone standing in a doorway across the street. He would have been invisible except for his carelessness. He was smoking a cigar or cigarette and the glow brightened as he drew on it. I wondered if it was the same man who had been watching this building soon after I arrived.

I tried to ease my concern by telling myself he was one of Sergeant Warren's men assigned to protect me. Except that if he had ordered a guard, he would certainly have told me.

I saw the man move out of the doorway, walk casually along the street until he moved beyond my line of vision. I actually smiled in relief.

So much to be done. I'd have to learn how to live alone. I would have to become a responsible adult overnight.

I would have to earn my own way. I doubted that my aunt's estate was large. My first concern was seeing to her funeral and that gave me a sense of uncertainty. Funerals cost money and there was little left of what I'd borrowed in Florence.

After those duties were fulfilled, I'd visit the art school and obtain from Mrs. Gardner a final judgment as to my ability to be a fashion designer. The more I thought about the idea, the greater the appeal it held for me. I'd never read about anyone who designed fashions, but certainly someone must.

I thought I'd momentarily dozed off in a parlor chair, but when my eyes opened, it was broad daylight and I lay on the sofa. I didn't even remember moving from the chair to the sofa. I moved quickly to my bedroom. My bedside clock told me it was midmorning and I'd slept a reasonably sufficient time. Certainly, I felt rested.

Of course all the sorrow and worry returned so that I had to fight off a feeling of deep dismay. Talking to the people at Aunt Celestine's bank would require a clear head.

I selected a subdued daytime dress from my wardrobe, then had breakfast in a small restaurant a few blocks away. Aunt Celestine and I had often dined there. I had to blink back tears and clear my throat before I ordered.

I called a carriage when I stepped out of the little

restaurant and I was driven to the bank where Celestine had kept her account. I'd often accompanied her so I knew the bank and some of the employees knew me.

There was one bank officer in charge of estates and trusts, a kindly, understanding man in his sixties who had liked Aunt Celestine and was indignant that the police had not yet arrested the men who had killed her. I learned from him that there'd been quite a few articles about the crime in the newspapers.

"Now," he said, "I've already examined your aunt's account records in view of the fact that I expected you'd be back from Europe soon. Just what is it you wish to know, Angela?"

"I've no money of my own. Aunt Celestine supported me." I didn't mention that the money she used for my upbringing and education had been supplied by my father.

"And you wish to know if she left anything. The answer is yes. Not a great deal, but enough to see you through this ordeal. I'm afraid you'll have to begin earning a living, my dear."

"What would the sum be?" I asked.

"Slightly more than four thousand."

"Thank you. She didn't maintain a safe deposit vault?"

"Not in this bank. I doubt in any other. Her income was regular and sufficient or she'd not have been able to save this much. She was not a woman with spendthrift habits."

"Could you tell me where her income came from?"

"No, I'm sorry. Every four months she would deposit a money order, usually the same amount or close to it. We don't keep any record of where the money orders come from or from whom. Now, it will take a bit of doing, but I can advance you a thousand now. The rest will have to wait until the Probate Court judge takes this estate in hand. I can expedite that, however, so we should be able to settle everything within a month."

"Thank you. That will give me the time I need to complete my plans, whatever they may be. I intend to remain in the flat."

"Yes, that's best I'm sure. Don't worry about the estate. If you'll wait a few more minutes, I'll arrange a checking account for you and deposit the thousand dollars in it. You'll have to sign a card so we have your signature on file."

I thanked him and, after signing the card and receiving a small checkbook, I left to visit the mortician whose card Sergeant Warren had given me.

Mr. Graham was properly sympathetic. He was a man of middle years, dressed in a black suit and black tie. When I identified myself, he brought me into his office and moved a small armchair over to the side of his desk.

Once he seated himself behind his desk, he expressed his sympathy at the shocking tragedy. Then he got down to my reason for being there. I appreciated that because it was difficult at best and I wished it settled as quickly as possible.

He then told me, much to my surprise, that my aunt, Miss Guillermo, had a funeral plot.

"I had no idea," I said.

"Oh yes." He had a meticulous way of speaking. It seemed to go with his clothing, yet his manner was proper without being patronizing. "She came to me a year ago and told me she had purchased a plot of ground in the cemetery one block from here."

"Is there just one grave?"

"No, Miss Gambrell. There are two. She said she had a niece named Miss Angela Gambrell. She asked me to write your name down. I did so—on her card. She left specifications for two funerals, yours as well as hers. And paid for everything."

The information shocked me. Certainly, at my age, one does not think of death or the possibility of dying, even though such a thing could occur.

Mr. Graham's lips moved in the semblance of a smile. "I know this comes as a shock to you, Miss Gambrell. However, I believe your aunt was one who left nothing to chance. Certainly she didn't expect to meet such a dreadful death."

"I'm sure she didn't."

"I would say she was thinking of you. If more families did it, this business wouldn't add to their grief. She even selected her casket. And, I might add, she left suitable clothing—for her. Not for you. When I read of the crime, I told the police and left my card. There is nothing for you to do except to tell me when you wish the funeral."

I did so, then wondered if I would be allowed a last glimpse of my aunt. It would seem the respectful thing to do.

As if reading my thoughts, Mr. Graham said, "The casket should remain closed. Remember her as she was when you left."

"Thank you, Mr. Graham. Was it that . . . shocking?"

"It was, Miss Gambrell, but try not to dwell on it. Her suffering is over. I will notify Father McDonald."

I told him I would like services at the church in an hour if possible. He assured me it would be.

I knew Sarah and Peter would be awaiting me in the lobby of the building. And they were. They got into the carriage with me and the three of us went to the church, where the priest said a low mass for my aunt. Then we moved on to the cemetery. We were the only mourners following the hearse with its black-plumed horses. The priest rode with the undertaker and the pallbearers.

I asked Sarah, a buxom, motherly type, to sit beside me. She did and held my hand until we reached the cemetery. Pallbearers were already there. They placed the casket on the ropes that would later be used to lower it into the grave and stepped back, lining up respectfully.

The priest moved to the head of the casket. I stood on one side, Peter and Sarah on the other. The priest intoned the last rites and recited a few prayers. A lovely bouquet of pink roses, my aunt's favorites, rested atop the casket. Apparently she had included them. When the services ended and Father McDonald, a kindly soul, expressed his sympathy, I bent down and slipped two roses from the bouquet. Once in the carriage, I gave one to Sarah.

"Thank you, Miss Angela. I'll keep this," she said softly. "If there's anything I can do, please say so."

"Thanks, Sarah," I said. "But I can't think of a thing."

"What about food?" she asked.

"I hadn't even thought about it," I said, giving her an embarrassed smile.

"I don't mean it to sound sacrilegious," she said, "but the living's got to eat. Your aunt would want me to look after you."

I opened my handbag and took out a bill. "Please buy something."

"I already got ice for you," Peter said.

"And I'll cook your supper," Sarah said.

"I can't let you. I know you did cleaning for my aunt, but there's little money left."

"Wouldn't take a dime from you," Sarah said. "But Peter and me are going to look after you so long as you live in Philadelphia. I expect that'll be the rest of your life."

I didn't answer, for I had no idea what I was going to do. I felt the shock of what had happened to my aunt all over again and I thought of her room. I mentioned it to Peter and related that Sergeant Warren also had told me not to touch it.

He said, "I went to the police station this morning and told them I believed you would be out this afternoon and they could come then and take what they wanted. So when we get back, I'll clean up that room."

"I'll appreciate it," I said. "Suddenly I feel very tired."

"After what you came home to," Sarah consoled, "it's going to take a lot of rest before you'll feel yourself again."

"No, it won't," Peter argued. "Miss Angela's young. She's got her own life to live and Miss Celestine would want her to do just that. Not sit and grieve over something that can't be undone."

Memories of my aunt sifted through my mind. Memories of happy days, of happy years. Yet I wondered if she had sensed danger and had prepared for it. I had no idea she had purchased a burial plot. And one with two graves! I tried not to read something into that gesture on her part, but I wondered if she had had some knowledge of where my parents were. If so, I was certain it had died with her. She would never have betrayed them.

I insisted Sarah use the carriage to shop for groceries. Peter came upstairs with me and waited until I entered my room before he opened the door of my aunt's.

However, I had to know if the police had come during

our absence. There was no sign that anything had been disturbed in the parlor. I asked him to check.

Peter opened the door of my aunt's room a crack, then wider. "They came," he told me. "They took what they wanted. I can clean up here now. You rest, Miss Angela. Sarah will have a good supper for you."

"I'd like you both to stay and eat with me," I said. "I feel a terrible emptiness here."

"So do I, Miss Angela," Peter said kindly. "And we'll stay."

"Thanks." I smiled my gratitude, entered my room and removed my hat and gloves. I glanced briefly at the ring I wore and gave a shake of my head. I couldn't see where any good luck was attached to it. Since I'd put it on my finger, my life had taken a drastic change, from one of calm serenity to one of violence and murder.

I went over to my writing desk and sat down. Carlo had to learn the bad news and the sooner the better. I took paper from my desk, but had to stop to fill the silver inkwell. I told him about the violent death of his sister, what had happened to the apartment, yet, despite that, I would continue to live here. I described her burial and concluded with the hope he had recovered from his injuries.

I wrote a longer letter to Vito, giving him details in full. I hesitated about appending a note that I missed him because, in truth, I had not thought of him except once, when I wished he was with me because his presence would have provided a peace of mind I needed. I was fond of him —I thought of him as a dear friend. Pleasant company, but that wasn't love. He did not provide that certain spark I knew would tell me when I met the right man.

I managed to sleep fairly well and the next day I first paid a visit to the Federal Courthouse where I applied for my first citizenship papers. In two more years I would be able to apply for my second papers and then I'd be sworn in as a citizen of the United States. After my experience at Ellis Island, I knew how necessary this was. That chore accomplished, I hired a carriage to take me to the art school.

Fortunately, Mrs. Gardner was not busy. She received me with a close embrace and, at the same time, she briefly expressed her sorrow over the death of Aunt Celestine. She didn't dwell on it, she asked no questions about the murder itself, or the apartment, and I was grateful.

"I feel as if I've been through too much to go back to my studies," I explained. "The day I left to go to Italy you suggested fashion designing. Do you still feel the same way?"

"My dear, as for becoming an artist, forget it. However, I've shown your full-length portraits to people interested in fashions and, to be quite frank, most of them never even noticed the subject you painted, only the clothes you painted on your models. Yes, Angela, if you study fashions and learn how to design women's clothing, I have little doubt but that you will become successful, even famous. I wish I had classes in designing. You'd be one of my best pupils."

"That's gratifying to hear," I said. "Only how does one go about learning how to design clothes? I never heard of a fashion designer. Even the term seems new to me."

"I would suggest that you talk to people in the garment business. The retailers, dressmakers and those in the big department stores, especially in New York. However, I would say the very best place to study clothing design would be Paris. All of our high-priced gowns come from there."

"I'd love to study in Paris," I said. "But it's out of the question. I'll have only a few thousand from my aunt's estate."

"With some degree of thrift, that ought to be enough to see you through."

"Then I'll go," I said. "It will be good for me too, getting me away from the tragedy."

"An excellent idea. Take my advice and do not be hasty, take the time to find out all there is to know about this type of work. Until you're certain you can persuade the people who control the business that your ideas in design are as practical as they are beautiful. The clothes you've painted on your models are revolutionary. You've been designing without realizing it."

"Thank you, Mrs. Gardner. The fact is, I clothed my models in garments that are less constrictive than what we are presently wearing. I seemed to notice it first when I was painting. It is my opinion that clothes should not get in our way."

Mrs. Gardner nodded approval. "Remember that and voice it whenever possible once you start your own establishment."

"I wish you were closer. I think I would move along much faster."

"I will be with you in spirit," she replied kindly. "One thing more. I recall a play the students put on about a year ago, for which you dressed several dolls. Do you still have them?"

"I believe so. In fact, I think they're here in the school, packed away in a box."

"Then I suggest if they still look fresh that you take them with you as your trademark. Continue to make them. When you get your establishment or should you work for others, set them in the showrooms. Besides being decorative, they will be an attractive advertisement for your talents."

The idea excited me. "You should charge me for that advice."

"You're one of my students. I always live with the secret hope that each one will have learned something that will help them sometime during their life. Not necessarily in painting. Geniuses are rare, gifted painters just as rare. But from learning how to bring a canvas to life, one can discover something that will be both helpful and stimulating."

"Certainly you have helped me. I never thought of designing clothes until you spoke of it before I went to Italy. Yet once you did, the thought kept slipping back in my mind, though not too seriously until I was suddenly confronted with the knowledge that I would have to earn my own living."

She regarded me strangely. "I have heard of your father. I read he was also wealthy."

"That is true," I said. "But he and Mama are traveling. They don't know yet about Mama's sister and I'm not going to tell them. Papa was greatly overworked and needed a holiday."

"That is very thoughtful of you to bear the entire burden of this tragedy," Mrs. Gardner said. "However, his money will be in your favor. If you run out of funds, you can always turn to him."

"I hope I shall become so successful I will have no need of his help. I would like to surprise him." I stood up, noting that Mrs. Gardner glanced at the clock on her desk. She was very sparing with her time and she had given me more than I deserved, particularly since I was no longer a student. "I will work very hard to be a success."

"If you work hard, you will make it."

"And I have you to thank for it." I spoke as we walked to the door. "You will have the gratification of knowing that you guided another of your students into a career."

"They're painfully few, my dear," she said. "Also, you may meet with many frustrations because you are a woman. Don't let it discourage you."

"I shan't. I'm going upstairs now to get that box of dolls. Thanks for remembering them."

I returned home to the flat where Sarah and Peter awaited me and told them of my plans. Sarah was excited about it, but Peter regarded me as if I were bereft of my senses. I didn't mind. They promised to look after the flat.

I departed the next day for New York City where I would make arrangements to set sail for Paris. I couldn't leave until I had received a check from Probate Court. I would stay at a small hotel on a side street I was familiar with. My aunt used to take me to New York three or four times a year and she always registered there. It was quiet and refined and used mostly by elderly people who were catered to by a kindly management, not because they had money, but because they had once been used to luxury, but now lived on a more modest income.

Before I left, I arranged to have my passport renewed and to make certain, without question, that this time there would be no difficulty in getting back into the United States.

During my spare time, of which I had a great deal, I made it a habit to visit all the big stores, especially B. Altman's on Fifth Avenue in New York. There I was able to study the styles and talk to people in the industry who could reasonably predict the future of women's clothing in America. More and more I realized this was the field for me. I found it fascinating but more than that, a field in which there were many opportunities because fashion designing had been sorely neglected, especially in the United States. Anything imported from Paris was deemed stylish and quickly sold, but clothing made in the United States hung on the racks until it grew limp from age. I meant to put an end to that if I could.

At long last I received word from the Probate Court and I was finally able to arrange my passage. I had already packed for a long stay and everything was here, including a shoe-box trunk, small enough to slide under my berth, and a regulation steamer trunk to be stored in the hold and delivered to whatever my address would be. I selected my clothing carefully for I was, by now, a fairly seasoned ocean traveler. For shipboard daytime wear, I set aside woolens of quiet colors. All ships, no matter what their reputation, are hard on clothes, and too much finery in travel is both vulgar and uncomfortable. I even sketched what I thought to be something suitable, something between these two extremes. For dinners I would wear woolen skirts with a waist of foulard silk or French sateen. For the more formal meals, a black silk finished with fine lace at the throat and wrists would be suitable. If I intended to enter the world of fashion, I had to act the part even though I was no more than a beginner.

I made a hasty trip back to Philadelphia. I was now the possessor of a fair amount of money, on deposit for me. The speed with which this had been accomplished made me think of the powers of the magic ring, which I wore constantly. It seemed to have served me well before and I wondered if it had been responsible for the dispatch with which this matter had been conducted. It didn't matter. In my loneliness it was a comfort to have something like this.

Now that everything was in order, I closed up the flat, left a farewell note to Sarah and made the journey to New York and to the pier where a French ship was due to sail. I'd already had a deck chair sent to the ship for my exclusive use. It cost two dollars, but I felt the comfort it would provide was well worth the money. One day, I supposed, these ships would provide such chairs, but thus far they had not. Perhaps I could sell it after we reached Cherbourg.

Some days prior to sailing, I'd written Carlo a long letter, telling him my plans, asking him to join me, and enclosing a draft sufficient to keep him until I arrived. He was to find a pleasant apartment for us in Paris. Sometimes I had doubts as to my wisdom in placing this responsibility on Carlo. Yet, if he overstepped, I had a letter of credit in my possession and I could find my own quarters later. Being utterly unfamiliar with Paris, I needed someone who knew the city and Carlo knew it—rather well, I assumed. Especially the livelier portions.

My stateroom was small, but on the upper deck which granted me sufficient light and air. The Promenade deck was just outside and I found the accommodations satisfactory, if not luxurious. I was not inclined to squander my money on things I did not actually need.

My deck chair, duly identified with my name, was in place and as soon as the sailing festivities were over and the great ship well out at sea, I provided myself with my blanket and went out to enjoy the sun and the ocean air. I had made up my mind that this voyage was going to provide me with enough rest and relaxation to last through the busy times I anticipated were ahead.

I'd done a rather strange thing, for me, after I first boarded the ship. I'd sent my luggage to my cabin and then I stayed close to the gangplank watching everyone who came aboard. I didn't know who or what I looked for, but I was still suspecting that I'd been watched right after I returned from Italy and found Aunt Celestine murdered. If I was right, then I was quite likely being kept under some kind of surveillance. Yet I'd seen no suspicious character following me. I knew the man or men I'd seen across the street from the flat were not police assigned to protect me. I'd made a brief call to the police station to check. Sergeant Warren informed me it was not the case.

I'd never before realized how varied the number of passengers who board a ship were. They came aboard via the gangplank, first cabin, second cabin, steerage. No one paid any attention to me for they were all too excited or too busy juggling their luggage. Only one man looked directly at me. When our eyes met, he smiled. He received no smile in return, though secretly I appreciated his attention, brief though it was.

He was a tall, rangy sort of man, with medium brown hair with auburn highlights. His eyes were a vivid blue. His face was rather long, but with good bone structure.

Now, as I approached my steamer chair, I found him spread full-length on it. He wore a shirt open at the neck, a pull-on sweater, cream-colored trousers, white shoes and a yachting cap. He looked up as I approached and once again he smiled. And once again I did not return the smile.

When he became aware that I was going to address him, he came to his feet. "Good afternoon," he said, in a voice equipped with a slight drawling accent which I couldn't place.

I said, quite crisply I'm afraid, "You happen to be using my chair, sir. If you look closely, you will see my name on it."

He turned about and looked. The name was printed on a bit of paper glued to the crosspiece on the back of the chair. The letters were so small they were barely visible, as if the stewards were aware that a woman, traveling alone, has no wish to advertise her name.

"So it is," he said. "I'm very sorry, Miss. I was of the opinion that deck chairs were not reserved."

"They are when the occupant has purchased them," I said.

"You bought the chair before the ship sailed?"

"And had it delivered aboard."

He shook his head. "I learn things every day. I apologize for this *faux pas*. May I make up for it by having the steward bring you a glass of orange juice or some other drink?"

"You may not," I said, still annoyed by him.

"I understand. I really don't blame you." He removed his yachting cap. "Once again, I apologize."

He began to turn away and as quickly I relented. He meant no harm. I'd been both priggish and rude.

100

"I'm sorry too, sir," I said. "My name is barely visible. Even if it were, it's a trivial matter."

He turned about quickly and broke out in a radiant smile which was infectious enough to make me smile too.

"That's great!" he said. "May I . . . well . . . try to find a chair and join you?"

"If you wish," I said, still under the spell of that smile.

He soon returned with a steward carrying a deck chair. The chair was set up, a gratuity was passed and the young man sat down beside me.

"We've been outbound three hours and the owner of this chair is seasick already. I feel sorry for him. My name is Stanton Talbot."

"How do you do, Mr. Talbot," I said. "I am Angela Gambrell."

"I'm delighted we could meet, Miss Gambrell. When I came aboard, I saw you on deck and wanted to meet you. I assure you, however, it did come about purely by accident."

"Thank you for the compliment." His manner was so disarming I had to caution myself to remain on guard.

"It's going to be a long voyage. And a boring one unless I find a pleasant companion. Are you traveling alone?"

"Yes." I again admonished myself to be vigilant.

"Then there is no reason why we should endure loneliness on such a long voyage. May I ask your destination?"

"Paris. My uncle will meet me there."

"I'm traveling on business. Something to do with foreign money exchange for a client of mine. Oh, I forgot to mention it. I'm an attorney."

I nodded. "That explains your inquiring mind."

He eyed me curiously. "The young lady has a suspicious one."

"A young lady traveling alone must be wary."

"And also discreet—which you are. I said it before you had the opportunity." He laughed. "I wish you could trust me a little. It would be more enjoyable for both of us. If you insist, I'll talk about torts, mittimuses and the rest of it, though I guarantee you'll find it a bore. I know I'd find it a bore. I'd rather know why a single young lady," he glanced at my gloved hands, "you are single, aren't you?"

"I am."

"Have you been spoken for?"

"You don't mind asking personal questions, do you?" I was becoming mildly exasperated.

"I'm afraid not." He wasn't the least bit embarrassed or affected by my show of irritation. "You see, I like you. I think we could have an enjoyable time together. How else can I get to know about you if I don't ask questions?"

I relented. "You can't, of course. So I'll tell you. First of all, I'm an Italian citizen. My name is really Gambrelli. I'm going to Paris to study dress designing. I will be under the chaperonage of my uncle. Before you ask, his name is Carlo Guillermo."

"Are you an orphan?"

"Good gracious, no," I exclaimed. "And will you please stop asking questions?"

He found my exasperation amusing. "I only asked because I wondered if you weren't, your parents must live somewhere on the continent. Italy, perhaps?"

"Yes. Just now they are on a holiday."

"But your home is in Italy."

"It is," I said firmly.

"Don't get angry," he said quickly, raising a cautioning finger. "I made it a statement. I won't ask why an Italian citizen speaks impeccably American English."

Despite myself, I smiled. "I was raised by my aunt in Philadelphia."

He was frowning.

I thought I knew why and said, "Her name was Celestine Guillermo."

He sobered even more. "She was brutally murdered. I read an account of it in the newspaper."

"Yes," I replied.

"Didn't the newspaper account state that you were out of the country at the time of your aunt's murder?"

"I have no idea of what the newspapers reported," I said. "But yes, I was in Italy. I had no knowledge of my aunt's murder until I returned."

"A dreadful shock for you," he said. "You're wise in getting away from it all for the time being. It will also help to immerse yourself in your studies. Dress designing, you said? You're the first lady I've met who is interested in making a name for herself in the business world."

"I hope," I spoke with trepidation, "I will be successful in doing that. It's daring."

"And a challenge. I've no doubt you meet it." He paused, then added, "May I escort you to the dining room tonight?"

"Yes. Just don't tell anyone what I've told you."

"I give you my word."

I wore a simple dinner dress. It had lacy frills on it, plus enormous sleeves and a bustle and an underskirt, plus numerous petticoats. As usual, I felt weighted down with it, but it was made of a soft fabric, antique gold in color, which complemented my olive skin and dark brown eyes. I wore my hair piled high on my head, which made me seem taller and gave length to my round face.

I'd watched my aunt apply makeup many times. She was so skilled in the art one wouldn't even realize she wore any. I had purchased some before I left, but I had no need of any except a film of powder which I touched to my face with a chamois. Excitement colored my cheeks and I touched perfume to my earlobes and my wrists, another trick I had learned from my aunt. The perfume I used had once been hers. It was a delicate floral essence that made me feel very feminine.

Mr. Talbot came for me and escorted me to the dining salon. I felt very elegant as the head waiter led us to a table near the captain's. Mr. Talbot had already told me I looked so enchanting I took his breath away. I felt radiantly happy. I'd never known such a feeling before. But then I had never felt so important before. Yet it wasn't really a feeling of importance. It was that I had a sudden awareness of the importance of being a woman. A sudden and complete awareness of it. I hoped the newness of this feeling I had wasn't revealed in my face. I wanted to appear sophisticated. Certainly Mr. Talbot was. I felt utterly confused. It wasn't rapture I felt and yet it was. My thoughts were getting all tangled up. I decided to concentrate on Mr. Talbot and forget trying to diagnose the change in me or what had caused it.

Our table was for two and it was partly secluded by artificial palms. Mr. Talbot suggested wine and I agreed. When our eyes met across the table as we raised our glasses in a toast, my heartbeat further quickened. His eyes held the same warm glow I felt in mine. Yet I knew he couldn't feel as I did.

We turned our attention to the dinner and both of us ate too much. However, we retired to the ballroom and danced to the strains of a string orchestra. When we tired of dancing, we took a stroll around the deck. Moonlight silvered the ocean and the sky was a myriad of stars. From time to time, the ship's bell rang the hour, but I paid it no heed until I had to stifle a yawn.

"I'm sorry, Mr. Talbot, but I do believe I am completely exhausted. I know I shall sleep well."

"Good. I'm not so sure I will." He led me out of the salon and we headed for my cabin. He was holding my hand lightly. The one on which I wore the ring. He raised my hand and held it so the moonlight revealed the ring plainly. "This is most unusual and quite beautiful. It's really an eye-catcher. I hope you don't mind my saying so."

"Of course not. It was given me by my father."

"Is it a family heirloom?"

"If so, he neglected to tell me."

"Perhaps it's a good luck ring."

"Perhaps. Though I never thought of it as such." My voice was barely audible. The magic of the evening had ended. I couldn't believe his statement was coincidental.

"Will I see you tomorrow?" he asked. "Rather, may I?"

"I haven't made my plans for tomorrow, so I can't answer that."

"Dinner then?"

"I'm not sure."

"Sleep on it. I'll be looking for you." His light mood was also gone and he regarded me soberly, studying my face. He seemed about to say something, then apparently thought better of it.

I withdrew my hand and opened my handbag for my key. He took it from me, unlocked my door, then stepped back for me to enter.

I was about to bid him good night when he spoke my name. Just hearing him say it made my heart race.

"Angela." He said it again.

"Yes?" I asked.

"Nothing," he replied.

"Then why did you say my name?" I noticed my voice was tremulous.

"I wanted to hear how it sounded. It's beautiful. Angela . . . Angela. Close the door, Angela. I shall go to sleep with the sound of your name on my lips."

I did close the door—fast. And I leaned against it, mostly because I thought if I took a step, I would fall. My knees seemed about to buckle. He spoke my name twice more. It seemed as if he had his mouth against the door, for his voice was muffled. I closed my eyes and pressed the palms of my hands against the door, as if by doing so, I could feel the touch of his hands against mine. Then I heard his footsteps as he slowly moved away. I stood motionless until I could no longer hear him.

Could it be I had fallen in love? I dared not think of it, yet I could think of nothing else. And in love with a man who might not only be my enemy, but that of my parents as well.

I must shut him out of my mind. It would be well to keep him at a distance. To ignore his presence completely. I could do it. I would make myself do it. It would have to be that way. He had made too great an impression on me. I was in love. Admit it, I told myself. You love Stanton Talbot. This crazy, mad, beautiful, wild feeling is love. Beautiful and miserable. Miserable because you should know better than to trust him. Beautiful because you can't wait for tomorrow when you will seek him out if he doesn't you.

We were together all day and most of the social hours in the evening. We walked miles along the deck, testing one another's endurance. We played shuffleboard, we danced in the evening, sometimes we watched slide shows provided to acquaint us with what France was like. There was even one night when we sailed through a violent storm and we clung to one another in defiance of the rain

105

and the winds, until we had enough and laughingly returned to the salon, dripping wet.

The lonely journey I'd expected was joyous and too quick in passing. It was the last night out and we were in no mood for dancing. Instead we sat huddled on deck, for it had grown cold, with blankets covering us up to our chins. It wasn't that we enjoyed this weather and the chill, but we wanted privacy. Going to a cabin was out of the question and there was nowhere else aboard where we could be alone.

"Want to go in?" Stan asked me after several minutes of silence.

"Not unless you want to. I'm comfortable enough," I replied.

"Good. I'm going to be quite frank, Angela. You must first know about me. I'm twenty-six. I graduated from a Northern law school and I'm an ambitious man. I firmly believe I shall be successful."

"I'm sure of it too," I agreed quietly.

"Thank you. That's going to help. Now, my home is in New Orleans."

"I knew you were from the South. Your accent," I said with a smile.

"Yes," he agreed. "It gives us away. My father is dead. He was a lawyer too, and he became a judge. My mother is wrapped up in social affairs. You name any society event and her name is there, if not at the top of the list, not very far down it. I have no one else. I intend to make my permanent home in New Orleans because I love that city. Now—do you know why I'm telling you this?"

"Suppose you tell me," I said softly.

"I adore you. I want to spend the rest of my life with you. Tomorrow we dock. Don't let me lose you."

"I have no address yet," I said. "If you can give me yours . . ."

"I will . . . it's a hotel and I'm not certain of it. I have to check my travel plans. In the morning I'll have it for you. Get in touch with me there and we'll do Paris. See everything. They say it's a city for lovers."

"Stan," I said, "there are things about my life that I'm not prepared to tell you now."

"Then don't bother," he said airily. "They won't matter."

"They do to me. I'll need a little time to think."

"But you love me?" he asked. He was watching my face intently.

"Yes. I think so. I'm not sure I know what love is. I like being with you. I'm sad when we have to say good night, even though I'll see you again in the morning. I do feel something that warms me and makes me want to see you again. I think I almost fell in love once before, but although I liked the man tremendously and respected him above anyone I'd met before, there was not the . . . I don't know what to call it . . . the same feeling I have when I'm with you."

"Was he in love with you?"

"Yes. Deeply, I think. He is a policeman in Florence, Italy. A ranking officer and a fine man. About your age and just as ambitious in his profession as you are in yours. He was kind to me, he was there when my uncle became involved in a little trouble."

"Yet with all he offered, all he did for you, it wasn't the same as you feel right now, with me?"

"No, not the same." I paused, searching for words. "Stan, I'm going to ask that you not press me now. There are things I must do. Extremely important matters which I cannot involve you in. I know it may be hard for you to understand this, but you must bear with me."

"In other words, you need time."

"Yes, it's precisely that."

"Shall we go in now?" he asked, rather abruptly I thought.

"Yes, it's late and we dock early in the morning."

He helped me up and we walked slowly around the deck just once, not saying a word. My own mind was running wild with a mixture of happiness because of what he'd said, and sadness because we would not be together again for some time. We reached my cabin and Stan unlocked the door for me.

Then, before I could enter, he took me in his arms and for the first time our lips met in a kiss of delight, wonder and passion. I held tightly on to him until I grew breath-

107

less. My resistance abated; my resolutions to resist him were forgotten.

I looked up at him and slowly ran my forefinger over his lips. "Now I know," I said. "I love you."

"Thank God." He closed his eyes for a moment. I stood on tiptoe and pressed my cheek against his.

"It should not end now," he said in a hoarse whisper. "It can only begin." He reached behind me and pushed the cabin door wide. Then he gently urged me inside and, without letting go of me, he kicked the door shut. I clung to him. I knew what I was doing. Knew full well what this meant, and I could no more stop myself than Stan could. I didn't even want to.

We needed no words now. We found our way to the bunk. He kissed me, this time with all the meaning he could put into it and I felt his tongue touch mine and then seek more. He tried to raise my gown but fumbled and I drew back slightly to loosen the bodice. I stood up and dropped my skirt and underwear.

My knees felt watery, as if they wouldn't hold me up. At the same time my body throbbed with the strongest desire of my life. His hands touched my thighs and moved gently along them. I closed my eyes, lay back and surrendered to him wholly. He was gentle and kind, and I loved him for it. My arms remained around his neck for a long time and I kissed his face.

Presently he laid his cheek down against my breast and he gave a great sigh. "Angela, I love you. Be sure of that. I may hurt you, but even though I do, I love you."

"My darling," I whispered, "how could you hurt me after this? Whatever I said about needing time . . . it's not true anymore. Because every moment of my time I must spend with you."

He raised his head. A lamp burned on the bureau, its wick turned very low, but I could see the agony written all over his face. I tried to raise myself, but his weight was too much.

"Stan, what is it? Why do you look that way? We're in love. We're happy. I'm not afraid anymore. There's only one step necessary now. Ask me when I'll marry you. I am your woman and you are my man."

He eased himself off the bed and began dressing. He kept his back turned to me so I couldn't see his face. I got to my feet, not bothering to reach for my gown. I touched his shoulder. He turned around slowly. I began to feel a sense of deep foreboding.

"Stan, were you only . . . playing a game?"

"I swear I have never loved anyone so much in my life and I never will again. Even if I lose you."

"If you lose me?" I asked. "What are you trying to say?" I gripped his shoulders. "Don't torture me like this."

"Angela, I'm engaged to be married next month."

I let go of him, backed away. My knees struck the edge of the bank and I sat down abruptly. I reached for my skirts to cover my nudity.

"I'm waiting to hear the rest of it," I said in a small, tight voice.

"This girl—in New Orleans—I don't love her and I never have. I never will. She's society . . . hand-selected by my mother to be my wife. I couldn't get out of it. There was no way."

"You, a man, couldn't tell your mother you would not marry this girl you do not love? Is it fair to the girl?"

Stan thrust his hands in his pockets. "I have to make you understand. Until a few years ago—two or three—I didn't even know how to live. All I did was study. I graduated *summa cum laude* from a law school where half the class fails. Then I had to take bar examinations. I spent another six months on them. I couldn't fail. You see, my mother expected me to get the highest grades in the world. I very nearly accomplished it, I think."

"So far," I said, "I've heard nothing that lets me forgive you for what you . . . no, we . . . just did. I didn't have to submit to you."

"I didn't mean it to be a seduction." His anguish was such that he couldn't stand still. He kept moving about the small confines of the cabin. "I went into practice. Oh, not in a small office to wait for clients. Not me! I went into the most prestigious law firm in the South. As a partner, not a novice. And as a partner I was expected to earn the lavish salary they paid me. I was up early, I went to bed early, and I saw no one except clients. Oh, I

109

earned my salary. I did the work of at least two partners, so they could relax and join their brown-skinned mistresses. One of them maintained two women."

"You procrastinate, Stan. I don't care about your partners. I want to know why you asked a girl to marry you and then took me to your bed."

"Her name is Mary-Lou. She's a well-protected, pure and innocent Southern girl. She's pretty. Not with your sultry type of beauty. She's like my mother. Sometimes I think that's why I asked her to marry me—I just accepted her. I didn't care. I was expected to marry and here was this girl."

"Do you love her?" I demanded, irritably now.

"No!"

"Still you asked her to be your wife and until tonight you gave no thought to not marrying her."

"The day I came aboard this ship and you were standing there, I knew I would not marry until you consented to be my wife. If that sounds silly, like the dreaming of a man who didn't deserve to dream, then you may regard it that way. Falling in love, to me, was something vague. It didn't seem to matter. Then I saw you. It all changed."

"You could have warned me," I said.

"Yes, and have you turn away. I didn't mean for this to happen tonight. I just wanted to kiss you, to taste the sweetness of your lips. That was all and then . . . it wasn't all. It couldn't be all there was to it."

"You speak of her as pure and innocent. That describes me—until you came into my cabin and entered my body. Now I feel cheap and common and used."

"You brought me alive, Angela."

"Yes," I said bitterly. "So you could marry her."

"No. I'll go home when my business is finished and tell Mary-Lou that I can't marry her because I'm in love with you."

"And after that?"

"I'll come to you. Or I'll marry you now. We're still at sea. The captain has the legal right to marry us. I'll take you back with me and present you as my wife and damned to the lot of them."

"Thank you, Stan," I said. I stood up and went to him.

I kissed him on the lips. "I love you. I want to be your wife, but not now. I've something to finish too. If I marry you now, I'll likely never learn what it is to succeed on my own. I want to be a fashion designer. I want to be looked up to and accepted as someone successful. Just as you already are. If nothing more comes of this night, I have no regrets."

"It will," he cried out vehemently.

"You must go back to your fiancée and tell her," I said. "It's the only thing to do."

"I know. Will you accept me when I come to you—wherever you are?"

"Yes, my love. But you will have to wait until I am ready. If there had been no one else, I'd marry you now. But since there is, the wedding—if there will ever be one—will have to wait."

"Why do you doubt me?" he asked.

"It isn't that I doubt you," I said. "I too have something on my mind. I can't talk of it at this moment. Perhaps I will tell you tomorrow. My mind is in too much of a jumble now."

He drew me to him. "Do you love me?"

"I will love you eternally," I said softly. "I am crushed at the moment, but I will get over the hurt of learning you are not a completely free man. But tonight, for a little while, we were one. I will cling to that memory."

"You said you have something on your mind. May I help?"

I cupped his face in my hands. "If you can't, my love, no one can. And yet . . . No, tomorrow. It must wait until tomorrow. I'll see you on deck in the morning."

He drew me close and his lips came down hard on mine. It would have been glorious to submit, but this time I pushed him away. It wasn't easy, but I managed.

"Be sure to bring the name and address of your hotel," I whispered.

"I will. Believe me, I didn't expect the voyage to end this way. But I'm glad it did. So long as you have forgiven me, I shall be eternally glad it did. Good night, Angela."

He kissed me and then left the cabin. I sat down on the side of the bunk and tried to assemble my scattered thoughts. I believed Stan. I had faith in every word he uttered. I loved him dearly. My life was now his. If we had to wait, that could be endured. Anything could be endured now. I was suddenly aware that I wasn't afraid any more. I wasn't alone any more.

I twisted the ring around my finger and wondered if it was responsible for my meeting Stan, and for what had happened tonight. Was this what Papa meant by calling it a magic ring? I brought it to my lips and kissed it, and then I quietly lowered myself to the bunk and lay there, still in the wonder of what love was.

I awoke early. The noise of the preparations for coming into port was partially responsible. I wasn't annoyed, only eager to get dressed and look for Stan in the dining room. I did take time to do some packing, resentful of every moment that would keep me from seeing his dear face and feel the touch of his hand as we discreetly met for breakfast.

I glanced out of the porthole as the racket grew louder. We were maneuvering toward the dock and the morning was filled with the sound of ships' whistles, the clamor from the crowded pier and, beyond that, the streets of Cherbourg which, I had been given to understand, were as crowded as those in New York City.

I entered the dining room hopefully, scanning the tables for Stan, but he wasn't there. No doubt he had extra work to be accomplished before leaving the ship. I was unreasonably disappointed. I went back to my cabin and finished my packing. A steward came for the luggage, which would be waiting on the pier after I disembarked. I checked the cabin to make sure I'd left nothing behind. I made up my mind to go to Stan's cabin and, if it proved possible, to enjoy a few more secret moments with him before we would land and be compelled to part. For how long I had no idea. My money and valuables were in a small valise and, carrying this, I made my way to his cabin.

The door was wide open and a stewardess was pulling the linen off the bed. She looked up from her work.

"Has Mr. Talbot gone on deck?" I asked, silently berating myself for not first looking for him there. He was likely waiting for me to appear.

112

"Not likely he would be, Ma'am," the stewardess replied. "He was taken off in a lighter about six o'clock this morning."

"He's left the ship?" I asked in amazement.

"Aye, Ma'am. Bag and baggage. He was off in a big hurry, I'd say."

"There is no message?" I looked hopefully at the bureau.

"Not as I know of, Ma'am."

"Thank you." I went back on deck, now rapidly clearing of departing passengers. There was nothing for me to do but join them. I saw no sign of Stan. I'd thought, perhaps, that he might have had urgent reasons for leaving the ship by lighter, but that he would be on hand when the ship docked and I'd come down the gangplank. I stopped for a moment at the rail to search the faces of those who were waiting to greet passengers.

I saw no sign of Stan there either, but I did quickly pick out the anxious face of Uncle Carlo. He was dressed as nattily as ever, a handsome man leaning heavily on a cane. Apparently his injuries had not yet successfully healed.

I walked down the gangplank, still turning my head eagerly just in case Stan emerged from the crowd, but he never did. I greeted and hugged my uncle instead and though my heart was leaden, I managed a smile of welcome. I felt a fool. I was a fool. Yet I loved him.

SIX

"I am not well," Carlo told me after we'd embraced. "I should not have left the hospital so soon, but I received your message . . ."

"Uncle Carlo," I said, "you were out of the hospital when I wrote you to find me a place to live and to come to Paris and live with me."

"*Si. Si* . . . but I was going to go back. My leg, my hip, my knees, and my ankle, everything gives me great pain. Even with a cane to support my weakness. I limp. I was very nearly killed, you know."

"Yes. You mentioned it several times. Have you seen Vito?" I was not going to allow him to indulge himself in self-pity.

"No. He cares nothing about me. In his mind I am nothing at all. He came to question me, but he did not come back. Only two or three times to inquire, but he wasn't really sympathetic. He came as a *Carabiniere,* not a man. Not as a friend."

"I think you're mistaken about Vito," I said. "He's a fine man. Now, we'll find a carriage, pick up my luggage."

"Oh, I have a carriage waiting, my dear niece. A fine carriage."

"Waiting? At so much an hour? How long has it been waiting, Uncle Carlo?"

"Well, the ship is an hour and a half late . . ."

"Very well." I should have expected this, knowing Carlo and his self-indulgent nature. "Have you found a nice place for us?"

He brightened. "Oh, yes indeed. A place which will suit your good taste. Depend on me."

I began to wonder if I'd depended too much. We reached the carriage, an open one of such splendor I wondered if I had enough cash to pay for it. Carlo sent the driver for the luggage and after it was aboard, we began the ride through the city to the railroad depot for the last leg of my long journey to Paris.

Carlo had accommodations on a fine train, an express. An entire compartment for us. I settled back to enjoy the trip through a country I'd never been to before. The busy city soon faded into lovely countryside with colorful villages and even more colorful peasants who often waved as the train sped by, sometimes to the accompaniment of the shrill whistle on the locomotive.

Carlo kept up a running conversation, mostly about his trials, troubles and pain. He was still a very frightened man, though getting out of Italy had helped calm him down somewhat. He was enthusiastic about life in Paris, as I'd expected he might be. I knew he had no money, or only a small amount left from what I'd sent him. Certainly he made no attempt to pay for the carriage which took us to the depot or for the railroad tickets.

He kept talking in Italian, but I now considered myself an American and I wanted to speak in English, a language he was as fluent in as I.

"Uncle," I said, "I have taken out my first papers to become an American citizen, which means I now regard the English language as my language. So I speak in English and you speak in Italian, our mother tongue, to be sure. However, we are now in France, so we will speak only English, unless we have to use our poor French to get by."

"I am a linguist," he informed me in English. "I speak many languages. French is my favorite, but, as you say, we will speak English. That suits me fine, for when we get to the United States, I will be used to speaking it always."

"You are going to the United States?" My surprise wasn't feigned.

I was sure his wasn't either when he said, "But surely you're taking me back with you, Angela. Otherwise where can I go?"

"We'll consider it later," I said. I had thought about it, but that was before I decided to go to Paris to study dress design.

I wasn't prepared for Paris. Not for its beauty, the stately and expensive facades on some of its streets. Nor for the wild traffic consisting of everything from lumbering vans to goatcarts. It seemed to come from every direction, then veer off to a thousand different destinations. What most impressed me was the softly pink haze that gave the city a magical air.

I shouldn't have been surprised to learn that another expensive carriage was at the railroad station to meet us. Uncle Carlo handled such matters with a diligence that never applied itself to the pocketbooks of those he was serving. This carriage, a soft green in color, even surpassed the one at Cherbourg. The seats were upholstered in lavender-dyed glove leather, the step was framed in what looked like gold. The woodwork was mahogany, highly polished, and the coachman was dressed in a lavender uniform as well, with a cocked hat sporting a lavender feather. I expected that feather was going to be costly.

Since I would pay for it, I might as well enjoy such luxury, for we were riding up the Champs Elysees. It was tree-lined and had an air of elegance and enchantment. The shops spoke of great wealth, the pedestrians were dressed in the latest fashion. Children played in the parks, watched over by their nursemaids whose uniforms were as chic as the clothes worn by their wards. Everything gave off an air of wealth and fine living.

But what attracted my attention more than anything else were the lovely carriages, exactly like the one I now rode in. And the women who sat, proudly erect, with their tiny, colorful, lace-edged parasols raised to shield them from the sun. Their gowns were elegant and voluminous as current fashion dictated. A few had gentlemen escorts as passengers. Men with high, gray silk hats, black dress coats and the huge cravats of the current fashion.

I came back to earth when I began to realize the carriage was not taking us to any modest commercial area, but was headed straight toward a hill, atop which were the rooms and tenements of artists, as I discovered later.

"Just where is this flat you obtained for us?" I asked.

Carlo fidgeted a trifle. "You would expect only the best, my dear niece. I would not allow you to live with riff-raff."

116

"I wouldn't expect to, but I don't think I belong among the millionaires either. I wanted something in between. I wrote you to acquire something that had an air of modest refinement."

"Wait until you see the suite."

"Suite? Are we to live in a hotel?"

"Not exactly a hotel, but then—yes, a hotel too, I suppose. Very exclusive."

"I cannot afford exclusivity."

He was dismayed by my sharp tone. "The proper address is extremely important."

"For you, Uncle Carlo. Not for me. I happen to be here to study, not to socialize."

"You will find it most important that you do so. Besides . . ."

"Never mind the besides. How much is it going to cost me?"

"I did not discuss the price, my dear Angela. After all, you are an heiress."

"I am not an heiress. I inherited my aunt's estate."

"She also happens to be my sister," he replied with an air of injury. "Did that thought ever occur to you?"

"It did."

"Is that all it means to you?"

Try as I might, I couldn't hold back my irritation. "What are you getting at?"

"Did it ever occur to you that my relation to her is closer than yours?"

"I'm aware of that. I still don't understand why you are upset."

"She left me nothing. Not even a token gift." He looked straight ahead as he spoke, then emitted a sad sigh.

"I'll be honest, Uncle. I never once thought of that. However," I went on, "though mostly everything in the apartment lay in ruins when I returned, there is the silver and a few other items remaining intact. Should you ever go to America, you may select anything you wish."

"I will do that." He spoke with quiet determination. "After all, I should have received something."

I thought of the many times she had sent him money at his request.

117

"Did you mourn your sister at all? She was murdered, you know."

"You wrote me about it," he said indignantly. "I mourned her and had two High Masses said for her. Though walking was extremely painful, I attended both and each time received the sacrament."

I reached over and covered his gloved hands with one of mine. "I'm sorry, Uncle Carlo. It was unkind of me to ask such a question. Perhaps, in the back of my mind, I did realize that you had received nothing from her. However, I am certain it was because I was so young and she knew that if anything happened to her, I would need what little she had to carry me. And that is about all it will do. I intend to work very hard toward achieving my goal. Once I do, I will need a lot of work."

"Plus the proper social contacts," he said. "Which I will provide. They come first."

I smiled despite myself and decided to further mollify him. "Thank you, Uncle Carlo. That is something I did not think about."

"As you said, my sister left everything to you because you were so young. I'm aware of that also and will look after you since, at the moment, there is no one else and you are a stranger in this city."

"It is a beautiful city, Uncle," I said.

"Everyone falls in love with Paris. Rome has grandeur; Paris has enchantment—for everyone, rich or poor. The rich have all the best of it, though the poor know how to enjoy it. Amour is the key word, though you have no knowledge of that yet."

"Don't I?" I asked. I forgot myself in the sudden surge of memory of that night in my cabin with Stanton Talbot. How little it had meant to him. I was merely a shipboard conquest, yet his love had seemed so real. Foolish innocent, I told myself.

I was suddenly aware of my uncle regarding me strangely.

I caught hold of myself quickly. "I am thinking in terms of loneliness. Some young ladies my age are already married and have begun raising families."

"Good gracious, don't think of such a thing until you

have experienced a little of *la joie de vivre*." His tone was one of stern disapproval. "One more question. Am I right to believe my sister was not wealthy?"

"Yes, Uncle Carlo. Not at all wealthy. And neither am I."

"What of your father?"

"Since we can't find him, we cannot rely on him for help. I have to earn my own way. And so do you, if I might say so. At least, I hope you will."

"I? But Angela, I am a sick man. I am too nervous and too weak to look for employment. I depended on you and the fortune my sister left. Are you sure she wasn't wealthy? Perhaps a secret bank account?"

"Nonsense. Goodness, the carriage is pulling up before this castle. Is it to be our address?"

"*Si,*" he said. "Unless you know of some other place."

"I do not. Though I'm certain you do."

The building was huge, likely a hundred years old and a landmark, no doubt. There were two liveried men to open and close the door. The people I saw going in and out were expensively dressed and carried themselves with the assurance of the rich.

The doorman came rapidly to take command of my baggage. As we stepped from the carriage, Carlo looked about, preened himself by dabbing at his temples, adjusting his rakish fedora at a stylish angle, then he granted me his arm. On the other hung his cane. He was about to make a grand entrance.

I said, "Uncle, you have forgotten to limp."

"For you, my dear," he said swiftly. "Only for you. I did not think you would like to be seen on the arm of a cripple. For you I suffer."

"Poor Uncle Carlo." My tone was sympathetic, though my eyes mocked him.

I sent him on with the baggage while I sought out the manager of this luxurious building. Monsieur Bernard was a portly, red-faced man of business who seated me in his office. I removed my gloves, noting a hole in the tip of one finger. I explained to him that my uncle had made all the arrangements while under the impression that I had fallen heir to a fortune at the death of his sister. I explained that

119

this was not the case, that I had come to Paris to study, and whatever the rent for this establishment was, I could not afford it and I would pay one week's rent while I found suitable quarters elsewhere.

"*Non,* Mademoiselle," he said sternly. "This cannot be, no. Your uncle signed a lease in your name for one year."

"At what figure, Monsieur, in American dollars?" I asked, and held my breath. It was fortunate that I did. The price he named was so far out of reach as to be ludicrous.

"I cannot pay it," I said bluntly. "Even the rent for a week will be a serious blow to my bank account. But I have a letter of credit so you can collect the week's rental."

"*Non,* Mademoiselle, a lease is a lease."

"But I didn't sign it."

"Your uncle signed it in your name. That is the same. You are responsible if he cannot pay."

"What if I . . . refuse? Just move out now?"

"Your letter of credit will find itself impounded, Mademoiselle."

"Then I'll have nothing."

"*Oui.* Only the privilege of living here for as long a time as your letter of credit permits. There will be no compromise, Mademoiselle. We do not compromise here. Not an inch."

"I'll think about it."

He held out his hand. "The letter of credit, Mademoiselle. To insure payment."

"If I do not choose to surrender it, Monsieur?"

His smile had the mirth of a crocodile's. "Your baggage will be held, Mademoiselle."

I handed over the letter of credit. His brows raised as he scanned it. In contempt, I supposed, but there wasn't much I could do about this. I left his office, crossed the ornate lobby, entered the grilled elevator and emerged into a wide hallway off which there were exactly four doors. Four suites on a floor of this size. No wonder the price I'd been quoted had rendered me momentarily speechless.

Carlo was moving about the drawing room, admiring it with nods of approval. The room was too large to be called a parlor. The size of it was four times what I'd expected of my entire living quarters in Paris.

"Uncle Carlo," I said, "sit down and let me tell you the good news."

"You like it, *si? Buono!*"

In Italian, I said sternly, *"E troppo caro.* It is too expensive."

His face fell into lines of defeat. "We will speak in English, *si?*"

"What made you do such a thing, Uncle?"

"But I thought there was great wealth. I thought your Papa . . ."

"You knew Papa and Mama have been missing for the past few years. No one really knows how many. It is possible they are dead and if they are, should it be they left anything to me, I have not been notified of that yet. Your sister left little. I am not rich."

"Refuse to move," he said flatly. "What can they do?"

"They have my letter of credit. All I have is American money in my handbag and there is not too much of that."

Carlo closed one eye and looked ceilingward with the other. "We will have to go, *si?*"

"Si. Si. Si. Si!" I replied irritably.

"A pity. It would have been nice here. There are splendid people and some of the middle-aged ladies look favorably upon me."

"You are the clever one," I said. "How do we get out of here and at the same time get my letter of credit back? The amount it represents won't pay the rent here for three months."

"You could send a cable to your bank and cancel the letter of credit. We could then live here until the manager got the news your credit is no good. By then we shall have another place, no doubt, and after we are ejected, we can go there and wait until a fresh letter of credit is issued to you."

"Uncle Carlo, you would have been a great confidence man. I'm afraid you're right. It's the only thing I can do. I will compose a cable and give you the money to send it."

"With proper transportation, Angela. One does not walk out of such a place as this. One only rides, in style."

I gave him sufficient money, knowing I'd never see the change if there was any. Carlo went off to perform this chore, with me hoping he didn't spend the money on something else on his way to the cable office. I supposed he had always lived by his wits and could not change now.

I unpacked some of my things. I did have the clothes for an establishment such as this and I made up my mind that so long as we were here, I'd act the part. Besides, it would be an education to watch the women here, with their latest fashions.

Among the purchases I had made before leaving was a miniature steamer trunk. In it were the dolls I had dressed for the play at school. I had let my imagination run rampant when I made their costumes. Some wore day dresses, tea gowns, dinner gowns, evening gowns, negligees, plus blouses and skirts. Others were dressed for tennis, croquet, swimming, or garbed in traveling suits. I held a doll in each hand and noticed how different their apparel was from any fashions today. The lines were simple without being severe. Most of all, I had made them as I felt women's clothing should be—to allow complete freedom of movement. That meant no frills or bustles or enormous sleeves. I liked dresses to follow the line of the figure. On impulse I placed some on the mantel above the fireplace. There was a long table placed against a mirrored wall. I arranged the remainder of the dolls on that table. I stepped back to survey them and exclaimed aloud at their beauty. I had no idea I was creating something very different in the line of dress. If only I could convince a designer that my ideas, though revolutionary in regard to female attire, also had appeal. Also, that in this modern day, freedom of movement in feminine apparel was not only desirable but necessary.

A firm knock on the door interrupted my musings. I answered it to be confronted once again with Monsieur Bernard.

When I made no move to invite him to enter, he said, "A word with you, Mademoiselle."

I stepped back and motioned him into the room. "What is it, Monsieur?"

He moved with brisk steps into the center of the room

122

before turning to address me. "Mademoiselle, I was thinking that perhaps you have something of value you might wish to leave with the hotel to insure payment, at least in part, of your lease."

"I have nothing of value, Monsieur," I said quietly, my manner just as assured as his.

He looked around him, studied me from head to toe. I thought his eyes lingered on the ring which Papa had given me. I placed my other hand over it, an indication I had no intention of letting him keep that until my financial position was better.

"You have my letter of credit, Monsieur," I said. "What more do you need?"

"Mademoiselle, you and your Monsieur Guillermo happen to be in one of our best suites. When such a thing occurs, it is customary . . ."

"Monsieur Guillermo happens to be my uncle."

He shrugged. "Of course, Mademoiselle."

"That is the truth, Monsieur." I was beginning to lose my patience.

"You have an American name. Monsieur Guillermo—your uncle, as you say—has an Italian name."

"I am Italian. The name is really Gambrelli."

He frowned thoughtfully. "It has a familiar ring."

I made no attempt to enlighten him. Since I had no idea of Papa's whereabouts, it would make little sense to say he would be responsible for any debt I might incur.

Then, all of a sudden, Monsieur Bernard's face lit up. He walked over to the mantel and picked up a doll. I might have told him to put it down, but he held it so tenderly and there was no mistaking the admiration in his eyes, though I wasn't ignorant as to the reason for it.

"Beautiful, Mademoiselle," he exclaimed. "It is so lifelike."

He was holding it at arm's length now. The doll he had selected was wearing a dinner gown, nile green in color, with soft folds of fabric falling from the shoulders. When he moved it, even gently, the chiffon touched areas of the form revealing lines which were heretofore concealed.

Still holding the doll, he studied the others on the mantel.

I said, "There are still more on the table."

His lips pursed thoughtfully as he went over and regarded each one. He spoke without taking his eyes off them. "You must have collected these over a period of years."

"No, Monsieur," I said quietly. "I dressed them myself."

"But their gowns and dresses—all so different. I have never seen such apparel. And I see the latest fashions in this hotel."

"I am sure you do."

"Who," he made circles in the air with his hand, "designed these clothes?"

"I did, Monsieur."

"So." He nodded knowingly. "You have come to Paris to display your creations."

I smiled enigmatically. "I brought only the dolls."

"Mademoiselle, I have twin etageres in the lobby—very large—which could hold these mannequins very comfortably. It would be good advertising for you and a feather in my cap that the designer selected my hotel for her stay in Paris."

I could scarcely believe my ears. "I will be glad to allow them to be on display while I maintain a residence here. Though it will not be for long."

"As long as you wish, Mademoiselle," he said. "Do you wish to bring the dolls down, or will I send a garçon for them?"

"I will place them, Monsieur. That is most important."

"I understand, Mademoiselle. Whatever you say. How soon will you bring them down?"

"I will replace them in this small trunk and you may send a garçon to carry it down. I will accompany him."

"I will go down immediately and order the etageres emptied of their contents—jade, Mademoiselle—so you know I am particular about what goes in there. The glass shall be washed and then you may display the mannequins as you wish."

"Thank you, Monsieur." I bowed graciously.

He returned the bow, saying, "It is you who must be thanked."

I returned the dolls to the trunk, taking my time so that

neither their hair—which was real and which I had taken pains to style—nor their gowns would be mussed. I had just finished when the garçon arrived. He was mature enough and strong enough so that I need not worry about his being careless in handling the trunk or dropping it.

The etageres were much larger than I anticipated. They had glass shelves and all four sides were glass, gleaming from a fresh washing. I took my time, placing each doll so that the raiment would show off to its best advantage. I knew my cheeks were flushed from this unexpected good luck and my heart was beating madly. The garçon stood close by in case I had need of him. When I completed my task, I nodded to him. He stepped forward to close each door, turn the key in the lock and pass it to Monsieur Bernard who had been standing in the background all the time, observing my progress. Now he stepped forward, still beaming, and gave me a respectful bow.

"I guarantee, Mademoiselle," he said fervently, "your designs will be the talk of Paris within a week."

"You flatter me, Monsieur," I said.

"Indeed I do not," he replied seriously. "You are a very talented lady. And since you are so young, you will go far. And you will not have long to wait."

I returned to the suite, still marveling at my good luck. Uncle Carlo would be surprised.

But there were other things to think about as well. Painfully, I brought my thoughts around to Stanton Talbot. Had he deliberately arranged for a lighter to take him off the ship to avoid our meeting again? Had he been playing a game? Was he a man to whom every woman was a challenge in seduction? Had he even lied about being engaged so that I'd not have thoughts about having any claim on him? If I had been hurt by the enticement, I was young. I'd get over it.

Yet, when I reviewed his behavior during those days we were together, I couldn't believe he had been insincere. It was true that I had had little dealings with men—none, in fact, except with Vito, who truly loved me and who held me in the highest respect. I wondered if he would now, knowing Stanton Talbot had enticed me.

Yet I could not blame Stanton for my fall from grace.

125

I had been a willing participant and I had no regrets. I still loved him even if he had been playing a game with me. In time the pain would leave me. I was mature enough to realize that and though at his moment it weighed heavily on my heart . . . time would heal the hurt.

I walked over to a window looking out at the foot of the hill atop which was the Montmartre section of the city, where I knew artists lived and struggled. That was where I'd fully expected Carlo to take me, but he'd certainly stopped at the foot of the hill where we now lived in a style I could not afford.

My irritation at Carlo started to rise again, but I quickly checked it by beginning an inspection of these premises. They were astounding. At the end of a corridor, bypassing my bedroom, bath and private parlor, was a suite of four rooms where Carlo had established himself. His expensive baggage was there and the closets housed his suits, hats and shoes. I shook my head in dismay, wondering if they were paid for. The man needed a millionairess niece, not an impoverished one such as I. I was in trouble and I knew it. Yet I knew Carlo's ways, so I had only myself to blame.

A month ago I might have thrown myself on the bed, buried my face in a pillow and cried my heart out. But not any more. If Stanton Talbot's deception had done nothing else, it had made me more resolved than ever to become a success.

I made up my mind not to be cross with Uncle Carlo. I believed his poor physical condition, which he spoke of in tones of self-pity, was as false as his good intentions. He was not truthful, but I couldn't help but be fond of him. He was at least a diversion. It might not be easy living with him, but it would be interesting and, at times, amusing.

I walked away from the window to sit down and begin planning exactly what I would now do. How I would handle my affairs. Also, I cautioned myself against becoming involved in any romantic entanglements. I would immediately immerse myself in my studies and also attempt to find some way to make a living. I could no longer delay. I could not depend on my luck changing just because the dolls were on display. Also, I knew Carlo and I would be evicted the moment Monsieur Bernard discovered the letter of credit was of no value.

For a few moments I thought of Vito. It would have been easy to return to Florence. With him I'd have a comfortable, peaceful life. One filled with his love for me. In time I would return that love, but it wouldn't be fair to Vito. Not now—when my heart ached for a mere glimpse of Stanton Talbot.

I tried to convince myself that some compelling reason had made him leave the ship abruptly, without his having time to let me know about it. He had not deliberately eluded me. He intended to search for me in Paris. All these factors favorable to him came to my mind and I believed none of them, though I wanted to with all my heart.

I was wasting time. I didn't have much to spend on idle thoughts or painful memories. I was here to study, to become a fashion designer and there was probably no better place to begin than in this very building where I lived under false pretenses.

When Carlo returned and, to my amazement, handed over change from the cost of the cable and the carriage, I told him to dress for dinner. I wished him to escort me to the elaborate dining room. It pleased him tremendously. Although neither of us had any business here, Carlo was able to blithely push aside such thoughts.

I selected one of the two gowns I had brought. Both conformed to the current fashion now on display. Lace frills on the bodice, very full double skirts, yards of lace and enormous off-the-shoulder sleeves to minimize the arms. One was of fine silk, the other of very stiff taffeta. I chose the silk. It was a deep pink which went well with my Italian heritage of black hair, dark brown eyes and skin of a blush of tan. White silk three-button gloves completed my costume. I tucked the hand part of the glove beneath the part which covered the wrist.

Carlo, in white tie and tails, looking quite the cosmopolite he was, surveyed me with a critical eye.

"Splendid," he said candidly. "It's the height of fashion."

I regarded myself critically in the long oval mirror hanging on a wall in the parlor. "I hope it won't be in a few years."

"Sometimes you dismay me, Angela," he said loftily. "Whatever are you talking about?"

"My gown." I tucked a silk rose of the same color as the gown into my hair which I had piled atop my head. "I hope to change the fashions."

He was standing behind me and regarding my reflection in the mirror. He tried to hide the smile which touched his lips by moving each of his forefingers against his mustache, as if one or two hairs were not in place— which they were. With Carlo, I doubted they would dare move.

"Do you like the present-day fashions?" I asked.

"I think they are enchanting," he replied seriously. "They lend a lot of mystery. Of course," he gave an expressive shrug, "there have been times in my life when the mystery was revealed and I. . . ."

"I do not wish to hear about your love affairs," I said sternly.

"I do not gossip about them," he said curtly.

"I should hope not." I laughed. "Uncle Carlo, let us not quarrel over a subject about which I know nothing. Though I would like to know if you lived all these years by your wits."

"I lived through the generosity and graciousness of your father. Also, Celestine—though her scolding letters were a trial to read. No woman should be without a man's love. But then, the cloistered life was of her own choosing. I suppose you had to endure it also."

"I loved Aunt Celestine."

"I'm sure you did. Just as I am certain she did not prepare you for life in the outside world."

"Then I shall learn."

"With my help."

"With or without it," I said. "Now, let us go downstairs. I wish to observe the ladies there and their mode of dress."

"You are in for an exciting evening," he said, extending his arm. "Allow me, my dear."

I said nothing about Monsieur Bernard's visit to the suite or the dolls now gracing the etageres.

The courtliness of the dining room was overwhelming. Gleaming chandeliers with shafts of light darting from their prisms, white linen cloths on which sat ornate silver, fragile crystal and beautiful china. The air was heavy with the scent of roses which graced each table. The fragrance mingled with the perfume of the elegantly gowned ladies. Everyone watched everyone else.

All eyes were on us as the maitre d'hotel led us to a table for two. It was almost in the center of the room and gave me a splendid opportunity to observe most of the ladies and their escorts. Once we were seated and questions were asked across the tables, followed by a shrug of the shoulders which indicated my identity was not known, the guests turned their attention to the next couple who had entered.

Carlo whispered across the table, "Did you see them stare, Angela?"

"Yes," I whispered in return. "Just as they are staring at each couple who enters."

He gave me a look of restrained patience, then turned his attention to the menu. He was so well versed in wines and food, he ordered without glancing at the wine list. I shuddered to think of what that bottle was going to cost.

We raised our glasses to one another. "For once, Uncle Carlo," I said, "I'm proud of you."

"Well, this is my element, dear niece. This is where I thrive and glow. If only I had the money to go with it. Manners are not easy to cultivate, but much easier than cultivating money to go with them." He paused, touching a rosebud appreciatively. "You cannot see them, but behind you is a table for four. Both ladies are discussing you, even though they are holding their menus over their mouths. One of them is now whispering to her escort. He is getting up. I believe he is coming over."

"Why?" I asked, knowing full well my question was foolish.

"How should I know?" Carlo could barely restrain his irritation. He could say no more for the gentleman stood beside our table. Carlo arose.

129

"Pardon this intrusion, Monsieur," the stranger began. "My name is Monsieur LeMont. Madame LeMont is enchanted with the mannequins in the etageres. Monsieur Bernard states they are your creations."

Carlo was completely bewildered for I'd not mentioned the dolls.

"Thank you, Monsieur. I am Mademoiselle Gambrell. This is my uncle—Monsieur Carlo Guillermo."

Carlo, though still puzzled, was once again in possession of his wits. He acknowledged the introduction and asked if Monsieur LeMont and his party would care to join us. I almost fainted at the thought, wondering how we would pay for the dinner.

"Some other time, Monsieur," was the gracious and, to me, most welcome reply. "Madame LeMont was wondering if Mademoiselle would do her the honor of coming to our table so she might meet the talented creator of those mannequins."

"My niece would be honored," Carlo said, bowing graciously.

"Indeed, yes," I said. I was already on my feet. Monsieur LeMont offered his arm and I slipped my hand around it. He led me to the table where the waiter was already placing two extra chairs. Once we were duly seated, Monsieur LeMont motioned for the waiter to pour champagne for the six of us.

Madame LeMont said, "I am Marie LeMont. To my right are my sister and her husband, Monsieur and Madame Croiler."

Madame Croiler said, "We are fascinated by the mannequins in the etageres. Did you really design all that raiment yourself? It is so different. Almost frightening, but it has great appeal."

"Yes," I replied, trying to restrain the pleasure I felt at their words of praise. "I feel the fashions of today are too constricting. Women are more and more becoming a part of the outside world. We do not lead the cloistered lives we once led and as that changes, so must our clothing. I like simple lines because they enable us to move freely and not be so constantly aware of our clothing."

Madame Croiler frowned. "I'm not sure I understand."

"I feel that clothes should follow the lines of our body. In that way, they will be far more comfortable."

She nodded slowly. "It makes a great deal of sense."

"It does indeed." Madame LeMont added her approval. "Where can they be purchased?"

"Nowhere just now," I replied. "I have come here to visit the Paris salons and to learn from them."

"Perhaps they should learn from you," Monsieur Le-Mont said. He raised his glass, adding, "A toast to Mademoiselle Gambrell. May you have a very successful future as a fashion designer."

"Thank you, Monsieur." I was trembling inwardly with happiness. I had never expected such a reaction to my designs. I took a sip of the champagne, we talked briefly, mostly about me, since Madame LeMont had quite a curious nature. She was, she said, amazed that I could fashion such creations when I was still so young.

Her husband said with a smile, "It's probably more than talent."

Monsieur Croiler said, "Genius is the word."

We thanked them and returned to our table, for our dinner had arrived. I forgave Carlo his extravagant tastes, for I sensed it would be all worthwhile.

Once we started eating, Carlo said, "Now, my dear, will you please tell me what this is all about?"

I explained in an undertone, though there was no need for it. A string orchestra was playing on a small stage and there was a hum of voices around the room, drowning out intimate conversation.

"Why didn't you tell me about the dolls?" he asked irritably.

"I didn't attach any importance to it," I said. "Even though Monsieur Bernard did."

"Which means we may stay here indefinitely," Carlo beamed.

"Yes," I agreed. "But we won't."

"How can you be so stupid?" Carlo argued. "Everyone comes here. You will be the talk of Paris."

"Splendid," I said. "But I still have a lot to learn. And my gowns have not yet been accepted."

"Where are they?" he asked.

"In the lobby," I replied. "I placed them there this afternoon."

He gave a resigned sigh. "You try my patience, Angela."

"And you mine," I said.

"Still," he went on, "we get along."

"Fairly well—so far."

"Are the patrons in this dining room well known?" I asked.

"Most of them. Some are courtesans. Very beautiful and very high-priced. It would do well to cultivate them. They set the styles, you know."

"When I have a salon, everyone will be welcome," I said. "However, I will not favor courtesans above others."

"It's easily apparent Celestine raised you," he said dismally. "Dear Angela, do you really not know what happened to your papa and mama?"

"No," I replied, suddenly shaken out of my delirium of happiness. "I wish I did, Carlo."

"But do you think they are dead?"

"At times I'm sure they must be. If they were not, they'd come to me by now, especially after Aunt Celestine died."

"If they knew she was dead," Carlo said.

"Yes, I have to consider that too. But in my heart, I think they are alive and some force, or circumstance, prevents them from coming to me. I don't know."

"Were they in contact with my sister, before she died?"

"I don't know that either."

"They were wealthy people. Whatever became of their wealth?"

"I don't know that they were wealthy, Carlo. I was told by bankers in Florence that there was nothing on deposit anywhere that they knew of."

"It is a strange thing," he observed with a shake of his head.

"Yes," I replied. "Very strange. And frightening."

"I ask this not because I wish to pry. But if you are alone in this world—as I am—then perhaps we should plan to remain together as a family. I shall protect you from the wolves of Paris, and I will do what I can to see that you meet the right people."

"Very well," I said. "That's how it will be. But Uncle, for the love of heaven, keep in mind the fact that I'm not wealthy. Even what I do have won't keep us a year. I shall have to find some sort of work in my own field."

"*Buono*," he exclaimed in great satisfaction. "I too will look for work, I assure you."

Which was one of Uncle Carlo's bigger lies, but I made no reply, possibly because I was about to face an even more serious matter. The portly manager of this hotel was threading his way between tables, heading straight for ours.

The manager signaled before he reached the table and a waiter promptly supplied him with a chair. Carlo, who had stood, sat down as the manager was seated by the waiter.

"Mademoiselle," he said, and his tone was surprisingly mild. "I am here to beg your pardon for the rudeness with which I greeted you today. I have here . . ." he placed the letter of credit on the table, ". . . your property. I have not drawn upon it and I do not intend to. Upon seriously considering the rude manner in which I acted, I have come to the conclusion that you must be granted the privilege of residing in your suite for a month . . . two months . . . or more, if you cannot find a proper place to reside."

"I don't understand," I said in bewilderment.

"Let me say it simply, Mademoiselle. I overstepped the bounds of propriety. Of course I do not own this establishment. I only work here, and I am strictly accountable for collecting the proper rentals. But when I informed those who do own the place, I was given a lecture in manners and told to see that you remain, rent free, as long as you desire."

"Thank you," I said. "Though I still don't understand . . . Is it because of the mannequins?"

"What of the dining room charges?" Carlo broke in.

"It has come to my attention that tonight you demonstrated consideration for all our guests by being most gracious when Monsieur LeMont came to your table. He and his party are important people, you see. They too have spoken to the owners. We would consider it an honor if you and your uncle will dine here each evening, at our

133

expense. I am very pleased to be able to provide our services and I assure you there will be no trouble if you wish to remain an even longer period."

I said, "Monsieur, I am as amazed as I am delighted and grateful, but I can assure you that we shall remain only so long as it requires us to find more suitable accommodations. And I will also say that I expect to be able to pay this bill in due time and I intend to do so."

"You are most kind." The manager rose. "I shall have a bottle of Napoleon cognac at your table at once. Please be in no hurry. Word seems to have passed about concerning your beautiful mannequins. I expect guests will be drifting in and out. I just hope they won't annoy you."

"They won't," I said. "I'll be happy to converse with them."

The manager gave a long sigh. "You have saved my neck, Mademoiselle. I too am grateful."

A bottle of fine cognac was delivered. I drank little of it, but Carlo was not bashful, though he didn't become tipsy. We talked little for we were both so astounded at this weird turn of events that we were unable to comment on it. The manager was correct in saying other guests would come in. They did so unobtrusively, on the pretense of having a nightcap here instead of in the bar. Once again a few of the ladies asked me about the mannequins and I answered their questions and stated my feelings about fashion.

When the dinner hour was over, we rose and were escorted out by the maitre d'hotel. There was no check to sign and be charged to our account. We returned to our floor and the sumptuous suite which was now ours without cost.

I sat down, still stunned by this strange event. "What do you think, Uncle Carlo?"

"There is but one thing to account for it. Someone informed the owners that an American with a new trend in women's style was here, and all the guests were talking about it. No doubt they will spread the word and their friends will come to see you and the mannequins. They will tell others and the hotel prospers, *capisce?*"

"It doesn't seem possible," I demurred. "But there's nothing else to account for it."

I turned the ring around and around on my finger.

I would be forever indebted to Mrs. Gardner for remembering the dolls I had made for a class play and suggesting I take them with me. They had seemed to work as much magic as the ring. Or was I just imagining things? It didn't matter. The fact was that things had changed drastically since our arrival in this hotel—and all for the better. I slept well that night.

SEVEN

I spent the next five days learning my way around Paris, with Carlo as my escort. I must admit I enjoyed his company. He had a sense of humor and there were times when I fell under the spell of his charm. He pointed out the leading salons, the homes of the famous and infamous and we sipped wine at a sidewalk cafe, watching the citizens, known and unknown, pass. I had never done this before, it was a pleasant way to pass the time. We visited the splendid cathedrals and museums.

Our evenings were spent in the lobby of the hotel and in the dining room where, from time to time, ladies accompanied by their escorts approached our table and complimented me on the mannequins in the etageres. Word of them had swiftly spread around Paris.

"You will be famous in no time," Carlo predicted.

"I doubt it," I said. "While it's true I have been complimented by the ladies, no owner of a salon has come to our table or even ventured into the lobby."

"I am sure they have sent spies." Carlo spoke with an air of mystery. "They are too proud and jealous to come themselves. And they wouldn't dare steal your gowns because they are so different from anything worn today."

"I never thought about them being stolen," I said worriedly.

"You needn't," Carlo said. "Any dressmaker who did would be laughed at. Everyone knows they are your creations. Though they do steal. It's a game. *C'est la vie.*"

"There's another thing," I mused. "While every lady has admired them, no one has stated she would wear my designs."

"True." Carlo smacked his lips delicately after tasting

136

his brandy. "Though it is just as well since you have no money to start a business."

"It's a frightening thought," I said. "And I may as well inform you I already have another."

"I'd rather not hear it. I want my dinner to settle."

"I'm not concerned about how your dinner will settle, though I am about where we are going to live. Tomorrow we shall begin looking for an inexpensive place. I would be thrilled to secure employment with a fashionable dress shop—even more so if a designer would hire me."

Carlo accompanied me on my search and, of course, found fault with everything we looked at. The rooms were too small, he suspected the presence of rodents, the wallpaper was not to his liking and the neighbors were the kind who were bound to make trouble.

I ignored his protests and I came upon a three-room flat with two more rooms down the corridor where Carlo could live. It seemed like a suitable arrangement to me. The three-story building wasn't new, but it was in a good state of repair. One disadvantage was that the stores and dressmaking establishments were not too close. A rather long walk, but the exercise would do me good. The furnishings were colorful and clean. There was a kitchen in each flat and the tenants seemed to be quiet, industrious people.

Over Carlo's continued arguments against renting, I made the proper payment and planned to move in quickly.

"You are giving up luxury for this?" Carlo asked in dismay. "I now have large, beautiful rooms, big closets for my clothes, everything of the best and it costs nothing. But you insist on moving to a place like this. You are mad, Angela. Mad and thoughtless."

"I am neither."

"Then you are stupid."

"I'm honest," I told him. "I pay for what I get. It's a matter of pride. You should acquire some. Besides, Monsieur Bernard would not allow us to remain there indefinitely."

"Stay for the rest of the week," Carlo urged. "Is that asking too much? Please, dear niece, let me enjoy this luxury a while longer. Here I am a man of importance. In this new place I will be nothing. Nor will you be. You are most unfair to me. To both of us."

"To neither of us, but I will stay the rest of the week." I gave in to his pleas. "However, on Monday be prepared to move. And meantime, I have to begin looking for work."

"You would be much more apt to get it if you stayed where we are now. Some designer might hear of the way you have impressed all those women, and come to you to ask that you work for him. Have you thought of that?"

"If it were so, Carlo, someone would have come to see me by now. No, the kind of good fortune that allowed us to remain without charge isn't going to continue. On Monday we go."

"Another week," he pleaded.

"No. I am uncomfortable living on the largesse of others."

I did spend two more days promenading up and down the Champs Elysees, enjoying the shop windows and observing the people. For someone interested in style and fashions, there could be no better place on earth to learn both the fundamentals and the final achievement in creating something new.

Carlo, using the pretext of his old wounds, aches and pains, remained at the hotel, mostly sitting in the lobby. I felt bold enough on the afternoon of my second day of promenading to enter one of the larger and more beautiful stores to ask for employment. They were gracious, but had no need for a new employee at that time. I knew very well I was going to receive the same polite but firm treatment in most of the places I would visit, but I was not discouraged.

Days were busy with my looking about, absorbing everything I saw. Nights were torture. After dinner, Carlo now remained in the lobby and the bar where, I presumed, he would have added up a high bill if everything was not free. So, alone, I sat in that luxurious suite of rooms and thought about my parents and Aunt Celestine. I remembered Vito and his kindness but, most of all, I thought about Stanton Talbot and that night of love when I became a woman and, in his arms, learned how great the joy of love could be.

In my wanderings about Paris I kept hoping for a sign of him. From time to time I would observe every carriage that passed. I watched people passing in and out of the lobby—all to no avail.

Over and over again I told myself that I had not been betrayed. I would find Stan one day or he'd find me. Some circumstance beyond his control had caused him to leave the ship clandestinely.

Finally I sat down and wrote him a letter. In it I expressed my faith in him. I asked for no explanations, only that he write me. I addressed it to Stanton Talbot, Attorney-at-Law, New Orleans, Louisiana. That was the only address I had, but because he was a lawyer with an office as well as a residence address, I hoped the letter might reach him.

It would take a long time before an answer reached me, if one ever did. Stan was likely still in Paris. Perhaps he might return at the same time the letter crossed the ocean. I had told Carlo pride prevented me from continuing to live at our present location. Apparently I had none where Stan was concerned.

Somehow, in spite of these tribulations, my failure to find work and Carlo's constant grumbling about the fact that we would soon move, I kept my head, forcing my problems out of my mind.

Two days before we were to move, Carlo and I performed our usual duties in the dining room. More and more ladies were approaching me to ask questions about the apparel on the mannequins in the etageres. I was elated at their interest, but the fashion designers still made no appearance.

Carlo walked me to the lobby and excused himself. "I will have one little drink in the bar and join you later," he said.

"There's no need, Carlo. Remain if you like. I know it's boring, and after we move, it will be more boring than ever for you, so make the most of it now."

He nodded agreement. I decided to take the air for a few minutes, but only in front of the hotel. I needed some exercise before retiring. I never ceased to marvel at the scene that was always passing the hotel, day or night. Possibly by night those who passed by glittered a bit more than those in daylight. I surmised the jewelry business must be extremely good in Paris.

Satisfied, I turned back to the hotel and walked through the lobby to the elevator. Flanking the elevator door were two tall, rather narrow mirrors which reflected part of the lobby. While I waited, I stepped before one of them to tuck a wind-loosened strand of hair into place.

Suddenly, in that mirror I saw a face. A man's head only; his body was hidden behind one of the thick Grecian pillars which graced the lobby. It was the face of my father. I was positive of that. I turned about swiftly. I could see no trace of him, but I threw all modesty to the winds and ran full speed across the lobby to that pillar. There was no one behind it. I looked about frantically and barely stopped myself from shouting his name. It had been no hallucination, no mental image of my father, for I'd not even been thinking of him at that moment. He had been in the lobby, present, looking at me. I was certain. When I'd entered from the street, he must have been somewhere close by, watching me. Perhaps he'd come with the single purpose of seeing me again, but he'd been unable to announce himself and, when he realized I might have seen him, he'd eluded me, escaped outside.

However, I searched the lobby floor and the dining room. I entered the bar and made certain he was not there. Then I went out to the street and walked up and down, studying each passing carriage and pedestrian. I spent an hour at this, a futile, heart-breaking sixty minutes, before I gave up. If Papa hadn't wanted me to see him, he'd succeeded. Whatever strange reason kept him from me—him and Mama both—must carry some sort of danger, either for them or for me, or both. Because if he was able to come here, he was not being held somewhere against his will. Yet, for some reason, he was afraid to make contact.

I wondered what Carlo would say were I to tell him. It occurred to me then that when I'd entered the bar, he had not been there. I returned to the hotel and entered the bar once again, quite conscious of the fact that women usually did not invade these premises.

I didn't see him and I stopped one of the waiters to ask him if Monsieur Guillermo had recently left.

"Mademoiselle," he said, "your uncle was not here all evening."

"But I saw him going toward the bar. He told me he was going to have a last drink before retiring."

"I know your uncle, Mademoiselle. He is here almost every night, but not tonight."

"*Merci,*" I said. "He must have changed his mind."

I could do nothing more, but when I walked down the corridor toward our suite I was more elated than I'd been in many, many months. I knew my father was alive. I unlocked the door and went on in. Carlo had not yet returned and I wondered where he might be. As I turned to close the door, I saw a large, folded piece of paper on the floor. Apparently it had been slipped under the door. I picked it up, opened it. There was a one-word message printed in the middle of the page: SILENZIO

That was all it said, in large letters. Silence! Did that concern the fact that I'd seen Papa? I decided it must, for I knew of no other reason for my being silent. I promptly walked to the bathroom, tore the paper into small bits and flushed them away.

I changed into a nightgown and robe, trying to puzzle out what all of this meant. So many odd things had happened to me in the past few days. The cancellation of all expenses in this hotel on the pretext I was bringing business to the dining room through my mannequins. Of course that was not true. I wondered what excuse Monsieur Bernard would have used, had I not brought them.

Now my father had appeared to me for an instant in time. If I'd been even slightly doubtful of my own eyesight, or that my memory of him had betrayed me, the message under the door removed that. Papa was alive and free. He'd come for a glimpse of me, knew I'd seen him before he vanished and he had caused this one-word message of caution to be delivered. It was obvious that whoever had slipped it under the door also knew Carlo was not in the suite and that I was on my way there, so the message would be seen by no one else.

I waited for Carlo's return with a happiness I hoped I could hide from him. The shroud of silence demanded by that one word must include Carlo too. He was a man who could keep no secrets from anyone. Therefore, he was not to know about Papa's appearance.

When Carlo finally returned, almost two hours later, I was engaged in packing my few things, getting ready for our move the next day. Carlo knocked and came in at my request. He threw his top hat onto a chair and slumped down in another one.

"Must we leave, Angela? Can't we stay longer? A few days, weeks . . . the manager did say months. You know he did."

"We leave tomorrow," I said. "You were a long time tonight."

"That's just it. I've made a lot of friends here. I was invited to do a little gambling. Nothing big, just friendly games. Perhaps I can make some money at this. We played tonight and I came out about even. These men are not very good players. I could win large sums if I played right and was blessed by a little good luck."

"Carlo, I went looking for you in the bar and I was told you were not there."

"Why were you looking for me?" he asked quickly.

"I only wished to remind you that we leave in the morning and you'd best get your packing done."

"I was in a private suite. That's where we played cards. Are you suspicious of me, Angela? Must you know everything I do?"

"Carlo, I merely asked out of curiosity, because you are late and I could not find you. Now stop this nonsense, go to your rooms and get ready. If you sleep late in the morning, I'll wake you with a glass of cold water on your head."

He smiled as he rose. "All right, my dear niece. You are in command. My desires are worth nothing. I will go. In the morning I will be ready before you are. But I think I could make enough to pay our way here even if the generosity of the management stopped. *Buona notte.*"

142

There wasn't much sleep in me this night. I moved restlessly through the suite and frequently went to the window overlooking the street, to peer down at the sidewalk across the road, just in case I might happen to catch another glimpse of a figure who was dear to me. The street had grown quiet after one o'clock in the morning. No one stood across from the hotel, watching and waiting.

I finally gave up, turned out the lights in the drawing room and went into the bedroom to get ready for sleep I knew might not come. A barely discernible knock sounded on the drawing room door. It was so faint that I hesitated, wondering if I really heard it. The sound came once more and my heart leaped for joy. Coming this way, in the dead of night and being very quiet, meant the arrival of someone who didn't wish to announce his presence to anyone else. Who else but Papa. He had found a way to reach me this time.

I ran to the door, unlocked it and threw it wide. A man I'd never seen before stood there. At sight of me, a smile widened his face. He was about twenty-five, I judged. Slender, wiry and quite handsome, except that his eyes were small and held a mocking look. Instinctively I distrusted him and began to close the door.

"Wait, Mademoiselle," he said in French. "I am Emile. I come from Vito."

At Vito's name, my fear quickly abated. "Of course, Monsieur. Is he in Paris?"

"No, but I have a message from him. May I come in for a moment?"

There was something about him I didn't like. So instead of stepping back to allow him entrance, I remained where I was, blocking the doorway.

"It is very late," I said. "You may give me the message here."

He took two quick steps forward and before I could slam the door on him, he pushed me backward into the room with such force I fell backward. When I tried to get up, his foot lashed out in a kick at my head. I tried to avoid it, but it struck my shoulder such a hard blow I moaned. I fell back and he placed a foot hard against my stomach.

143

"Don't move until I tell you to," he spoke with quiet deadliness, "or I'll kill you."

He struck a match, held it aloft a moment and saw a fat candle that was in a tall wooden candlestick. He applied the flame to its wick, blew out the match and tossed it to the floor.

He reached down, grabbed the front of my robe and pulled me to my feet. He pushed his coat aside with his right hand, and pulled out a sharp-bladed dagger.

He was agile and quick in his movements and the next moment his left hand held both of mine behind me. He forced me back until I struck the long table.

"If you cry out, you will get your beautiful throat slit," he said.

"What do you want?" My voice was a hoarse whisper.

"You," he leered. "And I will have you presently. I am Emile! Remember me. I need not say that. After tonight, you will not forget me."

The tip of the blade pierced the outer layer of skin and I felt warm blood run down. He moved his groin against mine and muttered one vulgarism after another. My revulsion outweighed my fear.

I opened my mouth and screamed. "Carlo!"

The man seemed disconcerted. Probably he had thought I was alone. I heard Carlo shout something. The man still gripped my hands, but not as tightly and he seemed as fearful of the voice that issued from Carlo's part of the suite as I was of him.

Then Carlo burst into the room. He wore a flopping robe over his nightshirt and without hesitation he darted straight at the intruder. I wrested myself free and hastily got out of the way. The man, apparently forgetful of the dagger he still held, whirled about and raced out into the corridor, heading not toward the elevator, but the stairway. Carlo went after him. I stepped into the corridor, wondering what would happen if Carlo caught up with him. Carlo was anything but a fighting man, though he was certainly displaying a great deal of courage tonight.

The man reached the door to the stairway and had it open when Carlo tripped and fell headlong, sprawled out

144

on the carpeted hallway. I ran to him. He seemed a little dazed as I helped him up. He stood there, out of breath, shaking a little, but with a look of pugnacious determination on his face.

"He used the stairway," he said, pulling away from me.

"Carlo, you can't possibly catch him. Neither could anyone in the hotel if we could get word down to the lobby. He's gone and I'm not harmed."

"Where did he come from? Who was he? What did he want?"

"I don't know where he came from. He told me his name was Emile. What he wanted was me! Thank God you were here."

"Such a one?" Carlo asked aghast. "In this hotel? I cannot believe it!"

"Come inside, Carlo. There's something else."

Apparently the commotion had wakened no one, or if it had, they were reluctant to interfere with whatever was going on. Carlo sat down in the drawing room of my suite.

"It was lucky I was not asleep, for I sleep very hard and might not have heard you scream."

"Uncle Carlo, when I opened the door, he said he was a friend of Vito and had a message from him."

"Vito?"

"The Inspector of the *Carabinieri* in Florence," I exclaimed impatiently.

"Him? I never trusted the man. He is a worm, a traitor, a no-good . . ."

"Stop it," I said indignantly. "I don't believe Vito sent him. I'll never believe that."

"But he knew of Vito and your regard for him. Why else would he have used Vito's name?"

"On the other hand," I said thoughtfully, "how did he know where I lived? Vito doesn't know."

"Don't be too sure. These police work together. Vito may have asked the *gendarmes* to hunt for you and let him know. It is not impossible."

"Vito is a kind and good man. He did not send this . . . this . . . intruder. I don't know how Emile knew Vito, but I can assure you it was not through Vito himself."

"Well, you know him better than I do. But from now on, keep your door locked and let no one in unless I am with you."

"I will agree to that," I said.

Carlo looked pleased with himself. "It is also a good sign that you need me around."

"Yes, that too, Uncle Carlo. Thank you for being so prompt in answering my shout."

"Will we still go in the morning?" His eyes pleaded with me to change my mind.

"There is no change in my plans," I said firmly.

"I think in a place of this caliber, you would be safer than that place on the hill."

"In view of what almost happened, I wouldn't say so. If you hadn't been here, I don't know what would have happened."

I checked the door to make certain it was secure before I returned to my bedroom. I lay awake a long time, wondering what was going to happen to me. Why had Papa let me see him? Would I ever be free of danger? Would they? Certainly they must be in peril because of something. Yet what?

I felt so alone. I assured myself I was, but I must not indulge in self-pity. I had enough of that with Carlo. I had come to Paris to seek a career. My doll mannequins were a huge success. Which reminded me, I must take them with me. Or would it be better to allow them to remain here, at least until I had made a contact of some kind? Would Monsieur Bernard allow them to remain in the two etageres? I'd not mention them to Carlo. He would adopt an injured air and say if I had any business sense, I would remain here. It might well be he was correct, though after what had just occurred, I'd had enough of this place.

EIGHT

I had to admit it was a complete change, but somehow I preferred these smaller and less splendid quarters to the opulence of the hotel which we had just left. Carlo, on the other hand, made no attempt to hide his displeasure. He complained of his small rooms, of the cheapness of the furniture and of the certainty the place must be infested with vermin.

"How long will we have to live in this hovel?" Carlo asked. "My dear Angela, how do you expect to become a success with such an address? And with so little money. You move out of the hotel where you could stay for no cost and move here where it is necessary not only to pay rent, but to pay for your food as well."

"Because here we are under no obligation to anyone," I said quietly.

"You were a sensation because of the doll mannequins. All the ladies came. Their escorts spent money at the hotel. You were earning everything that establishment gave us."

I repressed a sigh. "I will not debate the issue with you. The mannequins served their purpose. Anyway, this is where I wish to live. As soon as we are settled, I shall buy paints and canvas and see about renewing my lessons in art."

"I thought you were going to be a fashion designer," Carlo exclaimed impatiently. "There is no money in painting. Here everyone paints and sells their canvasses for only enough to buy bread and cheese. You have done me an injustice, Angela. I belong back at the hotel. Not in this hovel."

"It is not a hovel," I said. "However, all you have to do

is find a job that pays enough and then move back. You may feel free to go at any time."

He looked his disgust. "Who can earn enough for that?"

"I'm going to find work in some dressmaking establishment. Painting will be my hobby. In designing women's clothes, color and art are important, so my experience with an artist's brush isn't going to hurt me."

"How long before we go to the United States? I have already applied for a visa and they say I might make the next quota."

I was exasperated with him, tired of his complaining. I said, "Uncle Carlo, I cannot be responsible for what you want to do or where you go. I cannot return to the United States until I have become proficient in my field of work and that is not going to happen over a brief time."

He was seated in the tiny parlor of my flat, slumped in a chair. It was his usual posture when he was depressed or looking for sympathy.

"You don't care what happens to me. You forget I am not young any more and I am inexperienced in anything requiring work."

"I'm very well acquainted with your lack of experience," I told him. "Also with your lack of a desire to find work."

He eyed me resentfully. "You also forget that it was I who saved you from that crazy man Vito sent. Were it not for my being on hand, you might have been murdered."

"I haven't forgotten," I said, and I spoke now with more compassion. "But please don't say Vito sent him."

"If you have that much faith in Vito, why don't you write him? It's not far from Florence to Paris. Only a train ride."

"Because I don't want to bother Vito about my problems," I said.

"I'm not thinking of your problems. It's not right that you should be unmarried. You are eighteen now. What are you waiting for?"

"You are very rude," I said coldly.

He relented. "I'm sorry, dear niece. I admit I am a weakling."

148

Two weeks later I wondered if Carlo had been right and we should have continued to live on the largesse from the hotel. For days I'd walked the streets of the district where fashions were created and manufactured. I had faith in myself, fully believing I could equal anything being done in that line. Even better it. But as yet, here in France, there were no large factories manufacturing modestly priced dresses in volume. They were doing well in New York, but in Paris the designers preferred to make dresses, gowns and coats to order.

They were successful at it for there were enough wealthy women here to support these small industries. Nobody seemed to care much what the poor people wore. And there were many of them. I saw many ladies who dressed as smartly as those who came to admire the mannequins. They were gifted and sewed at home, copying the latest fashions, making them up in inexpensive fabrics.

The larger department stores had little interest in a designer. They either had their own or depended upon those in the dressmaking establishments. I was growing discouraged. Expenses were eating into my capital. I'd cashed the letter of credit and placed the proceeds in the small safe behind the owner's lobby desk. It was shrinking alarmingly, despite all I did to economize. Carlo was a considerable expense to me, but I didn't need his reminder to recall how he'd saved me from that man who tried to invade the hotel suite. As for painting lessons, I couldn't squander what little I had on them.

I began to long for the security I'd once known back in Aunt Celestine's flat in Philadelphia. The rent there was paid for some months from now. If I returned, I'd at least be comfortable and my expenses would not be as high.

I no longer believed the strange ring Papa had sent me brought luck. Each time I went for an interview seeking work, I would let one finger touch the ring. It did no good. If it had once possessed magical qualities, they had abated. It had probably all been in my mind anyway. I associated it with the love I bore my parents. That was sufficient.

149

Then, one morning, without even touching the ring, I found a man responsive to my request for a job. He was Henri Maspero, a small name in the fashion world, but kind enough to give me an opportunity. He operated on a small budget, but his creations were exquisite and he preferred to produce quality without regard to large profits that came from quantity.

He'd studied my drawings which I'd worked on faithfully whenever I wasn't out seeking employment, and been impressed. "I have designed my own fashions," he explained, "but it is exacting work and my wife insists I not stay in the shop half the night with my sketches. I cannot pay you in proportion to the skill represented in your work, but it is possible you will bring in profits which I will share with you, in proportion to your investment. In this case, it is represented by your creations."

"Thank you, Monsieur Maspero," I said gratefully. "All I ask is a chance."

"Then you may report in the morning, Mademoiselle, and we shall astound the Paris world of fashion with our new creations."

It didn't turn out like that, though after a month one of our gowns was accepted for an important fashion show. It was well received. So well that I worked endless hours creating more.

This involved everything from my skill in art to hand-sewing and fitting. We didn't even have a model, so I substituted for this as well. In six months we were beginning to see results. At the latest fashion show we had three offerings and they were also well received with orders following. Monsieur Maspero was talking about expansion. My pay was meager for the work I was doing and long hours I put in, but I was learning. However, Paris was not quite what I thought it was when I first arrived. The field of dressmaking was without glamor and composed of hard work, jealousies, the theft of ideas and the constant struggle to put something new over.

I was far from discouraged. From all of this, I would gain a perfect insight into the problems I would have when I began my own business.

I worked from early morning until late at night on the

six gowns Monsieur Maspero and I created, though he allowed me to include one of my own. He couldn't afford models, so he was reduced to requesting the help of high-priced courtesans to wear his creations at the finer restaurants or places of entertainment. If they caught the eye of a society lady, she would ask the waiter attending them to learn the name of the designer.

Not the easiest way to sell a creation, but when one was not yet a success, one had to be resourceful. The courtesans, of course, expected to be paid for such a favor. That left little profit for Monsieur Maspero and an even smaller reward for me.

Finally, a lady whose husband was high in the French diplomatic corps was giving a tea for the wives of diplomats from all over Europe. Even some from the United States. Monsieur Maspero was invited to show three of his creations. Much to my pleasure, two of them were mine, though he agreed to it only after I said I would give him the credit, should they be a success. At first, I was indignant that he would take such advantage of me. However, it took me only moments to realize it was the opportunity I had been seeking. I was young and versatile. I'd learned a lot in the time I had been with him. I could get an idea for a frock and transfer it to paper with a few rapid strokes of my pen. I reminded myself that I wouldn't be the first who had had to do this in order to gain recognition. If I really had the talent, I would move forward. At least Monsieur Maspero had given me a start. I only wished my pay wasn't so meager. There again, I reminded myself I was only getting started. At least I wasn't living in an attic. Though Carlo would have said we were.

He played a part also, consenting to attend the forthcoming show. It was by invitation only, but Monsieur Maspero was given two tickets. They were used by Madame Maspero and Carlo. She was very chic, though a little heavy through the waist. She wasn't too enthusiastic when her husband told her she would be escorted by my uncle. I suppose, knowing I had little, she figured Carlo would prove an embarrassment to her. But, being a dutiful French wife, she made no protest.

When Carlo made an appearance at the shop, dressed in the latest fashion, I thought she would faint from surprise. Carlo, not being a complete fool, knew she had expected a great deal less. He was most gracious and charming, as he had promised me he would be. In fact, he even flirted with her during the showing.

The mansion where the display of French fashions was held could almost have been called a palace. The models were courtesans hired for the occasion. I wondered if the ladies in the audience knew. If so, they didn't seem to mind. Their applause was enthusiastic. Both Monsieur Maspero and I were watching from the wings, for it was a ballroom which held a stage on which the models paraded, then moved down the steps to move among the guests so that they might make a closer inspection of the garments. Each model carried a card which had a number and the name of the designer. When the guests were especially pleased, they applauded politely. I was overwhelmed when sustained applause greeted one of my designs. Monsieur Maspero also beamed. And why not? His name was on the card held by the model.

I was pleased that Carlo evinced proud surprise when he saw both my models which he had already seen in drawings I had shown him. He forgot Madame Maspero and joined in the sustained applause. I felt a warm glow of affection for him at that moment.

When the show was concluded, the designers were allowed to mingle with the guests. Monsieur Maspero informed me I might have the remainder of the day off. He would return the gowns to his establishment. It was then I knew I would never achieve success in Paris. I belonged back in the United States. I felt at home there, far more than I had when I went to Florence. If the road to a career in dress design, especially by a woman, was to be fraught with frustrations, then I would prefer that I endure them in my adopted country.

Somehow, once I made that decision, I felt better than I had in a long time.

I didn't bother to return to the shop. I knew Monsieur and Madame would remain at the affair as long as possible. I felt certain he would be received with interest and accepted as well as his creations, some of which were mine, and it would prove profitable to him.

Back at my flat I stopped at the desk and exchanged a few words with the concierge who guarded the front door. She kept a tight rein on tenants, but she was friendly because I paid my rent on time and neither Carlo nor I made any trouble.

"I would like my envelope from your safe, *s'il vous plaît*," I said.

The woman shrugged her ample shoulders. "Mademoiselle, there no longer is an envelope."

"I mean the one with my money."

"It is gone."

"Gone? That's impossible. I haven't taken any money out in a month."

"Your uncle, he has been taking it out. I thought you knew this. He takes a little one day, a little more the next and poof!—it is all gone. You did not give him permission to do this?"

"Oh yes. I did," I spoke quickly, not wanting her to think me a fool, "but I didn't think he was spending it so freely."

"You will be able to pay the rent next month, *oui?*"

"Oh yes. I am employed."

"But of course. That uncle, he is one big man, eh? He has told me he has a fine job dealing in investments."

"Uncle Carlo is indeed quite a man." I attempted a smile, but was not too successful for I was seething with anger. He'd likely gambled away every franc.

I went upstairs and waited for him. After an hour of this, I prepared my supper and purposely neglected to prepare his. Half the time it had to be warmed over anyway, for he was notoriously slow and irresponsible. A set time meant little to him. Time was a commodity he had a great deal of.

It was shortly before midnight when I heard him making his way down the corridor. I could tell his step easily. I opened the door and confronted him.

"Ah, my dear Angela," he said. "Good evening to you."

"Come in," I said coldly. "We've something to talk about, Carlo."

He closed the door and leaned against it. "You have discovered all our money is gone, am I right?"

"How could you do this to me, Carlo? How could you steal the money by which we would have returned to the United States?"

"But *cara mia,* it was only to make more money. If I'd been lucky . . ."

"You were never lucky in your life at gambling, Carlo. I don't know what we are going to do. I want to go home and now I don't have the money. It will take months to earn enough. I have to pay our living expenses too."

"I will move out." Carlo was on his feet. "I know when I'm not wanted. My rooms cost money . . ."

"Yes, they do," I replied, untouched by his tone of self-pity. "Money which was mine."

"It was my sister's at one time," he said pointedly.

"Had she wanted you to have it, she'd have left it to you," I retorted. "I never went near that money except when the little I earned was gone. I've been supporting us on what I earned."

"I'm quite aware of it," he said impatiently. "You never let me forget it."

"You didn't even ask if you might borrow it."

He countered that with, "You would have refused."

"True," I snapped back at him. "I was saving that money to pay our fare to America."

"I spoke to you about going back," Carlo accused. "You didn't seem enthusiastic at the time. In fact, you told me you would be here months, perhaps years."

"I know what I told you, but that money could have been used for our return to the country of my choice."

"You have turned your back on Italy," he said, his tone one of disgust.

"I don't know Italy. I do know America and I love it. But that has nothing to do with the money you stole. You are a thief, Carlo Guillermo. Do you realize that?"

"You have made it very plain, Angela. Very plain. I am a ne'er-do-well."

"You are." I stifled my anger, knowing quarreling served no purpose. "What's done is done. But there is

154

nothing more, as you well know. I must work harder. I have no idea now when we may leave for America."

"How can you be so despondent?" Carlo exclaimed. "Your two creations received the most applause. Helped, in large part, by me."

I couldn't help but smile. "I saw you applauding."

"You're not angry with me, Angela?" Carlo's tone was placating.

"No. You will probably laugh at this. When I heard the applause, I decided this afternoon that we would return to America as soon as possible. I am getting nowhere here. If I am to have any success, I must go to the land where such a thing is most possible."

"But you are a success here, Angela," Carlo exclaimed, at ease now that my anger had abated. "After you left, Monsieur Maspero got order after order for the two gowns you created. I was standing beside him. The ladies loved them. In fact, Madame Maspero was jealous of her husband. He was basking in success. He will enlarge his salon now. He will employ seamstresses, models, errand boys and you will be his partner. After all, without you, he would still be a little fellow."

"And I am still unknown," I said quietly.

Carlo pointed a finger at the sketches piled high on my work table. "I have studied them. You have great gifts. These designs are beautiful. Different. They show off a woman's form. And when the form is not so good," he shrugged, "you design so its defects are hidden."

I couldn't help looking pleased. "You have noticed."

"I have," he said quietly. "Also, since you worked at Monsieur Maspero's, you have had the use of a sewing machine and you have made several dresses for yourself. You are now dressing too well for this place."

"Monsieur Maspero is kind enough to give me remnants," I said pointedly. "I could not afford such fabrics."

"No matter," Carlo said with a shrug. "It is good fabric. So why are you worried? You will have money now. You will be a partner."

I couldn't help but laugh. "I had to give both my creations to Monsieur Maspero. Otherwise he would not have put them in the show."

155

"Oh no." Carlo slapped his brow with the palm of his hand. "The crook. The dirty crook."

I could scarcely believe my ears, but I made no comparisons. "That is why I want to return to America. I realize I would never become successful here. I have learned a great deal. I will put it to good use when I get back—which won't be for a while. I will insist Monsieur Maspero give me more money. For that, I will give him more sketches."

"You can't do that," Carlo exclaimed indignantly. "They are so different."

I laughed. "I know that. That's why I'm not worried. He designs beautifully, but not as I do. And he never will. He designs for today. I design for tomorrow. I supervised the making of those dresses which were modeled today. He will need me around. And from now on he will have to pay. Only in that way will I ever get back to America."

Carlo became morose again. "I deserve it."

"What?" I asked.

"Being left behind."

"You may not be. It will depend on how much more I can wheedle out of Monsieur Maspero."

"I would like to punch his nose in for doing what he did.

"Please don't. I need the work."

"I promise not to gamble," he said meekly.

I shrugged. "There is nothing for you to gamble with."

"It was only to make more . . ."

"Oh, Carlo. If you'd not thrown it away, we'd have been on a ship a month from now."

"We could sell what we have," he suggested. "The clothes, keeping only enough to get by. I have a watch. You have jewelry. That ring you wear all the time. It is a monstrosity of a decoration for a woman. Not in the least feminine. But valuable, I am sure."

I glanced down at the ring. I'd ceased to think it meant anything more than a keepsake given me by my father.

"We shall see," I said. "I don't know what I'll do yet. Please go now. I want to think . . . alone."

That night I did some careful planning. Reluctant as I was to give up Aunt Celestine's flat, I would have to do so.

Most of her furnishings had been vandalized, but they had originally been quite expensive. Perhaps they could be re-upholstered. There were some months left on the long lease and if I could rent the flat, or make some accommodation with the landlord, I would salvage something from that. It would be close, probably not nearly enough, but I would have to chance it. Living in New York City was more expensive than in Philadelphia, but that is where I belonged. However, I would need money to rent some kind of space for the operation I intended to begin.

I couldn't afford to lose any more time because my creations had been seen and would be worn, but there was the present problem of finding enough money, quickly, to get back to the United States. I began to wonder if much else could go wrong.

My employer was sympathetic to my request for more money, but not very enthusiastic. As he explained to me—and I knew it was no lie—his wife was most extravagant and had placed him deeply in debt. In short, he couldn't afford to raise my pay.

Perhaps, with my little experience, I could have found a place with a larger and better-financed designer and dressmaking firm, but there too, the same reluctance would be shown once they got the idea it was short-term and I would soon leave France.

I kept telling myself I was young and I had the time, but I was also aware that fashions were bound to change and if I was to be a success, I would have to be in business very soon so my advanced ideas would be accepted first.

There were times I could barely tolerate Carlo when I recalled what he had done. Other times he was repentant and tried to be helpful—in his own way.

"If you could spare a small sum," he said. "A thousand francs for instance, I could bring it up to perhaps double that and then re-double . . . there are all kinds of gambling going on. Also, there are the races at Cannes . . ."

"Uncle Carlo," I said, "you never win. If you lose what little I have, we'll never get to America. Why don't you find work?"

"What can I do?" he asked, taking on an injured air. "I haven't the strength for physical work. I cannot find

157

employment as a clerk in a store, for my injuries are still too painful and I cannot remain on my feet."

"All right, Uncle Carlo. Go on doing nothing as you have been. I have no money to give you. I will work to support both of us and scrimp on everything so that one day we can sail for America."

"Then you still intend to take me." He looked relieved.

I smiled despite myself. "Perhaps, different as we are, we need each other. I just wish you were around a little more than you are."

He smiled. "There is a little coquette around the corner who has taken a fancy to me. She is harmless and she seems to like . . ." he shrugged.

"Your mustache, perhaps," I teased.

"You are making fun of me. You think I am unattractive to the opposite sex."

"*Au contraire,* Carlo," I replied. "I have watched you flirt with the ladies. Even when they are with another escort, they seem to enjoy it."

That soothed his ego. "So you noticed."

"Carlo, I realize you must have some money. You will call it a pittance, but it is all I can spare."

"However small, I will appreciate it."

I opened my handbag, took a few francs from it and placed them in his already extended palm. He regarded them, then switched his gaze to me. "As I said, however small, I will appreciate it."

"I hope so."

I worked long hours at the shop and after everyone was gone, I labored on a wardrobe for myself. Certainly I would have to dress so that my clothes would be noticed. I kept whatever I was working on behind bolts of material so that it wouldn't be discovered. The fashions were my own and they were certainly not, in any way, what they were wearing today. As each garment was finished, I brought it home and stored it in the back of my closet. I had acquired a dress for every occasion. I even bought hat frames and covered them with the fabric of the dress or suit. Fashion was a challenge and I found it very exciting. I forgot all my worries and frustrations when I worked on clothes.

From time to time, I was sent to the home of a customer to make alterations on a garment. Each one recompensed me and I accepted it gratefully. In my circumstance, I couldn't allow pride to get in the way of my goal.

Strolling home from such a task on a balmy night in late spring, I saw a man in a passing carriage suddenly stand up, despite the danger in a moving vehicle. The carriage turned toward the curb, slowing as it did so. Obviously I was the target of whoever was in the vehicle, for there were not half a dozen people in my line of vision and all of them were of the opposite sex. Instantly I was terrified.

"Angela," the man shouted when I turned to run away. "Angela, *cara mia . . .*"

I stopped when I recognized the voice and looked back. It was Vito, so fashionably dressed I hadn't recognized him. I ran toward him, calling his name over and over as he climbed down from the carriage. We met in the middle of the sidewalk and embraced shamelessly. He gave me an ardent kiss which I returned. I felt reborn. I'd had no one to laugh with or to share my problems with for a long time and now I did. It was too much. I laughed in sheer delight and reached up and touched his cheeks and then I cried and then I laughed again. He was very understanding, speaking my name again and again just as I had spoken his. He didn't speak until I quieted and then his thoughts were of me.

"It is good to see you looking well, Angela, though you are very thin."

"That is due to my long working hours which I thoroughly enjoy," I replied. I was holding on to him as though I feared he'd escape.

"So you study designing." His nod was one of remembrance, for I had spoken of such a thing to him in Italy.

"I am working in a small fashion house, but it is becoming more successful every day."

"Because of you, I'm sure," he said, laughing. He held me at arm's length. "Oh, let me look at you. You are like a dream come true."

"Please, Vito, let's go someplace where we can talk."

He grasped my elbow and led me to the carriage where

159

the somewhat surprised driver had witnessed our meeting with a smile that widened as we approached. Like all of Paris, he approved of love and what we had exhibited could only be that.

Vito said, "Drive anywhere. Through the parks where it is darker and more quiet. Just drive."

"What are you doing here, Vito?" I asked him.

"Business. I have come to return an embezzler to Italy. The French caught him for us."

"How long will you be here?"

"I wish it could be forever, but I have to pick up the prisoner tomorrow. So we have only tonight, Angela. And not very long. I have not been dealt such a cruel blow in my life. Tell me about yourself. Everything!"

I didn't know where to begin. "Vito, do you know a man named Emile? He is about twenty-four or five, slender as you are. He has a thin face, rather handsome, but cruel eyes."

"Emile? I have never known anyone by that name. It is French, not Italian."

"I think he is French."

"I have no acquaintances in France, except for a gendarme or two and they do not answer your description. What of this Emile?"

"He came to my door one night and told me you had sent him. When I still was reluctant to let him in, he pushed me aside and . . . he tried to . . . to. . . He had a dagger. Fortunately Uncle Carlo was close by and came to my rescue. Emile escaped."

Vito's features tensed as I talked. "How did he know you?"

"I haven't any idea."

"The French police have photographs of many molesters of women. They are very good at this identification business. Far better than we are in Italy. Would you examine some of these photographs?"

"No, Vito. I could not do that. Besides, I am not going to remain in Paris any longer than I have to. I must return to America if I wish to succeed. I'm on my own, Vito. I can't let time go by too quickly."

"What of your father and mother? Has there been any

change in your plans about them? Have you heard anything?"

Vito was, in my opinion, the only person in the world I could trust. I wished it was he I loved, not Stanton Talbot.

"I've said nothing about this to anyone, Vito. But I must tell you. About six months ago, I was in the lobby of a fashionable hotel—Carlo and I were living there; I'll tell you about it. Beside the elevator door were mirrors. I was primping in front of one of them when I saw a man move out slightly from behind a Grecian pillar in the lobby. I had a glimpse of his face—it was Papa. I couldn't have been mistaken. I looked for him, but he'd vanished completely. There was no sign of him, no hotel employee admitted to seeing him. I don't know where he came from or where he went, but it was my father I saw that night. I searched Paris trying to locate him."

"Good," Vito said. "Now we know he's alive and your mother must be too. Take heart in that knowledge, Angela."

"I still look for him. I study every man's face I see," I said.

"There is so little time for us," Vito exclaimed. "What can I do in one night? I cannot delay bringing the prisoner back. I cannot return once I have turned him over in Florence. I am a man with duties I can't shirk. One short evening!"

"Dear Vito, just being with you this brief time means more to me than you can imagine."

"If only you loved me," he said in a chagrined voice. "I warn you, I do not intend to give you up. I'll find you again . . . if you will give me your address, and I won't have to depend on my luck to find you. When do you return to America?"

I grimaced. "Just as soon as I can afford passage." Briefly I described the scrape Carlo's gambling had got us into.

"Poor child," he said, touching my hair. "Poor little angel. You look so elegant, so chic—I can't bear for you to work so hard. You know I love you. Won't you let me lend you the money?" Watching my face, he added,

"There would be no . . . conditions attached to the loan."

"No, Vito," I said sadly. "You know I can't."

"But why, when nothing makes me happy if you are unhappy?"

"Oh, Vito, *because*."

"You are stubborn. I must think of something."

"Short of robbing a bank I don't know what," I said.

"No, wait! Do you have any money at all?"

"A little . . . certainly not much."

"I have an idea, but you will have to be a gambler."

"Vito, that's how I lost what I had. Carlo gambled it all away."

"That's Carlo. But maybe we are lucky at that. As a policeman I know many things. For instance, I know an Italian horse is running in the races at Cannes next week. It is an unknown horse and if you bet on him to win, the odds will give you back ten or more times the amount of money you bet. I know of this because the whole thing is crooked. It has been set up by gamblers we have been trying to find proof against for months. The Italian horse will not lose. It is either set for him to win, or he is an exceptional horse and his speed is a secret. But when these gamblers in Rome bet fortunes on a horse, you can be sure it will not lose."

"Carlo," I said slowly. "He delights in gambling."

"You must take a chance," Vito said. "There is no other way. If you lose . . . well, so be it. You have lost before, but I assure you the chances are very small that you will. I think it is the best thing you can do."

"If you say so, then I will."

"The name of the horse—prophetic, I hope—is Chance. In French that means luck. The race is exactly one week from today. Don't enter the betting until the last possible moment. If you can, send Carlo there."

"If I am fortunate, I'll never forget you," I said. "Oh Vito, why can't I be in love with you?"

"For a simple reason. There is someone else. I can tell. For some reason you don't want me to know about him. Perhaps because you're afraid of hurting me. I'm a policeman. I've been hurt before and I see a great deal of hurting. However, whether or not you tell me about him changes nothing. Do you understand, Angela?"

"Yes. Do you understand, Vito?"

"I'm trying, *cara mia,* but it's not easy." He shrugged, then smiled ruefully. "Now, I'm sorry, but I've got to have you driven home. I'm late as it is. The driver must drop me off first because I have a meeting with lawyers and judges tonight, so I can get off to an early start in the morning."

"I wish you could stay," I said earnestly. "These few minutes with you have given me more strength and hope and courage than I've had in weeks. I'll write you as soon as I know when I'm departing. Once I reach the United States and am settled, I'll send you a long letter."

He nodded, somewhat glumly, I thought, but he maintained a fairly light conversation until the carriage pulled up in front of a stately government building.

Vito drew me to him and kissed me lightly on the lips. *"Arrivederci,* Angela. We will meet again soon. Please think of me as your protector. When I kiss you, that is. Then you will know I mean no offense."

He released me, left the carriage abruptly and didn't look back as he climbed the wide stairs to the building entrance. My eyes followed him until he disappeared inside. I gave the driver my address and as we drove off, I was engulfed with a wave of sadness. For a few minutes I had felt young and alive. I wondered if I would have eventually fallen in love with Vito, had Stanton Talbot not come into my life. But he had.

The next day, during my midday hour away from work, I ate hastily and visited my bank, where I withdrew my carefully hoarded savings.

That evening I gave Carlo the money and told him to bet it all on Chance, the horse Vito had named. To my surprise, he protested.

"What manner of nonsense is this, Angela? You know nothing about horse races. And what makes you think this particular horse is going to win? It's madness. Where did you even find out about the race at Cannes?"

"I didn't tell you because you were out last night.

163

Yesterday Vito Cardona was in Paris and almost like a miracle, we met."

"The *Carabinieri* man?" Carlo's voice took on a note of suspicion. "How did he know you were here? And how did you meet? Almost like a miracle, you said. Are you sure it was that? Or has he been keeping track of you?"

"That's stupid," I said angrily.

"No more stupid than betting on Chance."

"Uncle Carlo, Vito has no reason to be an enemy."

"Someone has," Carlo said. "Too many bad things have happened to you. I suspect everyone."

"I trust Vito and so must you," I insisted. "It was Vito who told me about this race. The Italian police know about it too. Apparently, the race is not to be an honest one. Vito suggested I take advantage of this fact. I will risk it. Everything I have, to the last sou, is for you to bet with. If we lose, then we begin again. But at present our situation is serious. I must take this risk."

"If you say so, I'll bet the money. I can do that here in Paris. I don't have to go to Cannes. Remember, this is your idea, not mine."

"Another thing, you must not talk about this. If too many people hear of it, the race may be called off, or so many bets will be taken on the horse the odds will go down. That's what Vito told me."

"If this works," Carlo acknowledged, "I'll stop suspecting him. And I give you my word I'll not mention this to anyone. If I did, and the horse didn't come in, you might lose all your money, but I might lose my life."

"Don't put the money on the horse until the last minute."

Carlo nodded. "I want to go to America even more than you do, Angela."

"Then pray the horse will win," I said. "It's our only hope."

Until the day of the race, I lived in uncertainty and doubt. If Chance didn't come in, I'd lose all I had. I'd not be able to return to the United States for at least another year. That presented a problem with the flat Aunt Celestine had leased, and paid for, far in advance. Also I felt that I was ready to strike out on my own. The more I saw of current fashions, the more I knew they were due for a change, and whoever accomplished that first was going to be very successful. I thought I knew what women would want. My sketch book and my mind were full of ideas. I needed only the opportunity to display them.

The day of the race I returned home from work as promptly as I could. Carlo was at a betting establishment where he would wait for the results of the race to be sent by wireless. I kept a tight hold on the ring and prayed silently. Carlo had placed the bet as close to the time of the race as possible so I didn't know what the odds were. Vito had indicated they'd be respectable, ten times what I bet if the horse won. I would be satisfied with half that, for it would bring in enough to pay my steamship fare and Carlo's. Not in first class, but I felt I could even weather steerage if it would get me back to America.

Early in the evening I heard Carlo run up the stairs. He'd never done that before.

"Tell me!" I said. "For heaven's sake, Uncle Carlo, was Vito's advice worthwhile?"

Carlo beamed. "We can leave for the United States whenever you wish, Angela. The horse not only won, the odds were the biggest I've seen in years. The race must have been as crooked as Vito said it would be. I have the money."

He placed it on the table. It didn't look like too much until I saw the denomination of the bills. I slowly counted out enough for first class passage and there was more than enough left over to go far in helping me establish a business of my own.

I kissed Carlo, mentally forgiving him for everything, and immediately began planning for the journey back to Philadelphia. However, fearful Carlo might want to gamble our fare, I went to the steamship company office and bought our passage. On my way back I stopped at Monsieur Maspero's and bade him adieu. I then returned to my flat and began to pack, for we were to sail in three days. No journey had ever excited me more. I'd never been happier. So when I heard unsteady steps in the corridor and Carlo's voice calling out something, I thought he might have been celebrating. I couldn't blame him. I

165

opened my door and cried out in horror at the sight of him. His face had been battered until it was almost unrecognizable. Blood was caked on his cheeks and forehead. Some fresh blood still oozed out of his nostrils. He was on the verge of collapse. He had to lean on me for support as I guided him into my parlor and onto the sofa.

I didn't ask questions. I filled a basin with water, supplied myself with towels and a half bottle of peroxide, luckily still potent. I bathed his face carefully, oblivious to his groans and sometimes sharp cries of pain. Apparently he'd fallen; earth seemed almost ground into the raw flesh.

I cleaned off the blood, studied the cuts to make sure they were not so wide and deep as to need suturing. The swellings and abrasions I could do nothing for except apply cold compresses. I did clean out the open wounds with peroxide, drawing more cries of pain, but this was necessary and I had to be ruthless.

Finally I had him bandaged and more at ease though he was groaning softly. I went to his quarters ignoring his protest of fear at being left alone. I found a bottle of brandy which I was certain he had on hand. I returned to pour him a generous amount of the drink and held it to his lips. His mouth was swollen and though some spilled, enough got into his mouth for him to swallow.

"What happened?" I asked him after he lay back. "That is, if you feel well enough to talk. You certainly were beaten up."

"The same people," he said. "They told me this would be the last time they would let me go. Next time they will kill me. Angela, I know they will."

"How much do you owe them?"

"I paid my debt to them. It is the cuckold's pride. Don't leave me behind, Angela."

"We're sailing in two days. I hope your face will not be as swollen by then, and the black-and-blue marks will have faded some. Have you gone to the police about this? You should."

"Angela, you don't understand. You have no idea how evil these people are—or how powerful."

"Well, you've shown me a good example, twice now,

of what they are capable of. It's lucky they didn't break any bones this time, as they did in Florence."

"There was talk of it, but they decided this was enough for now. But one good thing happened. Today I learned that I can enter the United States under the Italian quota, so we'll have no trouble there. My passport, everything is ready. Perhaps I can get away from these men forever."

"Then you'd best go to your own rooms and rest. Take the brandy with you. Tomorrow stay in bed and put cold cloths on the swellings. After tomorrow you won't have to worry. We'll go directly to the train for Cherbourg and in a matter of hours after that, we'll sail."

After Carlo left, I tried to reason it out. He claimed he had paid his gambling debt—how, I had no idea. But if he had settled that score, they should have had their vengeance. Would they really have beaten him again, after such a long time, for his affair with the wife? Admittedly, I knew little about men and their sense of honor. But it didn't seem logical. . . .

I turned my attention to the ring, raising my hand and pressing its cool metal lightly against my face. I was glad to have it and would always wear it. Yet I wondered if it had worked its magic when Chance won, or if Vito deserved all the credit. It had to be the latter. Nothing else made sense.

NINE

This time I met with no governmental red tape when Carlo and I arrived at Ellis Island. There was a slight delay with reference to Carlo, but we had prepared for that by having on hand all the necessary papers and answers to the innumerable questions asked of him. We cleared the Island in five hours.

Carlo, of course, was enraptured with New York. We stayed there overnight in a good hotel and spent hours roaming about the Fourteenth Street shops and the garment district further uptown. It was a small section of the great city, but I had a strong idea it was destined to grow as ready-made dresses were being sought after more and more.

"Do you like New York City, Uncle Carlo?" I asked, knowing full well he did. He seemed to be struck dumb and, for him, that was far from normal.

"There is such excitement here," he exclaimed enthusiastically. "I never was in such a place before."

"It is different," I agreed. "But then I suppose each large city has a special something to identify it."

"You are right, niece," he replied, still looking around. We were strolling up Fifth Avenue and had reached Thirty-fifth Street.

I said, "I intend to have a store here."

"That I know. But how soon?"

"As soon as I can raise the money."

"You have more than enough to open your shop. You said so." Carlo spoke impatiently. "So what do you mean —when you have enough money?"

"I will put some of the money into the shop, but I will try to get a loan from a bank. I must have some cash with which to operate."

"Oh."

"Also I want you to purchase a new wardrobe. You have a way with clothes and also with the ladies. You will be an asset to the salon."

He beamed. "Thank you, Angela. I already saw a men's haberdashery where I will have several outfits made for me."

"You won't need more than three," I said quietly.

"How many dresses did you make for yourself out of remnants?" he countered.

"They happened to be fabrics Monsieur Maspero discarded because they were imperfect. I was able to design and make the gowns so the defects of the fabric were hidden."

"Very well. It will be three outfits."

"As we grow successful, you may augment them with others."

He laughed. "Just think, Angela, when you become successful and someone asks you how you got your start, you can wave a hand loftily in the air and say—I owe it all to a crooked horse race."

"Uncle Carlo," I said sternly, "don't you ever tell that to anyone. We must be loyal to Vito."

"And who is that *carabiniere* loyal to?" he said disdainfully.

"Really, there are times when you make me so irritated, I swear I will never speak to you again."

"I am not worried at present. You have no one else to talk to."

"Don't be so smug," I said loftily. "That could change overnight."

He eyed me with fresh interest. "So? You have a gentleman friend here?"

"I do not. Nor do I have time for one."

The next day we took the train to Philadelphia. He was really shaken upon seeing the utter destruction which had taken place in Aunt Celestine's apartment.

"Were the murderers never caught?" Carlo asked.

"If they had been, I'm certain I would have heard from Sergeant Warren."

I showed him through the apartment, leaving Aunt

Celestine's bedroom for the last. Only the bedframe stood where once had been springs, mattress and bedclothes, all covered with a bedspread of pale violet satin. The wall beside the bed still bore blood stains. So did the carpet. It was not lost on Carlo. "Barbarous," he exclaimed. "No one will want to live here. I know I could not sleep in this room."

"There is a cot in the small sitting room off the large parlor. You may use it."

"Thank you, Angela. How soon will we leave for New York?"

"I want to see Peter and Sarah. Obviously they kept the place dusted and the floor cleaned. They were fond of Aunt Celestine, just as she was of them. I was unable to send them anything, yet they were very loyal."

"I didn't think Aunt Celestine could arouse warmth in others."

"That is because you never thought of her except when you needed money. I'm sure she never refused you."

"Never," he admitted. "Though each letter was a lecture about what a wastrel I was."

I made no answer. He had suffered enough of a shock. I looked around at the broken furniture.

"Certainly I cannot lease this flat furnished. I think I will call in a second-hand dealer and dispose of everything he will purchase. What he doesn't want, I will throw out."

Carlo said, "You told me I might have the silver."

"You may have anything you wish. Just remember we don't even have a place to bring it to in New York. But we can pack it and store it here until we have the room for it."

Carlo looked pleased.

"I will take you out and show you the city. Then I must see the manager of the building and learn if he knows of anyone who will take over Aunt Celestine's lease."

"Where will you take me?" Carlo asked.

"First to Independence Hall where I will show you the Liberty Bell."

"Ah yes. I understand it has a crack in it."

"It happened early in the century so now it is on display. Americans are very proud of that bell. As well they might be."

Carlo enjoyed his tour about the city and asked endless questions which I was proud to be able to answer. For once, I was the knowledgeable one. We stopped at a leading hotel for dinner, then returned to the apartment. I left Carlo there while I went downstairs to see the manager.

I explained my problem and, to my delight, he said there would be no trouble leasing it. A lady had already been there in the hope of doing that very thing and had asked him to contact her when I returned.

He had her name and address which he gave to me. I thanked him and without returning upstairs, I went outside and waved a carriage to the curb. The address was in a very old part of the city and I climbed a rickety flight of stairs to get there. A maid answered my knock and admitted me to a parlor so dim that I could scarcely find my way to a chair. I heard soft voices in the rear and in moments a buxom lady, dressed exotically in flowing robes, entered the room. She gave off a heavy scent of gardenia which was almost overpowering. She wore a band around her head with a peacock plume seemingly growing from the center of her brow. She extended a heavily jeweled hand and spoke my name in a crisp, cultured voice.

"It was good of you to see me, Madam Dainzler."

I had stood up when she entered, but she motioned me back to the chair and sat opposite me. "I am delighted you have returned, Miss Gambrell. I wanted terribly to lease the flat your poor departed aunt was murdered in."

Apparently she had no trouble seeing me, for she laughed at the surprise which must have been registered on my face. "I can understand your puzzlement. Most people wouldn't set foot in it, but I am a seeress. I might make communication with your aunt. Though I shan't seek to. I have my following and they know I will pay anything to buy up that lease."

"I want no more than what I am entitled to," I said. "I'm relieved to have it off my hands."

"There is one condition," she said quietly.

171

"Please name it." My heart sank. I hoped my voice didn't register the disappointment I felt.

"I must purchase everything in it."

"It's valueless—except for the silver, china and crystal."

"You may keep that. What I want is all that was destroyed. The manager allowed me to see the flat. I bribed him. Your aunt's spirit must be tortured, not only by what was done to her, but by what was done to her possessions. A seance, in the midst of such destruction, would be most unusual and, perhaps, highly rewarding."

I was so astonished I was at a loss for words. Even more so when she named a sum for the furniture that I considered astronomical. When I started to protest it was too much, she held up a hand and said it would have to be her way or she was not interested.

I accepted before she changed her mind. She wrote a check for the remainder of the lease, plus the battered furniture. When I mentioned the blood stains in the bedroom, she said they presented no problem. She did not want them disturbed.

I couldn't believe my luck. Back in the carriage, I looked down at my ring.

"Papa, did you have anything to do with this?"

I didn't even realize I had spoken aloud until the driver said, "What is it, Miss?"

I wasn't even embarrassed. I had never expected such luck. I would leave an envelope of money with the manager to recompense Peter and Sarah. He was honest and would see that they were paid for all they had done while I was away. I doubted they would set foot in the apartment once Madam Dainzler moved in. She was a little frightening. A seeress! I wondered how Aunt Celestine would have thought about her once-lovely furniture being used by a medium.

Carlo was pacing the floor nervously when I returned. "Where were you?" he exclaimed indignantly. "You said you were going downstairs to the manager. When you didn't return, I went down there and he said you had come and gone."

I brushed aside his pique and told him of our phenomenal luck. When I showed him the check, his frown was replaced with a smile. "You are right, dear niece. Our luck is holding. Are you sure your *carabiniere* had nothing to do with it?"

"How could he? Madam Dainzler left her name with the manager some months ago. She is probably going to conduct seances here."

"She should bring back my sister so she could tell who murdered her."

"I'm not interested in seances."

"I know. Only your salon. When do we leave for New York City?"

"As soon as I go through Aunt Celestine's possessions. That is, empty her closets. I will give her clothes to the manager. He will pass them on to some worthy organization."

"I have packed the silver, glasses and china. There is a beautiful candelabrum hanging in the dining room that would look gorgeous in your salon."

I dismissed that idea quickly. "We will take nothing from here that isn't personal. Madam Dainzler paid us well."

"Did she look Italian?" Carlo asked.

"I couldn't see her very well," I replied patiently. "The draperies were drawn. Why do you ask?"

He shrugged. "I am still wondering if your *carabiniere* had something to do with your getting that check."

"Uncle Carlo, if you don't stop nagging me about Vito, I swear I will walk out on you."

"I'm not worried. You have no one but me. You need a gentleman. One with polish—*savoir-faire,* as the French say. A family member. Once you are married, I will disappear."

I dared not hope for such luck. Aloud, I said, "I have no time to think of such foolishness."

"I'm surprised. You seemed to think a lot of that *carabiniere.*"

"Will you stop calling him that?"

"Why? That's what he is."

"There's nothing wrong with it."

"Nothing—except I don't trust him. He had you bet on a crooked horse race."

173

"You wouldn't be here if he hadn't."

"All the more reason to wonder about the man. It happened too conveniently. His coming to Paris, meeting you by chance. Knowing about the race which was to happen in only two or three days. I don't like it when so many things all fall into place."

"You're not being fair, Carlo. The plain fact is, you hate the police. Whether they are *carabinieri, gendarmes,* or even American police. You can't stand authority."

"That's not true. It's this policeman who happens to come by so conveniently."

I didn't want to argue any more. I said, "Oh, Carlo, at least I feel I'm ready to begin. To be on my own. I'm very excited."

Carlo nodded slowly. "Have you ever given thought that by coming here you may be giving up your chances to find your papa and mama?"

"Of course not," I said.

"Why would they come here? So far away from home? Paris, Berlin, even St. Petersburg—yes, they might go there. But to cross an ocean to a strange country where everything is so different, I don't think your papa would go to such extremes. Besides, your mama lived in Italy too long to ever leave it."

"They came to see me when I was eleven."

"Many years ago," Carlo said.

"Too many," I said.

His brow furrowed thoughtfully. "Where do you think they could be hiding?"

"Why do you think they are hiding, Uncle Carlo?" I asked.

"What else can it be? Do you hear of them going about? Sometimes I think they are dead."

I hesitated a moment. Carlo was my closest relative. An irresponsible, sometimes thoughtless man, but he and I were a family now. I thought he had a right to know about Papa. I'd sworn never to tell anyone, and that one word "SILENZIO" printed on a piece of paper slipped under my door had been a warning to say nothing. Yet it seemed to me he should know. If anything happened to me, he could carry on the search. Or be prepared if Papa and Mama did appear—or were found to be dead.

"I will tell you something in strictest confidence," I said. "You must forget it one moment after you hear it. I have been warned not to divulge this secret, but I can't see how that applies to you."

"You have heard your father is alive?" he asked quickly. I'd never seen him so excited.

"I've not only heard he is alive, I saw him."

"Here? When?"

"No, Carlo. It was in Paris. While we lived in that very fashionable hotel. I saw his reflection in a mirror, but I couldn't find him."

"You are sure, Angela? After all, just a reflection. You could be mistaken."

"I swear it was he."

"You hadn't seen him in years."

"Don't you think I remember what my own father looks like? I was not mistaken."

"Then why doesn't he come forward? What makes him hide like a wanted murderer?"

"I don't know. But whatever his reason, I swear he has committed no crime."

"A man hides only because he must," Carlo observed. "He hides to keep from being confronted with his troubles."

"You're hiding right now," I reminded him.

"Me . . . hiding . . . ?"

"From those people who twice nearly killed you and have threatened next time they will."

Carlo nodded. "You have made me see the error of my thinking. One sometimes must hide even though no crime has been committed. Perhaps your papa and mama are in this country after all. It is a big country and better to hide in than Italy or France."

"For once I agree with you."

"But what will you do about finding them? Have you a plan?"

"No, Carlo, I have no plan. They will have to come to me. There is no way I can find them. I tried and it could well be I only made matters worse for them."

175

"Perhaps I can think of a way," he said. "I'll try. Now I'm going to my room to get some sleep. At least my face has healed."

"And every hair of your mustache is in place."

He nodded. "*Si*. But bear in mind I have not been a well man since I was sent to the hospital by those people . . . those ruffians. And when they beat me the second time, some old troubles seemed to come back. The bones that healed in the hospital feel as if they are about ready to break again, and I'm sure I have a severe case of the rheumatics."

I suppressed a smile.

The next morning we began work immediately after breakfast, which I had to go out and get. We packed what we wanted. Carlo tired quickly, so I sent him out to buy some bread, sliced meat, cheese and coffee. He saw a cake he liked and purchased that. I wouldn't spare the time to go out to eat.

It was during the second day when I worked in Aunt Celestine's bedroom that I came across one of the greatest surprises of my life. I'd cleaned out some of her possessions before I went to Paris, but a few older things were left behind and in the furthest recesses of the long, narrow walk-in bedroom closet, I came across two ancient hat boxes. One contained old tissue paper. The second one was so old the lid was cracked and torn. Inside I found a hat which made me smile. It was at least twenty years old, with flowers and bows and ribbons that tied under the chin. She must have regarded it with affection because it was the only one.

I decided to try it on. But when I lifted it out of the box, I saw two bundles of what looked like money.

I carried them to the bureau and put them down. They were tied with faded ribbon and looked to be quite old. Most were goldback notes. Without counting them, I judged there must be a fortune here. I shouted for Carlo and he came quickly, recognizing the urgency in my voice. He stared, mute for once, at the sight of all that money.

"It was in an old hat box . . . in the closet," I said. "Aunt Celestine must have hidden it there. Carlo, that's a great deal of money."

176

"The way to find out," he said, when he got his breath and voice back, "is to count it."

He sat down on the edge of the bed, removed the ribbon from the bundles of cash and began counting. When he finished, he looked up at me in disbelief.

"Twenty-one thousand six hundred and ten dollars. A fortune, Angela. Celestine left you a fortune."

"But . . . but that's not like her, Uncle Carlo. To leave such a sum of money around like this."

"Well, she did it! It's a great piece of luck. What will you do with this?"

"Get my own shop started immediately. We will depart for New York as soon as I finish my work here. Now I can do what I wish to set up a beautiful store. I thought at first I would only have a small place where I would design and make gowns, but sell them to other shops. That's not the way to do it. The other shops take all the credit. Now I don't have to do that." My happiness knew no bounds at this discovery. "This means an end to all the bad luck we've had."

"Perhaps you will be good enough to give me a hundred dollars or so," Carlo said. "I need new clothes and if I am to be associated with your business, I have to look prosperous as well as handsome."

"You may have more than that. I agree with you on that point. We'll settle all that as soon as we're established in New York." I handed him a bill. "You should have money in your pocket. Please don't spend it at some card or dice game, or a horse race. We must be judicious in the manner in which we use it."

He tucked the hundred dollars into his pocket, tied up the rest of the money and gave it to me. "To have a fortune like this in my hands, if only for a couple of minutes, feels good, Angela. I think it's just a prophecy of what's going to happen. You will be rich."

"If that happens, you will not want. However, I don't care half as much about that as to have my creations accepted."

"Would you be angry if I went out tonight? Just a visit to a bar, or a good club, where I can talk to some people, learn a little about how they think. I swear I will not gamble."

"Uncle Carlo, certainly you can do whatever you please. If you think it's safe, by all means go out."

"If I think it's safe . . . ? I don't know what you mean."

"Have you already forgotten that your enemies attacked you in Florence, followed you to Paris and somehow found out where you lived. They could do the same here."

I saw his color fade and there was fear in his eyes. He turned away from me. "I haven't forgotten, Angela. But I'm also a man. Will you be afraid here alone?"

"No." Nor was I. I could accomplish more alone.

I spent the night at a desk, making estimates, consulting catalogues, tearing up one hasty prospectus after another until I'd finally settled on one that I wanted my store to look like. This done, I set about determining tentative costs. That dismayed me to a point where I realized that, even with all this small fortune Aunt Celestine had left me, I would have to be thrifty. I might even need to seek a loan. However, I did know bankers here and they knew me so, with this amount for a stake, I might find it easier to obtain one.

Thinking about that made me glance down at the ring. Could it have been responsible for my finding Aunt Celestine's money? It might easily have fallen into the hands of the killers. And its very existence here was so strange. Aunt Celestine always used the bank and, so far as I knew, there had never been any reason for her to conceal all this cash.

I removed the money from the drawer and looked at it. A pleasant sight to be sure, especially when I knew what it meant to me. One of the gold certificates seemed crisp and new. With an exclamation of horror, I recalled that there were people who actually tried to print money and pass it as genuine. I removed the ribbon and began going through the bills, studying them carefully. Most of them were old and no doubt genuine, but there were half a dozen fresh bills in the lot. I extracted them and placed them on the desk top. I got a magnifying glass for a closer examination. All of these were of current issue. The dates of issue proved they'd been in circulation less than a year.

But Aunt Celestine had been dead before these bills were issued. Someone else had hidden that money.

I thought of Papa. Yes, he'd once been wealthy enough to spare this amount, and certainly he'd have been eager to let me have it for a worthy purpose. But Papa was in France. Of course, he might have come here, but how? He would have to come as an immigrant because a man missing for more than seven years since he'd last used his passport wouldn't be likely to have it renewed. So it was reasonable to believe that Papa was still in Europe. Therefore, someone else had hidden the money, quite likely just before my return. Someone knew I was coming back, knew I needed money and placed it in the hat box.

Whoever did it knew I was determined upon a career and would have need of a large sum of money. I would think Aunt Celestine had hidden it. I knew better, but it was still another mystery to be added to a list that was growing formidable—and frightening.

We had almost a month before we had to vacate the flat. During that time Carlo and I made several trips to New York City where we spent hours looking for a proper location. I was aghast at the rentals asked. The store we finally decided upon, because it had room for a good-sized shop in back, was quoted at a hundred and fifty dollars a month, which we felt was unheard of. After we sought prices on other places and learned from nearby shops that the amount was well within a reasonable range, our consternation lessened.

I had enough cash on hand to pay a year in advance, for which I was granted a small concession. I bought new furnishings, not second-hand as Carlo suggested in one of his rare conservative moments. I searched for the best so the store itself would radiate the sort of luxury to go with the kind of merchandise I planned to make and sell. I even placed an expensive carpet on the floor and hung silks and satins from the ceilings to cover the cold, bare walls. The color scheme was a soft gray and pink, ranging from pale to deep—almost a salmon color. I covered one wall with mirrors, which would help show off my gowns.

It was the manufacturing part that took a great deal of capital. The new sewing machines were very expensive, but operated by electricity and so fast and efficient I knew they would pay for themselves very quickly. I splurged on three candelabra which would be reflected in the mirrored wall.

We also found a flat, six blocks from the store in a newer building, equipped with a gas stove, a large icebox, a porcelain sink, two modern bathrooms and a layout which enabled Carlo to have a small dressing room, though we shared the kitchen and the parlor.

My bank account had been depleted. I owed a fair amount of money but none of it pressing. So far I'd not needed to borrow, but with my investment I knew it wouldn't be hard to get a loan, even if I had no magic ring to count on. Besides, I had deposited a certain amount to see us through the first difficult year.

The ring had drifted into the category of the forgotten. I rarely thought about its influence on my good fortune, if such influence existed. I'd grown to give its powers serious consideration when I needed the luck the ring seemed to bring. Now that I had what I needed, the ring lost the importance it once held for me.

Finally, Carlo, with his new wardrobe, and I moved to our new flat. The salon was ready for business. I had purchased the necessary materials and hired two seamstresses. I paid them well once I knew they were capable. Then I set about turning into reality some of my designs that I'd spent so many months working on. I wore only my own creations and they were greeted first with shock, then admiration, albeit, in many cases, reluctant.

The present styles were cumbersome, even an impediment to moving with ease. Several times I had seen skirts become entangled between ladies' legs so that they had to bend down and pull them free. It was an embarrassment as well as an annoyance.

The high satin or linen collars choked one, and the wide, flaring skirts swept the sidewalks clean. The shirt-waist was an excellent and practical garment, if only the full, ungainly, above-the-elbow sleeves were eliminated. In wet weather one had to bunch the skirt in great handfuls and lift it to keep it from becoming soaked. These skirts bore the ridiculous name of rainsy-daisies.

For office wear, fashion decreed that the dress be almost always black serge; brown or dark gray was considered daring. The only relief from all this monotony and drabness was "Sunday Best" when a suit of silk or cotton was permitted, for use at church or concerts. These were provided at an average cost of fifteen dollars. For five more I knew I could turn out something in simple style, but colorful and fashion-cut to attract attention because it followed the lines of the body. Sensual, yes; but also pleasing to the eye.

My plans were to create something new, not too startling at first, for it would take courage to wear my clothes. Later I would introduce my more daring gowns. I even thought about exploiting the new bloomer fad which came about through the advent of the woman's bicycle, but I gave up the idea because there'd be little call for them. Not many women went in for athletics beyond the playing of croquet.

The one thing I was determined to do away with was the tight lacing which women had endured to bring their waist measure to the abnormal circumference of twenty inches, sometimes as small as eighteen.

It was my ambition to dress a woman who would be free of the constriction of corsets that gave one an enormous bosom and derriere while scarcely allowing one to breathe. This was the twentieth century. My sex was already beginning to fight for the vote. We were daring to enter the business world, though we were still scoffed at. My seamstresses were two ladies who had been widowed early in life. They had the responsibility of raising children still small. Fortunately, they had relatives who would look after them while they were at the salon. They were grateful not only because I gave them employment, but because I paid them a wage far beyond their expectations. They were well worth it and I informed them that as I prospered, so would their wages. Both were in their mid-twenties, but Mrs. Parks was two years younger than Mrs. Jameson.

They were already at work cutting out dresses from patterns I had made. I had purchased fabrics of every description and they were neatly stacked on shelves, some of which were cubicled and labeled. The idea was to save time when a customer or "client"—which was a label now being used to describe a potential buyer—might wish to be shown a fabric and have a gown made up from it. Also, we could make hats with the fabric matching the gown. And gloves. I had furnished the salon-proper with glass-topped tables that had drawers, the contents of which were visible. They held silk flowers, long silk gloves, combs and round hand-mirrors, some of which were small enough to sit comfortably in an evening bag. The drawers in other tables held jewelry in the shape of various small birds and animals, and evening bags. Some tables were mirrored-topped. On these rested crystal flagons in which perfume could be transferred from its original bottle.

I had had the wall opposite the mirror hung in shades of pink. In front of it were four-sided glass cabinets, in which we would show dresses. Once I had become established, I would hire mannequins to model my creations. Near the rear of the shop I had the workmen construct a small round stage which was reached in two steps. There my models would step up, pirouette slowly and step down to move among the ladies who were interested in making purchases.

Nor had I forgotten my doll mannequins. They were placed on small, separate, eye-high stands which resembled pedestals and stood before the mirrored wall, at a respectable distance from it, so that the backs of their outfits would be plainly revealed. The chandeliers with their glass prisms sent shafts of light through the room and were picked up by the mirrors, beautifying it even further. I was so proud of the final effect I could have cried.

Uncle Carlo, looking quite elegant in his finery, was as pleased as I. "You have done yourself proud, niece," he said. "I had no idea this was what you had in mind. Of course now I can see why you were worried about the expense."

"I'm afraid I became extravagant once I got started with the decorating."

"Don't worry," he said firmly. "I predict great success for you."

"I hope you are right, Uncle Carlo." I couldn't hide the concern which crept into my voice.

"How can you fail? You have worked so hard, your seamstresses are working night and day. They are very dedicated, though I think that is because you are paying them well."

"They're earning it. They want it to be a success as much as I."

"Well." He looked around the room at the few gowns hanging on forms, then eyed me with warm approbation. "If all your designs are as clever as these, you needn't worry. Also, I have watched you being observed on the street. The ladies eye your clothes. You carry yourself proudly, my dear."

I laughed. "I am trying to make myself look taller. That is why."

"Your clothes fit you so beautifully I don't even realize you are so petite."

"I like the clothes you bought, Uncle Carlo. And I am very pleased to have you around the shop. You give it class."

I had never heard him laugh so heartily. "I think my niece is beginning to like her Uncle Carlo."

"I have always liked you, foolish man," I chided.

"Not always. Sometimes I make you angry."

"True," I admitted. "But I'll not even think about it at present."

"Please don't. I like it better this way. Oh," he raised a finger in recollection, "your sign will be here tomorrow. It will follow the decor. Gray background with 'ANGELA' spelled out in pink."

Uncle Carlo became an asset to the salon. He dressed in gray trousers, black frock coat, a white ruffled shirt, a cravat, usually of a bright color. He wore white spats over his highly polished black shoes. His trim mustache gave him a princely look. Carlo knew exactly how to greet a customer and how to shoo away tradepeople I didn't care to do business with.

183

Still, even with the beautiful salon, plus the impeccable Carlo, I still needed something to happen which would draw attention to the salon and to my ideas in women's style. I spent hours trying to think of something. I had cards printed and mailed to ladies in society and the wives of politicians, a clientele from the moment I opened the salon. It grew, but not as fast as I wished or required. The money we took in went to pay bills and there was a mound of them staring at me whenever I sat down at my desk in the back room.

Besides, I was getting along with two seamstresses, one delivery boy and Carlo. I anticipated fifty seamstresses and a staff of saleswomen. Of course there could only be one Carlo.

So I had to find some way to get my salon known, even beyond New York City. All this work, this planning and hoping had kept me busy for several months. I wasn't tired or discouraged, but I was dismayed at the slowness with which my fashions were being accepted, mainly because so few knew of them.

Not every waking moment of those busy months was devoted to the salon. Not a day went by that I didn't think about Papa and Mama and wonder what had become of them. I received no news from abroad beyond an occasional letter from Vito who, unfortunately, had nothing to report about the absence of my parents, though his letters were warm, friendly and deeply appreciated.

I thought too of Stanton Talbot. There were times when I considered going to New Orleans to look for him, but my pride prevented that. After all, I had written a letter to him in New Orleans. Though it had no street address, I thought it should have reached him for there could hardly be two lawyers bearing that name in one city. I'd been sure to write my return address on the envelope in case the letter could not be delivered with an incomplete address. But the letter never came back and I had to assume it had been delivered and—disregarded.

I shut out my thoughts of Stan and my parents and started thinking of a way to make my salon and my fashions better known. I happened to buy a Philadelphia newspaper from a stand on Fourteenth Street where newspapers from all over the country were sold. I frequently bought one because Philadelphia had been my home and I enjoyed reading about its growth and its people.

This edition contained a long article about the Philadelphia Assembly, an annual cotillion at which debutantes were introduced into society. I doubted there was a more elaborate or beautiful ball anywhere. I knew for a fact it was one of the oldest in the world, having been in existence since before the Revolutionary War. It was held in the foyer of the Academy of Music. Being accepted as a guest was one of the great prizes society women sought. And only the top levels of society women were accepted.

Here the very latest in fashions were displayed, along with a treasury of fine jewels. And here the evening gowns cinched the waist, swept the ballroom floor, crowded the dining tables with the oversized shoulders. Women over sixteen were compelled to lean heavily on the arms of their escorts after even a brief dance until they'd recovered their breath. The tiny waistlines held in not only the stomach but the lungs as well.

I told Carlo about it one evening after the salon had closed and we were in the back room office discussing the day's events and our plans for tomorrow.

"If I could get into that ball," I said, "with a gown that exists only in my mind as yet, I know I could startle the lot of them. They're too stately and too dignified, and they know it, but these women must adhere so rigidly to custom. If I could change that and let them bring themselves out of their everlasting rut, we would establish ourselves, Uncle Carlo. We might make some enemies, true, but they'd not be enemies long if some of the others accepted our fashions."

"What you are saying then is that the problem is to get in?" Carlo mused.

"It can be done only by special invitation," I told him. "Everyone present knows one another. Those at the entrance would recognize a stranger's face at once. How can I get in there? I can't think of a way. Can you?"

"Why ask me?" Carlo demanded.

I gave him a knowing look. "Because you're basically

185

a confidence man with the ability to think of all sorts of tricks."

"Thanks," he said laconically.

I was persistent. "You know it's true. You must know of a way to get me in."

"How should I know about a silly ball you call the Philadelphia Assembly?" he asked irritably.

"Please don't be offended. This could be important to us."

"Very well." He acquiesced and furrowed his brow. "Invitation only. That means we must find a way to acquire one. Can they be bought?"

"Never."

"Then one must be stolen."

"That would not do either. I told you, those who attend are known to the people who stand at the door and study both the tickets and the guests who hand them in."

"That leaves but one way," Carlo said. "How to get a ticket legitimately. Once I got into an exclusive affair by posing as a diplomat. It was in Rome and I pretended to be from France. In place of a ticket, I had the aplomb of a nobleman, the air of a multimillionaire and the brashness of a statesman. No one dared challenge me and it worked."

"I have no doubt it did," I admitted, "but still you didn't need a ticket that time and in Philadelphia you can't get one to the Assembly unless you have been previously recognized."

"Then I will go to Philadelphia and establish myself. If there is time before the ball."

"The Assembly," I corrected him. "It isn't called a ball. You would have three weeks."

"I could do it in three days, but perhaps if I leave in a day or two I could well manage. It will require some money. Quite a lot of it."

"I'll gamble," I said. "How would you get me in?"

"Now would they deny the niece of an Italian nobleman and senator, especially if she is attractive and extremely well turned out? Before the ball—excuse me, Assembly," he bowed in mock apology—"you would join

186

me at the hotel where I will have the most expensive suite."

"Agreed—I will supply ample money. You may leave as soon as you can but . . . stay away from gaming tables. You're a loser at all forms of chance."

"Except one," he smiled. "I recall a horse race at Cannes . . ."

"Allow me to remind you that race was as dishonest as the plans we've just been talking about. And a further reminder—you had little confidence in that horse."

"I admit everything," he concluded. "However, in this case you must place your trust in me."

Two days later, Carlo, his luggage postered with foreign labels of hotels and ships, departed for Philadelphia. I could imagine his aristocratic entrance into the finest hotel, his demanding the best accommodations and setting the entire hotel staff on edge.

I didn't hear from him for several days and when I did, he somehow managed to transpose his pseudo-Italian statesman into the letter, as if it was censored and he had to carry out his pose. He had gained the confidence of several important people, one of whom was a member of the City Dancing Assembly and, in part, responsible for the Debutante Ball.

Two days later, he wrote that he had been a guest in the home of this assembly member and had spoken of his niece who might join him. There had been a few references to the ball, of which Carlo had at first pleaded absolute ignorance. Then he professed great enthusiasm for such an event, with the purpose of creating a duplicate of it in Rome.

And finally he wrote, briefly, that he had two invitations and he was returning for me. I felt that all the tribulations I'd experienced with Carlo had paid for themselves. I would attend the ball in a gown such as these people had never before seen. And I would pass the word that while I did come from Italy, I had already set up a salon in New York and I would welcome anyone who cared to come and see for themselves further results of my ideas for new fashions. I had no doubt that they'd come—and buy.

It was deceit, to be sure, and while I wasn't especially proud of it, there was no other way to get started in the manner I dreamed of. Philadelphia society thought itself superior to the society in New York City. But they respected New York and there was much communication among the belles and the grand dames of both societies. The word would spread—if they accepted my new fashions.

Pleased as I was with the arrangement, I paid a price for it too. With Carlo gone, I lived a solitary existence when the salon closed at the end of each day, and I felt my loneliness. Everyone I'd ever loved had gone out of my life—my parents still missing, my aunt brutally murdered, Stan Talbot apparently having forgotten me completely.

I tried to forget him when I turned all my efforts to decorating the shop, but he was still entrenched in my heart. The thought came to me that if my plans went well, word of my success could be spread as far away as New Orleans. Perhaps he would hear of the salon and be curious enough to pay it a visit. It was a foolish hope, but one which I nourished. It was over a year since that memorable night aboard ship. It seemed like a century. I chided myself for thinking as I did about him. He couldn't have cared—not really. Certainly he could have taken time to leave an address before he left the ship.

During the day, however, I was too busy to think of anything but the gown with which I hoped to astound the Assembly. My seamstresses, no longer shocked by my revolutionary ideas in design, were equally eager for its success and they cooperated in every way, ripping, resewing, fitting to the fraction of an inch. Finally the last stitch was taken and it received the last light touch of the iron.

It was really two gowns, both white. Nothing was ever worn at the Assembly except white. The satin gown was sleeveless and one-piece, held to my figure by boning. The skirt flared only a little and one side was split to my upper calf. Over the satin gown was another of white chiffon which had a high neck held in place with boning made invisible by tiny white satin bows. It hung free from the shoulders and was a mass of tiny pleats from shoulder to floor so that with my merest movement, the chiffon billowed and I seemed to float rather than walk. The sleeves, also pleated, reached to the elbow and would give a winged effect when my arms were raised for dancing. Long white gloves and white satin slippers completed my costume.

Possibly I would wear gardenias in my hair. I hadn't made a final determination about that. My heart was pounding with excitement as I slipped into the gown. I loved it, yet I was a little frightened. I knew it was daring, the satin gown. And also different. And though the chiffon gown covered me up to the neck, it was completely revealing, for it was a gossamer fabric. I had no idea what Carlo's reaction would be, but I would know in seconds.

Carlo had made a hasty return so he might escort me to Philadelphia. I insisted he turn his back until I had stepped onto the small stage where, one day, I would employ models to display my fashions. Both Mrs. Parks and Mrs. Jameson had remained behind to assist me in case there might be some last-minute alterations. However, not even a loose thread was visible. I wouldn't let either Mrs. Parks or Mrs. Jameson say a word until I was ready for Carlo to turn around.

Once he did, he was speechless for a few moments as I slowly pirouetted on the stage, then slowly descended the two steps to promenade the length of the salon. Though pretending not to, I did steal a few glances at the wall mirror and saw the gown float appealingly. I seemed to be engulfed in a white cloud, yet it did not impede my walking. Nor did the satin gown beneath, due, of course, to the side which was slit to the top of the calf. When I turned and Carlo caught a glimpse of my leg, he let out an exclamation.

"Angela, dear niece," he exclaimed in amazement, "are you going to wear such a daring creation?"

"I am."

He walked around me to view the gown from every angle. "They will think my niece is a graduate of Maxim's rather than a student of Monsieur Henri Maspero. That opening in the side. That show of limb . . . quite daring."

"Do you like it?" I asked. "The truth, Carlo. What is your verdict?"

Mrs. Parks and Mrs. Jameson stood side by side, their hands clasped, their features expressing the same concern I felt.

"You will be the talk of the Assembly," he said, flashing his most brilliant smile. "I will be proud and honored to be your escort."

"Do you think the gown will be admired, sir?" Mrs. Parks asked. She was a thin lady with large eyes that now revealed her nervousness. Mrs. Jameson was buxom and though just as diligent, more inclined to laughter.

Carlo walked over to them, planted a kiss on the cheek of each, then said, "Thanks to you both, my beautiful niece will be the talk of the Assembly. The gentlemen will be quite intrigued. The ladies—well, the ladies will be intrigued also—once they know they can purchase one like it."

"Not exactly," I said. "Each of my gowns must have something different. I insist on individuality."

Carlo walked over to a mirror-topped table and opened a square velvet box of a rather good size. He said, "I ventured down to Maiden Lane before I came here. As you know, I am a nobleman from Italy. I placed a modest deposit on a diamond tiara I selected for you."

He lifted it from its velvet bed and rested it carefully on my head. I had my hair up just as I would wear it at the Assembly. I glanced in the mirror and exclaimed aloud at the beauty of it, but then in a scolding tone, I told Carlo to take it off immediately.

"You know we cannot afford anything like that," I said.

"Of course, we can't," he replied unperturbed. "But the jeweler will get publicity. It is an exquisite thing, don't you agree?"

"Very. But I shan't rest until you return it."

"And I shan't return it until after the Assembly. And without me, dear niece, you will get no farther than the door. So what is it to be?"

I had no recourse but to consent. He meant well. He wanted me to succeed, though I knew well it was partly for his own peace of mind. He needed security as much as I. I did need all the help I could get and Carlo was all I had.

"Very well, I will wear it," I said. "But promise you will return it when we come back here."

"The very day," he said lightly. "Now I will put it back in its box. Frankly, it gives me a lovely feeling carrying it around."

"I doubt I will rest easy until it is back in the hands of the jeweler you fooled into thinking you were able to purchase such an item."

Mrs. Jameson and Mrs. Parks accompanied me to the rear of the shop where they helped me out of the gown. I was anxious to pack it and get home, for I needed rest. I was also eager to return to Philadelphia. I had no concern about the salon. Mrs. Jameson and Mrs. Parks could handle it while I was gone. I had designed a dress for each of them to wear on days when there was need for them in the front of the salon. They both took pride in their appearance and approved of the garments.

It was wonderful to be back in Philadelphia. Uncle Carlo had done himself proud. He had engaged the best rooms, eaten in the best restaurants and already managed to work his way into the homes of the most important names in society. Yes, he was already known and respected in Philadelphia.

We arrived the day before the Assembly and I confined myself to my room until the night of the ball. It gave me an opportunity to rest. Finally, the hour arrived for me to dress. I had to admit Carlo's instinct about the tiara was correct. It was the perfect touch and, except for the magic ring, the only jewelry I wore.

Carlo was delighted. "I have never seen anything like this. It is daring, God knows, but very chic. Certainly all eyes will be on you."

"It will look well on anyone," I said. "That's the beauty of it."

"Not anyone," Carlo corrected. "One needs the figure for it."

I drew on my long white gloves, snagging the right one

a bit on the ring. I was tempted to remove it, but I remembered Papa's admonition never to take it off. I managed to get the tight-fitting glove over it without further incident.

Carlo had arranged, as usual, for the best available carriage driven by a uniformed coachman. As we drove through the streets, I was reminded of my first visit to Paris when I watched, breathlessly, the beautiful ladies in their gorgeous gowns and little parasols riding in those large, magnificent carriages.

Outside the Academy of Music a crowd of onlookers had assembled. Mostly they just stared; it was impossible to tell what their true feelings were. But when Carlo helped me out of the carriage and I displayed my leg, I heard a few audible gasps and much whispering. I hoped it was favorable. A few people appeared shocked, though, and some eyed me with disapproval. However, I pretended not to notice. Carlo squeezed my arm gently and smiled down at me. It served to restore my courage and I smiled back.

We were graciously received at the door and passed on inside. I was stunned by the opulence of the ballroom, actually the foyer of this beautiful building.

Eight great chandeliers, illuminated by electricity, cast light and shadow to flatter everyone. The arched murals were meant to dazzle the eye, and they did. Chairs and small sofas set well off the highly polished dance floor were magnificent with their carved arms and legs and upholstery of heavy silks and damasks.

Here there was color, wealth, gaiety. We had deliberately arrived rather late to insure that my gown would not go unnoticed. The dancing was already in progress and the air was filled with the excitement of the evening.

On Carlo's arm I did my best to appear oblivious to the critical glances that were leveled at us from the first and to the whispers which almost subdued the sound of the orchestra. Naturally I ached inside to know what was being said.

Carlo spoke in Italian. "It is accepted, *cara mia*. There is a look in the eyes of every woman that gives them away each time. It is envy! That is what I see. The women here have everything—except a gown like yours."

"If only they have the desire to own one," I said, keeping my smile bright.

"Have you ever known a woman of wealth who did not? I think I shall stay here after the dance. For a few weeks. It is a pleasure . . ."

He suddenly steered me into the crowd of people sitting out the dancing. "What is wrong?" I asked, suddenly alarmed.

"If you look about—casually—so it will seem you are merely curious, you will see a small dark man with a vandyke such as the one I used to wear. He could mean great trouble for us, Angela. He is the Italian minister from New York and he will know in two seconds that I am not a deputy or a nobleman."

"Oh, Carlo," I exclaimed. "Why didn't you check the guest list?"

"The gentleman sent his card to our suite two days ago with a note that he would like to meet me. I avoided that, but I didn't think he'd come here."

"We have to face it," I said. "You will be at your best, Uncle. You will deceive him if you can. If you fail, we must make the most graceful exit possible. This is your responsibility. Your challenge may mean our future."

Accompanying the Italian diplomat were two of Philadelphia's most prominent men. It was clear they meant to talk to us. I clasped my gloved hand so tightly I squeezed the ring painfully against my flesh.

It came to me then that whenever this ring seemed to work its magic, it had to be in view, not hidden beneath a glove. I was unsure of this and it was no more than a fleeting idea, but I responded to it by slowly removing the glove from my right hand. Either I still had faith in the power of the ring or I was being reduced to a state of desperation.

"*Buona sera,*" the minister said, though not too cordially. It was clear he was suspicious of us.

Carlo greeted him, but instead of presenting me he began to talk rapidly in Italian. A ruse to try and confuse this small but important man. He was not to be confused. I could see the gleam of distrust in his eyes and the doubt that was contained in a half-smile. Carlo must have sensed it too, for he hurriedly turned to me.

"Angela, my dear, may I present to you the minister to New York from Rome. A very well-known and influential statesman."

I had by now peeled off the glove. I presented my bare hand and the minister bowed over it. When he straightened, the suspicion in his eyes had vanished. He took me in his arms and, to my complete surprise, kissed my cheek.

"It is wonderful to see you again, my dear Angela. You were a mere baby I held in my arms. Now you are a young lady. You look like your mother, as I remember her, though some years have passed since we last met. May I claim the next dance?"

When we reached the dance floor, I looked back to see Carlo seated on the small chair, speechless for the first time in his life.

I wondered if the minister had really known my parents. It almost seemed that he was entering into the deceit which Carlo had concocted. Of course it was the ring. It could be nothing else. When the minister bowed over my hand, it was a mere formality before he began to question us. But when he raised his head, his entire manner had changed and he accepted us, though he must have known we were both present under false circumstances.

During the dance we spoke of Italy. I did mention Papa, but he quickly changed the subject to questions about me. I was eager to inform him about my career and newly opened salon. And so the dance was successful beyond any of my dreams. The minister drew a great deal of attention for he was handsome and a superb dancer, and that became focused on me as well. When the dance ended, I was immediately approached by a small group of young women who congratulated me on my gown and asked me where I had purchased it.

"I created it myself. I am a designer; I have a salon in New York. I learned my business in Rome and Paris.

I became bored in Italy and decided on a career in dress design."

"Are all your designs so daring?" one woman asked.

"Would your clientele be so exclusive as to deny us the privilege of visiting your salon, my dear?" another demanded bluntly.

"Why, I'd be delighted to see any of you," I said. "It is for such as you that I design my gowns."

"Would you describe some of the ideas you have in mind?"

I was soon answering innumerable questions and listened to with respect when I described some of the gowns I would one day see on the backs of these kind of women. Someday I would use less expensive fabrics and mass-produce my products to be sold everywhere—at stores that dealt in lower prices and catered to millions of women, not the limited clientele imposed upon me by my small salon. They were genuinely interested in everything I said. It was a lovely feeling.

What had briefly threatened to become a disaster turned into one of the loveliest evenings of my life. I was claimed for more dances than there was room for on my card.

When the evening was finally over, the carriage pulled up for Carlo and me. We got aboard, still ogled by a few of the original crowd of onlookers.

Carlo said, "We performed nobly, wouldn't you say, Angela?"

"It was a wonderful evening, Uncle. And I swear I made a hundred contacts. This is what I needed to make my salon famous."

"I must admit I'm not sure what made the minister think he knew us. Had you ever met him?"

"How would I know? He said he held me on his knee. I think, being a diplomat, and not sure just who we were, he was taking no chances and accepted us at face value."

"It was my self-assurance," Carlo declared. "My expertise in putting myself over as an important Italian. *Si,* we fooled him. But I would not care to enter into a lengthy conversation with the man. He is not a fool."

"We'll leave early in the morning," I said.

"But why? It is pleasant here. You are in need of a vacation. You can promote your salon here. Your salon is in good hands."

"Yes," I agreed. "We have succeeded beyond my dreams, but we will not risk being exposed, for that would be the ruination of everything. We leave—without waiting for breakfast. We will eat on the train. Pack your clothes tonight. I will not listen to any excuses. There is too much at stake."

"*Si,* you're right, as usual. I will arrange for the tickets to New York before I go to bed. But it did go well, Angela."

"Yes, Carlo. I am indebted to you."

I felt I was far more indebted to the ring on my right hand. Searching for a rational explanation, I began to think it might be a design understood by certain people, a secret society, perhaps. But why would an important statesman be a member of a secret society? On the whole, believing that the ring's power was magical seemed no more foolish.

TEN

Within a month I had so much business from Philadelphia, I was compelled to hire more seamstresses and fitters. Word spread, as it always does, from Philadelphia back to New York.

Carlo and I were busy, he in greeting and flattering the customers, while I sought out fresh patterns in silks, satins, cottons. I also spent a great deal of time at my drawing board and, somewhat oftener these days, at my easel and canvas, for I'd not given up my painting. Working at it helped me with colors and designs and many of my inspirations for something new in a gown came to me while I was painting.

"I have," I said to Carlo one evening, "an old photograph of Mama. I think I could create, from that, a portrait of what she might look like today."

"To what purpose?" Carlo asked.

"I could hold an exhibition of my paintings. I now have enough fame and name to warrant it. I would rent an exhibition hall and invite the public to attend. I think with proper persuasion we could get the newspapers to give it great publicity."

"No doubt, but I still don't see why you want to go to all this trouble, Angela."

"I can't actively search for Papa and Mama, we've agreed, because I might somehow endanger them. But they don't know how to reach me, either. They may read of the exhibit and if they are out of hiding, they could get in touch with me. Or someone who knows where they are might recognize the painting of Mama. What do you think?"

I hadn't seen Carlo so excited about a prospective scheme since Philadelphia and the Assembly.

197

"Now why didn't I think of that? It's a fine idea! Certainly if the exhibit is given enough publicity, they will hear of it. The publicity itself will also be important to the salon."

"I've thought about something to make it even more widespread," I said. "I've been asked to give an interview to *Ladies Home Journal*. My picture, a photograph of the salon, drawings of . . . everything. That magazine has a big circulation. If they are interested, so will be *Women's Home Companion* and the *Delineator*."

"*Godey's* sells to women of fashion," Carlo added. "I have heard it talked about among some of our customers and you do keep copies of it in the shop."

"Carlo," I said excitedly, "I'm going to talk to writers from every one of those magazines. We'll begin work on it in the morning. We should be able to hold the exhibition in six months."

Putting this idea into operation taxed me to a point where I scarcely knew what time it was or what day it happened to be. I received wonderful help from the magazine writers and photographers. The articles were excellent, the photos very clear. All this brought more and more business and with my preparations for an art exhibit, I had to hire more personnel and prepare to increase the size of my salon.

I was now successful far beyond what I had anticipated and it seemed I was barely started. I only wished I had time to enjoy my success. Carlo did, for he spent many nights going about the city. He even took brief vacations, which I couldn't deny him. His aplomb was a decided asset to the shop and he gloried in it.

It was early summer when my art exhibition was ready to open. I'd been told that Paris newspapers were also running the story. Certainly Papa and Mama couldn't miss this kind of publicity. If they ever had any intentions of coming back to me, this would be the time for it. If I could have a one-minute talk with Papa, a few seconds in which to embrace Mama, I'd be satisfied.

The New York exhibition, at the Museum of Arts, opened on time. I hung a respectable number of portraits, mostly of imaginary people. One of them, featured above all others, was what I hoped was a portrait of what Mama would look like today. I'd titled it *Unknown Woman* and Carlo saw to it that this particular painting received the most publicity of all.

The exhibition was to last two weeks. During the time the museum was open, I neglected the shop entirely. I took to roaming about the great halls of the museum and I kept this up for three or four days before I noticed that there were some spectators who seemed to return again and again. They were men in dark suits and ties, wearing black fedoras. They prowled about as much as I did, and they rarely stopped to admire a painting.

I didn't like the looks of them and I told Carlo so. He was impressed with my suspicions.

"They seem Italian to me," I told him. "They remain at the exhibition for hours and when they go, others like them take their place. I think they're waiting for Papa or Mama to appear, just as I am."

"Tomorrow," Carlo said, "I'll go there and try to follow them when they leave. I'll find out who they are if I can. You've seen nothing of your father or mother?"

"If they wanted to come to the exhibit, those people who hang around would surely frighten them away. I've seen no sign of them. I've had no word from them. I'm afraid the whole idea is foolish."

"Not that, Angela. It has increased your fame and prestige. It hasn't been a waste in that respect."

"In others it surely has," I said. For I had still another reason for expending so much energy and time on this exhibit and the publicity preceding it. I'd hoped it might attract Stanton Talbot. I'd been watching for him almost as earnestly as I waited for either Mama or Papa to appear.

The next day Carlo joined me long enough for me to point out two of the men I suspected were not there because they enjoyed museums or art exhibits. I heard nothing more from Carlo until that evening. He came into the shop just before I was ready to go home.

"I will admit they were strange people," he said. "I followed one of them to the Waldorf Hotel where he is checked in. He is Italian, an art dealer no less. I didn't talk to him, or make myself known, but I think he is assessing your work with the idea of buying some of the portraits. The second man who left the museum with him and went off in another direction met the first man in the hotel lobby and they talked. In Italian, and this time I managed to listen. They are from Naples and Rome and they are interested in your work. Don't be surprised if they come to you with an offer."

The exhibition closed without fanfare. Nobody came near me to buy, or even make an offer. My purpose in trying to attract Mama and Papa—and Stan—ended in dismal failure.

"You must not give up," Carlo said. "Why not try another city? Perhaps Chicago. They have a fine museum there, or you could rent a hall . . ."

"I don't know, Carlo," I said. "I'm exhausted and it all seems so futile. I don't even know if Papa and Mama are in this country. Perhaps I'll try again. Give me a little time."

A month later, I opened the exhibition in Chicago, in their museum of arts. I received good publicity here as well, but I never allowed my hopes to rise. It was fortunate I didn't, for once again the whole thing was a failure in what I meant it to accomplish. This time I encountered only two men who came back again and again, and they did study my work intently. I thought they might offer to buy, but nothing came of that either. I dismantled the whole project and had everything sent back to New York where I had it all crated and placed in a secure warehouse.

Now I went back to my love of changing fashions, putting into reality the drawings I made on paper, studying the effects I was having on the class of buying public I catered to. Everything was going along well. I stayed ahead of the field in fashions. Not all of my ideas were successful. A few were even denounced from various pulpits, and social workers criticized the shamelessness of some of the gowns. All of which only served to make them more popular than ever.

I was getting business from all over the nation now and it was not unusual to hear western accents, or Yankee clipped voices, or Dixie drawls being spoken in the salon.

A Mr. Alistaire brought his wife and two daughters to be outfitted with a complete wardrobe. But of the greatest interest to the daughters were gowns for the debutante ball. Though I now did little selling myself, I decided to take care of them personally. I had some debutante ideas I wanted to try on them. There was no doubt but that the family was wealthy and quite likely socially important. I wondered where they were from. A large city would be preferable for my purposes. I hoped more prospective customers would attend the debutante ball where these gowns would be worn.

"We're from New Orleans," the man told me while the rest of his family were in fitting rooms. "Best darned city in this whole country and that includes New York, if you'll pardon me for saying so."

"I've heard about New Orleans," I admitted. "I've never been there, but I met a gentleman some years ago while on a voyage to Europe. Did you ever hear of an attorney named Stanton Talbot? With an office in that city?"

"Certainly have, ma'am," came the prompt answer and my heart began to beat madly. "Don't know him personally, but he sure comes of a fine family. His mother is about as high socially as a woman can go and that's high in New Orleans. We're a city of great culture. Most popular entertainment there is the opera. We got important openings and you can't buy a ticket a month ahead of time they sell so fast. I've heard tell of folks who pay three dollars just to stand in back."

"I've not seen Mr. Talbot in a long time," I said. "I met him only casually and we promised to write, though we never did. He's probably married by now."

"Can't say as to that. He's been pointed out to me several times and most often he had some girl on his arm. Can't remember if it was the same girl or he squires a whole passel of 'em."

I changed the subject before Mr. Alistaire could decide my interest in Stanton Talbot was more than casual.

For the rest of the day, my mind was filled with the chatter of the girls and their likes and dislikes. Finally

Mrs. Alistaire and her daughters made their purchases and were gone.

I saw them again when they returned for their final fittings. Mrs. Parks had the silver tea service ready for me to serve. The girls went directly to the dressing room and Mrs. Parks brought their tea in to them. I served Mrs. Alistaire and myself, inquiring about her health as I did so. After the social amenities were over, she informed me her first name was Ethel and her husband was a prominent politician.

She smiled cordially when I mentioned my surprise that her husband didn't know Mr. Talbot well.

"Oh, yes," she said, "Mr. Alistaire said you were acquainted with Mr. Talbot. I know his mother. Are you a friend of the family?"

"No," I said. "As I told your husband, I met Mr. Talbot on a voyage to Paris. I know nothing about his family. I merely mentioned his name after your husband told me you were from New Orleans. Mr. Talbot told me that is where he was from and spoke quite fondly of the city."

"He is not married. But then I suppose you know that." Her manner was innocent, but her eyes were calculating.

"I'm surprised to hear that. I seen to recall he said he was engaged."

"Oh, that! Well, he was, though the girl was his mother's choice. However, the young man isn't seen with the girl any more." She paused, then added in the tone of a confidant, "It happens I don't get along with Mrs. Talbot very well. I wouldn't make such a statement if you were a close friend."

"I've never met the lady."

Mrs. Alistaire sighed. "The problem is, she considers herself a cut or two above the rest of us. I don't know why. She doesn't come from a family better than ours, but she will try to dominate every social event and usually ends up doing it. If you ever meet her, you will see what I mean."

I smiled in friendly fashion. "I don't expect our paths will ever cross. If she is that difficult, I rather hope they don't."

She switched the conversation from Mrs. Talbot to Stan. "Mr. Talbot is quite successful and he is about to seek the political position of prosecuting attorney. My husband is all for him."

"But your husband told me he really didn't know Mr. Talbot."

"My dear, in New Orleans politics, that doesn't matter. Sometimes I think the nominating committee likes to pick an unknown because they can handle him better."

"What if Mr. Talbot surprises them by turning out to be his own man?"

She laughed heartily. "It would serve them right, wouldn't it? And he may do just that. He did not marry the girl his mother chose for him, though he hasn't selected any other either."

The appearance of her daughters from the fitting rooms, in their new gowns, put an end to any further conversation about Stanton Talbot. I was pleased with the gowns. They were off-the-shoulder gowns, though without low decolletage, so the girls looked delightfully demure. Dulcie, the blonde, wore blue. The skirt was made bouffant by means of several petticoats and had large pink rosettes scattered along the hemline. Beulah, the brunette, wore pink, with blue rosettes along the hemline. The puffed sleeves also were touched with rosettes. They wanted identical gowns, though in different colors. Mrs. Alistaire was as pleased as her daughters with my creative efforts. The remainder of their wardrobe would be ready the following day and would be delivered to their hotel. Mrs. Alistaire wrote out a check for the three wardrobes and they departed amid a flurry of good-byes and a promise to return.

That night I presented an idea to Carlo which had been brewing in my mind since the Alistaires left the salon. It was daring and I suppose I should have had more pride. But where Stan was concerned, I was willing to swallow it. I wanted to give an exhibition of my paintings in New Orleans.

"Why?" he asked. "Your paintings don't sell. You

have more business than you can handle. Why should you want to bother going down there? What do they know about art? Or culture of any kind?"

"That is a very cultured city," I replied with quiet firmness. "They love opera. All the great singers perform there and vie for the opportunity to do so."

Carlo shrugged. "So they love opera. Who doesn't? Will that make them buy your paintings?"

"That doesn't matter. Stay here then. I will go alone."

"Angela," he pleaded patiently, "you are not an artist. You are a designer of women's clothes and an excellent one. I am proud of you. You have made us enough money so we will never need to worry again. So why do you wish to go down to a wilderness to show paintings that no one wants to buy? You should have more pride."

"Yes," I said, thinking of Stanton Talbot. "I should. But perhaps Mama and Papa are in hiding there and when my work is on display, they will reveal themselves."

"Oh, my God. That again." He clapped his hand to his brow. "You are being childish. You are a run-of-the-mill painter. That is all you will ever be. When will you get that through your head?"

"It is through my head now," I retorted. "But I will still paint. I get ideas when my brush mixes the colors and touches the canvas."

"Then paint and get ideas, but don't go to New Orleans," he said.

"I am going. You may tend the salon while I am gone."

"I'm scarcely needed there. Mrs. Jameson and Mrs. Parks manage very well without me. In fact I am beginning to feel like an intruder whenever I go there."

"One would never get that idea from your behavior," I said. "You are quite the cavalier with the ladies. They like it, you like it and I like your gallant way with them. It is good for business."

He gave me a caustic look, but made no answer. It was just as well. My mind was made up.

I arranged for the shipment of my paintings and, through the museum authorities in New Orleans, I managed to set up the exhibit and gain proper publicity. It was the beginning of autumn when I entrained for New Orleans with both hope and fear in my heart.

All during the long journey I told myself that Stanton must have had good reason not to have contacted me. Certainly he must have heard of my establishment. Though he might be uninterested in fashion, his socially-minded mother wasn't. Nor were the girls he squired about town and I envied every one of them.

I wondered what I would do when we met. I didn't even question the meeting. I wasn't going to make the journey down there merely for the sake of displaying my paintings, nor did I expect to find Mama and Papa. I was going for one reason—to meet Stan face to face. I must know his feelings toward me. Or if he had ever had any. I was completely devoid of pride where he was concerned.

Would he even remember me? And if he did, would he admit it? It was about time I found out. It would be stupid of me to go through life waiting for the man of my dreams to come to me. Either he wasn't going to or he had no idea of where I was, and I might as well learn which.

My first impression of New Orleans was that of a beehive, with all manner of vehicles rushing haphazardly about the streets and congesting the squares to an unbelievable tangle. Yet everything seemed to keep moving and the tangles straightened themselves out. Sometimes that required rather lurid language on the part of dray drivers, but there was no real trouble.

I also learned that in New Orleans, any art exhibit is bound to be patronized. Everyone seemed interested in the subject and parts of New Orleans reminded me of the Montmartre section of Paris.

I checked into a fine hotel, as good as any I'd ever seen anywhere. My arrival had been preceded by publicity and I was quickly recognized at the hotel where I was treated as if I were royalty.

As I had arrived in the early morning hours and settled myself promptly enough, I went out to explore the city. I came upon the street art exhibit at a place known as Pirate's Alley. Some of the work was very good and I complimented the artists who stood proudly beside their works. Then I found myself in an unusual section of the city where the streets were very narrow and the houses seemed to rise directly from the sidewalks. They were wall-to-wall, yet each house was in pleasant contrast to its neighbors. Mostly, I thought, because of the way each was painted. The colors ranged from peach to lavender to shades of green. And each had galleries, two-storied mostly, with railings of ironwork in fascinating designs. They were supported by metal posts set into the sidewalks. Some of the houses appeared to have second entrances opening directly into large, heavily planted patios. And everywhere were the street merchants, some pushing or pulling carts or wagons, and all calling their wares in loud voices. They sold fruit, vegetables, all manner of nuts, candies, and even coal. The resulting din was such as I'd never heard before, yet it was not irritating, at least to a newcomer like me.

There was a wide river here too, with the streets formed to accommodate the turns of the river where more ships than I'd ever seen were tied up or majestically moving up or down.

My wandering took me to sections of white mansions and palm trees, where the wealthier people lived. It was a fascinating city, mostly because it seemed to be different from any I'd ever visited.

Then I found myself in the buisness area where the buildings were three and four stories high, the stores of such varied nature as to be confusing. I paid them only passing attention. I was here because this was where I'd find Stanton Talbot. I knew that I was in the process of breaking all social customs. That didn't bother me. I'd been breaking them with my fashions now for two years. I made inquiries, learned where the lawyers had their offices and came to a stop before a red brick building bearing a row of bronze nameplates beside the entrance. One read STANTON TALBOT, ATTORNEY-AT-LAW. I surmised that he'd left the law firm whose snobbishness he had derided when he told me about it. I entered the building and from a listing inside the lobby, I located his office on the third floor.

I climbed the stairs, each step a trifle slower than the

last, for I was beginning to lose my courage. So many things could have happened during the many months since we'd parted. I might be met with the greatest disappointment of my life, but I had to take that chance.

Standing before the door bearing his name, I felt weaker than ever. I was tempted a dozen times to walk away while I had the chance. To let well enough alone. Better to dream than awaken to a truth that would put a cruel end to dreaming.

Then it came back to me. The tenderness of the man. The way he'd held me and kissed me. I could not have been that deceived by him. I loved him and he had once told me he loved me. I had believed him then and I did now.

That recall of the finest night of my life gave me the courage to open the door and walk into a reception room where two middle-aged women were busy at work, one operating a typewriter.

The other, working on books, looked up with a smile. "May I help you, Miss?"

"I would like to see Mr. Talbot," I said. "I have no appointment, but I'm . . . an old friend . . ."

"I'll see if he can work you in, Miss. Please have a chair."

I sat down hard, because my legs buckled under me. I clutched my handbag tightly and then I touched the cameo ring. I even brought it unobtrusively, I hoped, to my lips. If ever this ring possessed any magic power, now was the time for it to prove itself.

The woman had entered the office, closing the door behind her. Now she emerged, looking rather stern. My heart sank.

"I forgot to ask your name and the nature of your business, Miss," she said.

"It is Miss Angela Gambrell."

Her mouth seemed to tighten. "Thank you, Miss." She walked back to the door and went inside. In a very short time she emerged.

"I'm sorry, Miss. Mr. Talbot has a very important client with him and won't be able to see you. If you like, I can make an appointment."

I rose. My knees weren't shaking this time. "Did you give him my name?" I asked, my manner still gracious.

"Indeed, yes, Miss. Please excuse me." She turned to go back to her desk.

I stood up and spoke quietly. "I do not believe you gave Mr. Talbot my name."

She turned and eyed me coldly. "You are presumptuous, Miss. I must ask you to leave."

I walked around her and moved rapidly toward the closed door. She followed me, clawed at my shoulder, but I never faltered a step. I opened the door and came to a stop just inside the office. Stan, seated behind a large desk, looked up, startled. He stared at me. I began walking toward the desk slowly. The woman who'd refused me entrance had closed the door behind me. To shut out the scene that she believed would follow, I supposed.

Stan arose. "Angela?" His voice changed from a question to a shout of recognition. "Angela . . . !"

He came around the corner of his desk, speaking my name over and over. When he reached me, he gathered me close and covered my face with kisses. Though I was delirious with happiness, I couldn't even smile. I realized I was speaking his name as he had spoken mine and I was murmuring endearments until his head lowered and his lips covered mine. We were both caught up in the rapture of the embrace. My arms were tight around his shoulders. We were trembling with the passion of our embrace and I knew how much I wanted him. His desire was as great as mine for his hands moved slowly down my back to press me tight against him.

"Please, Stan." I could scarcely speak, yet I had to gain control of myself. "We have so much to talk about. This can wait."

"You're right," he agreed reluctantly, his voice as tremulous as mine. He stepped back a pace. "Let me look at you. Oh, my darling Angela. I have lived for this moment. I searched for you. Truly I did. I never gave up. I kept returning to Philadelphia whenever I had an opportunity, but no one there knew anything of your whereabouts."

208

"I live in New York City now. I came here to look for you."

He took my hands from his chest and planted a kiss in the palm of each. "My darling girl. All this time. . . . We can't talk here. I'll cancel my appointments for the remainder of the day."

He was heading for the door when there was a light tap on it. He had his emotions under control and his voice was firm when he opened it to confront the woman who had tried to prevent me from seeing Stan.

"Mr. Talbot, I have typed my resignation. I'll leave the office within the next ten minutes. You may mail my check."

"What in thunder . . . ? Madge, what's the meaning of this?"

She pointed at me. "She can tell you."

Stan glanced my way. I said, "I don't know what she means, but she told me you were not available . . ."

"You mean when you asked to see me?"

"Yes. Somehow, I felt—perhaps from her manner— she was being dishonest."

"She was," Stan said. "She said nothing about you. Madge, why did you lie? Why didn't you announce Miss Gambrell?"

"Ask your mother," Madge said crossly. "She'll tell you, I'm sure."

Madge stepped back, gave me a final glare and slammed the door.

Stan shrugged. "I don't know what got into her."

I said, "Darling, did you ever get my letter from Paris? It was long ago, right after . . . we were separated."

"I received no letter from you, Angela. I don't understand this."

"I sent the letter without a street address. I think that woman got it and saw that you did not."

He stiffened. "My mother . . . that's what she said. My mother. Damn her!"

"Stan," I said, "let's not damn anyone now. Let's just try to make up for the lonely months of separation."

"Wait!" he said, and jumped up to return to his desk where he quickly removed a folder from a drawer. He

209

laid this on my lap, open. It contained a number of newspaper clippings from French papers with large framed blocks containing my name and a request that I reach him at the Hotel Grande.

"I never saw these," I said. "I didn't look in any of the papers. I thought . . . something had happened to take you away from me. I never lost faith in you."

"It was all my fault," he admitted. "Early on the morning when we docked, a lighter came to take me off. The people I was supposed to meet had to leave earlier than they expected and I was to come at once and conclude my business with them. It was vital to my client that I do this. Things happened so fast . . . oh, what's the use. I remembered I should have left a message for you when I was aboard the lighter and halfway to the dock. I gave a sailor a note and some money. He was supposed to see that you got it after he returned to the ship. I suppose he pocketed the money and threw the note into the harbor. Angela, everything went wrong that morning. Everything! And before the day was over, I was beside myself with worry. I didn't have your address and you didn't have mine. I stayed in Paris a week longer, and I spent all that time searching for you. I was sure you'd be somewhere on the Left Bank so I went there. It was no use. No one had heard of you."

"I was in an exclusive hotel, thanks to my extravagant uncle," I said. "Darling . . . did you shut me out of your mind and forget me from time to time?"

"Not for a fraction of a second. When I boarded the ship in New York, I saw you standing there and I fell in love. You've been in my heart since. These last months have been agony. I even took another trip to Philadelphia to search and . . . nothing."

"And I lived in fear that you'd married that girl you told me about."

"I realized you might think that."

He rose, as I did, and his arms enclosed me again. He held me tightly and as our lips met and held, our passion mounted. One of his arms loosened its hold on me and his fingers fumbled with the buttons of my blouse. I did it for him while he rained kisses on my neck and shoulders. He pulled the pink bow which held my corset cover in place and loosened it, releasing my breasts. He kissed and caressed them. Our soft moans mingled. His body had mine imprisoned against the desk. My arms lowered and my hand caressed his back beneath his coat and moved down to hold him close to me. In this way, the ecstasy of our love peaked, our passionate breathing as we clung to one another finally slowed and we felt both relief and contentment.

I broke the silence, my face close against his ear. "Oh, my darling love, don't ever let us be separated again."

He was fumbling with my corset cover, trying to cover my nakedness. It was amusing to watch him, but when I saw how helpless he was, I lifted the corset cover higher, drew the ribbons tighter through the embroidered openings and tied a bow.

When I started to button my blouse, he said, "No, let me." I noticed he managed quite well.

"So you are not completely in ignorance of how to do that," I said, feeling a pang of jealousy, but realizing he was a man and I couldn't have expected him to live the life of a recluse.

"Not completely," he replied honestly. "Do you mind?"

"I shall be as honest as you. I do."

"You needn't. It was infrequent and of no consequence. There will be no other. Now—or ever."

"That leaves me content."

"We shall be married at once," he told me. "We'll find someone to marry us. No big wedding. Let any wedding reception come later. We can go off for a few weeks, if you like."

"I can't, darling," I said. "I am here for another reason besides the one of finding you, though I was determined not to leave until I found out if you were married."

"What would you have done then?" he asked with a smile.

"I'd have quietly slipped away."

"When I returned from Paris, I called on Miss Fletcher —Mary-Lou—and informed her we would not be married, that I had met a girl and had fallen in love with her. Even if I had never found you again, I'd have been ever

211

grateful for having met you, for I learned then what kind of girl she really was. She told me exactly what she thought of me. Not that I didn't deserve it, but she behaved like a shrew. A lifetime with her would have been hell."

I smiled. "You mean she said ugly things about me."

"Without even knowing you," he said indignantly.

"Her pride was hurt, Stan. Mine was when you left the ship without leaving even a note."

"Yet you never doubted my love for you," he said wonderingly. "I'll always remember that because I feel I don't deserve it. And I have a correction to make. I didn't find you. You found me."

"I haven't forgotten what you told me about your mother. Your secretary's behavior seems to bear it out. I can't help but ask what your mother's reaction was to your breaking your engagement."

"Something in the same vein as Mary-Lou. She stormed, called me an idiot among a few other things. Warned me this could cost me important clients—which it did. I told her it didn't matter. That I'd find you and we'd be married. If necessary, I'd go elsewhere and start again."

"Stan, I don't want to come between you and your mother. I don't want to cause anyone unhappiness."

"Don't be concerned. My mother enjoys unhappiness. And being tyrannical. After I discovered I was unable to track you down, she gloated over the possibility that you had run out on me. My mother, darling, is in a class by herself. You won't like her. Most people don't, though they don't dare stand up to her. I want you to do that."

"Will I be in her company often?"

"I sincerely hope not. Let's speak of more pleasant things. Your painting. How did that develop?"

"Well enough for me to come to New Orleans to exhibit some of my work in a private showing."

His eyes revealed his admiration. "That's great news."

"But I'm not a really good artist. In fact, I'm really not a full-time artist. I operate a fashion salon in New York."

"Really? I remember you did speak of designing clothes. Have you done well at it?"

"Darling, if you read women's magazines, or the fashion section of newspapers—which you don't—you would have discovered I'm successful. Far more than I dared to anticipate."

"Then I won't have to worry about supporting you," he said with a laugh. "Well, my dear, you've now given my mother some ammunition to fire against you. High society in New Orleans includes no merchants. She will proclaim to one and all that I have married a business-woman."

"Will I harm you?" I asked.

"Not much of a chance. Not that I'd care. I'm sure you've heard of our Mardi Gras."

"It's quite an event from what I've read about it."

"It's the most important event staged by this city. Now the most exalted position in our high society is that of King of Mardi Gras. I have been selected, among others, and given to understand I will be voted. All of this to Mama's chagrin because it happened after I walked out on her."

"It's a great honor, as you just said. Stan, if you marry me before Mardi Gras, will that affect your chances?"

"I don't know," he confessed. "I don't see why it should, and frankly, I don't give a damn."

"You do," I said quickly. "And I don't blame you."

"Angela, how can being king of this silly Mardi Gras compare, in any respect, to marrying you? I'd be king for one day. I'll be your husband for life. Please don't be concerned."

"I wish I wasn't," I said. "Perhaps we should wait . . ."

"Not a chance. I don't intend to lose you for one minute of time. I lived too long missing you."

"Darling." I sat down to look up at him. "Finding you was not the only reason I came to New Orleans."

He resumed his chair behind the desk, regarding me with puzzlement. "I don't want to sound conceited, but what else would bring you here?"

"I will have no secrets from you. The other reason for my coming here may sound foolish, but it is of grave importance to me."

"Tell me, my love. Perhaps I can help. I hope so."

213

"When I was four years old, darling, my father and mother sent me from Florence, Italy, to live with my Aunt Celestine in Philadelphia. Seven years later, when I was eleven, they both came to visit me. Only for a short time, and then they were off again. Even at that age, I wondered why they didn't take me back with them. They wrote regularly, I answered. They sent gifts and money to my aunt to raise me. Everything seemed quite normal with them until I received a final letter from Papa which mystified and frightened me. It was then seven years since I'd seen them. So I decided to go back to Italy and find out what was wrong."

"You were on your way there when I met you?" he asked.

"No, Stan. I was searching for them then, yes, but I went to Italy months before that. Aunt Celestine objected to the trip and tried to dissuade me, but I had to know about my parents. So I returned to the house . . . a *palazzo* in Florence. That was where I'd been born. That was also where I sent my letters to my father and mother for years. I discovered they'd sold the *palazzo* soon after I was first sent to Philadelphia to live with my aunt."

"Do you mean your parents had vanished?"

"That's the word, Stan. A cruel one in this case. Papa was a political figure in Rome. He didn't run for office again, he sold everything he owned and, along with Mama, disappeared. No investigation was made because of a mixup. People in Rome where he had an apartment thought he'd resigned and gone back to Florence. In Florence, they believed he had elected to stay in Rome. No one discovered they were in neither place. That is, until my arrival."

"You found no trace of them? What about the police?"

"They instituted a search. It got nowhere. Nor did my efforts to find them."

"Do you think they may be dead? That something happened to them simultaneously, so neither was left to apprise you of the incident?"

"They are not dead. I have reasons for believing that. First of all, when I was in Florence, I was lured into a building where I was questioned about Papa's whereabouts. As if I knew where he was. They even . . . had one man partially disrobe me . . ."

Stan's features tensed and his face reddened with anger. "Go on. I know he didn't complete the act. What stopped him?"

"The other men. I guess they were only threatening me and called off the beast who manhandled me. Perhaps they thought if they let him go through with it, I might never tell them what they wanted to know."

"Go on," Stan said grimly.

"This same man, later on, burst into my suite. He hadn't been ordered to do so and came strictly on his own to satisfy the lust that he had built up since the first time. What he didn't know was that I was then under the protection of the police and two of them came in time. The man ran, but they shot him. He died. He was never identified that I know of."

Stan came to me, helped me out of the chair and held me close. His manner was tender and protecting.

"Darling, what's behind all this? Who is tormenting you this way?"

"I don't know. And I've never been able to find out. I don't even know why, except that I believe someone is trying to find my parents as diligently as I am, but their reasons apparently are different. Certainly their intent must be evil since they'll resort to anything. I'm sure they believe I know where Papa and Mama are."

"Did that second attack on you end your ordeal?"

"No—there was a third one while I was living in Paris. This man was no stupid hulk of a beast. He was young and strong and brutal. I barely escaped him. My Uncle Carlo came to my rescue that time."

"I couldn't have prevented the first and second attack on you, but I could the third. I was the stupid hulk," Stan exclaimed bitterly. "Leaving the ship so hastily, I forgot to leave a note."

"Don't berate yourself. Not even the police could stop it. It took on a more deadly phase. When I came back from Italy, my first time abroad, I found that my Aunt Celestine had been murdered. Tortured, and then killed. Our flat had been ransacked. You know about that. What

215

you don't know is that the only thing taken was a bundle of letters Papa had written me over the years."

"Wasn't that crime ever solved?"

"No. Whoever killed her left no evidence behind."

Stan looked skeptical. "Are you certain your parents are really alive?"

"I'm positive Papa is. I saw him, for an instant, when I was in Paris. I saw his head and shoulders reflected in a mirror in the lobby of a large hotel. He was looking directly at me. I turned and rushed to the spot where he'd been, but he was gone. If only I could understand the reason for this mystery and violence."

"Perhaps I can help," Stan said. "At least I can lend my efforts in helping you find them."

"Well—that's the other reason I'm here. In my collection of paintings is one I did of Mama, as I hope she looks today. I had an old photograph and worked from that. I give these exhibits with the greatest amount of publicity and I attend every showing to watch in case Mama or Papa has heard of the exhibit and cannot stay away. I also give prominence to Mama's portrait in case someone who comes by recognizes her."

"You mean you tried this before?" Stan's interest heightened.

"In New York and Chicago. I'd given up, but . . . frankly, I had some customers in my salon who came from New Orleans, knew your mother and you, and when I learned you had probably not married—they said you seemed to have different girls on your arm at social affairs —I made up my mind to come here. To find you and hold the exhibition too. It opens in two days. I must be there all the time. And so, my darling, let's not marry quite yet."

"The banns would prevent us," he said. "By all means, attend the exhibition. I will too, every spare moment I have. We'll both pray someone will come to give you more proof your parents are alive. It's a clever idea. Worthy of you."

"I'll feel much safer with you at my side," I told him. "In both New York and Chicago I noticed sinister-looking men. I think perhaps they're looking for my parents."

"We'll get to the bottom of it," Stan vowed. "It happens that I'm a candidate for prosecuting attorney in this city. I think I'll win, the opposition isn't very strong. If I do, I'll be in a fine position to track down these people."

My heart lightened. "I just hope you'll be in no danger."

"Not these days. There was a time, not long ago—about ten years ago, in fact—when we had a wave of violence here that wasn't easy to stop. It gives me a sense of shame to remember how it was ended, and I believe many of our thinking citizens feel the same way I do, though I decried it more because I'm a lawyer."

"I heard nothing of this," I said.

"You probably wouldn't have, being so young. We had a large number of murders, kidnappings and savage violence against many of our citizens. Those committing the crimes were known as the Black Hand."

"I have a vague recollection of hearing about it," I said.

"They kidnapped people and held them for ransom. They made merchants pay to keep their places of business from being wrecked or burned. They put their greedy fingers into all kinds of crime, and then they went too far. They assassinated our Chief of Police. The men were arrested, eleven of them. They were locked up and then, it happened. A large number of citizens, many of them prominent, stormed the jail, took out some of those men and hung them from the nearest lamppost. Those who tried to hide in the jail were tracked down and shot out of hand. Murdered! It's the only word to use. Nothing like that ever happened in New Orleans before—not in modern times—and hasn't happened since, thank God."

"That must have been horrible," I said.

"Now we're going out to dine," Stan said. "Have you tried any of our restaurants in the French Quarter?"

When we left, the outer office had already been closed up. One desk, Madge's, was bare. Stan shook his head.

"I see now how my mother had an uncanny knowledge of everything I did. No doubt, after I told her about you, she gave Madge orders to see that any letters from you

217

never reached me. It's outrageous and a little sad what my mother will do to get her own way."

"Perhaps she is only overprotective, darling."

"No, it's more selfish than that. She is now one of the top social leaders in this city, but she aspires to be *the* only top one. The *grande dame* who rules over every important dance and supervises much of our annual fiesta, the Mardi Gras."

We had reached the street by then and Stan suspended his further explanation until we were seated in the restaurant, an old one.

"It first opened in 1840," Stan told me, "and has been in the same family ever since. There are other fine restaurants, but this one seems to have just a little more. I'm going to order, because some of the menu will be a bit strange. That is, with your permission."

Our dinner was superb and in the enjoyment of its perfection, we did little talking. Not until brandy and coffee were placed on the table did we begin to contemplate our futures.

"What will we do?" I asked. "I have a salon in New York and your practice is here in New Orleans."

"My practice can shift, your salon cannot. That's the simple answer."

"But," I objected, "you'd be sacrificing too much. Besides, I like it here in New Orleans. I might find it very profitable to open a salon here, a branch of the New York store."

"What of the New York one then?"

"My Uncle Carlo can manage it. He's grown quite sensible lately and he knows the salon as well as I do. I've employees who would love to be promoted to saleswomen. The salon can handle itself. I'd like to try it. Unless you don't approve."

"I'd be for it all the way," he said. "However, you'll be faced with antagonism from my mother and, probably, from Mary-Lou. They both wield a great deal of influence and they could make your life here a hell on earth."

"I don't believe that," I said. "My gowns really are exceptional. New Orleans women will be buying gowns from a salon, not from me."

Stan said, "You know better than I about such things. Now let's forget them and talk about getting married. That's what is important to me."

"And about where we're going to live," I added. "I'm a complete stranger here. I have to depend on you in such matters."

"I'll look around for a suitable place. When will you close your exhibition?"

"I expect that if Mama and Papa do not respond in five days' time, they won't come at all."

"Then I'll see to getting the banns read and by the time you close the exhibit, we'll be ready to be married. The kind of ceremony is up to you."

"A quiet one. I've no one here, not even many people in New York or Philadelphia. The marriage is going to create problems for you so I think it wise not to make it a big issue."

"It will be done as you wish. But please, don't disappear on me again."

In answer I touched my brandy glass to his. "Never!"

ELEVEN

That night, in my hotel suite, I sat in awe and wonder at the abrupt difference in my life. During the space of three or four hours, everything had changed. I was no longer alone. I was loved; I was going to be married; I was going to leave New York and make a new life in this strange and fascinating city.

Already in my mind were plans for opening a new salon here. I needed only to look around me to realize New Orleans was a city where fashions were extremely important. My type of salon was bound to be successful.

The next morning, after discussing the beginning of my art exhibit with museum authorities, I walked about the streets where the more important stores were located and became even further convinced that this was where I belonged. I discovered a large, empty store located in the very center of the most fashionable shopping area. Such good fortune should be immediately taken advantage of. However, being a newcomer to the city, I decided to consult Stan about the location before I made any commitments.

It was fortunate that I did. Stan listened to me, approved the location after we inspected the outside of the store, but offered me some sage advice.

"Let me handle it. I'll say it's for a client who prefers to remain anonymous for the present. You see, the man who owns this store would listen if Mama told him such a store would not enhance New Orleans in any way. I'll handle the transaction today. Mama won't hear about our wedding next week until Sunday when the banns are read. By then, we'll have this settled so no amount of pressure can change anything."

I wrote Carlo a long letter telling him I was about to

open a shop in New Orleans and preparing him for his responsibility for the New York salon. In my mind I could see his gestures and outraged comments as he relayed the news to Mrs. Jameson and Mrs. Parks. I knew they would be as pleased as he was displeased. I wrote them also, giving them substantial raises. If he proved incompetent, they could take over. The New York salon was far too great a success to abandon.

Then there was the planning of the new store here in New Orleans. I made up my mind to duplicate the New York layout, for it had proven to be both attractive and functional.

I thought about my forthcoming marriage, and what Stan's mother might do to prevent it. Of course she could do nothing really, but making trouble seemed to be her way to interfere and I sensed she would find an opportunity for that. I didn't want more trouble, but I would face up to it if need be. Stan and I would be married and nobody could stop us.

Just now, my thoughts were on the exhibition of my paintings. It was to be held in a large room at the museum, but one free of pillars or posts behind which someone could hide. There were only two exits and one of these was not easily gained by visitors. So I'd be obliged to concentrate only on one door and that made it considerably easier.

I set up the exhibit, this time with help from Stan, whose comments on the quality of the paintings pleasantly touched my ego. The one I had painted of Mama, as usual, occupied the center of the exhibit. The more prominently it was displayed, the better.

"I'm not fooling myself that I think this will work," I told Stan the day the exhibit opened. "Yet I must take the gamble."

"Yes, it's a chance worth taking," Stan agreed. "I'll be around as often as possible. There are court cases coming up, trials I must attend, but other than that, the office can endure postponement of things without trouble. The day after you close the exhibit and we've cleared everything out is the day we'll be married."

Stan was true to his word. The first two days he and I wandered, separately, around the exhibition hall.

On the third day, late in the afternoon, just before I expected Stan to arrive, I left the exhibition hall for a drink of water. So it happened that I was approaching the hall, but still a considerable distance from it, when I saw a woman emerge. For a second or two she looked my way, directly at me. She hesitated for a second, began to raise her arm, but dropped it and walked briskly to the exit.

The woman was my mother. Though I hadn't seen her in years, I recognized her. And I was sure she had recognized me too. Possibly she'd been somewhere in the vicinity waiting for a chance to enter the hall and examine my work and when I left the room, she ventured into it for a few minutes. Yet why had she taken the trouble only to flee?

When I reached the street, I saw her turning the next corner. I broke into a run.

Again I was in time to see that slight figure turn, as if in desperation, to an iron grilled door almost flush with the street. She pushed it open and disappeared inside. When I reached that door it wouldn't open.

"Mama!" I called out. "Mama!"

There was no response. I yanked the bell pull a dozen times, creating a clamor somewhere within the premises. While I waited for some response, I peered through the iron grillwork into a large patio, so filled with flowers and greenery as to resemble a small jungle. There were clearings where tables and chairs were set up, but otherwise it seemed to be a garden. Everything had been freshly watered and the humid air was well perfumed.

An old man in a faded blue sweater came into view and advanced slowly toward the door. He wore an ancient cap which he doffed respectfully.

"There is no one home, Mademoiselle. The house is closed up."

"I saw a woman go through this gate not three minutes ago," I said. "I want to talk to her."

"But Mademoiselle, there is no one here. No woman

came in. I was inside and I saw no one. You are mistaken."

"I am not." I opened my handbag and thrust money at him. "Take this, but let me come in. Please! The woman I saw is my mother."

He accepted the money and unlocked the door, reluctantly and taking his time about it, but then he was very old and his hands had a tendency to shake, making the insertion of a key in the lock slow and difficult.

I hurried on by him, crossed the ample patio where the flowers gave off pungent, perfumed odors. The way into the house proper was by way of a French window, wide open. I went on in without hesitation.

I found myself in a large drawing room where the furniture was covered with dust sheets, giving the place a spectral look in the gloomy light. I looked about quickly and then went on to the reception hall. Here too were signs that the house was not lived in at this time. Even the great chandeliers were covered with cloth. There was a dining room, a music room, a library, all in similar condition. The kitchen hadn't been used in weeks judging by the accumulation of dust in the sinkboards and the oversize gas stove.

When I returned to the reception hall, the old man was there. He held out one hand as if to prevent me from going upstairs. "Please, Mademoiselle, there is no one here. I will give you your money back. I swear no one came in. It is all a mistake. You must not go upstairs."

My reaction to that demand became even more aggressive. It seemed he was trying to bribe me with my own money not to continue with the search. I brushed by him and ran up the staircase. At the top, I found myself crossing a brief gallery to the wing where I could see four closed doors. Each led into a bedroom, all equipped with covers to keep furniture in condition during a long period of disuse.

Finally I had to give up and I walked slowly down the stairs. The old man was still there. I felt sorry for him. He was on the verge of wringing his hands in anguish.

"You swear to me you saw no one enter the patio gate and then enter the house?" I asked.

223

"Mademoiselle, you have my word. I do not lie. No one came in. I have seen no one. You are the first person, besides myself, who has been in here in more than six months."

"Whose home is this?" I asked.

"That of Monsieur and Madame da Rimini."

"They are Italian?"

"*Oui*, Mademoiselle. They are in Italy now. I am the caretaker. No one came in. I swear to you."

"Very well," I said. "I was sure I was not mistaken, but perhaps . . ." I waved aside the proffered money. "You may keep that and thank you."

He bowed. "I will open the front door."

"That's not necessary," I said. "I'll leave the way I came."

Before he could stop me I left by way of the French window and crossed the patio. When I pulled back the grilled door to the street, I saw slowly drying footprints indicating that a woman with small feet had recently left.

I turned my head to look at him, then pointed to the footsteps. "Monsieur, you have lied to me, but perhaps there was need for you to. Needful or not, this has been a severe blow to me. *Au revoir*."

I hurried away, stemming the tears with an effort. I didn't return to the museum, but went straight back to my hotel. I used the telephone in the lobby to make a call to Stan's office. He was not there, but his secretary promised to convey my message when he returned, which she thought would be very soon.

Half an hour later, Stan came up to my suite. We embraced and I told him, between tears of joy and frustration, that I had actually seen Mama. When I finished, Stan looked pensive. "Is it possible you might have frightened the woman? No one likes to be pursued."

"Oh Stan, please believe me. I know I am overwrought, but I did not imagine all this."

"I believe you, Angela. But are you certain it was your mother?"

"I'm certain."

"Do you wish me to investigate that house and the old caretaker?"

"I'll wager you won't find him there, nor any trace of a caretaker ever having been in charge of the house. It might well be the Italian family that owns the house is in on this, but there won't be anything to show it."

"Then I'll let it alone. Have you seen any suspicious characters at the exhibition?"

"No. And I've looked. Of course, there could have been a dozen of them not resembling the kind of people I'd be looking for. I don't care now. Giving the exhibition worked. Mama did come. I'm happy about that."

"It's not enough," Stan said. "We have to determine what menaces your parents to the extent they dare see you only with the risk of considerable danger. Your father in Paris, vanishing the way he did. He must have had some route of escape planned. And now your mother —she knew you'd seen her and she had to vanish also. She had an entree to that house and a so-called caretaker to help her get away. What frightens them so?"

"I don't know," I said. "Well, the exhibition was a success, wasn't it, even if no one would buy my paintings. I'm satisfied. I'll close it and we'll go to New York on our honeymoon, if that meets with your approval."

"Of course it does. I've already arranged for any court cases to be postponed and I'll close the office for two weeks."

"That would be delightful," I said. "But let's make it one week. I know I've upset your schedule. Now you must go. I know I intruded on your day."

"You'll never do that, my love," Stan said softly. "I'd like to stay, but I'll be patient if you'll walk me to the door."

I did, but before he opened it, we became locked in a passionate embrace. It was only with difficulty that we broke it off.

"Forgive me," he whispered and was out the door before I could tell him there was no need for forgiveness.

In the morning, I prepared to venture into the business establishments to buy decorations and materials for the

225

new salon. I could afford the best and I promised myself it would be a busy but pleasant day.

I resisted the lazy way of having my breakfast sent up to my suite. Instead I went down to the restaurant and ordered a substantial breakfast, for I would be too busy to stop for the noonday meal.

I was seated in a booth, something that appeared to be more popular in New Orleans than in New York City. I drank my morning coffee, which was black and very strong. I would find it necessary to grow accustomed to this kind of coffee, but it did wake me up.

Without warning, a man suddenly sat down opposite me. I almost cried out in surprise and fear, for I knew him. The last time I'd seen him was in Paris, when he'd invaded my rooms and I was saved only by Carlo who answered my cry for help. Apparently the forces against me traveled the world.

"Good morning," he said. His voice was well accented. "It's been some time since we met, Mademoiselle. I am Emile. Remember?"

I said, "I don't know what you want, but if you are not out of this restaurant within one minute, I'll scream for help. This is not Paris and I'm no longer afraid of you or anyone else."

"Indeed, Mademoiselle. But I think you will let me speak to you without any hysteria." He reached into an inner pocket and withdrew a slender thong. He held each end and snapped the cord. I could see how strong it was.

"If you scream, I shall be compelled to put this around your throat. You will die in less than two minutes, well before anyone can come to help you."

"What do you want?" I was thoroughly frightened.

"Only to talk to you. No harm will come unless you lie."

"What do you wish to know?"

"Yesterday you were seen emerging from the museum where you have an art exhibit. Once you reached the street, you began running. You disappeared around the corner. Whom were you pursuing?"

"Why do you wish to know?"

"Mademoiselle, I ask the questions and you answer

226

them." His eyes were as cold as his voice. "I wish an immediate answer."

"Then here it is. There is no law forbidding anyone from running on the sidewalk."

"Don't be funny. You know me from Paris. Tell me who was running away from you yesterday and where you went, for you vanished."

So they hadn't seen me enter the patio. That meant they'd not seen Mama emerge from the patio shortly after. Knowing this gave me strength to defy this man.

"Let me inform you what will happen if you do not tell me," he said. "I shall come to you in the night with my little toy that will go around your pretty neck. But that won't happen until I am through with you."

"I am not without friends here," I told him in a firm voice, "and New Orleans is not without police. I shall be safe."

"I forgot to tell you," he said softly, "that before I come to you in the night I will assassinate a certain man you have been seen with often. If you think I cannot get away with that, you are much mistaken. It takes but a dark street, a single second in which to fire a shot and it is over."

I lowered my head, no longer able to hide my fear. I knew he was quite able to do what he threatened. I had to think of something quickly. And it had to sound believable. If I could get away from him now, I could warn Stan. He would arrange for my protection.

I raised my head. He was leaning back smiling, thoroughly at ease. This was a man to fear. In those cold eyes I found no spark of mercy. What he had threatened he would carry out remorselessly.

"What is it you want of me? What do you want and who are you really?"

"I once told you my name is Emile. That is sufficient for you to know. And you will tell me who you were running after. I will not ask again."

"A man had stolen a painting from my collection. I saw him leave with it and I tried to stop him."

"A likely story, Mademoiselle."

"A true one," I said. "My paintings are precious to me."

"Perhaps. But quite worthless." He leaned forward and spoke in a chill voice. "If you are lying, I'll come back. You are most attractive, Mademoiselle. I almost hope you are lying. It is not difficult to prove or disprove your story. It had better not be a lie." He paused, then added, "I suppose you reported the theft to the police."

"No. As you said, they're worthless."

He rose, stepped away from the booth and walked out of the room. What would happen if I screamed for help? Someone would stop him, surely . . . but I was certain he wasn't alone.

As I hesitated, a thickset man rose from the next booth. He didn't glance my way and I suspected that if I had screamed, he would have come to the rescue of Emile —and assisted him in carrying out the threat to kill me right there.

I was too shaken to eat my breakfast when it finally arrived. Emile would soon find out I'd lied. I must warn Stan, immediately, but he was in court this morning.

I went to my room and gave way to tears. I was shaking with terror. Once the spasm passed, I forced myself to move again. I washed my face and gathered my wits about me. I must go to the courtroom, find Stan and tell him of the danger he was in because of me. He must know before he went on the street.

A tap on my door brought back all the terror. Emile might have already learned that my story was a lie. I looked for something I could use as a weapon. The knock was repeated, more insistent this time. I approached the door. If it was Emile, he would have to break it down and perhaps make enough noise to attract someone.

"Who is it?" I asked.

"Miss Gambrell, I'm a policeman. I've got to talk to you."

I hesitated. He might be a policeman or he might be some cohort of Emile. However, it was not Emile's voice, that much I was sure of. I decided I must take a chance. I opened the door just enough so that I might look out, but be able to slam it shut if that proved to be necessary.

The man standing there was tall and athletic in appearance. He held out a badge for me to see. I breathed a sigh of relief, stepped back and opened the door for him to enter, but he made no attempt to do so.

"Miss Gambrell," he said, "we need you at police headquarters."

"Why?" I asked, immediately thinking of Stan.

"We've arrested a thief who stole a portrait from your collection at the museum. We need you to identify the painting."

I asked no further questions. The lie I'd told Emile had been somehow turned into the truth. By whom, or why, I didn't know, but I'd experienced these kindly forces before. My fingers caressed the cameo ring, for only the ring could have been responsible for this sudden and unexpected turn of events in my favor.

I accompanied the officer and at the police station I was shown a rough-looking, evilly dressed man and asked to identify him as someone I'd seen at the exhibit. I could not for, so far as I knew, I had never laid eyes on him before. I was also shown one of the smaller paintings which I'd hung at the exhibit. This I quickly identified and the police were satisfied. The painting would be returned to me after the trial.

It was totally incomprehensible. I told myself firmly that coincidences did happen, but I couldn't believe in this one. Why would anyone steal a painting of mine? And just when my life depended on a painting being stolen. Then, as I was leaving the station, I passed an open door. Behind a desk sat the big man who'd occupied the booth next to mine. This officer couldn't have been in the next booth by chance. So it must be he'd been secretly guarding me, just as I'd been protected in Italy. Yet by whose order?

I met Stan in the courtroom as soon as the trial was over. It was the last court procedure of the day and we sat down in the empty courtroom to talk. I gave him all the details of the day's events.

"These people, whoever they may be, seem to be everywhere. Emile, first in Paris, and now here. People in Italy turned up in France too. What can be so important as to keep up this awful search for so long a time?"

"They must believe either that you know where your parents are or that you can contact them if you become frightened enough. If that's true, they're only trying to frighten you. If they intend to use you as bait to draw your parents out of hiding, they can't very well afford to kill you."

"I'm not so sure of that," I said with a shudder. "Besides, some of the things they do are almost as bad as murder. Who can they be? What kind of motive can they have?"

"I can't answer that, Angela. However, it would be well to remember that you're more valuable to them alive than dead."

"And I'm just as confused about the way I'm mysteriously helped. It's like being caught between two powerful forces—one good, one evil—and I'm frightened."

"We'll get to the bottom of this," Stan promised. "But we've two other very important things to do—first, get married, second, set up your new salon."

"I'm afraid the risk to your life will be greater if you marry me."

"I won't rest until you bear my name. And my protection."

"I'd like to settle things with Carlo," I said. "As quickly as I can. That done, I can concentrate on opening the new store here. I'll have to arrange for buying stock and sending some of the finished gowns from the New York salon."

"Darling," Stan protested, "I can't get away immediately and I don't like you traveling alone. I'll worry about you from the moment you set foot on the train until you return."

I smiled. "It may sound ridiculous, but I have the feeling your love will act as a barrier against any danger."

Stan smiled reluctantly. "Thanks, darling. But it's not as simple as that."

"I know. Seriously though, I'm not so frightened now that I realize there was a detective in the dining room who could have acted quickly had Emile tried anything.

I can't walk around terrified of every shadow. And I'll not be alone in New York City. When I'm not at the salon, Carlo will accompany me. And we occupy the same apartment, except that we have separate quarters."

"I'd rather you stayed at a hotel. I think it would be safer. I'll send a telegram and make a reservation for you. Perhaps you are right. It might be a good idea for you to get away from here."

"Be careful, darling."

"I promise." His arms went around my waist. "And you must promise if you sense the slightest danger, you will send me a telegram. I'll come, no matter what, I'll come. In fact, send me a telegram each day you are in New York. In that way I'll know you're safe."

"I give you my word."

He nodded. "Go to the police if you even sense danger. But stay with Carlo. Have him escort you whenever possible."

"I will."

I went eagerly into his arms and we kissed with considerable passion. It made me realize how difficult our separation would be and how brief I would make it. I wanted to become Mrs. Stanton Talbot as soon as possible.

TWELVE

That evening Stan saw me to the railroad station.

"While you're away," he said wistfully, "I'll look for a place we can live comfortably."

"I should be with you to do that," I said.

"Then cancel this trip," he said quickly.

"Please don't tempt me," I said. "I hate our being separated. I'll make it brief."

He boarded the train with me and saw that I was made comfortable in a drawing room, as private a way to travel as existed.

"Don't open the door unless you know who it is," he warned me. "When you go to the dining car, try to move along the aisle with as many people as you can and be on guard passing from one car to the other."

"Stan," I said, "do you think they'd try to harm me while I'm on this train?"

"I doubt it, but being prepared for trouble is one way to avoid it, darling. I'd better get off now. Two more minutes and you'll be on your way. I love you. Be sure of my love, Angela. Come back as soon as you can."

We held each other close for a minute and made renewed declarations of our love. He had to run to get off the car before it started. He made his way along the platform until he stood beyond view of my window, and he saluted me with a little bow and a smile as the car I was in passed him by.

I settled down, unpacking what I would need for the journey. As it was a night train, I rang for the porter and had him prepare my bed.

Heeding Stan's warning, I remained in the drawing room while the porter finished his work. Then I locked myself in and settled down to read a newspaper Stan had provided

232

me with and examine the several books and fashion magazines I'd brought. I felt secure here, nothing could possibly reach me. I went to sleep early. The jolting and rail clicking didn't bother me in the least.

Morning sent me eagerly to the dining car for I was very hungry. I had to pass through three cars to reach it, but there were people all about me and I felt safe. I shared a table with two elderly women and when I studied the faces of the other diners, I saw no one who seemed to present any danger.

I spent my time making notes on what I had to do in New York, but my drawing room door was locked. I was following Stan's advice.

By the second day I was feeling more secure. That evening I shared a table with two more ladies on their way to Washington. They admired my traveling suit and I told them designing was my business. By the time I finished, I thought I'd secured two more customers for the New York salon.

On my way back to my Pullman, I felt the train slow down and instantly I grew wary. The conductor came toward me as I moved down the aisle of the car.

"Are we stopping?" I asked him.

"Oh no, just slowing down, Miss. This is where we take on water."

"Without stopping?" I asked.

"Yes, Miss. The engineer lowers a scoop that fits between the rails and along a certain stretch this scoop picks up water that's kept in a trough between the rails. Saves a lot of time, but it can't be done at sixty miles an hour."

"Thank you. I didn't think there was a depot anywhere along here."

I managed the next car, though the jolting of the slowing train sent me reeling against some of the seats and required a series of apologies from me as I collided with other passengers on my way.

I pulled open the heavy door to cross the small platform to the next car, which was mine. A blast of night air hit me, while the roar of the train deafened me. The gate must have been open off the car platform.

Suddenly a man emerged from the gloom, just as the

233

heavy door closed behind me. I was seized and pushed somewhat painfully toward the edge of the platform where there was only space between me and the ground slipping by as the train slowed.

I screamed, but only once, for a large hand came down over my mouth. My cries would never have been heard anyhow because of the noise. I was half lifted, half dragged to the open gate.

I raised a hand and dragged my nails along the man's face, eliciting a grunt of pain, but he didn't loosen his hold. I kicked his leg as hard as I could. The hand came down from my mouth as he staggered and lifted the injured leg.

I gave one hard turn and I was free of him. I started to pull open the heavy door to enter the car. He was at me again, throwing an arm around my neck and dragging me back once more. I seized the upper part of the open gate, which was fastened to the car by a locking device when open. It held and I clung to it.

The man suddenly let go of me and reeled back. When I turned around, I saw him falling from the now slowly moving car. Falling or jumping, I wasn't certain which. But he was gone and the danger to me had somehow passed. I was alive. Twenty seconds ago, I doubted I would be.

I leaned against the platform door on the opposite side of the car. I wondered if the man had been killed. The train was beginning to pick up speed, but when the man left the car platform, it had not been moving very fast. I hoped he'd not been killed. I was sure I'd not pushed him.

I made my way across that platform and the one leading into my car. Once I closed the drawing room door, I fell onto the seat and tried to compose myself.

Stan's theory must have been wrong; they *were* trying to kill me. That man had tried to throw me off the moving train . . . or had he? I tried to think calmly about exactly what had happened. He'd had me in a grip I couldn't break. When I scratched his face, he'd weakened that grip and I had escaped him for a few seconds. Then he'd seized me again, and I'd been sure he meant to throw me off the train. I was still too confused and shaken to recall just what had happened, only that the man had suddenly let go of me and fell . . . or jumped. I could establish in my mind only two reasons for this sudden change of mind. Either he thought he heard someone coming, or he'd somehow lost his balance.

It also came to me that he had known I was leaving on that train. How he knew this I had no idea, for I'd told no one and I doubted that Stan had any occasion to mention my trip north. I had to assume that I'd been followed, perhaps constantly. Perhaps even now, by a second man. The first one who had attacked me must have been looking for any opportunity to do me harm or, at least, to frighten me half to death. He'd certainly succeeded.

For several minutes I sat immobile in my drawing room, my mind trying to throw out the memory of those agonizing few seconds when I thought my life was about to end. I would be in New York in the morning but I was still worried enough to plan having my breakfast sent to my room.

At the railroad station swarming with people I felt utterly alone, a target for whatever assassin they'd sent. Once in a closed cab, however, I began to feel somewhat safer. The hotel had a suite reserved for me. I took time to send Stan a telegram and left immediately for the salon.

My employees greeted me with hugs and kisses and stories of wonderful sales, new customers, and a detailed account of the store in the *Delineator* with beautiful pictures. Mrs. Jameson and Mrs. Parks followed me to a private office in the rear and brought me further up to date.

It was not far from noon when Carlo arrived and he was all gestures and apologies.

"I have been walking the streets and the better stores to compare their merchandise with ours. I have found none to approach what we are doing in the way of new fashions."

"Sit down, Carlo," I said.

He'd not made any attempt to greet me with his usual embrace and I decided not to notice this. Perhaps he was

235

excited or plain scared that he'd been caught coming in so late. His nervousness subsided when he realized I was not angry about his tardiness.

"You are looking well," he said. "Tell me, was your exhibit a success?"

"As you expected," I said with a shrug. "No sales."

"I mean . . . the other. Did you see or hear anything from them?"

I had made up my mind not to tell him about seeing Mama. Carlo had a tendency to talk too much.

"No one came by," I said.

"It was all a failure then?" he asked. His dark eyes were studying me intently.

"Not exactly. I am going to be married soon."

Carlo didn't jump to his feet in shocked surprise, as I expected. Instead he eyed me with grim disapproval. "You don't mean that," he declared, knowing very well I did.

"I met this man on the ship going to Paris," I explained. "I knew he lived in New Orleans and practiced law there so I looked him up. We are very much in love, Carlo. The banns have already been read and as soon as I go back, we shall be married."

"You will bring him back here? That means I am out! There will be nothing further for me to do. I have given so much effort to this business and now it's all lost."

"Uncle Carlo, please stop talking and listen for a change. I am going to open another store in New Orleans. There's a wonderful market for the kind of clothes we make."

"You will close this store? Surely you don't mean to do that."

"Of course I don't. I'm going to place you in full charge. I expect wonderful things from you."

"I . . . in charge? I don't know, Angela. I'm not sure I want to assume so much responsibility. There will be too much to do . . ."

"Uncle, if you can't handle it, Mrs. Jameson or Mrs. Parks will. They gave me a good report about you."

He brightened. "Oh, I can do it. There is no doubt of it. Only . . . the hours . . . the responsibility, everything . . . but *si,* I will run it for you. Yes indeed. I am greatly

236

honored that you thought of me for the position." He smiled slightly. "Of course there will be a little more pay? So I may live in a manner befitting my position."

"We'll arrange that later. I'll be in New York only long enough to buy what supplies I need to be shipped to New Orleans. And I will take Alice with me."

"But she's the best seamstress we have. An expert."

"That's why I'm taking her—to teach the new people I will have to hire. Mrs. Jameson and Mrs. Parks agree all our employees are capable."

"I'll do the best I can," Carlo grumbled. "You should have given me more notice. You do things so impulsively, Angela."

"You don't have to accept the offer," I told him. "Mrs. Jameson and . . ."

"I am family," he said hastily. "I can't let you down. We can't have this salon failing while you establish another. You can depend on me."

I cut our visit short. Customers were coming in and Carlo was needed on the floor. I had already made a list of places I must visit to buy materials, machines and everything else that went with this kind of a business, so I examined the books and found them to be in surprisingly good condition. It would not have surprised me if I discovered Carlo had helped himself to just a little more than he was authorized to accept as his wages. It did seem to me that he had changed radically. In the old days he would have pilfered what he could and sold it elsewhere. Perhaps his newly acquired responsibility had been exactly what he needed. I felt now that I could trust him to take good care of the establishment.

For two long days I made my rounds and attended to the banking necessary to finance the new store. This time I had no need of the influence of the magic ring. I'd built up a reputation that was respected and honored so I had no trouble with finances.

Crates of materials and machines were being shipped out even before I would leave New York City. I had already telegraphed Stan to arrange for someone to be at the empty store to receive everything. Now and then I'd stop suddenly to gaze into a store window, to see if I could detect someone following me. If there was, it was expertly done.

The new telephone was of great value also and saved me many hours, though not all the establishments with which I did business had a telephone installed.

I wanted to get back to New Orleans well ahead of Lent to be in time for the Mardi Gras. I couldn't think of a better way to introduce my store than to feature a line of gowns meant for that gaudy and noisy affair. While I'd never seen one, Stan had described what went on well enough that I knew what would be in demand in the way of costumes. I even spent some time sketching harem girls, Dutch girls with pigtails and wooden shoes, a bright red Satan and an angelic gown in white. I studied pictures to help create the colorful dresses of Spain and rural France. I included daring ballet costumes in the hopes the weather would be warm. It was going to take some time to make up these garments and I intended to leave for the South no later than twenty-four hours from now.

There was much to do before returning. Instructing Carlo was one of these essential duties and I did that by taking him to supper at the ornate dining room at the Waldorf. One thing about Carlo, he was at his best in these luxurious surroundings with an aplomb that brought the maitre d' and the captains to brisk attention.

I suppose it was difficult for Carlo to take orders from me, especially when he was being shown so much attention. I had the feeling his mind was elsewhere as I talked about the unglamorous part of the salon.

"It is of the utmost importance not to antagonize any of the women who work at our machines," I explained. "Experienced seamstresses such as we require are hard to come by and I don't want any of them leaving."

"Well, you're taking the best one we have," Carlo complained.

"You know I need her, and I'm leaving you a first-rate staff. And be sure to keep the front of the establishment up. Our kind of trade is accustomed to fine surroundings and a certain amount of extra attention. That's where you excel."

238

"You will have no worries," Carlo assured me. "I know what I have to do and I know very well how to do it. As for the seamstresses, Mrs. Jameson and Mrs. Parks keep a sharp eye on them. I will make you a rich woman in no time, even if I am paid but a paltry amount for my work."

"You're paid more than you're worth right now," I told him in good humor. "What's more, you know it so don't plead poverty to me. Just keep this business going as well, or even better, than now. You surely won't be a poor man if you do—unless you go back to gambling your money away."

"I no longer gamble, Angela. That is, not for high stakes. Only as a pastime."

"You may have your brandy if you wish. I have packing to do."

"A walk after this sort of meal is essential," Carlo said with more authority than I expected of him. "You have your figure to consider, my dear, and I insist we stroll about for half an hour or so."

"That's surprising, coming from you," I chided him gently. "You're the one who usually hates exercise in any form. I think it's a fine idea, though I confess I wouldn't venture out alone after dark."

"There's nothing to fear," he assured me. "We won't go far anyway."

I signed the check and we walked slowly through the beautiful lobby of the hotel. I hoped everyone was looking at my gown, for it was one which had drawn quite a bit of attention in New Orleans.

Outside we found the autumn air to be cool, but not crisp. An ideal night for a stroll. Carlo enjoyed ogling the contents of the store windows on Fifth Avenue as much as I did. We were both very fashion-conscious and this was one of the best streets anywhere to study what was going on in the world of fashions.

The new B. Altman's department store, in the process of being built, would be the forerunner of many such stores, I believed. The Flatiron Building, rising high into the sky, offered more solid evidence of progress. And I'd heard of another big store being planned. Everything was moving uptown and this tendency had no doubt inspired the construction of the brand new St. Regis hotel. I was pleased our store was close to these new businesses.

Carlo and I chatted about everything, from our lives in Italy and France to my plans for the new store in New Orleans. He questioned me about Stan, but not with a great deal of interest. I had a feeling that he resented my getting married, though I'd softened that blow by placing him in charge of the New York store. We talked also of expanding it, by adding a floor above for a new workroom while we converted the entire first floor into the sales department.

We had turned down Thirty-fourth Street for a final walk around the hotel, which occupied the entire block. The side street was not as wide as the avenue and rather dark, but I had been so engrossed in our plans that I had forgotten there could be danger all around us.

So when a carriage turned the corner facing us, it caused me no alarm. Not until the driver whipped the horses into a frenzied gallop. I seized Carlo's arm as I sensed something was going to happen. The careening carriage veered to our side of the street, its wheels mounted the curbing and the frightened horse was almost upon us.

Carlo gave a shout of alarm and as the vehicle came straight toward us, he pushed me into a doorway, stepped in himself and pressed his body against mine to further offer what protection he could. The horse veered again, this time dragging the carriage back to the street where it continued to go wildly toward the avenue. It had come within a foot or two of riding us down.

I emerged from the doorway shaken, once again filled with all the terror I'd been forced to endure over the past many months. Carlo too was trembling, though his face was a mask of anger. I'd never seen him display this much rage before.

"They were trying to kill us," Carlo said. "No question about it."

"I agree," I managed to say. "Take me into the hotel now, before there's another attempt."

"We only have to return to the avenue," he said. "Walk faster, Angela."

We almost ran the distance to the hotel entrance and once inside I sat down in the lobby to recover my wits.

"Do you think we should report this to the police?" Carlo asked, in a voice as strained as my own.

"What would be the use? We couldn't identify the driver or the carriage."

"Who would do such things to us?" Carlo asked. "And why?"

"They're not after you. At least I don't think they are. I do know what they're after. By terrorizing me, they hope to bring Papa and Mama out of hiding in an attempt to protect me. That's why we must not go to the police to report what just happened. Papa and Mama must never hear of this."

"But Angela, there may come a time when they will despair of bringing your parents into the open by threatening you. Have you thought of what will happen? They'll kill you."

"I suppose what you say is true, but I think they'll continue these tactics for a while."

Carlo was seated in a chair beside me. He raised his hands, palms upward. "Now you are moving to New Orleans. Do you think they will follow you there?"

"I know they will. I'll have Stan to protect me there, so don't be concerned, Uncle."

He eyed me with contempt. "Don't be concerned," he mocked. "Until I meet this Stan of yours, I'll worry. How do you know what kind of man he is? Falling in love with a stranger. Stupid child."

"Once you chided me for not marrying."

"He's a stranger."

"I love him. Next time I come to New York, he'll be with me and you can see for yourself." I stood up. "It's time for me to go up to my suite and get ready for tomorrow. There's no need for you to come with me. I'll be safe."

"How do you know?"

"Whoever is behind these acts of violence is not stupid. They won't try anything more for a while. They'll wait and see if Mama and Papa will reveal themselves and spirit me away."

241

Carlo nodded. "You may be right. I'll stop by the bar for a nightcap. Perhaps two or three. After what happened I need them. *Buona notte,* Angela. Sleep well."

As he crossed the lobby toward the bar, Carlo wiped his face and neck of perspiration. The fear of what we'd just gone through was still with him. And small wonder. I was considerably shaken myself. I didn't fully relax until I locked the door of the suite after me.

I packed, hoping it would make me more tired, but when it came time to sleep, I found it almost impossible. I occupied those waking moments by thinking of Stan.

In the morning I slept rather late and the ringing of the telephone in the parlor awakened me. I staggered sleepily to answer it.

"Good morning, darling." Stan's voice came over the wire.

"Stan!" I cried out in happiness. "Oh Stan, I'm so glad to hear your voice. How extravagant you are. This must be horribly expensive."

"It's free," he said with a laugh. "I'm downstairs."

"Darling, how wonderful! Come up right away. Please hurry."

I first unlocked the door and then I rushed to unpack a negligee. I ran a comb through my hair, brushed my teeth and splashed water on my face. There was no time to do more.

When he took me in his arms there were no more problems, no fears, no lurking terrors.

"I grew worried," he told me after we sat down. "I don't know why, but I seemed to have a premonition . . ."

"Darling, then there must be something to premonitions because there were two attempts on my life."

He held me against his chest. "I should never have let you come here alone. I knew that minutes after you left."

"Oh, perhaps they weren't attempts on my life as much as ways to frighten me. But a man tried to push me off the train platform. I still don't know how I managed to get away from him. He jumped or fell from the train. It was moving slowly while it took on water from some sort of trough."

"I think he must have jumped. At the speed the trains

242

travel during that operation, he'd not be in any great danger if he way young and athletic. It would have been more dangerous for him to have stayed on the train for you would have had the crew searching for him."

"Uncle Carlo and I took a walk after supper last night. A carriage, running wild, almost ran us down. Carlo saved my life, or at least kept me from being severely injured."

"From now on," Stan declared, "I'm staying with you just as much as possible. All the time while we're in New York. In New Orleans, we'll try to find some way to keep you from harm. On that score I've a bit of news. Half pleasant and half not so good."

"Tell me the unpleasantness first and then the good news will help ease the blow," I said.

"It's nothing, really. I was advised, at a meeting of the Mardi Gras committee, that I was no longer being considered as king."

"I'm sorry, Stan. I know what an honor it is."

"Frankly, it means nothing to me."

"It means your mother knows of me and disapproves."

He said, "Yes, she knows. But the good news is, I'm the next prosecuting attorney for New Orleans."

"That's wonderful," I said. "I'm so happy. And very proud of you. I'm sure your mother was also."

"If so, I haven't heard," he said. "The job is an elective one, but the man who held that position died two weeks ago and the council had to appoint someone else. They're a hard-headed group and not to be intimidated by anyone, including my dear mother. I'll take office on the first of the month so I'll be in a fine position to see that you're protected, and I'll do my best to try and run down those who have been troubling you so much."

"Just so it doesn't interfere with your work. Oh darling, I love you so much."

"You can prove that by marrying me the day after we get back," he said softly. "I've arranged it all. I hope you don't mind. We have a house, not a flat. It's only partly furnished. You can finish the job."

"I was intending to return tonight," I said.

"Make it tomorrow. I want to meet Carlo, see your

salon and look about the city some. I'll arrange for tickets for tomorrow night. Now, let's have breakfast."

I put on my traveling suit, for my wardrobe was limited. I did plan, if we went to dinner tonight, to choose something from the salon. I wanted Stan to be proud of me.

We ate breakfast in the hotel and we had so much to talk about we kept interrupting one another, but we did decide on how the house would be furnished, at least to some degree, for I'd not yet laid eyes on the place.

From the hotel we went directly to the salon. To my surprise, Carlo was already there. I introduced the two men and I could see Carlo's doubts vanish.

"First of all," Stan said, "I want to thank you for saving Angela last night."

"It was an act of self-preservation too," Carlo announced. "My own skin was in danger. How do you like our little establishment, Mr. Talbot? Or may I call you Stan?"

"Please do, though I'll not call you uncle. As for the salon—it's colorful and feminine. I can understand why Angela wants to make the New Orleans store a duplicate of this one. It's charming. And there's nothing in New Orleans like this now. It should do very well."

"Carlo will show you around," I told Stan. "I've a few minutes work with the mail and some telephone calls to make. I promise not to be long."

I attended to the details in a great hurry, but even so, before I was finished Stan came into the office to sit down and watch me carry on the work I had to complete. I pretended not to notice the admiration in his eyes.

He made no comment until I had finished. "You're a businesswoman, Angela, and a good one. It's most unusual. Also refreshing."

"You'd best not like it too much," I said happily. "Because being a businesswoman isn't going to stop me from having a family, so be warned."

His laughter was hearty, pleasant to hear. "That's good news. I have a feeling life with you will be sheer enchantment."

"Now my day is complete, darling. If you have the patience I'm going to try on two or three gowns. One of them I'll wear to supper tonight. You haven't asked me yet, but I hope it will be Delmonico's or Sherry's. You may have the privilege of selecting either restaurant."

"And meanwhile?" he asked.

"We'll do the town," I said. "There is so much to do here. It will be a glorious day because you're with me."

My work was finally finished; the few leftovers I placed in Carlo's care. I selected the gown which Carlo promised to deliver to the hotel. Stan and I visited the Flatiron Building and from its top story we surveyed the city which revealed great structures in the process of being built on every side.

We had our noonday meal at Sherry's, leaving Delmonico's for the evening. We even paid five cents each to see a cinema and we rode the cars all the way to Central Park where we hired a carriage to drive us about. It was one of the loveliest days of my life.

The gown I selected was the one I'd worn to the Assembly Ball. It had been delivered and a maid had laid it out on the bed. I bathed and dressed leisurely. Stan had gone down to the lobby to read the daily newspapers before he went to his own room to change into formal attire.

Stan looked quite handsome in his white tie and tailcoat. I learned later that he had rented them because he'd not anticipated anything like a formal dinner at Delmonico's. He took my arm and led me through the lobby to a carriage for the brief ride to the famous restaurant.

There we enjoyed a fine meal, Stan vehemently claiming the quality of New Orleans food equaled this. I pointed out some of the more well-known people. They were mostly famous in the fields of finance and railroads, but their names were familiar. It was a pleasant evening, one I knew I'd remember for the rest of my life.

When we left the restaurant, there wasn't a trace of fear in me and I gave no thought to any possibility of danger. Stan was with me, my world was complete. Nothing could shatter the feeling of confidence he gave me.

It was such a beautiful night, I suggested we walk back to the hotel, just as Carlo and I had done. We did remain on the avenue, however, which was quite well lighted.

The two men walking toward us seemed in no way out of the ordinary. Anyway, we were too engrossed in each other to pay any attention to them. And so we were caught completely off guard when, without warning, a door to a store—unoccupied, as we learned later—opened. I was seized, an arm encircled my throat and I was dragged inside. The pressure on my throat was so painful I couldn't make the slightest outcry. My attacker's other hand had caught both of mine and held them securely behind my back. His leg, now wrapped around both of mine, rendered me further helpless.

At the same time the two men attacked Stan. I heard him cry out as he was struck and then they pushed or carried him inside the store. It was so dark I could see little. I tried to struggle, but the arm around my throat tightened its stranglehold, forcing me to remain quiet.

"Show her what will happen to him if she does not cooperate." The man holding me spoke in Italian.

I tried to struggle free of him, but it was no use. While I could see little of what went on, I knew they were beating Stan horribly and I winced at the sickening sound of the blows. Not that he didn't fight back for I heard one of the men give a cry of pain and then swear profanely in Italian.

There seemed to be three of them. One, who'd no doubt been hiding in the store, was holding Stan while the other two administered the beating. The man holding me kept prompting them in Italian, but his accent was odd. Suddenly I knew it was Emile.

Then it was over. Stan lay huddled on the floor, not even moaning. Emile spoke to me, this time in French.

"You are a lovely chicken," he said with a laugh. "I wish there was more time for me to know you better. One day I will. Now you see what we have done to this man you intend to marry. We could have killed him, or crippled him, if we chose, but I am a merciful man—this time. Unless you do exactly as I say, next time we will arrange it so that he will never be much of a husband to you. *Comprendre?* You will write, no later than tomorrow, a letter to your Papa. You will tell him unless he comes out of hiding at once, you will die, along with your husband. We are no longer patient. You have written to your Papa many times and received many letters from him. There is no use lying about that. We know what goes on. Remember—write that letter or you will wish to heaven you did."

He released his hold on my throat, seized my shoulders and spun me around to face him. My throat hurt too much to scream. As I stared at him in hopeless tears, he hit me on the chin so hard that there wasn't even any sensation of pain, only quick blackness and the sense of falling.

THIRTEEN

The face looking down at me would have confused
me under any circumstances, but when I again opened
my eyes, it was like seeing a ghost from the past.

"Welcome back, Angela, my dear." Vito Cardona
spoke in Italian. Vito, an official of the *Carabinieri*.

"Vito?" I asked. "What happened? Have I been ill?
Where am I? Vito, tell me!"

"You are in New York," Vito said. He spoke in English
this time. "You've been hurt. You are in a hospital."

"Stan?" I tried to sit up as it all came painfully back,
but the effort failed and every bit of me seemed to begin
aching. "Stan . . . he was hurt! They beat him! They
hit him . . . and me. . . ."

"He is all right," Vito assured me. "Carlo has told
me you intend to marry this man. I kept hoping that
one day. . . ."

"Help me sit up," I begged. "Then straighten out my
poor brain, Vito. I'm so confused. And my face hurts."

"It should. You were struck a severe blow. Perhaps
several." He bent down and kissed me lightly on the
cheek. His voice grew warm. "My heart is broken, Angela. I am sorry this has happened to you. I'm sorry
I lost you. And I cannot even kiss you on the lips because they are too swollen."

"Please don't be angry with me. You're my true
friend and I have need of as many as I can find."

"I know," he said. "Forgive me." He gently raised
me, puffed up the pillow and eased me onto it so I might
sit at least half erect. "That's better. Now—if it doesn't
hurt too much to talk, tell me what happened."

"I know the man who attacked me and ordered Stan
beaten up."

248

"No . . . no . . . no," he said gently. "I mean this man. This Stan—whatever his name is—tell me about him so when I cut his miserable throat I will feel no remorse."

"Don't make jokes about him, Vito. He was badly beaten . . . my fault. I love him, Vito."

"And you do not love me!"

"No, Vito. But you always knew that. Just as you know I am very fond of you. Tell me," I implored, "how badly he was hurt."

"He was beaten severely, but the doctors say he will recover. I'm sure they will let you see him some time today, though someone may have to tell you who he is, for he is well bandaged."

"Nothing permanent? They spoke of making him a cripple the next time."

"No doubt they meant it." Vito sat down and his hand closed over mine. "Did you see any of them? From the size of this Stan, there must have been six or more who attacked him. He is one big man."

"He never had a chance. They struck him before he could raise a hand to defend himself. It was awful. They dragged us into . . . some place or other. . . ."

"A vacant store, very handy. They must have followed you, realized the route you'd take walking back to the hotel and they found the empty store, broke in and waited. You must have walked very slowly."

"We did. There were four of them, I think. Two were on the street, two were inside. One held me so I couldn't scream or struggle. I had to listen to them beating Stan. I know the one who held me."

I suddenly remembered the orders I'd taken from Emile. I had to write a letter. It was necessary that Vito know about it. Here was a man I'd trusted long ago and I still did.

"Vito, the man who held me is a ruffian named Emile."

"From Paris?"

"That's the one. He said I have to write a letter to my parents and tell them to come back from wherever they are. If they do, they'll be killed. I can feel this. I know it! What shall I do?"

"You have to gain time. Write the letter. I can just

about guarantee your Papa will not come back. You will have to take a chance. And in the letter be sure not to say anything about me being here, or discuss any other matter. Merely beg your father to come back. Do this in Italian. Don't try to hide another message. It won't work."

"Do you know whom we are dealing with?"

"No! I don't even know what they want of your father and mother."

"Vito," I said carefully, "I think you do."

"Poor Angela, so full of suspicion. You don't even trust me."

"You're wrong, dear Vito. I trust you without question."

"*Grazie*." He bowed his head slightly and changed the subject. "Carlo tells me you are a successful business-woman."

"Please don't change the subject. How did you happen to come here at precisely this time, when I needed you most?"

He shrugged. "It was the will of God, I suppose. All I know is that I got off the boat last night and I immediately tried to find you without success, until this morning when I was able to visit your beautiful salon. I found Carlo there. He is a popinjay, that one. With a chest that sticks out almost as much as his stomach. A proud man! Maybe he deserves it, but I remember him too well to accept his taking a large measure of credit for the success of *Angela's* salon."

"Vito, he's changed. He's a fine businessman now and a great comfort to me."

For the first time Vito smiled. It was meant to humor me, I know. "Well, anyway, Carlo had already learned of your being taken to the hospital last night. The police found your hotel key in your handbag and traced you that way. Carlo told me what happened. That is, what he knew about it—what the police told him. It seems someone came by and heard you crying out. You were taken to the hospital with your Stan."

"Are you sure he suffered no permanent injuries?" I asked.

250

He patted my hand. "Except for two black eyes, a loosened tooth, swollen face and a soreness of the body from the beating, he will be himself in about a week or two. When are you to marry this southern gentleman? That is what Carlo called him, though I thought I heard disapproval in his voice."

"In two days," I said glumly.

"The wedding will have to be postponed. He won't be able to stand up until after that."

"May I see him now? Please, Vito."

"You will have to ask the doctor, but my advice is against it. Not because I don't think you can stand seeing him without fainting, but you yourself are in no condition to get up and walk about."

"I feel good," I lied. "Help me up."

He pulled down the bedcovers, eased my legs off the bed, got his arm around my shoulders and lifted me. I was on my feet, but swaying badly and I fell back to sit on the bed again.

"You're right," I admitted. "I wouldn't get to the door without falling down."

"That," he said, "is what I wanted to prove to you. There is plenty of time. Your Stan is not going to run away. Perhaps later in the day they will let you go to him."

"Did he—ask about me?"

"The doctors told me it's the first thing he asked about when he regained consciousness."

"Vito, I don't understand why are you here?"

"*Cara mia,* I came to marry you. I told myself I could no longer exist without you. I hoped perhaps you might, with the passage of time, have grown to love me, but I am no sooner here than I learn you are pledged to another. Truthfully, I grew very tired of police work in Italy. They promoted a man, lower in rank than I was, over my head. I . . . just resigned. I will find something to do here, though it is not of any great necessity, for I have money enough. I am essentially a lazy man and I will likely not even look for a job until I am good and ready. I will stay close by you, Angela, just in case this Stan changes his mind."

251

"I don't wish to hurt you, Vito, but I hope he will never do that."

"I am only teasing you," he admitted. "I know he loves you. As for me, do not concern yourself about my broken heart. It will heal. Enough of me and my foolishness. We have serious things to talk about. The letter they told you to write. Do it."

"How will they know whether or not I write it?" I asked, thoroughly perplexed. "And please—tell me who 'they' are."

"I cannot, because I do not know. However, from what has happened, the way they can follow you about, plan ways to hurt you, seemingly be everywhere, I think they will know whether or not you write the letter."

"But where shall I address it? I don't know where they are."

"Where did you address all the other letters you wrote them?"

"To the *palazzo* where I was born. But someone else lives there now. I told you."

"Address it there, Angela. They will know about it. It's possible they have spies also, even among the *Carabinieri*. Who knows?"

"All right. Please help me up again. I want to see Stan."

"You've rested from your first effort for all of five minutes. You will have to wait for a doctor to say you can get up. Let your body rest. Also let Stan rest."

"You're right, of course," I agreed, as Vito eased me back on my pillow. "Do let Carlo show you about the city. That is, if you are a stranger here."

Vito laughed softly. "Your uncle actually seemed glad to see me. He was quite shaken by what happened to you. At first he blamed your Stan. Then he relented when I reminded him of what had happened in Italy and France."

"He fusses about Stan."

"He expressed his feelings about you marrying a stranger and going down South to live with savages. His words, not mine."

"I know how he feels about my coming marriage. He thinks it's too hasty."

"Isn't it?"

"I met Stan on the boat when I went to Paris. We fell in love, but we—we lost track of each other."

I explained briefly what had happened.

Vito nodded slowly. "Why didn't you ask me to see if I could find him when I was in Paris?"

"First of all, such a thought didn't occur to me. Even if it had, don't you recall apologizing because you could spend only a brief time with me?"

"You have a good memory."

"There is one thing I didn't tell you," I said. "And it is important. I saw Mama in New Orleans. She came to my exhibit. And Emile—he was there too." With Vito asking a few questions, I told him the whole story.

"You look tired," he said at last, "and your voice is weakening. I let you talk too much. But thanks for telling me everything."

I raised my arm and let the palm of my hand rest lightly against Vito's face.

"I'm fond of you, Vito. I always will be. I'm glad you are here. I wished many times that you were by my side."

He moved his face so that his lips could kiss the palm of my hand. Then, with his own, he lowered mine to the bed. "Get some sleep, dear Angela. I've not eaten today and I'm starved. But I want to make certain you are going to rest before I leave."

"I promise I'll not leave this bed. I doubt I could, even with help."

"*Arrivederci*," he said, and he kissed me lightly on the cheek.

I think I fell asleep before Vito left the room. It was late afternoon when I awakened to find him seated beside the bed.

"Well," he said, "you put in a hard day. Carlo came by to see you. He couldn't stay, but he asked me to tell you he sold something he called the 'gold and silver thing'. . . ."

"It was a very expensive gown," I said. "What of Stan?"

253

"He's taking nourishment. Liquid, because his jaws are too sore to stand chewing anything. As soon as you're fit, you may see him."

"I'll try in a little while, but first my hair . . . my face . . . I must brush my teeth. . . ."

"I'll go outside and send in a nurse," Vito said. "When you're ready, we'll put you in a wheelchair and I'll do the driving. Please take your time so you won't tire. Remember, you are still weak from your ordeal."

"I'll be careful," I promised. "And I know I'll feel better when I see him."

Vito looked noncommittal. "Don't expect him to look himself. I had a talk with him. He isn't very good at talking. He mumbles, but I think the swelling around his mouth may be responsible. Just brace yourself. You'll know what I mean when you look in the mirror."

The moment Vito left the room, a nurse entered. After my initial shock at seeing my swollen jaw, she helped me bathe and put on a fresh nightdress and Watteau negligee. My jaw looked ugly and it was extremely painful when I brushed my teeth, but I managed. With my hair combed and neat, my face more alive with a little color, artificial though it may have been and applied gently, I was ready.

Vito came with a wheelchair and helped me into it. I felt weak from my efforts, but his compliment at my changed appearance raised my spirits. He wheeled me down the hall to the men's side of the hospital. I knew by now it was a private one about ten blocks from the hotel where we were checked in. A passing doctor opened the door to Stan's room and I was wheeled in. Stan was sitting up in bed, his face well covered by bandages, but his eyes brightened at sight of me. His lips were badly swollen. He held out a hand to me.

"Angela, darling," he said. His voice was thick.

"You see," Vito teased, at the same time eying Stan with sympathy. "He does mumble."

"Who is this man?" Stan asked in mock anger. "He tells me he came here from Italy to marry you. Have you been deceiving me all this time?"

"You're both mad," I said. I bent and kissed the back

254

of his hand which rested on the bed. "I'm sorry, darling, that's all I can manage in the way of affection."

"We will make up for it later." His speech was thick and I knew it must be painful for him to talk.

Vito said, "I'll be outside," and left the room.

"This is a hell of a way for a man to greet his bride-to-be," Stan said. "How could I have let this happen? I came to New York to make sure it wouldn't."

"Stan, you couldn't help it. Let's not talk about what happened. Instead, tell me more about our new house. It's a good time for me to consider how I'll complete furnishing it."

He told me it was a large house, as most New Orleans homes are. It was equipped with a patio like the one I was already familiar with. The first floor consisted of a double-size drawing room, spacious enough for a moderate-size ball. The dining room could accommodate two dozen people with ease, double that number if necessary. The kitchen was modern in every detail, with a gas instead of a coal stove. Upstairs were six bedrooms, a sewing room and a nursery. Stan described the house well enough so that I could actually visualize what kind of furniture would best fit such surroundings. We agreed that the furnishings that came with the house would, for the most part, be disposed of.

Stan talked slowly, indicating how sore his face must be and the painful effort it took to speak. Yet he insisted on my remaining with him. His presence did much to restore my confidence and eliminate most of the fear which had stayed with me.

"About the letter they demanded you write to your father," Stan asked. "Have you written it?"

"Not yet. Vito thinks I should do as they said. What is your opinion?"

"I think so too. Your father and mother aren't going to come into the open after all these years of hiding. Certainly they wouldn't consider it without consulting you first."

"Or arranging with those who have been helping them," I added. "I know they have friends, some of whom are looking out for me. I don't know who they are, but it

255

seems to me they are people of consequence and power."

"Write it then."

Later that day I wrote a brief letter to Papa telling him that people whose identity and motives I didn't know threatened me and my future husband with harm unless they came into the open. I didn't offer any advice or suggestion. I made the letter quite formal, not like my former ones, because I knew Papa would realize I was determined never to give in to these people and neither should he and Mama. I asked that he write me at once and I gave the New Orleans address of what would be our home. I addressed the envelope to the *palazzo* where they had once lived and where all my other letters had been sent. I also wrote the return address in New Orleans where I would be.

I was free to leave the hospital and when Carlo came to visit me, I sent him in to talk to Stan while I dressed and made ready to attend to all the business I'd so far left undone.

Carlo had a carriage waiting and we rode directly to the store. It pleased me to see half a dozen well-dressed women talking to my salespeople who were showing my gowns. In the office I read the mail, wrote three business letters and began to wind up things.

"This letter they ordered you to write," Carlo said. "Did you send it off?"

"Yes, this noon, at the hospital. I mailed it to Florence. I have no other address."

"Let me know what happens," Carlo urged. "Remember, they're after me too, it seems, and I have to protect myself. That means I have to know what's going on."

"I'll let you know," I promised.

I barely completed everything I wanted to do before Stan and I boarded the train for New Orleans. Vito had stopped by to wish us good fortune, but he didn't confide any of his plans to me. Carlo grew more and more nervous as the time came for him to assume complete command of the New York venture. Stan, still wearing some bandages, had regained most of his strength and occupied a compartment with a connection to my drawing room. We disregarded convention and during the long journey we had time to make our plans and contemplate the future.

Once, during a lull in our conversation, he took my hand and examined the cameo ring.

"It's an heirloom, I think," I said. "Papa sent it to me. I don't go anywhere without it."

"I noticed you don't. Is it valuable?"

"I've no idea," I said, and once again I obeyed Papa's edict not to discuss it.

"Speaking of rings—I sent a wire to Father LeMans, asking him to be ready to marry us as soon as we arrive. I know you are tired from the journey and from what was done to you, but I'll feel better with you close. Especially at night."

"I want to be with you, my love," I said. "And thanks for not being angry for what happened to you."

"My God, you couldn't help that," Stan exclaimed, almost indignantly.

"True," I replied. "But it happened because of me. You know the story. So before we enter into the sacrament of matrimony, I want you to give serious thought to the constant peril you will be in because of me."

"My concern is for you, my love." Stan's arms were around me as he spoke. "That is why I would like us to go directly to the church from the train for the ceremony."

"That sounds wonderful, though we will have to make one stop—at the salon. I want Alice Keane to be my bridesmaid. I don't know if I told you I sent her to New Orleans as soon as I arrived in New York to supervise the decorating and furnishing of the salon. It wouldn't surprise me if she had completed it."

"Fine." Stan suddenly laughed. "Good thing we decided against an elaborate wedding."

I gave him a wry look. "It would scarcely be in keeping with our appearance. How will we explain it?"

"We were taking a ride through the park and the horse became frightened by an automobile."

"Good. Do you have a best man available?"

"Yes. Jacques Fayette, an attorney and friend of long standing. He'll be at the church, as will Father LeMans."

And so, in the presence of a very astonished Alice Keane, my principal seamstress, and a completely surprised Jacques Fayette, we were joined in marriage.

257

Our traveling attire was somewhat rumpled, our bruises still showed, and we both could have done with a bath. But none of it mattered. Stan, his face still partially bandaged, stood beside me and proudly repeated the words that would make us one throughout our lives. I didn't dwell on that last thought—not after what had happened to us, plus Emile's threat to me.

After the ceremony we went to one of the hotels for a brief wedding supper. Alice and Jacques seemed to enjoy each other's company which was good because Stan and I had eyes only for each other. Though it was early evening, Alice insisted on being brought back to the shop. Jacques said he would remain with her.

"I'm impatient to see our new home," I told Stan after we'd parted from Alice and Jacques.

"I think you'll like it," Stan replied. "It's typically southern."

"I shall love it," I assured him. "And we shall bring our love into it."

And we did. A full moon revealed large white columns, two stories high, spaced equally around the four sides. The structure was three stories high and, as Stan said, the third floor was for servants, should I want them to sleep in. Just now I wanted the house to ourselves. Servants could come in to do day cleaning. Stan paid off the driver of the carriage, took out the keys and opened the door.

The interior was as Stan described. I had no fault to find with the furniture, it being French and very delicate, ornate and beautiful. A wide staircase led to the second floor which looked down into the enormous reception hall.

"I wanted to carry you over the threshold and up the stairs," he said. "But it will have to wait until my ribs heal."

"Oh, *dear!*" I exclaimed, stricken. "As you say, your ribs must heal. Perhaps we'd better not . . . We can be patient."

"Not that patient," he said indignantly.

"Then cautious," I urged with a smile. "I must take a bath."

"Then let's go upstairs. We've wasted enough time talking."

258

Stan used the bathroom across the hall, leaving the one adjoining the bedroom for me. Neither of us lingered.

We forgot our bruises once we were together. Stan closed the sitting room door behind him and came directly to the bedroom where I awaited him. He lit a candelabrum beside our bed before he turned off the gas jets at either side of the bed. Then he removed his robe, revealing his nudity. I held up the covers for him.

"I want to see you in candlelight." He brushed back my hair which had slipped down to partially cover my face. "I love you, Angela. Even more now than the night we consummated our love. Do you know why?"

"Tell me," I whispered. His hands had drawn me close and were caressing and exploring my body. My hands were doing the same to him, though I was careful not to touch the area where his ribs were fractured.

"All I knew of you then was your beauty and charm. Now I know how brave you are, how loyal, how resourceful . . . Thank God, we found each other again."

"I shall thank Him every day of my life," I vowed.

He lifted my hand on which he had slipped the ring Jacques had purchased for him, and kissed it. "Now you are really mine."

He drew me closer, slipped off my nightdress, kissing my body as he did so. His hands caressed my shoulders, moved down to my breasts which he held as he kissed them. He was all gentleness. My hands moved down to his thighs as he pressed me down until I was on my back. I helped him, for his fractured ribs made him awkward. I moaned with pleasure as he entered my body. Our cries mingled as we again consummated our love. Afterward we lay side by side, sometimes quiet, sometimes murmuring endearments, but always conscious of the exquisite love we bore each other.

I never once thought of the fear of what we had undergone in New York City. Again and again we forgot our fatigue in the joy of possessing each other. Only once did the pain in my jaw become evident. That was when Stan's kisses became more demanding as his passion rose. But I soon forgot, for my passion was equal to his.

We didn't even take the next day off. Stan went to his office to attend urgent business and arrange for his being sworn in as the new prosecuting attorney. I went directly to the salon. Alice had made splendid progress. Girls were already trying out the heavy new machines sent from New York. I had little to do beyond setting up my drawing board and my desk.

The store was larger than the New York establishment, but otherwise it was a duplicate so far as furnishings and color schemes were concerned. Also, we had more elaborate dressing rooms, both for our models and our hoped-for customers.

Everything was progressing so smoothly it worried me once I found the time to think about it. In the next week, Stan assumed command of his new staff and civil duties. I had deliberately avoided any kind of publicity about our wedding, but with the store it had to be different. I placed advertisements in the local newspapers. In return, they gave me some fine stories, including the success of my New York salon. At my suggestion, the reporters also wrote that I would be prepared to serve anyone who was interested in unusual Mardi Gras costumes or ball gowns.

When the store opened for the first time, Stan stood with me to greet people at the door. There was a surprisingly good crowd in attendance and they were served coffee or wine, little cakes and miniature watercress and cucumber sandwiches once they were seated. I was about to give my first fashion show in this famous and fashionable city.

"It's going so well," I said to Stan, "I can hardly believe it. Did you hear them stop their chatter when the blue silver-spangled gown was shown?"

"I was too busy watching the model," Stan said with a grin. "I'm sure it's going well."

The following day, after the success of the opening, word got about and even more ladies came. Stan insisted on being with me. At this time of year every woman in New Orleans was style-conscious and interested in Mardi Gras costumes and ball gowns. I was showing some of them in the afternoon, standing back to allow Alice to

260

control the showing. I was near the door when I saw a white-haired, slim, aristocratic-looking woman enter in company with a younger woman. She was also slender, with lovely blue eyes and pretty face, except for her mouth which compressed when she observed Stan and me standing side by side. I knew I was about to meet Stan's mother and the girl to whom he had once been engaged.

I decided it was better to meet trouble head-on, but befor I could move, Stan said, "Come, darling. You have to meet Mother sooner or later. Also, Mary-Lou Fletcher."

We approached them and Stan made the introductions. Mrs. Talbot gave me a cool nod. Mary-Lou expressed her pleasure, though her face remained unexpressive.

Mrs. Talbot addressed Stan. "What happened to your face?"

"I took Angela for a ride in a cab in New York City and the horse bolted. We were thrown."

"You look as if the animal stepped on you," Mrs. Talbot replied coolly. "Have you seen our doctor?"

"Not here, Mother. Everything is healing nicely. There will be no scars."

"I shall carry them, my son," Mrs. Talbot said, giving me a cold glance. "To my grave. You have humiliated me beyond belief."

"I don't understand, Mother."

"I am referring to your marriage. I wasn't even notified, much less invited."

"Would you have come?" Stan asked calmly.

"No."

"Then the invitation would have been a waste, wouldn't it?"

"Yes."

"Why did you come here, Mother?" he asked.

"So I might see my son. I heard your appearance was that of one who had been badly beaten."

"If that were true, you can also see I am none the worse for it. If you and Mary-Lou came to see the fashion show, please take a seat. If not, please leave."

"You've learned impudence since you met this woman." She gave a nod of her head in my direction.

Stan smiled. "No. You are the expert at that. So I must have learned it from you."

Mary-Lou said, "Your mother and I came to meet your wife, Stan. Please don't make a scene."

"I had hoped there wouldn't be one, Mary-Lou," he said.

Stan turned the talk to the fashion show. I ignored Mrs. Talbot's rudeness and said I hoped they would enjoy the show. Mary-Lou urged Mrs. Talbot toward the few seats left available. Every eye was on the four of us. The gossip would be all over the city by nightfall. I didn't know if it boded good or ill for the salon.

But I wasn't to get off so lightly. I had had a copy of the gown I'd worn to the Assembly in Philadelphia sent down with others. I somehow felt it was my good-luck gown. Certainly it caused audible gasps when it was shown. It was modeled by a tall and graceful girl who had been hired by Alice. She had stated she had modeled in Paris and from the way she posed and postured, we both believed it.

The audible gasps came when the side slit in the white satin gown revealed a flash of leg. They were followed by looks of either admiration or shock. However, above them rose the cold, disapproving tone of Mrs. Talbot.

"This is a gown one would expect to be worn either by a northerner or a quadroon. It is in very bad taste. If it is an example of what the establishment is going to put out, I doubt New Orleans couturiers need worry about competition from a northerner and an alien. You are an Italian, are you not?"

She didn't deign to call me by name, but since her remark was addressed to me, I had to answer.

"I am, though I have taken out papers to become a citizen of the United States of America. I grew up in this country."

"That explains your lack of accent," she commented. "It also explains your lack of good taste in dress. Your Italian origin."

"I will let the good ladies of New Orleans decide that."

"You will be gravely disappointed," she said.

"Only time will tell," I replied serenely, though I was far from feeling calm inside. "Now let us get on with the show."

An attractive woman in her late thirties rose and turned to regard Mrs. Talbot. "Of all the nonsensical criticisms," she said in a calm voice. "We are known in this city for our open minds and for our love of Parisian fashions. I feel this salon will become an instant success. The designs are clever, original, daring and beautiful. Mr. Talbot's mother does not dictate what we women wear, though she would like to."

Stan's mother half rose, but another voice brought her down to sit and listen to the new charges. These came, surprisingly, from a motherly-looking woman with black hair, severely coiffed, wearing the black so prevalent in Italy. Her accent, while not too noticeable, still gave her away. She was an Italian.

I had no idea who she was, but apparently she must be important in social circles for no one tried to interfere with her halting comments.

"Please," she said in a mild, chastening voice, "Mrs. Talbot, we all know your son married the young lady who owns this establishment. You must know from the newspapers, she is a talented girl who has already made a great success of her work. I know about her New York store. I have been there and it is as lovely as this one. And her gowns are in great demand by women who know good clothes. Perhaps that is not for me to comment on, for I have not the figure or the youth to do justice to the gowns I have seen here this afternoon. I am a simple housewife who does the best she can in the way of her clothes, but when I see beautiful things I have to say so. Excuse me, please."

She sat down, apparently embarrassed. Mrs. Talbot rose, along with Mary-Lou, and stalked out. I made my way to the front of the room and faced the audience.

"I'm sorry for this unpleasantness, ladies. I hope you will judge me on the quality and originality of my designs. Now we will continue our show and hope you like what you see."

The models resumed displaying the gowns as if nothing had happened. No one left and as soon as the fashion show was over, the salespeople began taking orders and seamstresses came from the workshop to take the ladies in back to take measurements. It was going to be a profitable day, despite Mrs. Talbot's efforts to see that it was not. I quickly forgot the hurt I'd endured from Stan's mother.

The lady who had spoken first was admiring the Assembly gown as I approached her.

"Thank you," I said. "You did me a great service, though I'm sorry there had to be unpleasantness."

"Mrs. Talbot, you would have had a perfect right to have her ejected. Such unreasonable comments! Still, I'm surprised she let me get away with it. I was braced for a caustic reply. She's good at it."

"Your manner was so gracious, you placed her at a disadvantage."

"On the contrary. You're new in this city so you cannot know that a quadroon is never accepted an equal, even in this day and age."

"I'm afraid I don't understand," I said.

"My dear, there was a time when I'd be called a *femme de couleur*. My great grandmother was black, I have been told. To Mrs. Talbot, being criticized by me was an insult of the worst type."

I put my arms around her, my cheek next to hers. "You are one of the loveliest women I have ever seen," I said. "I hope one day you will be my friend. I feel as if you are already. I would like to present you with any gown of your choice."

"Mrs. Talbot, I cannot accept one as a gift, but I will buy the blue one. The last one modeled. Later we shall talk and I will tell you about the past history of this city. You will understand us more then."

"Please come back soon," I said. "I'd like nothing better than to be educated in the ways of New Orleans. The old and the new. My name is Angela. I hope you'll call me that."

"I am called Suzette." She spoke as she made her way to a clerk to order the gown. I went over to sit down beside the somewhat embarrassed woman who had risen to my defense.

I spoke in Italian. "Signora, I am forever in your debt. And I'm proud that I am an Italian, just as you are."

She displayed a broad, happy smile. "I am ten times glad I told that woman what I thought. I could not help it. My Pietro tells me, always say what you think and don't be afraid. This is the first time I did."

"It was wonderful," I said. "Tell me, how long have you been here? What part of Italy do you come from? There are many, many questions I would like to ask."

"I am from Aleria. A small place of little importance, I'm afraid."

"Corsica?" I asked. "I am sure that's where it is."

"*Si*—Corsica. A poor island with poor people."

"I am from Florence. My name, until two days ago, was Gambrelli."

"*Si*—*Firenze*—Florence. I have been there. So beautiful."

"All Italy is beautiful," I said staunchly. "You live here in New Orleans?"

"Ah!" She clapped a hand to her forehead. "I have not the sense God gave me to introduce myself. I am Laurari Liggio. *Si,* I live here with my husband and I have a little one. A girl. I came today to learn more about clothes. I do not know how to dress well. Not as well as I should."

"From now on, you will," I said. "At little expense too. It will be my delight to show you how a woman of your age and figure can look as glamorous as . . . well, anyone here."

"No, Signora, that would not be possible, but I am willing to try," she added hopefully.

"Fine. Next time you come, plan to spend a few hours. And bring your daughter. She too should learn how to look her best."

"I am most honored," she said. "Most honored. I will come in two days and you will come to see me. *Si*—I will give you my address. Come whenever you like. My husband is a man who appreciates beauty and he will like you."

So despite the scene Stan's mother had made, the day

was a good one. Stan felt worse about what happened than I did. In retrospect I believe she did me a favor. Whereas many came out of curiosity, her rudeness swayed their sympathies in my direction and my orders grew far beyond anything I had dared hope for.

FOURTEEN

We ate at Armand's that evening, for Stan and I would be dining out until my salon and his new position had settled down to provide the time for me to employ a good cook. We discussed his mother's behavior.

"Don't blame her too much," I begged him. "After all, you did marry me against her wishes. She is hurt and taking it out on me. One of these days she'll accept me."

"Thank God you're so understanding. Not many daughters-in-law would be," Stan said. "There's little I can do about it, darling. That's the way she is and nothing is going to change her. At least Mary-Lou didn't contribute to the unpleasantness."

"She's beautiful. I hope one day we can be friends."

Stan looked dubious, but said, "I hope so."

I reached across the table and placed my hand on his. "Try not to be unhappy because of what happened. Tell me about quadroons. I don't understand."

"It's a long story," Stan said. "And not a pretty one. Their ancestors were mistresses to white men, mostly very rich white men who kept them in style and provided for them and for the children they begot. A few became quite wealthy. Usually the children were sent to Paris to be educated. There they were treated as equals, which is not the case here, worse luck for them—and for us. Anyway, there used to be quadroon balls where the loveliest of the girls met the men who would support and love them, in their particular way, while they also maintained their wives and families and were considered quite respectable. It was all a sorry business, but it happened. A few whites regard quadroons as a race apart. Ugly nonsense."

"The woman who defended me today, Suzette Larkin, I

regard as a friend and I hope she'll become a close one. Do you object, Stan?"

"I encourage it. You need a woman friend. Make no mistake, she's as much a lady as . . . as Mary-Lou. But this girl will be highly intelligent and unless I'm sadly mistaken, you'll grow to like her more and more. As for me, it's lucky you're as attractive as you are, because those girls can be most beguiling. I'll be her friend too."

"A casual friend," I said with a smile. "Stan, it really went over well. You've no idea how happy I am. I have a wonderful husband and before me is a good life. The best. I only wish I could solve the mystery of my father and mother."

"We'll be settled soon, Angela, and we'll get to work on this mystery. We'll find the answer and we'll get rid of whatever danger they face. I give you my word."

"Then my happiness would be complete," I said. "Now tell me about the Mardi Gras. There's not too much time left. How would you like me to appear? Are we all masked?"

"Oh yes, masks are worn. Otherwise there might be a great deal of embarrassed people next morning. There's a lot of kissing and love-making going on, but if you don't know who your partner is, what of it? Mardi Gras is not for a lifetime, only one day and night. I can't advise you as to a costume. You're better at that than I."

"What do you favor?" I persisted.

"I haven't thought about it. What I'm thinking about right now is home. I want you to myself. I want to hold you. To make passionate love—as we did last night."

"And will every night. Oh Stan," I said in fresh anguish, "I'm so sorry about your injuries. I was afraid of it ever since I met you here in New Orleans. The danger that surrounds me now includes you."

"Darling," he said confidently, "this is New Orleans. I'm the prosecuting attorney. I've more authority than your Vito when he was with the Italian police. By the way, did he ever tell you what he intended to do with himself?"

"Not one word. Vito used to be very outspoken, gregarious, but since he came to the United States he seems to have changed. He joked and teased, but I have a feeling he's a very worried man."

"Well, if he contacts you, welcome him to New Orleans whenever he wishes to come. I like him. And pity him— because he lost you to me."

"I wish I could understand him," I said. "He loved working with the police, yet he left it. Out of pique, of course. As for his loving me, somehow, it doesn't ring true. He's a strange man, darling, but I shall always be fond of him. Let's walk home."

Stan eyed me in mock resentment. "Woman, you torture me."

Nonetheless, we left the restaurant and walked home.

It was a warm night for January and we strolled hand in hand. We bought pecans from a man with a cart, whose strident voice rang all through the square we were crossing. I was without fear for the first time since I'd begun the hunt for my parents.

There were many days and nights like this. Everything appeared to have settled down. Whatever pressure had been exerted against me had been released and I felt free. And marvelously happy with Stan.

My letter to Papa came back marked addressee unknown. So Emile's plan had failed. I'd promised to let Carlo know about this and I sent the letter to him along with other mail which passed almost daily between us.

Carlo gave me fine reports on the New York store, with further favorable comments from Mrs. Parks and Mrs. Jameson. I was, from time to time, tempted to go there and see for myself, but I hated to leave Stan for even a day. He was extremely busy with his office and staff and, from what I could read in the newspapers, he was doing a very good job and had been commended several times. He never talked much about his work.

The store was a success, but not quite as great a one as I'd wished for. I wondered if Stan's mother and Mary-Lou could have been responsible. It meant I must try harder. I held no grudge. Suzette stopped by, not to purchase, but to talk to me and I was grateful for her company.

I had an idea one day and I summoned Alice Keane, who now practically ran the store, to my office. I wouldn't have hurt her for anything in the world, but I had an idea she was not completely at ease with her work heading the sales department.

"Alice, in a short time I'm going to expand and take over the floor above. I'll turn that into a bigger workshop and enlarge the first floor so sales takes it over completely, except for my office."

"That's wonderful news." Alice approved the idea. "I know we're getting crowded already and we've been in business such a short time."

"You're as familiar with the business as I, Alice. I want you to have a free hand here, take over anything you wish. But I am going to have to separate the selling and the tailoring end of the business. Do you think you can handle both?"

"No, ma'am," she said promptly. "I've got my hands full right now."

"Then which division do you wish to assume control of? The tailoring shop upstairs, or the selling?"

"The shop upstairs." She chose promptly. "Just let me take those drawings of yours and turn them into garments. To me that's far greater fun than selling them. Just to see them come to life from a drawing board. I love that."

"The job is yours. We'll begin the change-over immediately. There's another matter. You've seen Suzette Larkin here often. What would you say if I hired her to supervise sales?"

"She'd do better than I," Alice said promptly. "She's a beautiful woman, she loves fashionable clothes and knows the proper accessories to complement them. But I hear she's . . . well . . . not fully white. Maybe you know that."

"She told me so a long time ago. I don't see how it would interfere, unless she would object. Would you approve?"

"With all my heart. She would be an asset to the salon."

"Good. She's coming this afternoon to pick up that pale green street dress. I'll talk to her then. What about the evening gown Mrs. Liggio ordered?"

"It is almost ready. She's going to be very pleased with it. She does have an inclination to look—well—dowdy."

"She's Italian, brought up in a small island town. Every woman there wears black. Don't ask me why. But I doubt they'll ever change. I'm going to try and get her to change. I'm starting with something not too light—no pastels yet. A medium gray serves to set off her hair. Also it's fitted to her figure which really isn't bad. The clothes she's been wearing are what makes her look dumpy. I just hope her husband approves. Some Italian men have a tendency to be old-fashioned." I paused, then added, "Where their wives are concerned."

"She won't look old-fashioned in this gown," Alice assured me with a laugh.

"I think I'll deliver it myself," I said, purely on impulse. "She's a dear lady and I'd like to know her better. Besides, I'll get an opportunity to speak Italian before the language leaves me forever."

Suzette came by during mid-afternoon. I'd given instructions that she be brought to my office. She entered, looking slightly puzzled. I quickly came around my desk to embrace her and set her at ease.

"Please sit down," I said. "I'd like to talk about something important to me. I only hope it's just as interesting to you. But first—I've never asked you any personal questions. You've bought two—or three—gowns. I know you don't work . . ."

"I'm not anyone's mistress either," she said. "Those days are gone."

"Would you like to work in this shop?" I asked, without further delay.

She raised her head in surprise and by the look on her face I knew what her answer would be.

"Why, I never thought of such a thing. I . . . no, that's not quite true. I did think how nice it would be to work here, because I love beautiful clothes and I like to be around people. We . . . my kind . . . don't have too many friends in New Orleans. Not the kind of friends I wish."

"You'll manage the entire sales end of it. Alice wants to run the seamstresses upstairs. I'm going to expand the store. You'll be in full charge. We'll talk about wages later. Right now I only want to know if you are interested in my offer."

271

"I've had some experience," she said. "In Paris I was a model and I did some sales work as well. Models sometimes do both there, as you probably know."

"I have to ask this, Suzette. Will . . . ?"

"My color—so-called—will it make any difference? Oh yes, I knew what you were going to ask. Thank you for making it so easy for me. It will not make any difference because of one very obvious reason. We—my kind—are accepted so long as we do not aspire to anything great. Here, selling gowns, I will be accepted with pleasure. Because they know I can advise them, but they will always be higher in social rank than I, and that will make the difference. I assure you there will be no trouble. I know every single rule they've made and I've broken none of them."

"It might have been well if you had," I told her. "When you work for me, Suzette, there will never be a need for you to bow your head to anyone. If such people come into this store, disregard them. Let them take their business elsewhere."

"Thanks, Angela. I'm not destitute by any means, but I do have to live rather frugally. My father provided for me, and rather well, but over the years such payments do dwindle. I'll be delighted to work here."

"That's settled. I'll let everyone know. Thank you very much. I'm relieved I have someone I can depend on."

That evening I told Stan about it and he approved. "She'll do well and give you more time to yourself. The idea is excellent."

"Darling, what about your own work? You don't talk about it very much. Is it going well?"

We had finished our supper and, as we often did, we relaxed in the parlor where I had done a little refurnishing. There was a pale blue sofa where we had grown accustomed to sit and enjoy our coffee while Stan smoked his evening cigar.

"It's been going fine," he assured me. "Up to now. However, there's a new—but old—trouble rearing its ugly head. I think I told you some time ago about an organization that used to prey on small merchants, mostly the Italian ones. They'd demand tribute every month or the

272

store would be set afire or broken to pieces. Sometimes the owners would be beaten severely."

"I remember. It ended in a horrible way."

"Yes. These outlaws became too bold finally and they murdered the Chief of Police. That broke the back of our citizens' patience. A group of them invaded the jail, hung some of the gang, shot the rest to death in their cells. That put a quick end to this kind of trouble—until now. It's come back."

"Oh darling," I exclaimed. "As bad as before?"

"It's growing, and will be if we don't do something about it. I think perhaps they've started again because they probably regard me as too young, inexperienced and maybe too weak to challenge them. I'm going after them. Every last one. The trouble is, they are very hard to convict. People are afraid to testify against them. A man gets beaten within an inch of his life, in broad daylight, with a dozen people looking on. He swears he has no idea who did it and all the witnesses went blind at that particular moment. It's very exasperating."

"Is it dangerous? I mean to you. They did murder the Chief of Police."

"I'm not afraid of them. However, the people they prey on are deathly afraid. All they have to do is send some reluctant victim an envelope with a piece of plain paper in it and on that paper, the imprint of a man's whole hand, in black ink. They've become known as the Black Hand."

The thought sent shudders through me. "Darling, I hope they won't come after you."

"They won't. They learned their lesson after what happened to the Chief of Police. They confine their banditry to little people who are afraid of them. A family that gets a Black Hand in the mail, or finds it imprinted on the door of their home, loses their eyesight and their voice immediately. I think they go deaf as well. We can't get them to admit anything. They live in a state of terror from then on."

"I know what that is," I said. "I've lived with it for years."

"Things seem to have quieted down," Stan said. "I meant to talk to you about that before. That is, it's been quiet—unless you've been holding back something you don't want me to worry about."

"I promise I will never keep anything from you—except the customary women's secrets you've no business knowing. But if anything happens, no matter how small, you'll be the very first to know, as quickly as I can reach you."

"Good. Remember that I'm in a unique position now. I've got the police, the judges and everybody else behind me. I'd be a hard man to intimidate and I'd be very quick to respond."

"I've noticed you carry a gun," I said with a smile, because I knew he'd been trying to hide that from me.

"I didn't want you to know," he said. "How did you find out?"

"When a husband returns home to his loving wife and she greets him with a kiss and a hug and he presses her close, she is bound to discover he carries a gun in his vest pocket."

"It's a very small gun," he said. "A derringer. Because I wanted to keep it from you. Now that you've found out, I'll be carrying a larger one. It's a good precaution."

"I agree. I wish you had had one in New York when those cruel men hurt you."

"I don't think they'd given me a chance to use it. I wasn't alert then. I'd had no experience with them. I wonder why they've suddenly grown so quiet. I think about it and wonder if they'll let you alone now that you are married."

"I wish I knew. It's either that or it means they're hatching some scheme."

We talked for a while about my parents and the chance that they would someday emerge from hiding. "I hope we find them and they are safe," I said softly. "I want them to meet you—and our child."

"I hope so too," he said. Then he looked at me. "Wait a minute! Do you mean they're going to have a grand-child?"

"Something of that nature."

"You're not . . . just talking about what might be . . . ?"

"Well, Dr. Thornley doesn't seem to think so. I saw him yesterday."

"You didn't tell me . . . yesterday! You didn't tell me."

"I wanted to think about it for a few hours, all by myself."

He said nothing for a few moments and then he drew me to him and kissed me with a warmth and a love that made me sigh aloud in pleasure. Then he drew away, his brow furrowed. "Who else have you told?"

"No one. Stan, I wouldn't tell another soul until you knew."

"That was wise of you. Keep it a secret as long as you can."

"But why?" I asked. Then I gasped. "Stan, if they find out somehow—Papa and Mama . . ."

He nodded. "Something like this is more apt to bring them out of hiding than an art exhibit, for instance. And this time they'd hardly be able to arrive for an instant and vanish again. When those forces—whatever they are—seeking your parents, hear you are having a child, they'll be more alert than ever and they'll watch you constantly. Apparently they have spies everywhere."

"Now I am worried," I said. "I'm glad you thought about this, but it's not going to make it any easier."

"I know. And when it becomes necessary, you're going to have the heaviest protection you can imagine. Until then, keep quiet about it. That means to everyone. There's some very important reason why these people are trying to find your father and mother. I don't know what's behind it, but as I said, trust no one."

"I'll be very careful," I agreed. "I'm going to carry on with the store just as if nothing is different. Right up until the time I can't hide the secret any longer."

"Good. When that time comes, we'll take necessary precautions. So long as the word doesn't leak out, there won't be any danger, and when the news has to be made known, you'll be so protected no one can get near you."

Yet, despite all his assurance, and my absolute trust in him, Stan had turned my hour of bliss into something akin to a nightmare. I couldn't sleep. I tossed about and finally I got out of bed without disturbing him. I went to a window looking out onto the quiet residential street and I remembered other windows, other years, when some shadowy form lurked in the darkness, ever present and ever dangerous.

I knew that when Papa and Mama heard about my child, they would come to me, no matter how perilous it might be for them. They'd all but given me away, reluctantly, I knew now, when I was only four. They'd kept in touch with me by mail and risked a visit when I was eleven. I suspected there were many times when they saw me and watched me growing up. Times I never knew about for I'd never suspected there was anything wrong until I made that trip to Florence.

What motive could exist so many years? What lay behind it all? Forces strong enough to compel two fine people to destroy what had once been a pleasant, comfortable life, to turn into fugitives, hiding in fear of their lives.

It had been important to me to discover the truth and eliminate the danger so they could come back to me openly and without peril. Now it became more important than ever. I tried to think of some plan, some scheme by which I could let them know, and yet beg them at the same time not to risk their lives.

I finally crept back into bed, but I didn't sleep for another hour or more. In the morning I knew I was sleepy-eyed and I made certain not to let Stan notice it by keeping up a lively conversation at the breakfast table.

"I'm going to deliver a gown to that nice Italian lady I told you about," I said. "She's so strange. She dressed so dowdily until now. Yet the clothes she wears are expensive. Most of them are silk. She seems to have no lack of money. I've yet to have her ask what something costs, and the two dresses—simple ones—which she bought so far, she paid for in cash. She's such a dear woman that I must find out about the life she lives so I may know how to dress her."

"Good luck," Stan said. "Tell me about it tonight."

We were driven to the City Hall where Stan got out. The carriage continued on to the store. I found myself looking about nervously, just as I used to do when everything seemed to be closing in on me. I had to stop that, for I'd give away my fears and if someone watched, he might wonder why I had suddenly grown so nervous.

I tried in vain to forget that I was now carrying a child. I even laughed softly to myself, as if to tell myself how impossible that could be. Yet when I touched my abdomen, I was certain I could already feel life inside me. And a glorious feeling it was.

The gown for the Italian woman was ready and boxed. Suzette was on hand, I suspected from the moment the store opened for business, to begin her duties. Everyone in the store admired her and they seemed quite content, even pleased, to have her operating the salon where the gowns were shown and the sales made.

I called another cab and, with the attractively boxed gown beside me, I gave the driver the address. The route he took surprised me somewhat. Even though I guessed Mrs. Liggio had money, I didn't think we'd be heading for the section of the city where there were nothing but the estates of extremely wealthy families.

The carriage pulled up before the grilled double gates leading to a slightly curved, tree-lined driveway. Beyond this stood a mansion, set far back, and looking like something out of a dream.

A man at the gate came forward. I told him who I was and what my errand was. He nodded, without saying anything, and he entered a small booth-like structure just inside the gate. I saw him pick up a telephone, crank the handle industriously and then hang up. I'd never seen a private telephone like this before.

He emerged and waved the driver through the gate which closed behind us. The mansion was probably one of the largest and costliest in New Orleans. A maid in a black uniform came out to greet me and carry the box inside. Mrs. Liggio met me at the door with a fond embrace and much excitement.

"It is so nice of you to bring the gown," she said, "but it was not necessary to put you to all this trouble."

"Mrs. Liggio," I said, "I want to see it on you. It is to be worn this evening, you told me, and if it is not right, I want the time to fix it. I am clever with a needle if I say so myself."

"I am nervous about it," she admitted. "I have never

277

worn anything like this before. I know it is beautiful, but I am not . . . you see . . ."

"Wait," I said, "until you have the dress on. Then tell me you're not beautiful. And tell me this also. When did you ever see an Italian who wasn't beautiful?"

She laughed and led me into a drawing room about the size of my entire store, reminding me of those days when Carlo and I lived at that terribly expensive hotel in Paris. This mansion was of the same plush style.

When I exclaimed at the grandeur of the place, she shrugged and gestured, Italian fashion. "It is nice, but too big. For me, much too big. My husband, he likes it. He says if you have money, you show other people you have it. Or what's the use in having it? He is a little crazy, that one. But he is nice. You will see. He is home and I know he will want to meet the so-kind lady who treated me so well. And who is going to make me beautiful. Ha!"

"Let's get the question of the fit settled right now," I said.

"*Si*, upstairs. Later I will show you the rest of the house. And also the peacocks."

"Peacocks?" I asked.

"*Si*—there are six of them and they chase me whenever I go out. And they scream at me. I hate them, but my husband says they are stylish. You ever hear of a vain bird that is stylish? Eh?"

Upstairs, in a delightfully furnished room—so different from the rest of the house—we removed the gown from the box and she made ready to try it on. I looked about the room and I couldn't help but clap my hands in applause.

"The house is New Orleans," I said. "But this bedroom is Italian. Everything is as it is in the old country. I love it."

"I asked only for this when my husband brought me to this house. I wanted to have something that reminded me of simpler days when I was even happier than I am now. All in this room came from the home I grew up in on Corsica. Everything, even the carpets and the pictures. They are all holy pictures, as you can see. There are others in this house for which my husband paid a great fortune, but they cannot compare with these which may

278

have cost five hundred lire and no more. This room is me. And I am afraid the gown you have created may not be me."

"Wait until you put it on," I said. "Turn away from the mirror and don't turn back until I tell you. I'll help you get it down over your head . . . Good. Hold still while I fasten it. Now stand up straight . . . walk two steps. Don't turn until I see how it hangs . . . It fits perfectly." I tugged at the waistline. "Yes . . . perfectly. Now close your eyes, turn around to face the mirror and then look."

She obeyed me and took a few seconds before she had the courage to open her eyes. She gasped and walked closer to the mirror, as if she couldn't believe it.

The gown had changed her from a woman who looked fifty into a woman of no more than thirty. When she had her hair properly arranged, her face made up, at least a little—I doubted she would permit makeup to be obvious —she would attract the eye of any man.

She brought her hands to her face and began to cry silently. I put my arm around her shoulder. "You see, a woman is like one of those peacocks you told me about. She needs lovely clothes to complement her physical attributes. The gown does that for you."

The skirt was a dove gray satin, richly embroidered. The bodice was a deep green velvet with ostrich feather trimming which also ran down one side of the skirt and encircled the hem.

"I feel like I'm someone else. On Corsica they would ban me from Mass, perhaps stone me for being an impure woman. But here . . . oh, it is lovely. You were right. I am not that old I should wear always this black, but it is the way I was brought up. I have to remember that here in America it is another world."

"The next time you come into the store," I said, "I will show you a bolt of silk in a deep maroon. It is a warm color, but still conservative. The color would complement your black hair and brown eyes."

"*Grazie,*" she said and impulsively hugged me. "First we will see what my Pietro has to say."

Her eyes kept switching back to her reflection in the mirror.

"It will please him as much as it does you."

"Yes," she agreed. "I have watched him look at women in bright dresses. He would never think of . . . flirting, as you call it . . . but he is a man who likes to look—and admire. Now he won't have to look far. At least, not tonight."

"Tonight you will be the most attractive woman at your ball."

"All because I stand on my feet and say what I feel to that woman. That is why you do this for me."

"It was a favor I'll never forget."

She led me into the hall and there she shouted her husband's name. Probably it was necessary. If she tried to open all the doors on this upper floor, it would have taken her some time.

He came out of one room—a short, dark-featured, typically Italian man in a bright red smoking jacket. He approached us and then stopped. I could see the wonder forming on his face, and then the smile, followed by a great shout of joy as he moved to take his wife in his arms and, in voluble Italian, tell her how lovely she looked and how much he loved her.

Just as impulsively he hugged me and kissed me on the cheek. "You are the Italian girl Laurari tells me about. She says you are making a dress which scared her, and I said she should never let such a thing as a dress scare her, but to put it on and see how it looks."

"Does it please you, Mr. Liggio?" I asked.

"It pleases me so I cannot talk about it. For a long time I have told my wife to dress like Americans, but she says she has no shape for it. She is too old. Forty years too old? *Mama mia,* she is no more than a well-grown child. And now, in this dress, she looks like the girl I married. Ah, this is one fine day. Come, you two, we shall have some wine and then, Mrs. Talbot, you shall tell me about Italy. It has been so long since I was home."

"You two go down and I will come soon," his wife said. "If you think I am going to drink wine while wearing this gown . . . never! Nothing must happen to it. I should put it away with my wedding dress and I keep it forever."

He nodded and winked at me. "She is a little crazy, that one, but so beautiful. Come . . . I have wine from Italy. All you want. And do not forget to give me the bill for the dress. No matter what it is. You will make more for her?"

"We've already talked about another," I said. "Please, speak Italian, Mr. Loggio. I will feel completely at home if you do."

He never spoke another word of English that day, not while I was there. We talked of Corsica, a poor, barren land on which people would starve if they were lazy. We moved on to Florence where there was an abundance of everything. And Rome, beautiful Rome, with all its antiquities and its people, so volatile and uninhibited. He did most of the talking. He seemed eager to talk of the past. I was an eager audience.

"I became a wealthy man in Italy," he told me. "Once I was so poor I had no shoes and my father's pants were so big when he gave them to me to wear that I was ashamed of even going to church in them. Until it came to me that every other boy wore the same kind. So I married my Laurari, and I made up my mind we would one day never be poor again."

"She's a charming lady," I said, just before she came downstairs in her somber black. "And a happy one."

"*Si*, I think she is happy now. I am not sure. Sometimes she cries because she is homesick. I am too, but I do not cry. I build something else or I buy a painting, or do over part of the house. It is good to have money. Sometimes I think it is too good and a man grows uncomfortable with it."

"I've not enjoyed that experience," I said.

"Your papa was poor like me then?"

"No. He was well-to-do. He was a member of the House of Deputies in Rome."

"His name, if you please?"

"I'm sorry. I should have told you before. He is Luigi Gambrelli."

Mr. Liggio nodded. "I think I have heard of him. He enjoys fine health, I hope?"

"I don't know," I said. "I haven't seen him in many years."

"Your papa . . . you have not see him?"

"Pietro," his wife scolded him mildly, "mind your own business."

"No . . . no," I said quickly. "I have no secrets. I don't know where my father and mother are. They sent me to America to be raised by Mama's sister. I was only four and I don't know why they do not join me. There has to be a reason, though it's a puzzle to me. I can answer no questions because I don't have the answers. Someday I hope they will return."

"You don't know where they are?" He seemed amazed by what I said and looked as if he couldn't believe it.

"I have no idea where they are," I said.

"You saw them last when you were a little girl?" Mrs. Liggio asked.

"As I already told you, I went to live with my aunt when I was four. Papa and Mama came to see me when I was—eleven. That was the last time."

"How strange! And how sad!" Mrs. Liggio said. She was obviously a highly emotional woman for I saw the beginning of tears. Her husband also noticed them and quickly did his best to divert them.

"Now, Mama," he said, "we must show Mrs. Talbot our joy—and our surprise."

"*Si, si,*" she recovered promptly. "Of course. I had forgotten. The gown, it made my memory so poor. You must meet Amorita. I will bring her at once. You have the time?" she asked anxiously.

"Yes," I said. I did have a great many things to do, but I felt comfortable here and I was enjoying myself. Mrs. Liggio hurried away. Not calling her daughter, but going for her.

"She is a fine child," Mr. Liggio said. "Mama is so careful of her that she is not allowed to run around. I say that's wrong, but I do not argue much. For years we thought we could not have a child and then, by heaven's grace, it happened."

I almost gave away my own secret, holding back only because of Stan's warning. It seemed impossible that a

282

family like the Liggios would have presented any problem if they learned I was carrying a child, but I took no chances.

Mr. Liggio went on. I could see how devoted a father he was. "This little one, she is going to be a beautiful woman. I know this, and I shall be very proud of her. Perhaps by the time she is a woman I will be an old man, but that will make no difference. We prayed for her, Mama and I, and now we have her. And I tell you, Mrs. Talbot, there is nothing going to happen to her. It would kill Mama if it did and sometimes I think maybe I would not live either. That is from being old when your first-born comes."

I heard the childish voice and a moment later Mrs. Liggio entered, holding the hand of a lovely little girl with raven hair and large, deep brown eyes. She was dressed in white and she was, no doubt, a very lively child. Behind Mrs. Liggio and little Amorita stood a large man, both in height and girth. He was well-dressed and watchful. I took it for granted he must be Amorita's tutor. This proved to be true when I was introduced to him later on before he led Amorita away. Her parents had interrupted her studies so that I might meet her.

She was a sweet child and very well-mannered. She had been told I would make a dress for her and she asked me about it. After I answered her questions, she was led away by her tutor. I spent another half hour with the Liggios and drank a little sherry with them. I was to receive a report on how the gown went over at the ball they would attend that evening. I declined an invitation to it, though it would have been an interesting evening and perhaps a profitable one as well, for I would surely meet new customers there. But I had made up my mind, except for Mardi Gras, not to accept any invitations for the duration of my pregnancy.

Not that I was so afraid for myself, though that did have some bearing on my decision. My concern was that the more invitations I accepted, the greater the risk of my pregnancy being discovered. With that would come the danger that Papa and Mama would hear of it and risk coming out of hiding. I had to prevent that until Stan and

I cleared up the mystery and removed this strange menace which seemed to confront them.

There was something else I had to do before my figure became ungainly. I had begun to realize that I must visit the New York store soon and make certain Uncle Carlo was managing it in proper fashion. His reports were good, the profits had increased, but knowing Carlo from old, I didn't quite trust him. He could go only so long at some important task before it became boring to him and he would begin looking for diversions which, ultimately, became extremely expensive.

Stan was against the trip. He was unable to accompany me because, as a prosecutor, he could not ask for postponements and take days off from his work. If I had to go, it would be alone. I decided to think it over.

The New Orleans store was in excellent hands. Suzette had proved to be a natural saleswoman and administrator, with a love of fine clothes and the ability to transfer her feeling for them to the customers. At no time did anyone ever question her background or color. So long as she was in no position to enter the social life of the ladies she served, she was accepted. Sometimes I thought this color line was there because these girls were unusually beautiful with their golden skin and sylph-like figures. They'd certainly present a degree of hazard to the comfort and domestic tranquility of the ladies.

Even Stan realized the importance of visiting New York now. It was essential I check on Carlo, and soon my condition would not permit the long trip. I made train reservations and prepared to go.

FIFTEEN

I'd not notified Carlo that I was coming. I wanted to walk in on him and discover just how he was managing the store. I found New York somewhat changed in the months since I'd been here. There seemed to be more people, the streets were more crowded. The horsecars were being displaced by electrically driven trolley cars, and there were quite a few smoke-belching automobiles, with their loud motors and honking horns adding to the din.

I checked into the Waldorf-Astoria because I knew it so well, and it was among the finest. I could well afford luxuries now and it was part of my business to keep abreast of fashions by going about as much as possible, to places where fashionably dressed women would be.

I reached the city at night and I was so tired that even going down to supper seemed too exhausting. After a light repast I spent a restful night. In the morning I had the doorman call a carriage and I was driven to the store. I dismissed the carriage a block away and walked the remaining distance to gain, for myself, a perspective of the store which I hadn't seen in so long a time.

I was gratified to note that the windows were expertly and tastefully decorated. It was too early for much business to be in progress. When I walked in, a salesgirl whom I'd not seen before and who, obviously, didn't know me, approached with a polite greeting.

"Is Mr. Guillermo in?" I asked.

"No, madam, it is too early in the day. He will be here just before noon if you care to return."

She was gracious, a definite asset to the salon, and so I smiled as I spoke to put her at ease. "I am Angela. That is my name above the door."

There was confusion and excitement after that, for the employees I knew came hurrying out to greet me. It was a warm and satisfying welcome and I was overjoyed that I'd come. What I heard from them was also welcome news. The sketches I'd mailed to them had been well received. The store had been doing a better business than ever, and gowns bearing my name were to be seen at almost every social event. I was shown a list of names and my customers appeared to be from some of the most important families not only in the city, but the nation. Angela gowns were known and accepted all over America. Mrs. Jameson even suggested I open a branch in San Francisco.

Carlo arrived, dressed in the height of fashion as always. He was first overjoyed, then dismayed to find me in the office.

"You did not tell me you were coming North," he complained, after he'd greeted me affectionately and with true warmth. "Have you been dissatisfied with the way I run the place?"

"Carlo, I'm proud of you. I came because I felt I should pay you a visit in case there were problems, or suggestions you wish to make. There could be any number of reasons why I wanted to come, but the most important is one I hope you will be as overjoyed to hear as I."

He sat down after tossing his gray, English-style derby onto a nearby chair. "What could that be, Angela?"

"I am going to have a baby."

"*Mama mia*, what a surprise!" He came to his feet quickly and brought me to my own feet to be kissed and hugged, making certain he handled me gently. He was, in fact, more demonstrative than Stan had been, though considering his nature that was normal.

"It is about time," he concluded, after he had eased me back in the chair.

"You should criticize?" I challenged him. "A bachelor —in your middle years!"

"Me?" He looked askance at the very thought. "What kind of father would I make? What . . ." He stopped and

286

grew solemn. "Angela, do your papa and mama know?"

"How could they? I can't get word to them. I still don't know where they are."

"If they hear of it they will come. I know them well enough to be sure of that."

"I have the same feeling and it frightens me."

He nodded. "It should. They will come to you if they learn of your condition."

"That's why you are the only person, outside of Stan, who knows about this and I have told you only because it is necessary for you to understand why I will, before long, not be too active in the business."

"I will go back with you to New Orleans," he said promptly. "Mrs. Jameson and Mrs. Parks can take charge here, as you well know. I will go back so you can take all the time off you wish."

"And mingle with the savages?"

"I'll make every sacrifice for you."

"No need, Uncle. You will stay here. I have someone in New Orleans who is quite capable of handling the store. It's more important you remain with this one. And now I'd like to see the books, talk to the help and generally find out how my drawings are being carried out in the creation of new gowns. You've sent me precious few letters lately, Carlo."

"There isn't time to write you! I socialize and bring more and more customers. Also there are things you must be told about. Right now, I think. Do you have the time?"

"That's what I came North for, to find out what is going on."

"There will have to be some changes. You see, there are more and more stores being opened. Some are very big and very fashionable. They sell made-to-order dresses like we do. Though not as stylish I will say. However, they also sell to people who cannot afford the kind of garments we turn out. Many ready-to-wear factories are being started. They provide these big stores with very good dresses, evening gowns, robes. Not in our class, but they are not expensive and people can afford these when ours

287

are out of their reach. Do you follow me, Angela?"

"I'm listening," I said. "I've known about that for some time. It's even begun in New Orleans. Boston, Chicago and even Philadelphia are a part of this expansion. Are you suggesting we begin manufacturing this kind of merchandise?"

"We will come to it eventually, Angela. Otherwise, all your work may fall by the wayside."

"It has good points as well as bad," I said. "We'll grow so big, things won't be as they are now. So we won't go into that yet. As you say, eventually we may have to, but we operate well now on a record of originality in our dresses and we deal with customers on a more intimate basis. When the time comes to change that, we'll know, and take whatever steps are necessary."

"As you wish, dear niece," he said. "To be truthful, I like it better this way."

"Good. Now, what have you been doing with yourself, Carlo? Are you happy and content?"

"I would say so."

"Do you gamble as much as you used to?"

"Not often. You must realize I am a man of the world and I need certain outlets. However, it is for me alone to accept the fact that I am getting old. I dye my hair now. Does it show?"

"Not in the least," I told him. "You still look very handsome. And quite continental."

He nodded. "That is my greatest asset. My virility."

I laughed. "Certainly it isn't modesty."

"Modesty may be a virtue, my dear, but it doesn't bring in the business."

"Uncle," I said lightly, "you must create havoc among the American ladies."

I regarded him with amusement, for he loved to hear such things. He smiled reflectively.

"American women respond to the polish of a European. Especially an Italian."

"More especially if his name is Carlo Guillermo."

"Modesty prevents my responding to that." He rose. "I'd better get started before the help begins to adopt

288

my ways. Seriously, I'm delighted you're here, Angela. May I ask you to supper this evening?"

"I'll be ready at seven-thirty."

"I shall look my best," he said. "Of course I will pay the check with company money."

"Of course," I agreed. Then I changed my bantering mood to one of seriousness. "Uncle Carlo, I have your word not to mention to anyone that I am to have a baby?"

He grew serious also. "I swear. I will not reveal your secret. I know how serious it might be if the news got out. I will forget you told me."

"Tonight then, at seven-thirty. I'll be leaving the store soon to do some buying and to look over anything new on the market."

I settled down to work on the books which Carlo had sent in. I spent the afternoon with the fabric wholesalers and I was considerably impressed with the trend toward ready-made dresses. Surely it was going to be a vast business and enable women of more moderate means to look well without the long hours spent in being fitted again and again, dealing with temperamental seamstresses and dressmakers, and then being charged an exorbitant price well beyond their means. Soon they could quite likely obtain a fine dress for a cost no greater than they now spent for only the materials.

We dined at Sherry's where Carlo seemed to be quite well known to the captains and waiters. He was saluted by people at several tables as well. When I studied the menu and noted the prices, I wondered if Carlo dined here regularly and, if he did, how he managed. While I paid him a handsome salary, I knew he spent much of it on clothes and a fashionable flat in one of the best parts of the city.

"Have you kept in touch with Vito since I left New York?" I asked Carlo.

He made a wry face. "That . . . policeman!"

"He was very kind to me," I said. "And to you as well. You don't seem to have a very long memory, Uncle."

"He haunted me," Carlo sighed. "But yes, I suppose

he did see that I got protection while in the hospital. He was very much in love with you, which I suppose you are well aware of."

"Yes, Uncle, he was. Vito is a very kind and compassionate man. I used to wish I loved him, but it was not to be."

"Just as well. A cop is always a cop." Carlo had clearly never gotten over his hatred of authority. "No, I've neither seen him nor heard a word from him. If he was in love with you he would not be likely to hang around, seeing you are now married. I give him credit for that much sense anyway."

"I would like to see him again. If he does come by, please tell him he's welcome to call on Stan and me in New Orleans any time."

"A woman, inviting a man who loves her to come by, could be a dangerous thing, wouldn't you say? Especially an ex-lover."

"A man with your suspicious mind no doubt would think so. I happen to think otherwise. I would like to see him any time. I would also suggest you not call him my ex-lover. Love is something to be shared and it was never that way between Vito and me."

"I know, I know. You tease me. I tease you back," Carlo said. He closed his eyes for a moment while his mind went into the past. "You know, it seems so long ago. Remember how we lived for nothing in that very luxurious hotel? And then moved up the hill to those flea-bitten rooms? I don't remember those days with any degree of happiness, but I will admit they were interesting."

For the next two days I was extremely busy. I wrote Stan every day and on the third day I had a brief note from him saying everything was fine and if all was well, I need not hurry back, though he would wait impatiently for news of my return.

Nonetheless I made up my mind to return the following day and I informed Carlo of this fact when he entered the salon around noon, his customary hour, it seemed. We made an engagement for that evening, this time at

Delmonico's which was still one of my favorite places to dine.

At eight there was no sign of Carlo. By eight-thirty I was growing impatient and upset. Carlo could be depended on only for a limited length of time before he displayed his carelessness in keeping appointments. I thought that had all changed, but apparently it had not.

By nine I knew, of course, that he wasn't coming so I went down to dine alone in the hotel dining salon. I had little appetite. I thought Carlo could have shown more consideration not only because of my condition, but since this would be the last time I'd see him for months.

Back in my suite, I began to pack. Once the room telephone rang and I sprang to answer it, but it turned out to be someone calling my suite by mistake. At ten-thirty the phone rang again. By that time I was comfortable in a robe and nightgown, reading the evening papers before going to bed.

It was likely Carlo, full of apologies and excuses. A man's gruff voice announced his name was Harnell, that he was a Lieutenant of Police and did I know one Carlo Guillermo.

"Yes, he's my uncle," I said with a sinking feeling. "What's happened to him?"

"He's been injured. Seriously, but not fatally. We sent him to Bellevue. You may see him there whenever you wish. And I would like to speak to you later."

"I'm leaving for New Orleans tomorrow morning," I protested.

"You may change your mind, Mrs. Talbot."

"Is it that bad? Is my uncle able to talk?"

"Yes. He told us where to reach you. I suggest you go to see him immediately. Is that your intention?"

"It is, Lieutenant."

"Very good. I'll be there too and we can have our talk. Then, if you wish, you may go on to New Orleans."

I dressed hastily, telephoned for a carriage and was driven to the East Side where the big red brick municipal hospital was located.

Inside, the files had to be searched for Carlo's name

and then I was told he was in the prison ward on the top floor.

"Prison ward?" I cried out. "Is he under arrest?"

"I don't know, Miss," the woman at the desk told me. "He's locked up. That's all I know."

I found the prison ward and faced a locked, barred door before which a uniformed policeman questioned me.

"Carlo Guillermo?" He consulted a list. "Oh yes, you can come right in, Miss. He's expecting you. Lieutenant Harnell telephoned you'd be here."

"I don't understand. Why should my uncle be locked up?"

"Oh, that! We got orders, Miss. The Lieutenant is afraid the guys who beat him up might come here to finish the job. He's locked up for safekeeping."

"Thank heavens for that," I said in relief.

I was admitted and led to a private room. A nurse, ministering to Carlo, finished dressing a wound on his face before she left me alone with him.

His face was cut and bruised and I suspected the injuries from his shoulders down were more serious. He was weak and groaning, especially when I entered the room. Before then I had heard him talking in a joking sort of way with the nurse, so he was obviously putting on an act for my benefit.

"How badly are you hurt?" I asked.

"I am near death as you must be able to see."

"Carlo, you're far from that. You're going to be all right in a day or two. Now I want to know who did this so the police can go after them and put an end to it."

"How do I know who it is? The orders came from that old enemy of mine, I am sure, but he is in Paris and you cannot reach him. The hoodlums who waylaid me were local. They spoke only English, such as it was, without a foreign accent. They were hired and one of them told me I had not much longer to live. That was before he broke my leg."

"Broke it? As serious at that?"

"Well, I think it's broken. The doctor said he doubted it, but I know my own body and I say the leg is broken. Perhaps in more than one place."

He was exaggerating again, though he certainly had been severely punished and his condition was nothing to take lightly. I sat down to wait until the Lieutenant arrived, and to keep Carlo company for awhile.

"I never saw them very well," he said. "There were five. A whole gang—to half kill me. They didn't say much. They just dragged me into an alley and pushed me against a wall. I was hit everywhere and when I fell, they kicked me. It was awful. Worse than any of the other beatings I received. Next time . . . next time will be the last. I can feel it. They will surely not stop until I am dead."

"We're going to have to do something about this, Uncle. Perhaps have the Paris police round up this man who has sworn to kill you. And warn him if you are killed, he will be held responsible. We are not going to stand by and do nothing. I can assure you of that."

"What can be done? This man can send any number of murderers to kill me. I can't be protected all the time. It's impossible."

"Stan could see that you were," I said thoughtfully. "He's the prosecuting attorney now and he works with the police constantly."

Carlo struggled to sit up, moving his legs, though gingerly, showing he was not as badly injured as he pretended to be. "Angela, take me back there with you. Please! If I stay here I'll die. I know it. I am getting old. I can't stand any more of this. Next time it will be the end. Take me back there and let Stanton protect me. At any rate, they won't find me easily. Going back with you will delay them, at least."

"I did give it some thought just now," I said. "I could send Suzette to take charge here. She's proven her worth and I know she can handle it."

"Take me back. If you value my life, if you love me as an uncle, don't make me stay here."

"Get better first," I said. "We can decide later."

"You are going back in the morning," he protested.

"No, I'll stay a few days more. Until you're well again and until we can make up our minds what to do. It may be that it would be best if you left New York."

Any further conversation was interrupted by the arrival of Lieutenant Harnell, a middle-aged man with a paunch and little remaining hair, but with a professional approach and a no-nonsense manner.

"We can be more comfortable in the waiting room," he said. "If you don't mind, Mrs. Talbot."

I bent down and kissed Carlo on the forehead, one of the few spots not bruised or lacerated.

"I don't see why you can't do your talking in front of me instead of behind my back," he complained.

"You're too weak to hear the sordid details," the Lieutenant assured him with a grin. "The doctor just told me you have to rest and you can't be interviewed until tomorrow. So go to sleep, Mr. Guillermo. You're well protected here and you need have no fears."

"I hope you are right," Uncle Carlo mumbled.

In a small, plainly furnished waiting room on the same floor, Lieutenant Harnell got to the point at once.

"Your uncle was quite badly beaten," he said. "I've seen worse, but this was neatly done. He must feel as if there are a hundred red-hot bolts inside his chest and stomach. I want to know why it was done and by whom. He is not in the least cooperative. I trust you will be."

"He told me," I said. "This is not the first time it happened. Actually, it's the third. Twice before he was badly assaulted. That was in Europe and some time ago. Perhaps two years. I don't remember the exact dates."

"Who and why?" Lieutenant Harnell repeated.

"He never told me the name of the man responsible. I doubt he ever will. My uncle used to be quite a gambler —a bad one, by the way. He also had an active eye for the ladies. I think the man who has ordered the beatings was owed a great deal of money my uncle was not able to pay. And it seems my uncle had an affair with this man's wife. Whatever happened, the man swore he would have my uncle beaten up several times before he ordered him murdered. It seems this man has a long arm. Extensive enough to reach across the ocean."

"I see. Hired thugs did it, eh? That means we'll likely never solve this thing with an arrest. See if you can get

294

the name of the man who paid for this. Perhaps we can do something through the gendarmes in France."

"It is a suggestion I already made to my uncle. I'll see what I can do."

"It's the only suggestion I have, Mrs. Talbot. Incidentally, I notice that you use the past tense in telling me your uncle was a gambler. He is now—a rather extensive one. I think you should know."

I shook my head in consternation. "I suspected as much. He is not a man to change entirely I'm afraid."

"When he was subjected to this beating he'd just come out of a gambling place. I was told he was a steady visitor and he'd lost quite a lot of money, but he never welched on a loss. There were no I.O.U.'s."

"I don't believe I can stop him from that vice," I said. "I will try, I assure you. Thanks for all you've done. I think I'll take my uncle back to New Orleans with me."

"That's the best idea yet. And don't leave any forwarding address for him."

"Thank you again."

"I'll see you home," he said. "There's a carriage waiting for me."

When I reached the hotel, my mind was still in a turmoil. Carlo had done very well in New York and I was reluctant to displace him, even with Suzette. But in New Orleans I had no real need for Carlo, though of course I would have to give him the same authority he had enjoyed up to now once he had recovered.

Bringing him to New Orleans was not going to remove the temptations that gambling always presented to him. Gambling was a favorite vice in New Orleans and was conducted quite openly, being a gentlemen's game, as it was called.

Also, moving Carlo hundreds of miles from New York didn't guarantee his safety, for if his enemies had tracked him from Paris to New York, certainly they'd find him anywhere he went.

It did seem to me this individual who was behind Carlo's woes appeared so vindictive as to be unreal, yet

295

I supposed there were men whose vanity, offended by someone like Carlo, nurtured an everlasting rage that could only be satisfied by the death of the offender. Still, they'd had chances to murder Carlo, but had stopped short of it, though not by very much.

I reached my suite, unlocked the door and went in. As I closed the door behind me, I had a feeling that someone was inside, waiting in the darkness. I checked the door from closing all the way and kept a hand on it so I could turn and run.

"Who is in here?" I asked, feeling slightly silly in case there was no answer and my feeling of not being alone proved false. Someone laughed softly. I pulled the door wide.

"*Cara mia,*" the voice said softly. "Don't tell me you are afraid of me."

"Vito?" I asked. "Vito . . . is that you?"

He turned on the lamp on the table beside the chair where he was seated. It was Vito, as debonair and relaxed as always. I closed the door. I was very glad to see him, but very annoyed because of the circumstances.

"How did you get in here?" I asked. My voice certainly displayed my annoyance. Vito had never taken such liberties before. I'd been through too much to allow being frightened like this to pass without expressing my displeasure.

He arose and came toward me, smiling as always. "Have you forgotten that I was a policeman and I know all the ways of criminals? A mere hotel door could not prevent me from entering. But are you not glad to see me?"

I quickly relented, knowing he meant no harm. "You know I am," I said. I embraced him and kissed his cheek. "You frightened me, that's all."

"You look lovely as always, Angela. And I'm sorry I frightened you. I did not care to meet you outside. It is safer for you this way. How is Carlo?"

I removed my hat and gloves. Vito helped me with my coat. He draped it over the back of a chair and resumed his seat once I sat down. I regarded him thoughtfully.

296

It seemed to me that he looked older, less carefree. As if he'd been under a considerable strain and it was beginning to show.

"So you know about Carlo."

"Oh yes. I've made it my business to keep an eye on him."

"A pity you couldn't have saved him from the beating."

"I'm as sorry about that as you."

"He'll recover," I said. "They hurt him, but not as badly as they did in Paris."

"They came close to killing him."

"Has Carlo ever named the man he claims is responsible for all these beatings?"

"No."

Vito looked thoughtful. "I wonder if he paid the gambling debt. Or if he did, did he consider the possibility of buying this man off? Giving a bonus—or paying a penalty. It would soothe the man's ego, at least where his wife is concerned."

"He told me he had repaid the man."

Vito looked skeptical. "It's hard to believe."

"I'm going to take Carlo back to New Orleans with me. Perhaps he'll be safer there."

"Only if you lock him up where he cannot escape and no one can get at him. Finding him in New York wasn't difficult. Finding him in New Orleans will be even easier."

"At least it will take them a while to locate him. Besides, Stan is now prosecuting attorney there and he has the power and the influence to offer Carlo more protection than he's ever had."

"True! Congratulate Stan for me. And how is he? I must say you look radiant."

"Stan is well. You look well also."

"I am."

"What are you doing these days? I thought you might have gone back to Florence and resumed your police career."

"Oh no. I like it here. I pick up a few dollars now and then. I'm comfortably situated financially. And you?

Why do I ask? You're dressed in the height of fashion. Yet you have a different look. More mature perhaps. And your figure. Nicely rounded out. Yes—marriage agrees with you."

I smiled with pleasure. "Vito, you have no idea how you've lifted my spirits."

"I cannot say the same. I have had to learn to live without what my heart desires most. When will you return to New Orleans?"

"As soon as Carlo can travel."

"Have you heard anything from your father and mother?"

"Not a word."

"Did you actually see one of them at the exhibit you held in New Orleans?"

"Why do you ask that?" I was instantly suspicious of him. I didn't think anyone knew I had actually seen Mama.

"Angela *cara,* this is Vito. From way back, when there was no Stanton Talbot. Don't you trust me any more?"

"Strangely enough, I do," I told him. "Though sometimes you say things I didn't think anyone else knew about."

"I am a detective, first and foremost. I always will be. Did you see either one of them at that time?" he persisted.

"Yes," I said. "You see I do trust you. Now it is up to you to trust me. How did you know?"

He gave me a disarming smile. "I guessed. It was pure guesswork, Angela. I believed, as you did, that your exhibit was bound to draw either one or both of them."

I said, "Vito, I am beginning to get the impression that you are actively involved in whatever happened to my parents—and probably to me. What I wish to know is, whose side are you on? The police, or those who are trying so hard to find Papa and Mama so they can destroy them?"

"It's time for me to go," he said. He stood up and extended his hands. I placed mine in them without the slightest reluctance.

"You didn't answer my question."

"I told you I am a detective first. I ask the questions."

"I should be angry, but I'm going to trust you. You couldn't be associated with those who have made my life so troublesome. You're my true friend."

He released my hands and let his rest lightly on my shoulders. His smile was warm and friendly. "Angela, thank you for not being angry; also, for your trust in me. Please, I implore you, be on guard and trust only your husband. *Arrivederci, cara mia.* My life and my happiness have been improved by seeing you again."

He kissed my cheek lightly and left without another word. I sat down slowly, puzzled by him. And puzzled by my own conflicting attitudes toward the man. I felt I could trust him and I had told him so, but . . . I'd not made any mention of the fact that I was going to have a baby. There was now something about Vito that made me hold back. I wondered why. I never had before. He'd even mentioned I looked different. Did he suspect I was going to have a baby?

Carlo, of course, had been told. Living with us, as he would be, or even if he chose not to, he would soon have known. I stayed over two additional days until his pain eased and his strength returned. He remained in the hospital where he could be guarded in the prison ward.

He'd limped out of the hospital, using two canes, and casting many fear-ridden glances to right and left. We went directly to the train, timing ourselves to arrive just minutes before departure. Once the train was in motion, he lost some of his anxiety, but he was still very tense.

"Relax, Carlo." I patted him lightly on the arm. He was still nervous and, of course, very pale. I had gotten adjoining compartments and we were seated in his, facing one another.

"Would you like a glass of sherry?" I asked.

"Two, if you please," he said seriously. "It would take that many to relax me."

I rang for service and ordered two glasses of sherry. We received prompt service and Carlo gave a quiet sigh of approval at sight of them. The table was set up between us and the glasses placed before us. I had no intention of having any and I was pleased to see that despite Carlo's nervousness, he sipped his like the connoisseur of good food and drink that he was.

"Won't you have even a little?" he asked.

"No. I think it's wiser that I refrain from any alcoholic stimulant while I am *enceinte*. But I think it will do you a world of good."

"It will, dear niece. And I appreciate your thoughtfulness. Do you know I still haven't gotten used to the fact that you're going to have a baby."

"You don't sound too cheerful about it," I scolded him mildly.

"I'm not," he replied in his usual blunt manner. "It makes me too aware of the years that have passed. Also, I think you chose a very bad time to have a baby."

"I did not choose, Uncle," I said remindfully. "It is God's will."

"Ah, yes." He reached for the second glass. "I am thinking of that Emile character."

"I prefer not to think of him," I said quietly. "Instead, I will tell you a little of New Orleans."

"Good." He settled himself back carefully on the plush seat. "I may as well learn about the savages since I will have to live amongst them."

"There are no savages there," I said impatiently.

"Peasants then."

I gave him a chiding look, picked up a magazine and turned my attention to its contents. Carlo didn't mind. He gazed at the passing countryside.

I'd written Stan the circumstances which led me to take Carlo back with me. He telegraphed by all means to bring him. Stan met us at the depot with a carriage and had the driver go through the center of the city so that Carlo could see how different it was from New York and Paris.

"Well," Stan asked him, "what do you think of New Orleans?"

"Delightful," Carlo said. "Somewhat provincial, of course, but otherwise I'm sure I shall like it here. Especially the weather. February in New York City is not the best time of year. It is warm here and very pleasant. Also, the peasants don't seem like savages. They're fashionably dressed."

Stan smiled tolerantly. "I'm glad you arrived before Mardi Gras. You will see something New York hasn't got. I'd suggest, if you wish to take part, you find yourself a costume. Everyone is masked and the costumes sell out or rent early. You may have a problem finding one to suit you."

"If I am able to go." His voice took on an injured air as he addressed Stan. "You understand, of course, I was severely injured."

Stan said, "Angela wrote me about it. I'll do my best to see that it doesn't happen again. Your injuries will have two more days to mend. It isn't until Shrove Tuesday, the day before Lent."

"Which doesn't give me much time either to mend or to get a costume."

I said, "We'll give you the names of costume shops you can canvass."

"Thank you, niece. Now there is one more thing I would ask. I have not yet seen your home and no doubt it is large and lovely. But I have lived by myself so many years I would have a difficult time adjusting. You know, Angela, even in Paris and New York, we had separate flats."

"I know," I said quietly.

"Is it possible for me to find a small flat, or a hotel, in keeping with my way of life?"

"Which means luxurious," I said pointedly.

"Yes, dear niece. You know I like to live as well as I can. But alone, so I will not have to feel I must account for my movements and interfere with your lives. Especially with the baby coming."

"I'll have a place for you in two or three days," Stan promised. "So Angela told you about the baby."

"Well, naturally," Carlo said indignantly, "since I will be its great-uncle. Besides, I'm sure I would recognize the symptoms, given another few months."

"Of course," Stan agreed good-naturedly. "Will you work in the salon?"

301

"I could be of help," Carlo said promptly. "Angela would find it somewhat difficult in the near future. I have done well with Angela's New York venture."

Stan turned to me. "I told Suzette about your plans to transfer her to New York and she is very excited about it."

"Good," I exclaimed. "I believe she will be happier there."

We arrived home and when the door closed behind me, I felt a wave of relief and a feeling of safety. Stan showed Carlo about while I bathed and changed into fresh clothes. We had eaten a mid-day meal on the train so we weren't hungry. Stan and Carlo were enjoying cigars and brandy when I came downstairs.

"I neglected to tell you," I said, "that I met Vito in New York."

"Vito!" Carlo exclaimed. "You saw him? He is here?"

"He was in New York," I said. "As for being in New Orleans, I don't think he had any plans to come South."

"How is he?" Stan asked.

"He looked very well. I don't know if he is working. He seemed quite evasive when I asked him even a simple question. I believe it was just a social call, to pay his respects and find out how we're getting along."

"Did you tell him I'd been hurt?" Carlo asked.

"I didn't have to. He knew."

"How?" Carlo asked excitedly. "No one else knew. The police were not making it public."

"Carlo, I don't know how he knew, but he did." I spoke softly in an effort to calm him, though from the worried look on his face, I knew I'd failed.

"It is odd how he stays out of our way and appears only when he wishes to," Stan commented. "If he came down here, I'd certainly see to it that he was offered work on our police force. They'd welcome a trained and experienced man."

"I wish you'd mentioned it at some time," I said. "I'd certainly have suggested it to him."

"You . . . just met?" Carlo asked and snapped his fingers. "Like that?"

"He was waiting at the hotel when I got back from

the hospital," I said patiently. "That was the night you were attacked. Perhaps, being an ex-policeman, he wanders around police circles and heard about it. It may be that's why he looked me up. He did wish to know how badly you'd been hurt, Uncle."

"He never showed much consideration for me before," Carlo said grumpily.

"You're being unfair," I said sharply. "He had you guarded in the hospital in Italy."

Stan seemed amused by Carlo's peevishness. "Shall we plan to take Carlo out to supper at one of our favorite places?"

"I'd love it, and I'm sure Carlo would too. I wish there was time enough to visit the salon."

"There is, darling, if that's your desire."

"Not without me," Carlo said. "After all, I want to see the place I'll manage."

Stan, practical as always, said, "I've some work to do at the office. I'll pick up both of you at the salon at seven. All right?"

"Will you go off by yourself, darling, or will you wait for us?"

"I'd better get back as soon as I can. We're studying ways to counter the Black Hand. They're getting active again."

"Black Hand?" Carlo asked, puzzled by the term.

"They're a band of extortionists. Recently they kidnapped the five-year-old son of a wealthy family and they were paid ten thousand dollars to let him go unharmed."

"Why are they called Black Hand?" Carlo asked.

"Because they send their demands in notes signed with the imprint of a hand in black ink," I explained. "Thank heavens they haven't approached our place yet."

"If they do," Carlo said ominously, "they'll find trouble they won't be able to handle."

"Don't be too sure of that, Carlo," Stan warned. "They're a formidable gang who don't hesitate to murder. So far they prey on their own people, small storekeepers, families with a little money in the bank. This kidnapping is the first time they've overstepped themselves since the

303

massacre in 1893. That stopped them for a while but, like everything else, the memory of that night has faded."

"A vigilante group killed eleven of them," I told Carlo.

"Maybe that's what should be done again," Carlo declared ominously.

"My uncle," I told Stan, "is bloodthirsty and, perhaps, with reason. Let's just hope we won't become involved with such things. If you're a bit late picking us up at the store, darling, don't worry about it. We'll have a great deal of business to discuss."

Carlo was fascinated with the street merchants crying out their wares, though he sniffed with disapproval at the dresses worn by many of the women. But he did admire the store as the carriage came to a stop. Once inside, he completely forgot his aches and became fascinated by what he saw.

I introduced him to Suzette who was still in a state of high excitement at the anticipation of being transferred to New York.

"Carlo will give you all the details you'll need to know," I told her. "At the same time, you can show him around here while I look over the mail."

"Oh yes," Suzette said. "A strange man came . . . two, three days ago. He said he was a friend and he left a note for you. It's in an envelope on your desk."

I turned Carlo over to Suzette and went to my office. I didn't realize how much I missed it until I sat down at my desk. I loved both the salon and the city. A moment later my happy mood was shattered. I opened the unmarked letter and removed the single page. On it was a brief message that made my heart pound.

Of course you remember Emile! I wish to thank you for writing to your father. When the letter was returned to you because he was not known at the address, I realized you told me the truth and you are ignorant of where he is. But we will find him, never fear. And one day I will come back to see you.

Emile

304

I tried to forget the note, but it spoiled an otherwise pleasant day. I worked on the books, added a few strokes of my pen to a sketch for a new evening gown, answered some business mail and ended up feeling tired. I felt the strain from the journey and lay down on a couch Suzette had thoughtfully provided. I wondered if she suspected.

Stan came for Carlo and me just before eight. I said nothing about the letter from Emile until we had finished our supper and the men were on their cigars and brandy while I sipped my sherry.

"It would be interesting to learn how he found out the letter came back undelivered," Stan observed.

"Yes," I said.

"Why did he admit it?" Carlo asked. "If he has some way to examine your mail, he would have been wiser not to reveal the fact that he could get at it. What does he mean by that last sentence?" Carlo scrutinized the letter again. " 'I will come back to see you.' "

"He has sworn that some day he will possess me," I said frankly.

"Darling," Stan said softly, though anger colored his face, "if you see this man anywhere, get help and have him held if possible. I'll see that he spends so many years in prison you'll never need fear him again. That is, if I don't kill him."

"Who is he?" Carlo asked. "How is he mixed up in this?"

"He's trying to find Papa and Mama," I said. "He's part of the plot. That's all I know about him, but I'm more afraid of him than of any other man alive."

Stan said, "Tomorrow, give me a full description of him and I'll have the detectives who are posted at the railroad station and the docks keep an eye out for him."

"I'll do that," I said. "I'll have it for you tomorrow. Now let's talk about something more pleasant. My return to New Orleans hasn't been exactly something to celebrate."

"The most pleasant subject in New Orleans today is the Mardi Gras," Stan said. "Which takes place in two days. You're going to see the city transformed into a miracle of color and excitement. From tomorrow on you might as well close up the store. There's very little business done except that concerned with the carnival."

"Then the salon is concerned," I said. "We're still making up at least a score of costumes which were ordered a bit late. Mine is ready. As I told you, darling, I shall go as a Dutch milkmaid with wooden shoes, pigtails . . . everything. Did you get your costume yet?"

"I've had it since last year," Stan explained with a chuckle. "You don't throw away those things after a single use."

"Unless you are a woman," Carlo added. It was the right comment to lift our spirits. Except that Emile's note, in my handbag, seemed to weigh heavily.

Carlo would obtain his costume in the morning. Stan would go as a pirate and when he described his outfit, I couldn't help but feel sorry for him.

"You'd have gone riding on the most important float, dressed as King of the Mardi Gras," I said. "Oh, Stan, I'm sorry I spoiled that for you. I've been here long enough to know what a great honor it is."

"Don't fret," Stan said. "I'd far rather have you than be king. Besides, I'd have to wear tights and my legs are skinny and knobby. No! It's better this way. Besides, all the real fun is in the crowd, not on the float. We'll attend the ball, however, because I still hold enough importance to get in."

"Not if your mother or Mary-Lou is present," I said flatly. "I don't want any more encounters with them or anyone."

"They'll be there, but masked, as we will be. I know what Mama will wear and I can steer us away from her at unmasking time. You'll enjoy the ball, Angela. And so will you, Carlo. I'll get you in."

"I shall enjoy it," Carlo said. "If I am masked, I cannot be held accountable. It's a very nice idea. I'll probably go as a bolero dancer. The costume is seductive. And a beautiful lady is always a challenge to me."

"Please," I cautioned, "note first if she is wearing a wedding ring. Many duels were fought here over a lady's honor."

Carlo nodded. "I knew there were savages here."

Stan laughed, though his words to Carlo were serious. "We hold our wives in high esteem, Carlo. Be wary."

"I shall be," he replied. "I've taken enough abuse for awhile."

SIXTEEN

Until the morning of Mardi Gras, I was too busy to think of anything but the salon. I had a number of last-minute costumes to get out, besides several ball gowns. I had my own costume to make ready and I had to supervise alterations in the outfit Carlo had procured.

Everything else was closed. It was, it seemed, the most important day of the year in New Orleans. And news of it seemed to have spread, for people were here from all parts of the nation. Hotels were sold out weeks in advance, private homes took in boarders at handsome rates. People even slept in wagons and cooked their meals in the open.

But aristocratic New Orleans went about its preparations without a hitch. The floats were ready, the ballrooms prepared, bars began a flourishing business at dawn and never stopped until the last straggler went home.

"The whole idea," Stan explained, "is to go about the streets, kissing everybody you fancy. Wait for the parade and when it comes by, be sure to duck the souvenirs which are thrown from the floats. Some of them are rather big and made of metal. There have been fist fights when the man on the float happens to hit the wrong person with one of the larger objects. Then, after the parade, it's dinner. A long one with so many courses you stop counting. Finally, there's the ball when the king appears and walks down the aisle to meet his queen. It's an elaborate, colorful ceremony. It's the Comus Ball, the most important of all."

"If the king has good legs," Carlo said.

Stan chuckled. "Believe me, I'm not sorry I lost the honor. Now if we'll all get costumed, we can go about celebrating."

My costume was more cute than elaborate. A Dutch cap on my hair, center-parted and braided, with the braids brought to the front and resting on my shoulders. I wore a white apron over a colorful Dutch dress with heavy white cotton stockings, a fine idea because the weather contained a chill. I decided to wear square-toed shoes instead of wooden ones, which might go well with the costume, but be impossible to dance in.

Carlo, resplendent in his Spanish bolero outfit, was going to conquer a few hearts, especially after the unmasking at the ball. Stan, as a pirate, would have plenty of company, I presumed. A whole frigate's crew of pirates was bound to be on hand, for the costume was popular.

I resolved that this was one day when I would think of nothing but having a fine time. A carnival spirit came over me as we came to the already crowded street along which the parade would pass. I knew I'd have little opportunity to enjoy something like this again for a long time. After this holiday I intended to begin taking things easy and work lightly, so the carnival was like a last fling. Which was exactly what it was meant to be, for in the morning would begin the lean days of Lent.

I maintained a firm grip on Stan's arm. Soon the crowds became so dense that Carlo vanished somewhere in the midst of them. Stan steered me into a crowded cafe. There were no empty tables, but he approached a man at the door, spoke to him, and a table was found somewhere and set up for us. It was isolated too, so some of the hubbub and noise was reduced.

"No sense overdoing it," Stan said. "The parade is apt to be long and when you get tired, we'll find a place to sit down. Will it be a julep?"

"No, darling," I said happily. "I'd rather have a sazarac. I'll not cater to my so-called delicate condition. This is a day for fun and I intend to have my share of it."

"Good for you." He approved the idea, then added, "Up to a point."

"For just one moment," I said, "let's go back to our troubles. Do you think Emile could be here?"

"Since everyone is masked, it's possible. He might be sitting at the next table."

I shuddered. "I wish I hadn't brought it up. Stay close to me, darling. Don't let me roam. I want you at my side all the time."

"I'll do my best," he said, "but when the bands come by and the dancing begins, you may be claimed by anyone."

"I don't wish to dance with anyone but you," I said. "I can't help it, Stan. I've a feeling something is going to happen."

"Not if I can help it. I even doubt Emile would try anything here—the crowds are too great. Even masked and in costume he'd have a hard time getting away. You may not know it, but in this pack of merrymakers are as many policemen as we could round up. Some even came down from Baton Rouge and other cities to help out. They're in costume too, some of them, and along with those who remain in uniform, they're all watchful. If anything happens, yell. The chances of one of them hearing you and recognizing it as a cry for help are very good. I wouldn't worry. Get into the spirit of Mardi Gras and have a good time."

"I'll do my best. As you say, Emile wouldn't have an easy time of it."

"Besides," Stan added, "how does he know who you are? How can he pick you out?"

"Of course. I'm being silly. Let's finish our drinks and go back to the crowd. I've made up my mind not to be afraid any more. I wonder where Carlo went."

"We'll likely not see him again until the ball. He'll find us. My pirate costume and Carlo's Spanish outfit seem to be very popular."

We reached the street and I looked about. The crowds were now all over the street, thicker than ever, and there was much horseplay and some impromptu dancing. One man seized my arm to claim me for a dance, but Stan said something and the man desisted at once.

"You're right about the pirate and bolero costumes," I said, "but I would say the most popular of all is the toy soldier. They seem to be everywhere."

Stan stopped to look about. "You're right," he agreed. "I just counted four . . . no, five . . ."

"Behind you are two more," I said. "I can see why they're popular. They're so colorful. And they fit as if they really are soldiers. The red coats and the blue striped pants, and the silly helmets with the feather. Oh, there . . . to your right. Who can that haughty-looking woman be in her Napoleon court gown? And the tiara. When the sun hits it, you'd think those are real diamonds."

"I'm not sure," Stan said. "She could be . . . my mother. She usually wears something like that. But no— she wouldn't be on the street. That's not for her. She'll be at the ball and she'll be wearing real diamonds. One of these times she's going to be robbed. It's happened at these balls, even on the street. Anything that draws big crowds also draws thieves."

"They wouldn't dare rob the prosecuting attorney."

"Not if they knew who he was. I'm just another pirate when I wear the mask. Did I tell you the mask you have on is very attractive and it shines like diamonds with all those stones you had sewn into it?"

"Thank you, darling. Oh look—two more toy soldiers," I exclaimed.

The sound of music from a strolling band grew louder and the dancing became more prevalent. Stan took me in his arms and I abandoned myself to the fun and the pleasure of dancing with my husband.

Within the next ten minutes I found myself dancing with a clown and then a robust gentleman dressed as a southern planter. How it all happened, I didn't quite know. The street was so crowded that Stan must have let go of me for an instant and I was swept into the arms of another dancer. I was nervous, though really I shouldn't have been. It was all in the spirit of Mardi Gras fun and the men who held me were perfect gentlemen. But there was too much anonymity around me. Anyone could be Emile, for instance.

Then, when I had managed to frighten myself thoroughly, I saw Stan, not dancing, but wandering about, searching for me. Without a word of apology to my startled partner, I pushed him away and edged through the crowd until I heard Stan's cry of relief and I was in his arms.

311

"Oh, darling, I was scared," I said. "How did we become separated like that?"

"I don't know any more than you do. All of a sudden I was dancing with a woman so drenched in perfume I'm still slightly giddy from it. Are you growing tired?"

"A little. The crowd is getting so thick."

"In half an hour or so, the parade will come by. I've an idea. I know who lives in most of these houses. I'm going to try and move to the banquette."

"The banquette?" I asked.

"I guess you've not been here long enough to know that's what the sidewalks are called. Anyway, if we can reach one of those houses down the street, we may be able to get inside and watch the parade from the gallery. It's also a fine place to see everything."

Even as we struggled through the crowd, I had to resist several attempts to get me to dance. Finally, Stan pushed open one of those grilled iron gates to a spacious patio.

"Stan," I asked in wonder, "how did you do that? Aren't those gates kept locked?"

"I'll confess," Stan said. "This is my mother's house. I brought along the key in case we wanted to use it."

I held back. "Stan . . . she hates me."

"She's not here. I swear it. She always takes charge of some of the goings-on at the main ball. We'll have a box seat to the parade. Nobody will be home. The servants take off. You couldn't pay them not to join the fun."

Stan led me into a large, exquisitely furnished drawing room. He gave me little opportunity to observe much more than the somewhat staid-looking family portraits adorning a wall.

The reception hall was spacious too, with a single huge chandelier hanging just above the base of the curved staircase. As we ascended it, we could hear the sound of lively music coming closer. Once we reached the gallery, Stan's arm enclosed my waist and he urged me on. Obviously he wanted us to see the parade from the beginning.

Entrance to the white-painted grillwork gallery was through a large, high-ceilinged bedroom. We stepped outside and the deafening noise of the crowd again made my ears ring. One minute later the first float came by. It was a lovely creation of flowers amongst which were pretty girls posing like statues. Stan stood at the rail, but I sat in one of the many rockers which adorned the gallery. The float was followed by a band, a large one, its members in gaudy uniforms. The dancing had stopped for the duration of the parade, but Stan assured me it would begin again after the last float passed by when people crowding the banquettes would spill over into the street again.

The parade was quite long and Stan finally sat down beside me. I felt like a princess seated in regal splendor to witness the entire festivities. It went on until the afternoon began to fade into evening. The last float was that of the king. He sat atop a throne, high on a lumbering wagon drawn by twelve white horses. He wore ermine, or something that resembled it. He carried a scepter, wore a crown somewhat atilt, and he kept hailing the crowd with sweeping gestures.

"That's Billy Enders," Stan said. "I think he's had a little too much cognac, but he'll survive. If he gets too drunk they'll dunk him into a tub of cold water."

"Darling, that's where you would have been except for me. You'd be riding that float sitting on that big throne. Oh, I did spoil it for you."

"Tomorrow," Stan said lightly, "nobody will remember who the king was. Mardi Gras is strictly for fun. Enjoy it, darling. Are you rested?"

"Yes. Very much so." I put my mask in place for we'd both removed them as they were inclined to be quite warm.

Stan said, "The time between now and the start of the ball is going to be noisy and rough. Stay close to me. Keep your hand in mine all the time. If we get separated, we'll never find each other."

"I'll do my best," I said as I stood up. "Stan, look—the toy soldiers again. It certainly is a popular costume."

"I thought the pirates would outnumber all the others," Stan commented.

He led me back into the house. This time I had a better opportunity to observe how grand it was. Stan's family had been here a long time. The paintings attested to that, and

313

the family must have been illustrious in the days when the city was founded and beginning to grow. This was, I judged, the home of French aristocrats before the whole area was sold to the United States.

"It's a lovely house, Stan," I said.

"Yes," he agreed. "Though it wasn't much fun to grow up in. It reminds me of a museum, on a small scale. As a boy I resented the perfection Mother insisted on. Every stick of furniture had to be dusted each morning and I was not permitted to lay a hand on any flat surface or to sit in any of the petit-point chairs. Mother had her rules and they were to be obeyed."

"How long has your father been dead?"

"Since I was sixteen. He wasn't like Mother. He enjoyed laughter and good times. Well, Mother loves to entertain. So long as the guests maintain a proper decorum which means an almost formal behavior. If one gets out of line, he is not invited again. So Mother usually has no trouble, for she entertains infrequently and her invitations are sought after."

We headed for the double doors which opened on to the street. Before Stan could open one, I placed a restraining hand on his arm.

"What is it?" he asked.

"Would you object if I paid your mother a visit?"

"Darling, I don't want you hurt. Especially now."

"I'm willing to risk it. Perhaps when she learns about the baby—the likelihood of her becoming a grandmother —she'll change. I don't like the thought of having come between you and your mother."

He nodded slowly. "It would make things less difficult all around. I'll go with you. I don't want you hurt at this time."

"No!" I objected promptly. "Let me go alone. Right after Mardi Gras I will pay her a visit. If she refuses to see me, at least I have tried."

Stan said, "It'll take a great deal of courage, but I know you have that. All I can do is wish you luck."

"Then that's settled," I said. I slipped my hand through his and said, "Now let's join the fun."

We stepped out directly onto the banquette to merge

with the crowd now once again engaged in boisterous romping. They'd been well-behaved during the parade, at least for the most part, but now it was time for un-restrained joy.

Stan's arm encompassed my waist in a protective gesture. There was no use in trying to carry on a conversation. The din was too loud and too general. I felt light-hearted, free-spirited. I wanted to join in on the fun. I had a fine husband who loved me as dearly as I loved him. I had a business more successful than I'd dreamed it could be, and I was going to become a mother. It was a complete picture, distorted only by my anxiety over the fate of my parents. Some jostling around us caused us to be separated.

Before I could call Stan's name there was a hard tug on my arm. Suddenly I was pulled into a spacious doorway to a darkened opera house lobby. I couldn't even see who did it. Before I could offer any resistance, a man in the costume of a toy soldier had me in his arms and moved me back into the street.

I tried to fight him, but he was strong and I was unable to break his hold on me.

"Angela," he whispered, with his lips close to my ear. "My dear, don't struggle so. I won't harm you. Just dance with me."

I drew a sharp breath. I tried to make out the face behind the large mask. I found my hopes soaring to the heavens, but I didn't dare give way to them, though I did stop struggling.

"You have grown into a lovely young lady," he said. "I'm as proud of you as your mother is."

"Papa?" I asked in a whisper. "Papa . . . is it you?"

"Yes, Angela. How I've longed for this day when I could take you in my arms. The last time was when you were still a little girl. At Aunt Celestine's. Do you remember?"

All doubt left me. I brushed his cheek with my lips and I hugged him. I was filled with joy. "Papa . . . oh, Papa, I don't know what to say. What about Mama? Is she all right?"

"Yes. She is here too, and right now she's looking at

you and I wish she didn't smile so broadly. We've enemies everywhere and they might correctly interpret that smile. Ah, she's lost it. I think she also realized what she was doing."

"I want to talk to her."

"I'm afraid that's not possible. My dear Angela, we know how difficult it's been for you. Thank you for understanding. We beg forgiveness for what you've been through because of us."

"For what I've been through. What of you two? Papa, tell me what this is all about."

"At this time I cannot. I wish I could. I'm risking much just to be here. I felt it was worth the chance to talk to you. To warn you and advise you to be cautious."

"Papa, what of my husband? It seems to me we were separated deliberately."

"You were," Papa chuckled. "He's a good man, that one. He's been told what's going on and I'm sure he approves. In a little while, you'll be back in his arms."

"I'd rather be in yours," I said. "For now, anyway. Tell me all you can, Papa. I want to know where you've been, where you're going."

"Your mother and I have been everywhere, it seems. One day it may be possible to tell you the whole story but for now, I cannot. Please try to understand."

"I do, Papa. I know it's something very serious, even dangerous that you're faced with. But try to dance me to where Mama is. I just want to touch her."

"My dear Angela," he said softly, "we've longed for you. We took risks to come to your exhibit here. I saw your painting of your mother and it's beautiful. She saw it too, but of course you know that. They almost had us that time."

"She was in that patio, wasn't she?"

"Yes. How did you guess?"

"I saw the wet prints of her shoes leading out through the gate."

"She wondered. I'll tell her how observant and clever you are."

"Clever? No, Papa. I'm not very clever. And I'm frightened. For you and Mama."

"I know. That's why I can tell you so little. They are trying to find us through you. They will do their utmost to force us to come into the open. So far we've not done so. So if you know nothing about us, where we are, or what we're doing, who our friends are . . . then they cannot make you reveal anything."

"Yes, Papa, I understand."

"I wish you didn't have to go through this. We sent you away, sacrificed the best part of bringing up our lovely daughter, to save you all this. But they discovered where you were. They—murdered Aunt Celestine, damn them."

"Did she know where you were and what this was about all the time?"

"She was as ignorant as you, dear Angela. I heard they tried to make her tell what she didn't know, and then they killed her. One day they'll pay for that."

"May it come soon," I said fervently.

"I notice you wear the ring."

"Of course. You told me to."

"Do you regard it as magic?" His lips parted in a smile.

"Well, yes," I said. "Certainly it's performed wonders for me. Is it really magic?"

"Continue to regard it as magic and it will continue to perform as it has in the past. One thing more about the ring. If you ever see a duplicate on the finger of another, trust that person. Do you follow me?"

"Yes, Papa. I don't dare look. Are we close to Mama?"

"Lower your right arm and reach out for a second. Do it as if it's just an accidental contact. Now!"

Cool fingers closed around my hand. A voice whispered in my ear. "We love you, daughter. Be brave."

Then the contact was lost and Papa danced me away into the thick of the crowded street. For a few minutes I was content just to be held by him and I hated to have the mood break. Almost all my life I'd waited for this moment. I looked up into his deep brown eyes, visible even behind the mask.

"This day I'll never forget, Papa. Please tell Mama what I said and that I love her too."

"She knows that, daughter. We're proud of you and all

317

you've accomplished." He chuckled and held me tighter. "How close you came to finding me in Paris. I had little more than a look at you before you saw my reflection in the mirror. I had to run—because I didn't know if you were being watched."

"Papa," I said, "is it true that you will come to me soon?"

"We hope so, your mother and I. We can't be sure, but matters are beginning to go our way. The trouble is that we never can be sure."

"You took a great risk in coming."

"Yes, but your mother wouldn't have been content to let this rare opportunity go by. Masked and in costume, among so many thousands also masked and dressed in all sorts of ways—well, we expect to get away with it."

"Please don't leave me yet. There's so much I want to know."

"I think I can risk another few minutes. I've seen no one apparently interested in us. Not yet. They won't know me, but they know your Dutch girl costume and if we dance too long, they might guess I'm not just some stranger who took you away from your husband."

"Will you and Mama be able to get away safely?"

"I think so. There's not much more time. What do you wish to ask me?"

"Do you know Emile?"

"I know of him and what he has done. I'm sorry we could not stop him. He is an evil man."

"What of Vito Cardona, who used to be an officer in the *Carabinieri?*"

"My dear, all I can say is, trust no one. Not even those you are sure of."

"I'll remember that. May I tell Uncle Carlo you and Mama were here?"

"Not even Uncle Carlo. If he knows nothing, he can tell nothing."

"Is that why he's been beaten so badly? So many times? To make him tell where you and Mama have been hiding?"

"It's possible. I don't know. To be entirely safe, do as I say. Trust only your husband. I shall dance you back to the opera house lobby where we met. Another man will take you in his arms. Don't fight him."

"Then let me say only this," I said. "You and Mama should know and it does my heart good to tell you. I am going to have a baby."

He drew a sharp breath. "I wish this good news were not so. I am overjoyed, but also afraid. It gives them just another way to reach out in our direction. Take good care of our grandchild, Angela. And now it's time to say good-bye. Not for too long I trust and hope."

He bent his head and touched my cheek with his lips. He tightened his hold on me into a warm, affectionate embrace. Then we were across the banquette and into the lobby. It all happened so fast, it seemed unreal. One second I was in Papa's arms. I seemed to slip from his embrace into the arms of someone dressed exactly like him. Once again I was swept out into the crowd. Suddenly I was aware of all those men in the costume of a toy soldier, closing in from all sides and then, just as suddenly they seemed to be gone.

"Do I know you?" I asked the man who danced with me.

He didn't reply but he held me tighter, as if he expected I might break away from him. Suddenly I was afraid of this man. I knew Papa had slipped out of my embrace to allow this man to hold me, but I was still frightened. Why hadn't he let Stan dance with me? How did Papa know who this masked man was?

Someone bumped against us. The man who held me stiffened. Then, with a groan, he slumped against me. I tried to support him, but his weight was too great. As he started to fall, my fingers encountered something moist. I felt the man's knees buckle beneath him. He was going down. There was no way I could support him. He was out of my arms now. My right hand slipped away from him and when I saw it, I stared in amazement. My hand was drenched with blood. At the same time that I threw my head back and screamed, the man fell to the pavement.

Strangely, no one seemed to be upset, and then I knew —they must have considered that he was drunk. I looked about. The men in toy soldier costumes had all vanished. I saw Stan shoving aside people to get to my side. By the time he reached me, I was kneeling beside the man who had been my partner. As Stan knelt, I removed the man's mask.

"Vito!" I shouted. "It's Vito!"

Stan moved me aside, tore open the toy soldier costume and placed his head against Vito's chest. He looked up at me.

"He's alive. We need help quickly."

Stan stood up, removed a silver whistle from a pocket and sent its shrill note loudly above the sounds of the revelry. Others realized something desperate and unusual was going on. When masked, costumed men scattered some of the crowd in an effort to reach us, people got out of the way. Two uniformed policemen appeared. Stan gave crisp orders and the pair went off, their batons held over their heads as if to threaten anyone who didn't move out of their way.

"Is he badly hurt?" I asked.

Stan said, "I'm afraid he is. Are you certain this is the man you know as Vito?"

"Stan, you saw him before."

"I only want to be positive. Can you identify him without any doubt?"

"Of course. Stan, don't let him die. I don't even know what happened."

"He was stabbed in the back," Stan said.

"Stabbed?" The grim reality told the story. "They thought he was . . . my father."

"Yes, they did. No question about it. By now they know they made a mistake."

" 'They'! Again it's 'they.' It's always 'they'."

"I know. I know that, Angela. That's how it has to be for now. I can assure you these people I call 'they' are not far off. They never are. Stay at my side. Don't move away whatever you do."

"Vito . . . he looks so awful . . . aren't you going to do anything?"

"I sent for an ambulance. That's all I can do."

"Is he going to die?"

"I don't know. From all the blood he lost, it must have been a deep wound, done with a very sharp knife." He drew a handkerchief from his pocket and handed it to me. "Your hands, Angela. . . ."

I gasped at the sight of the blood, on both hands now. I wiped as much off as I could. I bent down and talked into Vito's ear.

"Please, Vito, hang on. Please . . . help is coming. Angela is with you."

I placed my hand against his cheek. It was so cold. He made no reply. I knew he was unconscious. I breathed a prayer for him.

I thought of Papa. That heightened my terror. "Stan, did he get away? You know who I mean."

"Apparently, or we'd have heard more commotion than this."

The distant clang of the ambulance bell was scattering the crowd. The ambulance couldn't go fast. There were too many people, some of them reluctant to move, regarding all of it as just a part of Mardi Gras. The season when everyone was mad.

Then it drew up beside us and Vito was carefully lifted onto a stretcher and placed aboard the vehicle. The driver pulled an upright lever that rang the bell loudly. He used his reins to get the horses into motion and he kept the bell clanging as the ambulance headed for the hospital.

"Stan, I want to follow him. Please. . . ."

"All right. The hospital isn't far. We'll have to walk. Only an ambulance could get through this crowd, and even that almost didn't make it. Come, darling. Leave your mask in place."

He grasped my hand, helped me to my feet and led me to the outskirts of the crowd, where it thinned out enough that we could walk faster. There was no one pressing close to us now and we could talk as we walked rapidly down the street.

"All those men in soldier costumes were meant to confuse anyone who tried to stop Papa. They were all on our side, isn't that so?"

"So I presume. I wasn't in on any of this. It was all as much of a surprise to me as it was to you."

"Vito changed places with Papa," I said. "Oh, why didn't he just let Papa get away? There was no cause for Vito to sacrifice his very life. . . ."

"Angela, if Vito had not danced you into the crowd so whoever watched would think your father was still dancing, your father might not have gotten away. It was all a well-planned scheme to give your father a few minutes with you. Did he explain anything?"

"Nothing. Mama was there too. I managed to clasp her hand, but that was all. Papa said it would be too dangerous if I spoke. Stan, who are these people? These murderers! Do you realize Vito deliberately drew their attention?"

"Of course I do."

"I told Papa I was going to have a baby."

"I expected you would. Perhaps that news will comfort both of them."

"Papa said . . . now they have something more to strike against."

"How well I know," Stan said grimly. "We'll have to take every precaution to see you are not placed in danger."

He stopped talking to lead me up the wide stairs to the wooden building that was the city hospital. There were uniformed police all about and I noticed that some had followed us quite closely.

We were taken in charge by a young doctor who led us to the second floor. There we entered an emergency room to find Vito stripped to the waist, lying on his stomach and still unconscious while a doctor carefully probed the wound with a silver instrument. He withdrew it, studied the distance the blade had pierced and shook his head.

Stan said, "I'm Talbot, the city prosecutor. How is he? What chance does he have?"

"It's not easy to say, Mr. Talbot. It's a deep wound. If it was made with a blade not dangerously infected, he may have a chance. I'm not sure yet what organs were pierced. We'll determine that shortly. There's one thing in this man's favor. Look at the muscles on his back and shoulders. He's in excellent physical condition and that means a great deal."

322

"Doctor," I asked, "how long will he be unconscious?"

"Long enough for us to make our needed determinations, I hope. Please. That's all for now, if you want this man to live."

"Doctor," Stan said, "it's of the utmost importance that he lives. This was no ordinary knifing. It was an attempted assassination. Do the best you can."

"You may wait if you like. As soon as we finish and get him into bed, you may see him. He'll wake up by then."

Stan and I walked the length of the long hospital corridor to stand at windows overlooking the street where the crowds were as noisy and intense as ever. All the pleasure had gone out of the celebration for me now. We found chairs and sat down. I wished the unholy racket from the street would cease, but I supposed all the patients in this hospital wished the same thing.

"If only I knew the meaning of this," I said. "The reason behind it. Will it ever stop, Stan? If they can do this, they can reach Papa and Mama. . . ."

"Not unless someone leads them, and so far as I know, nobody is aware of where your father and mother are at this moment."

"All we can do is wait. Pray for Vito, darling. Please!"

"I have been. We'll soon know how bad his condition is. As the doctor said, if no infection develops, he'll have a good chance. He is strong and in fine health."

"I hope so. Stan, do you realize that recently I suspected Vito of being in league with whoever is trying to kill Papa and Mama? It's true! Vito showed up too conveniently. While I regarded him with respect and affection, I still wondered why he gave up his career in Florence. Why he came here so unexpectedly and then disappeared again. I didn't know he was down here."

"We'll settle that question before long," Stan assured me. "As soon as he is able to talk, we'll find the answers. Right now try to relax and rest. We still have the ball tonight."

"Must we attend?"

"I think it's imperative that we do."

"Provided Vito is out of danger."

"Of course. Now rest."

I let my head touch his shoulder and, with his arm about me, I once again felt a sense of security. I closed my eyes and, while I didn't even doze, I could feel my strength coming back.

I wasn't sure how much time passed. The din from the street still prevailed, but glancing toward a window I could see that it was dark and street lights were now lit.

"How are you, darling?" Stan asked.

I raised my head. "Oh yes. Forgive me for being so preoccupied."

"You've maintained a remarkable calm. What you went through would make many women—especially in your condition—grow hysterical or faint."

"I must remain calm. I have our baby to think about."

"I do have a question I would like to ask."

"Of course." I gave Stan my full attention.

"When Vito was stabbed, did you notice who was behind him? I mean what costume the man wore?"

"No, darling. It happened so fast."

"I doubt anyone else noticed the assassin. I'm sure he was away before Vito started to fall."

"I felt Vito give a start and utter a moan. That was all. I didn't even know he'd been hurt until he began to fall to the ground and I saw the blood on my hands." I looked at them. They still bore traces of blood. "Stan . . . there must be somewhere I can wash."

Stan nodded and beckoned a passing nurse, who led me to a washroom where I scrubbed my hands and washed my face. When I left the washroom I saw that the doctor was with Stan.

"He's awake," the doctor told us. "He's weak, though I don't think he knows that. The knife missed any vital organs. I'd say now he has a good chance. No infection, no internal bleeding. If these do not develop, he'll be out of here in a week or so. You'd better go in and see him. He threatened to get out of bed and look you up if you don't."

Vito seemed pale and wan except for his eyes which flashed in recognition as we approached his bed. His voice was a sorry substitute for his usual strong delivery, but there was fire in him yet. It was easy to see that he entertained not the slightest doubt that he would soon be better.

"Vito," I said, as I bent down and kissed him on the cheek, "it was a brave thing you did. I shall never forget it. Never!"

"Brave? It was foolish," he said. "I should have been on guard. I was supposed to be protecting you."

"You can't fool me, Vito," I said. "You knew the danger of taking my father's place."

"Do you have any idea who tried to kill you?" Stan asked. "I'm speaking officially now."

"I never even had a glimpse of the man. Not even what kind of costume he wore."

"It was all cleverly done," Stan observed. "Those men in costumes the same as Angela's father wore stayed close to him so when he was ready to leave he could merge with them, and if the assassin or assassins realized there'd been a change and you had taken her father's place, they'd have a hard time identifying him with twelve to one chances against them."

"Clever, oh yes," Vito said with a sardonic smile. "Only they never realized I had taken the place of Angela's father so they thought that blade was being thrust into his body, not mine. The would-be murderer had only one chance, one strike with the knife because of the crowd all around us. I was lucky. One more stab and I'd have been finished. I don't remember falling. I was barely conscious of you trying to hold me up. What a dreadful weight I must have been on you. Were you injured?"

"No, Vito. I didn't know what had happened until . . . you fell."

"She saw to it no time was wasted," Stan said. "We had you on the way to the hospital within fifteen minutes."

"They tell me I'll be here for some time. I don't think so. What did they tell you?"

"Vito, you are not to rush this. You were seriously wounded. It is nothing short of a miracle that you are alive. I'll be very angry if you leave this bed without the full consent of the doctors."

"Right now I don't think I could sit up," Vito admitted,

and his voice was a trifle weaker, a signal we should be letting him rest. "If you don't mind, I'll have a little nap. Come back soon. Or don't leave at all. It would be nice to wake up and find you here, Angela."

"I won't promise," I said. "Because you need a great deal of rest. But as soon as they tell me you're stronger, I'll be here. I'll spend all the time you wish at your side."

"God bless you both," Vito managed as his eyes began to close.

"Good night," I said. I doubt he even heard me. Stan and I moved noiselessly out of the room. Once again Stan admonished the doctors to do all in their power for Vito.

We stepped through the hospital door and the racket came rushing at us again. Mardi Gras was still in full swing.

"Do you want to go home?" Stan asked.

"We have to," I reminded him. "I must change into my ball gown."

He looked chagrined. "Do you know I forgot about it?"

"I didn't. You're an important man in this city and the ball is the biggest event of the year. You must be present and as your wife, I must be well-dressed. Vito is being well cared for, which means I won't need to worry about him. So we are going to the ball."

Stan didn't appear convinced. "Thank you, darling. I don't quite know how to put into words my pride in your behavior today. But remember your condition. You should get some rest. There will be Mardi Gras balls for years to come."

"And we will attend them, darling, just as we will attend this one. If I didn't feel up to it, I would tell you. But think of it this way. Papa assured me that they were both well and considered themselves reasonably safe. It's the best news in the world, and even what happened to Vito can't change that."

"You're right, of course. About Vito. While I have no official word on this, I believe him to still be an active member of the Italian police and he was sent here to do what he could to protect both you and your parents,

326

and to locate and handle the people who are responsible for all the evil that's happened to you."

"So that's it," I said. "It explains his concern about work. It also explains why he was around often. Perhaps even more often than we were aware of. He is a true friend, darling."

"He's all of that. We'll be indebted to Vito the rest of our lives."

"How well I know."

"As for now, we must bear in mind there's a murderer somewhere in this crowd of masked people. By now he probably knows that, first of all, he made a mistake, and secondly, he didn't succeed even in killing Vito. He'll likely be a desperate man."

"What can we do?" I asked.

"I'll handle it," Stan said. He called a waiting carriage. "Take us to the police station," he ordered.

"Aren't we going to the ball?"

"Yes. But not until I arrange for a strong guard to be placed at the hospital."

The driver got to the station, though he had to make several detours to avoid the noisy street crowds. Once we were there, the arrangements to protect Vito were quickly made. After that, we returned home. Stan insisted I rest for an hour before dressing. I didn't protest. Once we reached the sanctity of our home, I discovered I was trembling.

I bathed and dressed, paying careful attention to my toilette, though my mind was on Vito and my parents. I thanked the Almighty I was no longer alone. I wouldn't have known how to cope with the danger all around us. I knew Stan was as much in danger as my parents and I were. Vito would be safe as long as he was in the hospital. I only hoped he would obey the doctors and remain a patient there for whatever time they deemed necessary.

I wore a maroon satin gown with lace trimming at the shoulders and around the waist. Ostrich feathers, dyed black, surrounded the off-the-shoulder neckline and succeeded in camouflaging my bosom, which I deemed necessary for my breasts were already swollen due to my pregnancy. Feathers decorated the edge of the hem. I had dispensed with a train, for two reasons. It would be a nuisance when it came to dancing, and it impeded one's progress. I still followed the freedom-of-movement idea when it came to clothes.

SEVENTEEN

Stan said, "First we'll make our way as close to the ballroom as we can. From there we can see Comus, the final parade. The big one ruled over by the king of all kings, King of the Comus Ball. The floats in this last parade are especially beautiful."

We watched as the first float came into view with the king seated atop his high throne, glittering scepter in hand, rhinestone-studded crown on his head, robed in what looked like ermine. These floats were lovely and the noise and excitement helped to dispel some of the terror which had overcome me only a few hours ago.

At the specified time, we entered the great ballroom and joined the ranks of those who stood in line to welcome the Comus King when he made his regal entrance. At the far end of the line, his queen sat in state, with a gown of rich white fabric studded with pearls and rhinestones. As someone who knew what such a gown cost, I wondered how the father of the queen ever found the money to pay for it. Her mantle alone was at least eight or nine yards long.

The king strode majestically down the aisle and his subjects bowed formally while he saluted them with his scepter, in grand style.

"You should be wearing that crown," I whispered to Stan.

"A crown on my head is nothing. You on my arm is everything. Remember that, my lovely wife, and enjoy this evening."

The formalities over, the dancing began, to end with a late supper. Stan pointed out his mother, richly dressed in the black lace of a Spanish senora. We danced quite close to where she was seated. I knew she recognized us despite our masks, but she deliberately turned away to look in the other direction.

Stan's hand covered mine, which rested on his arm. "Don't let her spoil your evening. You know what she is like. I would rather you didn't pay her a visit. I don't want you hurt."

I squeezed his arm reassuringly. "We'll see."

I was disappointed but not dismayed. And I had no thought of changing my mind about visiting Stan's mother, though I preferred Stan not know. I didn't want him worrying.

Stan and I cut our attendance short and we were driven back to the hospital where we discovered that Vito had not awakened from the sleep he'd fallen into before we left. But he was being watched and his condition was listed as stable. That was encouraging and so was the sight of the policemen stationed in and around the hospital. Any assassin with the idea of reaching Vito, or the man he believed was my father, would be promptly dissuaded by one look at all those uniforms. Truly, my husband could exert influence.

The following day Carlo and I walked to the hospital before going to the store. Carlo was aghast at learning Vito had been seriously injured during an attempt on his life.

"But why?" he asked. "Vito may have been a policeman in Europe, but not here. Maybe he's been getting himself mixed up with the wrong kind of people."

"To be truthful," I said, "I didn't even know it was Vito who was dancing with me when the attack happened."

"How did it happen?"

"I was dancing with Stan. All of a sudden this man pushed Stan in the lobby of the opera house on Charles Street, seized my hand, dragged me out to the street, and began dancing with me. I've no idea how he found out who I was, but he intended to surprise me. He certainly did."

"I don't see any reason why someone would want to kill him. Do you?"

"None. Perhaps he was mistaken for someone else. He

330

wore a toy soldier costume and they seemed to be very popular yesterday." I didn't like being deceitful with Carlo, but I felt it unwise to let him know about my parents. He might drink too much and talk.

"Maybe," Carlo said doubtfully. "I'm more inclined to think Vito has enemies we don't know about."

"Speaking of enemies," I said, "have you heard anything more from those people who all but killed you more than once?"

"No. They wouldn't let me know they were around. When they strike, I'm clubbed and dragged somewhere and beaten. I hope I never hear of them again."

"So do I. Now be nice to Vito. He's a sick man."

Carlo was carrying a paper-wrapped package. I didn't comment on it even when it accompanied him into the sickroom. Vito was sitting up. On a table beside the bed was a breakfast tray; apparently a rather substantial breakfast had been served to him and he appeared much more fit than he had last night.

"Bend down and let me kiss you," he said. "Carlo look the other way."

"You're being foolish," I told Vito as I kissed him gently. "That's good. It means you're feeling better."

"I feel fine except where the knife nicked me. That area hurts some and I have to be careful it doesn't start to bleed. Carlo, you look lovely."

"Lovely!" Carlo said defensively. "That's a word used to describe women. You may say I look handsome."

" 'Lovely' is the only way to describe a man who wears white shoes, cream-colored spats, striped pants and a reddish, long-tailed coat over a yellow vest. I'll admit that black derby looks well on you, but somber."

"You do tire me out sometimes," Carlo said. "Perhaps if you dressed better, you'd not get into this kind of trouble. People take you for a ruffian."

"That's what I am, essentially. Being well dressed hasn't saved you from being beaten. Angela, how did you survive the Mardi Gras?"

"Quite well," I said. "It was beautiful, Vito. I have never seen anything so elaborate."

"I've been told the parents of the queen of the principal

331

ball sometimes go into bankruptcy after the festivities are over."

"I can well believe it. She wore a gown I'd be reluctant to try and make for anything less than four thousand dollars, and that doesn't include the mantle which was a work of art in itself."

"Tell me something," Carlo broke into our light banter. "Why did somebody try to kill you?"

Vito eyed him impatiently. "Have you forgotten I used to be a policeman? Those of us who wore a badge made enemies."

"That follow you all over the world?" Carlo's tone was skeptical.

"There seem to be certain people who follow you about, Carlo," Vito replied.

Carlo nodded. "I'll not argue that. What I do not understand is how did they know you when you were wearing a mask?"

"I've no idea. If I did, I might find the man who is responsible."

"Why did you quit the *Carabinieri,* Vito?"

I thought it time to interfere. "Carlo, you ask so many questions you're acting like an interrogator."

"Well, I am curious. And I haven't forgotten that Florence hospital. Do you remember, Vito? Coming two or three times a day, to ask me a thousand questions. When I couldn't answer them, you grew angry—and worse—you insulted me." Carlo turned to me. "Now, dear niece, you know why I resent your dear friend."

"All right," Vito said with no loss of his good nature. "Now I'm in bed and you're asking the questions. Go ahead and insult me. Then we'll be even."

Carlo shrugged in defeat. "I'm no match for you, Vito. To be honest, I've come to like you. Only a little, remember, and that because you have been hurt and maybe you saved Angela from harm. It might well be the knife was meant for her."

Vito's eyes flashed. "That is not amusing, Carlo."

"I didn't mean it to be. Anyway, I've got to get to the store. I'll drop by again if I have the time and the inclination. Here's something to keep you company."

He handed the package to Vito and left abruptly, as if he was afraid of being thanked. It turned out to be a very expensive bottle of the finest cognac.

"Well," Vito said in surprise, "this one is a puzzler."

"Carlo talks a lot. Actually, he's a very sentimental man. Don't judge him harshly."

"Oh, Carlo's all right. Except that at his age he ought to know better than to spend most of his free time gambling, especially when he's so bad at it. The man loses his week's pay in half an hour sometimes."

"Vito, you must be wrong," I said. "Carlo pays his bills on time and he's never been in any financial trouble."

"Then he must allot a certain amount to gamble with and make sure he never carries the rest of his pay with him. Sit down, Angela. I don't recall our conversation too well last night. I was a bit fuzzy in the head. Was the Mardi Grass ball really exciting?"

"It was beautiful," I said. "There were many gowns there which I had designed. Fun and profit, that's what my evening consisted of. I enjoyed it once I was assured you were going to be in no danger."

"I'm glad what happened to me didn't spoil your evening."

"It would have been more enjoyable if you hadn't been injured. Did the doctors tell you when you might leave?"

He smiled. "If all goes well, I'll be out of here in two or three more days."

"I'm glad. Where will you go?"

"I've things to do," he said evasively. "Many things."

"You won't be too fit the first few days. You could stay with Stan and me."

"Thank you, that's very generous, but I won't leave the hospital until I'm completely well. Then I have to go elsewhere."

"Vito, I don't believe that you just gave up your position in the *Carabinieri*. You came here because you're trying to help protect my father. Tell me the truth! How can it do any harm?"

"My dear Angela, it would be harmful to me, to you

333

and especially to your father. And your mother. I admit no connection with them."

"I'm sorry I asked that question," I said promptly. "Will you remain after you're well?"

"Here in New Orleans? I may. Just now I'm not certain what I'll do."

"Stan said you would have no problem getting on the police force. If you're interested, he'll speak for you."

Vito raised my hand to his lips. "Thank him for me. I'll think about it."

"I must ask this," I said. "I hope you will answer. Is the danger to Papa and Mama any greater now?"

"Che cosa?" he asked.

"Very well, Vito. You don't hear the questions you don't want to answer. Now I know you are still a policeman and you always will be."

He smiled, but said nothing.

"I am going, this afternoon, to pay a visit to Stan's mother. She turned away from us last night at the ball, but she is his mother and she will be grandmama to our child soon and I hope it will soften her attitude toward me."

"That she-bear may eat you up," Vito warned. "I've heard of her."

"There's not much you don't hear about, is there? I'm glad of that. But she doesn't frighten me."

"Be sure to tell me how it goes. Or come if only to lick your wounds. Seriously, Angela, I wish you luck."

"Thank you, dear friend. I'll be back, if not today, tonight with Stan."

"Sì. Buono. I will be here."

I walked the distance to the store, enjoying the air and watching with interest the massive clean-up after the parades and the excitement. The city seemed so still this morning. Only the street cleaners were in evidence, though it was a business day. There were throngs around the churches, however, for it was Ash Wednesday, the first day of Lent. I also noticed two men in civilian clothes across the street. They had been keeping pace with me. They were police, evidence of Stan's handiwork in protecting me while he tried to prevent me from being worried.

334

Carlo was in full charge of the store, though there was little actual business except to make ready for the summer fashions which would soon be placed on display. We were already planning a fine showing for our best customers.

My work at the desk was brief, the mail contained only a report from Suzette and it was more sound evidence of her ability to manage the New York branch. I was truly fortunate in having met her.

I decided to omit my noonday meal for we'd eaten very late at the ball and there'd been food and drink in huge quantities. Instead, I called a carriage and gave the driver the address of Mrs. Talbot's home, from the gallery of which Stan and I had watched some of the parades.

I wanted to get this over with before I lost my courage and I prayed sincerely that this haughty woman would bend sufficiently so that we might at least have a friendly, if casual relationship.

The door was opened by a trimly dressed maid. She offered a silver tray and I placed my name card on it, though I had already identified myself verbally. She'd made no answer, though her eyebrows raised perceptibly. She ushered me into the stately drawing room and informed me it might take a few minutes.

Instead of sitting down, I wandered about the room, being especially interested in the oils adorning the walls on either side of the fireplace. I wasn't quite sure that I liked being a member of this austere, mirthless family. How grim the faces were! I had not seen many paintings of my own ancestors, but the few Aunt Celestine had owned revealed a gleam of interest in their eyes, a brow raised rakishly or a mouth meant for smiling.

The carpet under my feet was thick and very soft. The bare flooring beyond the limits of the carpet was of fine, highly polished dark wood. Knowing fabrics well, I recognized the curtains as coming from one of the best—and most expensive—factories in Belgium. The purple draperies, drawn back to display the beautiful curtains, were heavy and supported by ornate window hardware.

There were two large sofas and three small settees. I didn't count chairs, but there must have been a dozen overstuffed ones and as many straight-backed chairs covered in petit-point. Doilies were likewise of Belgian manufacture and the assortment of tables of various sizes and purposes were all mahogany. Two large chandeliers had been converted to electricity.

"Good afternoon," a quiet cultured voice spoke. I turned around. I hadn't heard Mrs. Talbot enter the room. I approached her with my hand extended, but I lowered it when she gave no indication she wished any physical contact with me. I was determined to remain calm.

She was taller than I, more fair skinned, and her eyes were the same shade of light blue as Stan's. Her face was narrower than his and she had the supple figure of a much younger woman. She was the kind of person who dominated everyone near her, whether purposely or by the very nature of her personality, which was strong.

"Good afternoon, Mrs. Talbot," I said. "May I sit down?"

"Certainly. Though I can spare you but a few minutes. I was not expecting you."

I had hoped she would sit down, but she maintained her regal stance before the fierplace.

Something began to churn inside me. "Mrs. Talbot, I am married to your son, your only child. It would be better for him, for me, and for you if you would be kind enough to meet us on even terms."

"I have no idea what you mean by that," she said, her voice icy.

"Then I shall inform you of the reason for this visit, but first I would like you to know that my father was a member of the House of Deputies in Italy, which conforms to your Congress. He was a banker, heading a large and highly successful bank. He was a graduate of the finest colleges in Rome. My mother came of a family devoted to sciences. Her father was a surgeon of considerable note. We lived in Florence, Italy, in a *palazzo*, which means a mansion not a great deal smaller than this house."

"Why should that interest me?" she asked coldly.

"Because your attitude is that of a person who believes herself to be on a social and economic pedestal

336

rising high above that of anyone else. I can inform you, quite candidly, that your family ancestry can go back no further than mine, nor were your people more illustrious. Personally I wouldn't care if Stan came of peasant stock and lived on a farm. I married a man, not a family history."

She said, "I abhor impudence. We will terminate this visit now, if you please."

"I abhor rudeness," I said. "Despite your breeding, you excel in it."

"Good afternoon." She turned, about to leave the room.

I managed a smile. "Not quite yet, Mrs. Talbot. There is yet another reason why you are entitled to know of my family background because mine—and yours—are going to be shared by my child—your grandchild."

She checked her departure abruptly and turned around. "You are with child?"

"Yes," I said.

"I see."

"No, you don't see," I said sharply this time. "My own father and mother are in some sort of enforced exile, for what reason I don't know. Not yet. My child will be born sometime this year and it is my fervent hope that he or she will be blessed by a grandparent. Since mine cannot come forward, there is only you. I had prayed you would possess the . . . shall I call it maternal instinct . . . to welcome this child into the world and to share with your son and me the pleasure we shall find in raising the baby."

She slowly closed her eyes and sighed deeply. I rose. "I'm sorry my prayers were not answered."

I walked past her toward the door. She hadn't moved as I spoke, nor opened her eyes.

"Angela!" She spoke in a low voice. I stopped and looked back. Her eyes were open. She sat down slowly. "Please don't go. I wish to talk further about this."

"Of course," I said. I walked back to resume the chair I'd just vacated.

"Are you aware that my son was engaged to another girl before he met you?"

"Quite aware, Mrs. Talbot. It was one of the first things he told me."

"As an Italian, perhaps you were not familiar with our social mores."

"If you are referring to daughters-in-law being selected by the man's parents, it's usual in Italy too. Far more so than here, and especially in the less-prosperous regions. It is an ancient problem which should have been eliminated a century ago. Or longer than that. It is, Mrs. Talbot, an abomination in a civilized world. Stanton and I fell in love almost upon sight. I know that is regarded as happening only in fairy tales, but I assure you our love was not the fairy-tale type."

"Can such an encounter have lasting effect, Angela?"

I smiled. I knew she was turning my way and I had to insure the continuance of this change. The best way was to shock her.

"Aboard that ship, soon after we met, Mrs. Talbot, we knew how much in love we were and before the ship docked, we consummated that love."

She regarded me somewhat stonily. "I see."

"Do you? Really? Stanton and I were parted the next morning, neither of us knowing where the other would be, depending upon meeting again before we went ashore. That was not to be. Stanton was called off the ship before morning. So we lost each other. For many months we neither saw each other or even knew where each of us was. I wrote one letter, addressing it to Stanton as an Attorney-at-Law in New Orleans, and I prayed for days it would reach him. It never did because someone in your son's office confiscated the letter, possibly at your request. So I received no answer."

She nodded, as if to acknowledge that she knew about the letter. I went on talking, with the intention of not losing the momentum my surprising announcement of being with child had created.

"I came back to the United States. I began a business of my own which flourished sufficiently to allow me to open a branch store in New Orleans. Before I even considered whether I would open the store or not, I went directly to your son's office. We beheld one another and in the space of a few seconds we each knew the other had never forgotten, never ceased to hope we would again

338

meet. Our love was renewed as quickly as it had begun aboard ship."

"Quite romantic," she said. "You and Stanton are both romanticists of course."

"Of course," I agreed. "You can rest assured that we are in love. None of this would have happened if Stanton had married the girl he was unofficially engaged to. So his life would not be one of contentment as it is now and her life would have been depleted, for she would have been a wife without love. At this moment, Mrs. Talbot, there are no two people in New Orleans, or anywhere else, more in love and happier than your son and I. If I have offended you with this long speech, I'm sorry. I said what was necessary. Whatever the outcome, it is up to you."

"You have confused me, Mrs. Talbot."

"I'm glad of that."

"You're a most unusual girl. Quite enterprising as well. I believed when I first entered your establishment with the purpose of demoralizing you, that I'd succeeded. Oh, not in upsetting you personally, but I thought—well— you'd not last out the month. But it didn't turn out that way. I'm going to confess something that once irritated me no end. You recall Mary-Lou?"

"Of course." I wondered what she had to do with this conversation.

"She . . . sent a friend with her exact measurements to buy a ball gown. She wore it at the Comus last night."

"I'm flattered. Mrs. Talbot, I know there are many dances and formal dinners held in this city and you are almost always in attendance at one or the other. May I make your gowns from now on?"

Her lips moved, her mouth began to lose its customary grimness. In a moment she was actually smiling.

"How beautiful you are," I said, and I meant it. That smile transformed her.

It was a false smile. "If you are trying to entice me into accepting you, Angela, it will not work. I cannot forgive you for taking my son away from me, nor my son for flouting my wishes."

I drew a long sigh. "Mrs. Talbot, I have not taken him away. You have sent him away. Can't you realize

339

that? He loves you dearly, if you would give him half a a chance. How you feel about me is not important, but how you feel about your son is another thing. Even more important than that, how you will feel when your grand-child is born."

"I love my son, Angela. I will love my grandchild. You have yet to earn my love, especially after your ad-mission of . . . of. . . . I'm sorry. I wish to terminate this talk."

She walked out of the room as I rose. When I reached the door, the maid was standing there with it open. She favored me with a semblance of a smile which I couldn't return. Apparently she'd overheard and did not exactly disapprove. I departed as disheartened as when I went in. Yet there'd been a few moments when I thought Mrs. Talbot was coming round. Now I felt sure that if the news of a grandchild didn't make her change, nothing would.

That night, over the supper table in our favorite restau-rant, I told Stan about my visit.

"For a moment I thought she was won over," I said. "Then she changed back, for some reason."

"I'm afraid inviting her to have her gowns made at your salon offended her. You probably implied that this would be at no cost, or she thought you did. Mother will accept nothing from anyone. I wish it had gone better, but at that I think you made some giant strides in dealing with her."

"She did seem concerned about the baby," I mused. "I think perhaps when the baby is born she may change. I hope so. You know, there was a moment when she ac-tually smiled and I thought she looked quite beautiful and I told her so. It didn't last long."

"Keep at it," Stan advised. "Now what's to be your schedule for the next few months? I know you can keep working for some time yet, but when you can't—then what?"

"I'll stay home and be lazy. Stan, we've never had a servant in the house because we're there so little, but that's going to change. I think we'd best have a maid to

340

sleep in. We've the room for her. And later on, probably a nursemaid."

"I'll look into it right away. Let me handle hiring the maid and the nursemaid later on. I want to be absolutely certain as to the qualifications of both, and especially their backgrounds."

"You're afraid that when the baby comes, it will be a tempting target for those people who are after Papa."

"Something like that. A baby makes a mighty powerful hostage and these people are ruthless."

"Papa thought the same thing," I told Stan. "Darling, nothing must ever happen to our baby. We must see the baby is protected always. Oh, I wish whatever keeps Mama and Papa away would cease to exist so they could come back and everything settle down to a peaceful life."

"I know exactly what you mean. Try not to worry about them. You've been through enough today."

"I've noticed you're in court more often these days, and you're even away in the evening a great deal. Is there that much crime in New Orleans?"

"There's more than we can handle, it seems. The Black Hand is increasingly active. We're trying to do something about it, but picking up the small fry isn't very productive. There were two murders last week—we think both were victims of the Black Hand."

"I'm not complaining, Stan," I said. "I'm going to be very busy myself. Easter is coming up and that's the season for new gowns. The orders have been coming in for a month and business is very good, and will be from now on until summer."

"Is Carlo handling it well?"

"Oh yes. He's really good at it. If a shy woman, for instance, enters the store, Carlo can put her at ease in no time. Before he's finished, she feels as if she's a princess. That sort of thing sells garments, darling."

"And Suzette in New York?"

"Doing better than ever. I've thought of going back for a visit and an inspection, but I've changed my mind. It's better if I don't try to do too much. If Suzette needs help, Carlo can go."

"After the baby is born and old enough for the nurse-maid to take in charge, we'll both go to New York and celebrate. I've thought about that for a long time."

"It may yet be a long time before we manage to go," I warned.

"The time will pass swiftly, my dearest. I'm sure of that."

EIGHTEEN

Stan was wrong. When I was compelled to stop visiting the store and confine my outings to brief walks, the time went by with painful slowness. And I slowed down too, which was probably what was really responsible.

Some days Stan was working fifteen and sixteen hours. He was in court all day and was occupied with extra work with the police by night. I knew he was worried about the way crime appeared to be multiplying and growing bigger in its operations. The Black Hand especially was functioning as if controlled by some expert in crime. The Italian colony was more close-mouthed than ever, refusing to cooperate out of plain terror.

I knew what that was. I was alone so much—even Emily, our new maid, was of little comfort to me—and my solitude brought back too many memories. As much as I longed for our child to be born, I was also afraid.

Stan knew this, though I tried not to mention my worries. Before I was due to enter the hospital, he hired a nursemaid, a compassionate and understanding middle-aged woman who was robust enough to put up a brisk fight if anything interfered with her charge.

Jennie Atkins proved to be capable and as warm and talkative as the maid was reticent. Jennie would be with me at the hospital and come home with me and the baby.

When Alexa was born, a seven-pound healthy little girl, everything else in the world stopped for me. It was not a difficult delivery and when my baby was brought to me for the first time, no such things as crime, Black Hand, a reluctant mother-in-law, or anything else, important or otherwise, existed. There was only Alexa, and Stan was as delighted as I.

All during my waiting time, Mrs. Liggio and her little daughter had called often to help me pass the time, as she put it. I was delighted to see her, not only because I regarded her as a good friend now, but we could talk in Italian.

Little Amorita had grown into an adorable child, doted on by her father and, as Mrs. Liggio put it, her reason for living. I looked forward to her visits. But another visitor was a complete surpise. On the third day of my confinement, Stan's mother walked into my hospital room. Without pausing a step she came directly to the bed, bent down and kissed me on the cheek. I was too startled even to smile or welcome her.

"That was for providing me with a grandchild." She kissed me again. "That is for driving some sense into my silly brain. I'm sorry for the way I behaved."

All I could say was, "I'm pleased, but I'm at a complete loss."

"You've a right to be. I came here merely to make a duty call. After all, my son is a rather famous man in this city. My friends would ask me about you and the baby, so I had to at least be able to tell them what the child looked like. My reason for coming was purely selfish. She's not very beautiful, I must say."

"Wait a few months," I said. My astonishment was slowly fading.

"Yes, of course. Stan was homely. Well, I came here with the ever-present chip on my shoulder. I asked to see my grandchild and she was brought to me. I needed one look and I seemed to melt inside. That little bit of human life taught me more than all the priests in this world could do. That's all I have to say. Don't you ever dare tell anyone I could make such a confession."

I held out my arms to her. "I'm glad, Mrs. Talbot. I wanted your friendship and good will more than anything, especially now, when we've something to share."

"When my son gets here, don't you tell him what a silly idiot I've been. Just let him know I'm no longer angry with him. And you might as well call me Clare. Though Alexa must call me grandma."

344

"Of course," I said. I couldn't wait to tell Stan every word she'd spoken. He'd be delighted.

"When will they bring the baby to you again? I'll stay here all day if I have to, but if they delay too long, I'll go out there and growl."

Though the baby was brought to me for nursing several minutes later, Clare remained most of the day. She was with me when Mrs. Liggio called and the two got along famously, though I suspected that only yesterday Clare would have frozen in anger if Mrs. Liggio were as friendly as she proved to be.

"Next time I bring little Amorita," Mrs. Liggio promised. "You be here, Mrs. Talbot, *si?* I wish to show that I too have a lovely child."

"I am sure you have," Clare said. "Tell me when you're coming and I will be here."

"Tomorrow afternoon?" Mrs. Liggio asked hopefully, looking across the bed at Clare.

"I intended to come. I'll be here. And I do think it's time for us to leave now. I've a carriage waiting. The poor driver must be put out with me . . . waiting all this time. I'll be glad to drop you off."

They left, chattering away, and I was happy for all of us. Stan would be too. And he truly was when he visited me that night. They gave him Alexa to hold and she slept contentedly in his arms.

"I'm not really surprised," he said. "My father wasn't the type to marry a perpetual grouch. I think his death embittered her. Anyway, I'm glad she finally relented."

"How's the salon going?" I asked. "Did you drop by?"

"Every day. Carlo complains about being too busy, but actually he turns most of the work over to the clerks and the seamstresses. I'd say your establishment is doing fine. Carlo told me letters from New York say business is better than ever."

"What of Vito?" I aked. "Is there any word from him?"

"None. He vanished. When he believed he was well enough—even before he should have been released, according to the doctors—he got up, dressed, paid his bill and walked out. He hasn't been seen or heard from since."

"Poor Vito. I owe him so much. I wanted him to see Alexa."

"He'll be back. I'm certain of that."

Stan kissed me and left. I had another visit with my brand-new daughter and then I fell asleep with the thought that my world was almost perfect. All it lacked was the presence of my father and mother. I had a strange feeling this dilemma was going to be over soon, one way or another. I shuddered a bit in thinking that things still might go wrong, but I had to trust in whatever forces had so far kept them from evil.

I rotated the ring around my finger, wondering if it was possible the ring had something to do with the favorable events that had happened recently. My brief conversation with Papa hadn't enlightened me very much on the influence of the ring, but he'd been frank enough that I doubted he attached any mystical powers to it. Especially when he told me anyone who came to me and displayed a similar ring could be trusted without question. That seemed strange, for I'd never seen a duplicate of that ring since I possessed it.

Normally the hospital was quiet in the morning. The doctors made their rounds and the nurses were busy changing linen and bathing the patients, but there were no visitors. It afforded me a few precious hours to catch up on newspapers and read the latest novels. I was in the middle of *The Call of The Wild* by Jack London, a dog story of the outdoors which was exciting, but more of a man's type. I had yet to begin *The Little Shepherd Of Kingdom Come,* by John Fox. That promised to be more my style.

I was actually dozing when I heard a scream, then a loud shout and the sound of running footsteps. There were more shouts and the beginning of a confusion that grew louder and louder.

Whatever possessed me to think my baby was in danger, I don't know, but I got out of bed, staggering a bit from weakness. At the door to the corridor I froze in absolute terror.

A nurse lay on the floor screaming. Another stood by uncertainly, a blanket-wrapped baby in her arms. Two

346

detectives, guns drawn, were chasing a man down the corridor, which ended in a large, at least triple-size window.

At their shouts to stop he looked back and I added my own cries to the confusion because the fear-ridden face I saw was that of Emile. I knew then that the baby in the arms of the nurse was Alexa and that Emile had been trying to kidnap her.

Suddenly he seemed to realize there was nowhere for him to go. The detectives were gaining on him and he knew it. With a last wild look behind him, Emile suddenly thrust out his arms to protect his face and dove headlong through the big glass window.

It made a dreadful noise, followed by a shrill scream from Emile. He had to be at least half-mad, or he'd forgotten that this was the third floor of the hospital.

The two men, detectives I assumed, turned and raced for the nearest stairway. The nurse holding the baby saw me and ran toward me. I took Alexa from her arms.

"That man must be insane," the nurse said. "It was so awful. He just seemed to appear from nowhere. I was bringing the baby to you for mid-morning feeding when he just—suddenly stood before me. He pulled the baby from my arms and when I screamed, he started to run. He must have thought there was a stairway at the end of the corridor because that's where he headed. Just then, Ellen"—she pointed to the nurse lying on the floor—"came out of one room and the man ran full tilt into her. He dropped the baby . . ."

"Is she hurt?" I asked anxiously.

"I don't think so. She was swaddled in a heavy blanket."

"We must find out if she was injured," I said. "Please get a doctor."

She followed me into my room, placed the baby on the bed, removed her blanket and clothing and examined her practically inch by inch while little Alexa cooed and enjoyed the attention.

"She's fine," the nurse said. "I'll have a doctor look at her now."

"Later. I'm satisfied she's not hurt. Go on with the story of what happened."

"Well, right after I screamed, two men—the two you saw chasing the man—they came out of a room and ran after him. I guess that's all. Whoever he was, he must be badly injured, if not dead. There's quite a fall from that window."

I took Alexa and sat down in a chair beside the window. "I'll take care of her now. Thank you very much. I shall ask my husband to consider some sort of reward. Without doubt, you saved the life of my child and I'm grateful."

"I don't want any reward, ma'am. I'm just glad I could stop that insane man. If you need anything, just ring. The floor will be over all the excitement in a few minutes. I have to make a report on this. Be assured she'll be examined by a doctor."

"Thank you again," I said.

I snuggled Alexa's face against mine and I wept tears of joy that I had held back until we were alone. I rocked her gently and she fell asleep. I took her to bed with me, for I felt a bit groggy after all the confusion which had ended so happily for me and my daughter.

Half an hour later Stan came into the room, his face wet with perspiration. He removed his jacket and I saw that his shirt was soaked.

"Excuse the way I look," he said. "I've done some fast footwork and it's a hot day. I heard all the details from the nurses. Do you have anything further to offer?"

"Not much. The man was Emile. Is he seriously injured?"

"Dead. He landed on his head and shoulders and he died instantly."

I shook my head. "I can't weep for him or even pray for him. He had actually taken Alexa from the nurse."

Stan said, "I doubt even prayers would help a man like that, so don't concern yourself over what happened to him. In a way it's unfortunate. We've been trying to find him for days. I thought once he was captured, we might get him to talk. He was likely one of the few men who knew the person who heads the organization here. Now we'll have to try to find someone else and that's not going to be easy."

"Alexa wasn't even scratched," I said.

"I know. We were lucky, darling."

"But it scares me. I'm worried they'll try again. There's no real and sure way to protect her from another attempt."

"We're going to try," Stan declared. "I'm arranging to double the number of men on duty at the hospital. One will be outside your door every moment of the day and night, and when Alexa is brought to and from the nursery a guard will be with her every step of the way."

"I have a feeling this is coming to a head," I told Stan. "If and when Papa hears about this, he's going to take some kind of action. That scares me too. I know if it comes to that, he'll sacrifice his life for Alexa's."

"Let's hope it won't come to that," Stan said somberly. "Darling, I have to go now. So much to be done. I'll be by tonight. Can I bring you anything?"

"Only yourself," I said before he kissed me and left reluctantly, though his footsteps along the corridor were hurried. I was still trembling a bit when Mrs. Liggio arrived with a small cake she'd baked for me.

"What is happening?" she asked. "There are so many people around and a man downstairs stopped me to ask questions. So did another at the top of the stairs. And now, at your door, I was again stopped until one of the nurses assured the man it was all right for me to go in."

"A dreadful thing happened," I explained. "A man tried to kidnap Alexa."

"Kidnap? Is such a thing possible? Why would he do this?"

"I think he was part of the Black Hand," I said.

"*Mano Nero!*" she exclaimed. "I have heard of them, *si*. They must be monsters."

"They're all of that," I agreed. "But Alexa wasn't hurt."

"They have arrested the man who did this?"

"No! He was trapped after dropping Alexa and rather than face arrest he . . . jumped through the big window at the end of the hall. They told me he died as a result of the fall."

"Thank God!" she said fervently. "Such a thing to happen to nice people like you. It is almost enough to

349

make a woman wish to go home to Italy. Except that there is no difference there."

"I'm afraid you're right," I said. "I'm glad you didn't bring Amorita. She's at an age where she'd be frightened to death by the story of what happened. Especially if she'd heard all the screams."

"My husband took her to the gardens in the park. I think, sometimes, he is jealous when I go off with Amorita and leave him home alone. I am glad he does take her out now and then. He is not one to go out much himself and he makes few friends so it is well when he does not stay home."

Recognizing that I was still unstrung by the excitement, Mrs. Liggio didn't stay long, excusing herself because she wished to go home and do special housekeeping chores that were difficult when her husband and daughter were underfoot.

Stan's mother had no inkling of what happened when she arrived for her daily visit and she was beside herself with anger.

"Why did Stanton permit such a thing to happen? That is my granddaughter he was supposed to be protecting. What manner of guards did he place on duty to allow this ruffian to even get into the hospital?"

"It wasn't Stan's fault," I assured her. "This man who tried to kidnap Alexa was very clever and completely ruthless. I'd had encounters with him before. Guards, short of standing two feet apart all around the building, couldn't have stopped him."

"Thank heaven it ended as it did," she said. "At least he won't try it again."

"He was but one part of a large group," I said. "This won't stop them."

"But why?"

"As I once told you, my parents have been in virtual hiding for years. These people want to reach them, I think, to do them harm. They tried to use me to trap them, to force them to come into the open. Now they will try again, with Alexa as a hostage."

"You will come to my house to live," she said promptly. "I'll hire my own guards . . ."

350

"No, Clare," I told her. "I'd rather go home with Alexa. We can be guarded there, I hope. You are very kind to make the suggestion though."

"Well, I certainly want to do something. I'll speak to Stanton about it. The idea—kidnapping my grandchild."

On the heels of Clare Talbot's departure, I had two visitors in a row. First came Jennie Atkins with news that at home everything was in readiness for me and Alexa. She'd heard nothing of the attempted kidnapping. The newspapers had not had the incident long enough to print, though when they did, the stories were sensational.

I told Jennie about the incident, shocking her, but only strengthening her vow to give Alexa the best of care. Jennie was strong and sensible. I regarded her as an asset.

Carlo had heard the news by word of mouth from a customer whose version was even gorier than what actually happened.

He mopped his face after he learned the truth. "I don't know how such wild stories get out. You say it was Emile who tried to kidnap the baby? The same Emile of old? The one of Paris?"

"The same. He's dead. Did you hear that?"

"I heard that something drastic happened to him. I thought perhaps the police . . ."

"Emile jumped through the window at the end of the corridor, glass and all. The fall killed him."

"Which is no loss to society. Someone should have killed him long ago." He looked drawn and suddenly old. "When is it going to stop?"

"I have no idea, Uncle Carlo."

"I wonder if your papa and mama heard of it."

"I sincerely hope not."

"You've heard nothing from them? No word at all since this happened?"

"None. It would be too dangerous for them to contact me."

We talked for some time about the store, about a minor problem which Suzette had written about and needed advice on. Everything was going very well.

"I intend to be back at the salon in about two weeks," I said. "Then you can take a vacation if you like."

"Vacation? Me? I'm not the type. I wouldn't care about going off somewhere. I feel my job calls for conscientious attention all the time. Besides, I wouldn't know where to go."

"Well, you may suit yourself, Uncle. It was only a suggestion."

"I'm not taking any time off. Oh, a day now and then, but no extended periods. Isn't my work good enough to warrant my staying around?"

"Of course it is. You've done wonders. Without your help it would all have been much harder. And slower, so far as our success is concerned."

"Thank you. I didn't wish to bring that up, but I do believe I've done as well as anyone. I am thankful for your faith in me. Nobody ever had any before. Certainly not my sister Celestine, Lord rest her soul. To come to such a terrible end." He crossed himself.

"What of this man who has vowed to punish you? Have you heard from him?"

Carlo wasn't feigning the fear he evinced. "No. As I told you before, I never have warning when his men are coming."

"If you get even a hint that you are going to get another beating, let Stan know. He will see that you receive protection."

Carlo looked dubious. "I don't think he did too well here."

"This was different, Uncle. Different people and a different motive. Also the kidnapping was foiled."

"Just luck," Carlo replied, still sounding unconvinced. "Well, I'll get back to the store now. Business is good, but we're soon going to need new designs so I'll keep your drawing board dusted."

"I've been thinking about new designs," I said. "I'll put them on paper very shortly. Did you stop to look at Alexa?"

"She was sound asleep. You better warn her, when she comes to work at the store, I'll stand for none of that. My clerks must be alert at all times."

"Even if their boss isn't," I teased.

Carlo left indignantly without even a backward glance.

While the element of danger to my daughter had been extremely great, the outcome did make another such attempt increasingly difficult. The baby and I were under heavier guard than ever.

NINETEEN

We went home, Alexa and I, to find everything in readiness, with Jennie Atkins in full charge. Alexa seemed to take to her at once, and I was relieved of some of the duties of motherhood.

My convalescence was slower than I had expected, and sometimes I became depressed. But Stan's mother had lightened some of my days. Mrs. Liggio and Amorita came almost every day and I'd grown very fond of them. Amorita, now four, was an alert, highly intelligent child with her mother's warmth. Mr. Liggio never came and Mrs. Liggio was careful to explain that her husband rarely went outside the estate. Apparently supervising its care and expansion took all of his spare time. And, just as clearly, he was wealthy enough to indulge himself.

Stan, of course, was wonderful, shouldering every responsibility he could handle. And he doted on our Alexa no less than Amorita's father doted on his daughter.

A month went by, very slowly it seemed. I had my drawing board and supplies brought to the house where I set everything up in a spare room, but I found it difficult to concentrate.

I was too worried about the next time they'd strike against my daughter. I was concerned about the absence of my parents, about danger to Stan, who was exposed to it every day. In the face of this, Alexa thrived and grew chubby and acquired a smile that, if it lasted, would one day charm every boy she met. She was a contented child too, and Jennie a superior nursemaid. All was well with my world, for both stores were doing an increasingly better business. Stan was gaining a growing reputation as a prosecuting attorney and was certain of being elected to a full term.

By the time Alexa was two months old, I was more than ready to go back to the salon and my work. Even then, I left the house reluctantly, although it was guarded at all times, Jennie was alert, and the maid would help in time of trouble.

Gradually then, under the pressure of business and the hours at my drawing board, some measure of calmness came back to me. It would have been easy to settle into a feeling of confidence that nothing else would happen. It would be easy and also foolish. Somewhere, in or out of the city, those forces that had haunted and tortured me all these years were still there. Waiting to strike out again— and the next target was bound to be Alexa. They must have known by now that even if I was tortured beyond human endurance, I'd be unable to tell them where my parents were. They'd tried in every possible way to force them to reveal themselves and that hadn't worked either. The only thing left was to threaten the life of my daughter, and when they did that, Papa and Mama would appear, no matter what fate awaited them.

I knew Stan was worried too, though he took pains not to display it. At night one detective was posted in the kitchen, another just inside the front door. By day, detectives moved about the neighborhood.

Then, one day while I was at the salon concentrating on my designing, someone entered the room. I sensed a presence more than I heard anyone enter and I turned about abruptly, ready for anything.

It was Vito, and I came to my feet to rush toward the man and greet him as I always did, with a hearty kiss and hug which was returned with equal warmth.

"You ingrate," I stormed at him. "You never let us know where you were, what you were doing. Where have you been?"

"In many places," he said with a grin. "I keep myself busy. How is Alexa?"

"She's fine. Wonderfully well and thriving. You'll see her as soon as I bring you home."

"Not this time," he said. He sat down as I did and he seemed to me to be older. As if he'd outgrown all of his more or less youthful exuberance. There were wrinkles

355

around his eyes and his mouth seemed to have tightened somewhat. His forehead was furrowed, like that of a man living too intensely, under far too great pressure.

"What do you mean?" I asked indignantly. "You must see Stan and Alexa."

"I'm sorry. This is only a brief visit and I have come to ask a favor of you. A most important favor."

"Vito, you know perfectly well that I'll do anything you ask of me. So what is it you wish? Could it be financial?"

"No, no." He laughed at the idea. "This is a very personal thing to be done without telling anyone. Not even Stan. It must be the tightest secret you have ever been asked to keep."

"Does it concern my parents?"

"Everything concerns them. We are coming to the end of it. All these years, and finally we begin to see the light. A few things are missing. We cannot act until they are cleared up. Also, you will ask no questions."

"What is it you wish of me?"

"You may not even want to do this, but I assure you, it is very necessary."

"Vito, don't keep me in suspense. You sound as if you're about to ask me to murder someone."

"In truth, it may come to that. Not you doing the killing, but, well . . . I can't go any further. I know I have your cooperation. Tomorrow, in the mail from New York, bearing the markings of your salon, but designated very personal, will come a package. It will contain two cameras. You are familiar with photography? With a Kodak?"

"Yes," I said, now completely mystified. "I've taken photographs of Alexa with one of them."

"Good. Now both cameras will contain film. They are identical. I want you to place one of these cameras in a large handbag, something like the things women carry their knitting in. The second camera you will keep in your hand."

"Yes, Vito," I said. "So far it's easy enough."

"So it may seem. You have, in your workshop, a new gown for Mrs. Liggio. Is that true?"

"Yes, though I can't understand how you found this out. And what could her gown have to do with all this?"

"I ask that you deliver the gown personally to Mrs. Liggio at her home. Take along the camera in the bag, and the camera in your hand. Tell Mrs. Liggio that you wish to take her picture in the new gown and you would also like to take photographs of Amorita."

"Whatever for?" I asked.

"Do you think you can do this?"

"Of course. Mrs. Liggio is a very good friend of mine."

"I know, that's what makes this so difficult. When you take those photographs, get Mr. Liggio in at least one of them. A picture by which he can be easily identified."

I sat erect. "Vito . . . is he part of this conspiracy against Papa and Mama?"

"We don't know. That's why we ask this of you. We have tried to take our own pictures of him, but he rarely goes out and when he does, it's with no advance notice. You can get in the house, see him, and quite possibly take his picture."

"Vito, they are friends of mine," I protested.

"I know that. But if what we suspect is true, believe me they are not friends. At least Mr. Liggio isn't. What we have learned so far is very inconclusive. We may be on an entirely wrong track, but we cannot take any chances. If there is nothing wrong with the man, we'll all be happy and he will never know of our suspicions."

It was still difficult for me to accept. "I hate to take advantage of my friendship with them, but I suppose I must. Oh, Vito!" I wailed.

He patted my hand absently. "Now—and this is of extreme importance—tell no one you are going there. Don't even give a hint, though you may place the camera on your desk—one of them. Let nobody know that you have a duplicate. After you take the pictures, place the camera in that large bag where you have already concealed the duplicate. Once in your carriage, after leaving the Liggio estate, remove the one with the exposed film and with Mr. Liggio on it, and hide it. Sit on it, place it under the seat. Anything, so long as it is out of sight."

"Someone is going to steal the camera and will get the wrong one," I said.

"That may happen. We're taking no chances."

"On the other hand," I said, "I could take pictures with one camera, perhaps exchange it for the second one and take more pictures with that. So I'll have him on both films."

"If you can manage that, fine. You have to improvise, Angela. He may take some kind of action to prevent you from leaving the estate with his picture. So it's necessary that he does not know you have two cameras."

"So you honestly believe he is involved."

"If he takes any action to prevent you from having a photograph of him, we can be sure he is."

"I'll do the best I can. Will you be here?"

"Only until after you bring back the film."

"When will I receive the cameras?"

"We estimate they'll arrive the day after tomorrow."

I refreshed my memory from my calendar. "The gown will be finished in four more days, two days after I receive the cameras, if they come on schedule. Is that too long?"

"Do you have an appointment with Mrs. Liggio?"

"Yes. She is to come here." ·

"Go to her. Unless you manage to get Mr. Liggio's picture, this whole plan will be worthless."

"Could it be possible Mrs. Liggio knows about her husband?"

"Angela, you know how these old-fashioned Italians behave toward their wives. They tell them nothing and they tolerate no questions. Maybe she knows, more likely she does not. And there's an even chance Mr. Liggio won't know what it's all about either. He could be innocent. But we must investigate everyone we think might be involved."

"Can you tell me anything more? I know there must be others working against Papa and Mama. Is Mr. Liggio just a small part of something? Or is he as big as his wealth seems to indicate?"

"I don't know. We're not sure of anything. That's why we must have these photographs."

"Do you have someone who can say yes or no about Mr. Liggio?"

"We believe we have."

The thought of practicing deceit on my friend was terribly distasteful, but I knew I must. "I'll do my best and hate myself for doing it."

"Think of your parents. That might make it less painful," Vito said curtly. "Expect the cameras then and remember, it's vital no one hears about this. Not even Stan or Carlo. Especially Carlo. He talks too much."

"I know Carlo does. But why can't Stan know?"

"He wouldn't let you do it."

I nodded agreement.

"I'll either pick up the film or have someone else come for it. Keep it in this office, well hidden. If someone takes the second camera from you, don't actually resist. Act indignant and a little frightened to make it look genuine, but don't get yourself hurt."

He rose, walked over to me and gripping my shoulders lightly, lifted me out of the chair.

"Now I have something else to tell you, unless Carlo has heard about it and already informed you."

"Carlo has told me nothing. I assume it concerns you."

Vito smiled. "Very much so. It's strange Carlo hasn't heard about it. I've spent quite a lot of time at your New York salon. I have discovered a beautiful, intelligent and compassionate lady there."

"Suzette?" I asked, knowing what he was about to tell me.

"She is a gentle, sweet, loving person—and spirited when she has a mind to be—very much like you. I love her."

"Does she love you?' I asked, needlessly, since his eyes bespoke his happiness. "I am happy for you both." I stood on tiptoe and kissed Vito's cheek.

"Perhaps," he said, "we will soon put an end to this longstanding trouble. *Arrivederci,* Angela. God be with you."

Then he was gone. I sat down and reviewed all he had told me. I didn't like not being able to speak to Stan about it, but I had given my word and I intended to keep it. No one would know what I had to do.

Two days later the package arrived. The return address on it was that of the New York salon. It was all properly labeled and addressed to me personally. I opened it to find the cameras. I'd already provided myself with a large, heavy cloth bag, duly decorated to pass as a ladies' handbag. I placed a number of personal items in it, none of them valuable, since the bag might be either stolen or forcibly taken from me.

Once that was done, I ordered Mrs. Liggio's gown made ready for delivery. On the day I'd promised it would be ready, a carriage brought me to the gate. I had been there so often I was passed through without the usual telephone call to the house.

A maid summoned Mrs. Liggio while I sat in the drawing room, one camera on my lap, the boxed gown beside me. I felt like a traitor and I prayed that, for once, Vito's suspicions were without foundation.

"My dear Angela," Mrs. Liggio said, "it was good of you to send word you would come with the gown, but I could have called for it."

"Not this one," I said. "It has to fit perfectly and there were several final fittings set for this afternoon, plus a bridal party. I wanted no distractions when you tried this on. I'm concerned about the side buttoning. It may pull a little. I won't have that."

"You've been very kind to me, Angela. Always I get such attention."

"With a customer such as you, and a friend besides, I find it no bother to bring it here. How is Amorita?"

"She's fine. A good little girl. And a happy one."

"I'm glad. And Mr. Liggio?"

"Like always, a man who has too much time on his hands."

I opened the box and removed the gown, separating it from the tissue paper and shaking it to free it of its folds. I had deliberately moved the buttons so that they would pull the gown out of line. I held the gown up to her and studied it while I shook my head.

"There's something wrong with the lines of the gown.

Whatever it is I can fix in five minutes, but you'll have to try it on first."

"That will be my pleasure," she said, admiring the gown as I held it before her. "It's beautiful. Like all of the gowns you have made for me, but I think this one is the prettiest, though it looks a little small."

"I'm not sure what it is, but I know it can be taken care of."

"I hope so. My husband is pleased with the clothes I get from you."

"I would like to know his opinion of this one. Please ask him to come and see it."

"I will try, but I can't promise," she said. "I will go now and change. Amorita will come to see you. And I will try to get my husband to come also."

Amorita arrived promptly and with her was the large, very alert man whom I had seen before and who was supposed to be her tutor. He looked more like a bodyguard.

Amorita, as always, ran into my arms. I hoped my Alexa would be as affectionate when she grew older.

"Look, darling," I said, "I have a camera and I'm going to take your picture."

"Oh, that's nice," she said. "I'll keep it forever. Thank you, Mrs. Talbot."

"Stand over by the window," I said. I pulled aside the drapes and the curtains for maximum light. The big man, standing close by the window, quickly stepped out of camera range when I held the box camera to take the first picture.

There were six exposures on the roll and I was on my third when Mrs. Liggio and her husband came into the room. I thrust the camera into my large handbag without referring to it and displayed annoyance with the way the gown pulled across the front.

"I see what it is," I said. "Two of the buttons are out of line. A simple matter."

Armed with needle and thread, I made quick repairs and then I stepped back.

"Now, Mr. Liggio, we have a problem for you to solve. Laurari thinks this is the loveliest gown I have made for her, but I just remembered a blue ball gown I had made about three months ago. I sort of favor that. What is your opinion?"

Mr. Liggio fell into the spirit of the thing. "Always the newest is the best. So this one I will say is better, but not by much."

"I'm defeated. But I'm grateful to you anyway," I said with a gesture of resignation. "Now that I see this on you . . . Mrs. Liggio, I have an idea." I reached into the handbag and took out the second camera. Before anyone could protest, I aimed it and took a picture. Mr. Liggio stood beside his wife and I knew I had trapped him on film. I immediately thrust the camera into the handbag.

"Now we have a picture. Next time we'll remember how this gown looked."

Mr. Liggo said, "You must let me have the film developed, Mrs. Talbot. I insist."

I removed the first camera. "It isn't necessary, Mr. Liggio, but if you wish, we might as well take more pictures. Please—stand with Laurari and with Amorita. A family group . . . yes, that's what it will be."

I had them stand together. I purposely raised the camera so that I could see, in the finder, only Mr. Liggo and his wife. Amorita, being small, wasn't tall enough to be included.

I said, "Mr. Liggo, please turn your face toward your wife." I aimed and snapped the shutter while I called loudly for Amorita to stand up straight. I hoped my loud voice concealed the sound of the shutter, for now I had on this camera which would be sacrificed, a photo of Mr Liggo and his wife, in almost the same position as the pose when I took the other picture, which was now in the second camera.

I aimed again, took two more pictures, including Amorita. Mr. Liggo approached me and held out his hand. "You must allow me to take a picture of you with my wife and with Amorita. It will be treasured."

"Wonderful," I said. I posed. He was clumsy with the camera, showing he had little experience with this new type of picture-taking.

"That's the last picture," I told him.

362

"How do you remove the film?" he asked. Before I could reach him, he had the back of the camera open. The film was, of course, ruined.

"Oh Mr. Liggio," I complained, "that is what you must not do."

"I did something wrong?" he asked, looking at me innocently.

"The camera must only be opened in a dark room."

"Ah, Pietro," his wife said in dismay, "you have ruined the pictures,"

"Is that the truth?" he asked me.

I removed the roll and let it unwind from the spool. "It's worthless, and I haven't any other film."

"Next time," he said. "I will buy film. I'm sorry. I am a clumsy man, but these new devices are sometimes more than I can understand. Excuse please. I am so sorry."

I dropped the camera into my bag. "Oh, it's really nothing. As you say, next time. But they would have been very good pictures."

"Will I be in them next time?" Amorita asked.

"I'll bring two rolls and take a whole roll of you," I promised. My purpose now was to get out of here before some accident revealed the fact that I had two cameras. I began putting my sewing things away.

"The gown is perfect," I said. "I hope it is a great success."

I talked for a few more minutes and then begged off having wine or coffee. I gathered up my large bag, made a point of removing one camera to shift it into a better position and smiled at Liggio as I did so, as if to mildly reprove him for having ruined the film.

Moments later I was driven away, but I didn't stop worrying until the gates to the estate closed behind me and I was on my way home.

I wondered what Vito intended to do with the photograph, whom he would show it to, and if Mr. Liggio was identified, what then?

Late in the afternoon Vito returned. "There is one picture of Mr. Liggio in the camera," I said. "I took several other pictures with the second and Mr. Liggio

363

opened that camera, by mistake he claimed, and the film was ruined."

"Pictures of him were on the exposed film?" Vito asked.

"Yes, several."

"Then there is not much need to have his picture identified. Though of course we shall do that at once. It seems to me he is guilty."

"Of what?" I asked.

"At this moment I can't tell you, but things are going to happen now. After all these years, we're coming to the end of it."

"Does that mean Papa and Mama will be free to come back to me?"

"It could happen. Don't depend on it."

"Vito," I asked, "are you involved in this as a policeman, still working for the *Carabinieri?*"

He nodded. "Yes. I was assigned to come to the United States because everything seemed to be moving here. I tell you this in confidence and I would not admit it except that you are as much a part of this as I am. Trust me a little longer, Angela. But trust no one else. No one!"

"I will do as you say," I promised. "All I want is to set my parents free."

"Then pray for all of us," he said. "We are fighting the most formidable group of enemies any police agency has ever had to face. I will try to come back soon."

Three uneventful days went by. Stan was actually growing very optimistic about his program for driving crime out of New Orleans. To my relief, Mrs. Liggio came to the store to report the gown was a huge success. If Mr. Liggio had suspected I was attempting to get his picture for reasons harmful to him, I doubted he'd have allowed his wife to come to see me. I was glad things remained as they had been for I could not, no matter how hard I tried, believe that Mrs. Liggio was a part of any sort of conspiracy in which her husband might be involved.

Stan and I still ate out often, mostly at our favorite restaurant. Naturally it was well patronized by tourists and visitors, and we usually played a game, choosing one or two and speculating on where they came from and why they were in New Orleans. The fact that we could seldom verify our conclusions didn't diminish the fun of guessing. One evening our subject was a woman of about thirty-five, eating alone, and by the way she studied the menu and questioned the waiter about the food, we knew she was a stranger.

"I say she's a recent widow," Stan decided. "She's here to forget and try to move back into society."

"On the contrary," I opined, "she's not yet married. She's a successful businesswoman and so attractive that if she weren't deeply occupied in business she would have married before now."

"Which of us is going to ask her?" Stan said.

"Not I," I rejected the idea. "We're probably both wrong anyway."

Stan and I were accustomed to take our time dining, for we had much to discuss over the supper table. As usual, I excused myself to visit the lounge. As I did so, the woman we'd been talking about also rose and followed me at a discreet distance.

There were two other women seated before the mirrors, tending stray locks or applying touches of eau de toilette to their brows. When they left, the woman sat down next to me and as we spoke, we addressed ourselves to our mirror reflections.

"I have certain instructions, Angela Gambrell-Talbot," she said.

"Indeed?" I replied. "I am not accustomed to being given instructions by someone I've never seen before."

She raised a hand to touch her hair and in the mirror I saw the duplicate of the magic ring.

"I have seen the ring before," I said.

"Good. You will ask no questions because I won't answer them. I am no more than a messenger."

"Very well. I understand."

"Tomorrow you will receive a letter from Suzette Larkin at your New York salon. It will ask that you make a quick trip there to settle some difficulty. And, in fact, you will make that journey, taking the evening train. Reserve a drawing room for the entire trip, but do not unpack. When the train slows for the first stop after it leaves New Orleans, you will get off as unobtrusively as possible. Someone else will take your place and take charge of your baggage. She will also check into your customary New York hotel under your name and leave your baggage in the room assigned you."

"And when I leave the train?" I asked.

"There will be a carriage at the depot. It will be drawn by a matched pair of black horses. You will get aboard. I will be inside. I will then tell you the next step of this plan."

"Do you know where you'll be taking me?"

"I know, but you shall not. At least, not until this is all over. Ask no further questions. Please leave first."

"May I tell my husband?"

"He should only know you are going to New York on business. And wear your dark blue traveling suit with its matching hat."

"May I ask one more thing?"

"Of course. Provided I can answer it."

I touched the ring on her finger and placed my ring finger alongside it.

"Is the ring really magic?"

She laughed softly. "There are times when I came to believe it was."

"I've had the same experience," I confided. "Thank you."

I returned to our table. Stan was enjoying a cigar and we resumed our conversation at once. The woman soon returned to her table, but she didn't stay long.

"We should have asked her," Stan said. "Why didn't you? The two of you were in the lounge at the same time."

"My dear husband," I told him, "I do not go about asking questions of strangers. Now tell me about the case you're trying in court today."

It was a routine case, but he loved to talk about every one and I had become a devoted listener. When we left the restaurant, I looked about, but I saw no sign of the woman. Stan and I walked home, enjoying the warm night.

I slept fitfully, but I took care that Stan didn't know it. In the morning, when I reached the store, the mail was already in and Carlo presented me with an already-opened letter, presumably from Suzette.

"This would not have happened if I had remained there and in charge," he told me. "She wants you back in New York as soon as you can get there. It's a banking problem. There's a mixup and only you can straighten it out. Suzette is not too exact about what happened, but I suppose you'll have to go."

I read the letter and nodded. "I'll leave tonight. I'll go to Stan's office and tell him. Please reserve a drawing room for me on the early evening train. You can handle things here, Carlo."

"Well, since I have been all along, I suppose I can continue to do so," he said in his customary grand style, but knowing him I realized he would have preferred going in my place. I immediately went to work on the other mail and tidied my desk before I made an early departure. I went to Stan's office and told him I was leaving.

"Isn't this rather sudden?" he asked.

"Of course it is. Suzette and the bank have some kind of a dispute and I'm the only one to settle it. I'll give you the details when I get back."

"I'll miss you. How long will you be gone?"

"I don't know, but you can depend on it, I'll take the first train back after my business is completed. No more than four days, including the journey."

"Send me a telegram and I'll be at the depot to meet you," he said. "I'm sorry I can't take you to the train. There's a meeting and it won't be over in time."

I went home, packed two suitcases and stayed awhile with Alexa. I would dine on the train, so I left right after six o'clock. I was wearing a dark blue traveling suit with a matching hat, the outfit I'd been requested to wear. Someone, identically dressed, would probably take my place.

TWENTY

I had my supper in the diner. Again I was watchful, to see if I could notice anyone studying me a bit too closely—or even too casually. No one seemed to pay any attention to me.

Back in my drawing room, I made ready to leave the train. It was running on time and two hours out of New Orleans it was due to make its first stop to take on passengers for the North.

I made my way to the end of the car as the station platform flashed below the windows. I opened the door and stepped out. The porter was waiting to get off first and set up his little stepstool to make leaving or entering the car easier.

As I stepped onto the depot platform, a woman, dressed the same as I, got aboard. She didn't look my way, but I knew she must be my double for the rest of the train ride and the reason I'd been asked to wear the blue suit.

I looked about. The closed carriage drawn by paired black horses was there. I approached it. The driver got down to help me aboard. Inside the carriage, where all the curtains were drawn, the lady of the previous evening greeted me with a smile.

"Thank you for carrying out everything exactly as it should have been."

"Now may I ask what this is about?" I settled myself for a ride of indeterminate length.

"I can't tell you just yet. Also, I'm sorry but I have to apply a blindfold. It's night and quite dark, but we have important reasons for your not knowing where we are, or what the route will be. Do you mind?"

She handed me what looked like a Mardi Gras mask without eye holes. I was none too pleased with this as

368

pect and I had begun to worry. Papa had told me to trust whoever wore a duplicate to the magic ring on my finger, but there could be many of these rings. How was I to know someone else hadn't discovered I would trust whoever wore one.

Despite these growing doubts, I placed the mask over my face and tried to relax as the carriage began to move. I felt it turning and then it rolled over what seemed to be a paved road. This continued for about half an hour. Then there was another turn and the road became rougher, like a country road full of ruts.

Now and then I heard the sounds of night insects and the croak of frogs. I could feel the chill from some large body of water as well. Then I could smell dewy fields. Twice, some large vehicle made the carriage driver maneuver to give room and the vehicles that passed by sounded as if they were heavy farm wagons.

I wasn't sure why I was storing up this information. I must trust the wearer of the ring. Once, when the carriage gave a rather violent lurch getting out of an exceptionally deep rut, I was thrown against the woman. I cried out and seized her arm, letting my hand drop to her wrist and pass over her hand. There was no ring on it and I began to really worry. I knew, of course, she was the same women who had started me on this strange journey, but she must have removed the ring and that concerned me.

"May I ask how much longer I must endure this blindfold?" I asked.

"Be patient," she said. "It's all very necessary as you will see. Have you any idea of where we are?"

"No. How could I?"

"You've been listening to every sound," she said with a gentle laugh. "We are well into the countryside. It is quite isolated here and the carriage cannot move as fast as it might because this is a very dark night and the only illumination is the lantern that swings below the carriage. Please bear with it, Angela. You will find it worthwhile, I promise."

"I hope so," I said. I lapsed into silence, which the woman seemed to respect. Then I felt the carriage begin to really slow down. It made a turn to the right and soon came to a stop. I judged the journey had taken about an hour.

"Please leave the blindfold in place," my companion requested. "I will lead you inside. This is an ordinary farmhouse, if you must know."

"I'm grateful for even that bit of information, small as it is."

"Thank you for behaving so well. Under the circumstances, I don't know if I could have. Stay where you are now until I help you down."

I felt the carriage move as she and the driver both got off. Then she touched my hand, took it in a firm grasp and assisted me to the ground. She held my arm and led me along a rough walk. I heard the squeal of rusty gate hinges, felt the gate itself brush against my side.

"Four steps up," my companion warned.

I climbed them, heard a door open, and I was escorted into a warm house smelling faintly of freshly baked bread. Later I recalled the thought that flashed through my mind at that moment. Anyone who baked her own bread could not be a criminal.

"You may remove the mask now," my companion said. "Keep your eyes closed for a few seconds and open them gradually. The room is well lighted and you have rested your eyes for a long time."

I reached up and removed the mask. When I was able to see once more, I found that I stood alone in an old-fashioned parlor with a pot-bellied stove from which warmth emanated.

The room was furnished with a round table on which stood an oil-burning lamp. There were two others close by and on the small mantel above the fireplace were two more. Chair arms were covered with lace doilies and antimacassars were on the backs of the stuffed chairs. The table was crowded with curios and so was the mantel. Pictures and dried flower arrangements covered the walls almost entirely.

"It is not like our *palazzo* in Florence, my dear," a voice spoke behind me.

370

I almost spun around in my excitement, for I recognized a voice I hadn't heard in years.

"Mama!" I cried out and went into her arms. I cried and so did she. When I raised my head, I saw Papa standing behind her and I went to him. I couldn't talk. I could barely see for the tears.

"Isn't she a lovely young woman?" Papa asked Mama.

"I saw her at the Mardi Gras, remember?" Mama said. "Of course she wore a mask, but I knew she was our daughter and I knew also that she was lovely."

Papa said, "We are having a special supper tonight, just the three of us. Mama has been cooking and baking all day."

"And will someone tell me what this is all about? The need for such secrecy?" I asked. I still clung to Papa as if I feared he might vanish.

"Yes. It's time for explanations."

"I'll get the food on the table," Mama said, "and then we will eat and after that we will talk."

"It will probably last until morning," Papa chuckled. He kept his arm around me. I was still fighting tears as he escorted me into the dining room.

It was small and plainly furnished, but the aroma of fine Italian cooking aroused my appetite. We ate and I praised Mama's cooking. I loved these two parents of mine so much it was hard to refrain from getting up to hug them over and over again.

Papa poured red wine at the close of the meal while Mama removed the dishes. Then she returned to join us, taking off her apron as she did so. I knew one day I'd look much like her. I had her mouth and eyes, though my nose was certainly my father's. Papa had become almost bald, but he was still a handsome man.

"Now," he said, "for some truths for a change. First of all, we are grateful for the way you have behaved through all of this. We know what you suffered, what they tried to do to you."

Mama said, "I kept trying to make your father take me to you no matter what happened. He refused and I see now he was right."

"Tell me from the beginning," I begged. "Never mind my part of it."

"When you were still a little girl—four years old," Papa said, "I was a politician and a banker. In those days we lived a pleasant life in Florence. But on Corsica and elsewhere in our fine country, things were happening that disgraced all Italians. It began on Corsica years before. Many years before. Wealthy landowners became afraid of the peasants who worked their lands, and they brought in strong, tough men to guard them. After a long time, the guards became more powerful than the landowners and by then they had also frightened the peasants to a point where whatever the guards did became a law. They killed when they were strongly opposed. They ruined others financially, until they bowed to their will.

"Finally it came to a point where these guards appointed leaders who acted as governors, mayors, judges, police . . . anything you care to name. They governed ruthlessly, but they were wise too. Those who worked with them or maintained silence about what was happening—these people prospered and were left alone. Until finally everybody was under the thumb of what became known as the Mafia. You have heard of these people, no doubt."

"Yes, Papa, often. My husband is fighting the Black Hand now in New Orleans. Once before they were powerful here, but they were driven off. That was ten years ago. About ten years."

"How well we know," Mama said. "It was a terrible thing."

"But I will have to say it was also necessary," Papa added. "I don't know if those who suffered were guilty. If they were, they could have been only minor people who, as usual, bore the brunt of violence. Those who ruled and made the big money, they got away."

"Did you have anything to do with that, Papa?" I asked.

"No, not directly. Let me go back again to Italy and Corsica. The Mafia found it profitable to keep growing and they expanded to other places. It became so bad something had to be done. All this I knew about, but it meant nothing to me. I was successful, I had nothing to worry about. They didn't bother me. I had my lovely wife and my little daughter. For me life was beautiful."

"But they came to us," Mama said in a tone of resignation. "We should have known."

"*Mafioso*," Papa said, "is anyone bearing himself with great pride. But Mafia, that is something else. They killed a friend of mine. He regarded them as a joke and they made an example of him. Another—a man who fought his way to wealth—they took his wife and his two sons and when he finished paying to set them free, he was a poor man. Later he killed himself. And then, as Mama said, they came to us."

"Papa, were they going to kill you too?"

"Oh no! I was something different. I was a member of the House of Deputies and I was an officer of a large bank. They needed a bank through which they could place their money, obtained by murder and kidnapping and robbery. They needed a man in government they could trust. Oh yes, they came to me. They told me I would grow richer than any man in Florence if I helped them. They said I would be powerful and rise in government. All I had to do in return was to keep them informed, answer any questions they put to me, and see to it that no stringent laws were passed against them. I would also publicly discount their activities as mere nuisances. I would insist they were of little danger. I would keep the image of them soft and obscure."

"I think they have such people all over the world," I said.

"True enough. There are always those who see only the wealth that will be theirs, without any chance of their being actively involved themselves and, therefore, feel in no danger of being punished."

"I think, Papa, that you have just answered all the questions I might put to you."

"I thank you for such kindly thoughts, but let me give you the details. I went to the highest government officials and told them what was going on. They had already recognized the seriousness and potential power of the Mafia. We set up a plan. I would agree to join them. I

373

would furnish them certain information, not too dangerous to the government. I would cooperate with them and I would use what power I had to rise as high in their ranks as possible. Then, when I knew everyone connected with the conspiracy, especially before some very great project was about to take place, I would denounce them and reveal myself as an agent of the government."

"Is that what did happen then?" I asked.

"They had a scheme which could have resulted in the overthrow of a government, or could at least so weaken it, the Mafia would be in power. Can you imagine what that would have done? I denounced it. That was the moment when I had to assert myself and reveal the fact I had never been one of them. But, in joining their ranks, I took a vow of silence on penalty of death. I had broken that vow, so now, according to their rules, I must be killed. We knew that and we had arranged for me to testify against them and go directly from court to a hiding place which one man knew. Only one, very high in government, but a man who would never be suspected of having this information."

"Papa," I said sympathetically, "they continued to flourish and they never stopped hunting you."

"They couldn't. They still can't. Their organization calls for my assassination and the sentence of death against me will never be revoked unless the highest authority in the Mafia agrees. I doubt that will ever happen."

"We thought we were safe," Mama said. "We hid on a farm in Sardinia. We received word they'd found us and we moved to Paris. From there it was Vienna. Six months later, they were on our trail. We continued to run, ending, of all places, in St. Petersburg. We thought they'd not yet penetrated Russia and the courts of the czar. Again we were mistaken. Then we continued to run, finally to Canada."

"That was when we risked a visit to see you and Aunt Celestine," Papa continued.

"How wonderful it was to see our daughter again," Mama said. "But it couldn't last. They were moving against us."

374

"By then," Papa went on, "we realized how widespread this organization was. We didn't go back to Canada but remained in the United States. This time we were successful in keeping hidden for years. But as always, questions were being asked about us. The agents of the organization were closer on our trail."

"What an awful penalty to pay for your fight against them," I said.

"It wasn't pleasant. About the time we had to pack up once more, there was a great drive against the Mafia in New Orleans, complete with lynchings and arrests. This so frightened them that they left New Orleans and we decided to go down here to live, on the hope that with few or no agents of the organization in the vicinity, we would be safe."

"They haven't found you, have they?" I asked.

"No," Mama said. "Not yet."

"They will, before long," Papa added wryly.

"Will you have to disappear again?" I asked in horror.

"Hopefully not this time. Thanks to you, Angela," Papa said.

"I? What did I do?"

"A great deal. More than you know. And we are proud of the way you held out against them when they were centering their attentions on you. In Paris, New York, everywhere."

"Papa," I said, "there was nothing heroic on my part. I couldn't answer their questions because I didn't know where you were."

"That's why you were never told. But they came to realize that perhaps you were telling the truth and our whereabouts was being kept from you too. So then they attacked you, thinking we'd hear about it and decide to sacrifice ourselves to save you. So we had to keep you safe and ourselves still hidden."

"All of which was placed in the hands of Vito Cardona. Am I correct, Papa?"

"You are. He was sent here to cooperate with an organization of our own. This was set up to protect us, in the beginning, but as the Mafia grew in numbers and power, so did we. Ours is now an organization even more

375

secret than that of our enemies. We have representatives all over the world, many of them in strategic places. That was one way we were able to stay ahead of the Mafia in their search for us and for other, even more important matters."

"I'm beginning to understand the magic of my ring," I said, and I extended my hand to show them the round band on my finger. "Its magic was represented by your own organization."

Papa smiled. "True enough, Angela. The ring identified you and we saw to it that where you were, or where you traveled, we had our own people ready to help you if the Mafia struck against you."

"Even in banks?" I asked. "Even at Ellis Island when I found myself in trouble?"

"At Ellis Island the man who befriended you had been there for a long time. His duties as our representative were to keep track of both our enemies and our friends coming and going. He was not there to help you alone, but when he recognized the ring, he knew who you were and took steps to set you free."

"And the bankers. Those who turned me down when I needed help. They changed their minds when they saw the ring."

Papa nodded. "You needed help, without security, and you went from one bank to another. You were bound to contact one of ours and then you'd be taken care of."

"The Society of the Rings," I mused. "I'm disappointed. I came to believe it was possessed of magic powers."

"It is the only time we have used the ring," Papa said. "I doubt we will ever use it again."

"I'm not giving this one back," I said.

"Of course you may have it, Angela."

"Dear Angela," Mama said, "my heart was broken when we learned how that terrible man tried to kidnap your baby."

"I'm afraid," Papa admitted, "that if the plan had succeeded, and we were given the choice of surrendering ourselves or having the baby killed, we'd have come forward."

"These people are inhuman," I said bitterly.

"They have to be. They cannot afford to allow one turncoat to go on living, for it will encourage others, and if the organization is exposed completely, it will cease to exist. So they are ruthless and they never give up. We will be pursued until we die a natural death, or they kill us."

"Mama, how are you so involved?" I asked. "Must they kill you too? Because Papa turned against them?"

Mama smiled and I thought there was some satisfaction in it. "I was also part of them. Sometimes a woman is necessary for such deeds as carrying secret messages to places where their own people could not go."

"Messages we read before those who received them," Papa said, adding, "Your mother was a great help to us."

"They murdered Aunt Celestine, didn't they?" I asked.

"Yes. They found letters I'd written to you and they knew we were still alive. There is something else I must tell you, warn you about. We believe someone we didn't suspect has been giving information to our enemies. Whether out of fear, or for money, we don't know. But . . . there must be someone because we have too often been close to being captured and some of our activities have been known to them."

I said, after a brief moment of consideration, "Would it have to be someone close to me, Papa?"

"I'm afraid so."

"No one employed in my stores could possibly have been able to provide any information about you and Mama. The only person close to me has been Vito."

"No, not Vito. We're sure of him," Papa said promptly.

"Stan? My husband?" I asked, almost in terror.

Mama shook her head and waved her arms, Italian style, to discount the suggestion. "Of course not."

"His mother? Or someone close to her?"

"No, Angela," Papa said.

My eyes widened in disbelief. "Not Uncle Carlo! Surely not he."

"Why do you say that?" Papa asked.

"When I went to Florence to find you, he came to me. I was glad. I was worried about you both. He was severely beaten three times that I know of—but I see now that this was done partly to keep my sympathies alive for him. Or perhaps to keep him faithful to those who both threatened him and paid him. I recall how he stole all my money one time in Paris. Now I wonder if he was ordered to do this so I would be in such financial trouble I would have to go to you for help. That was when they thought I knew where you were. I think they even arranged to have that awful man come to attack me while Carlo was close by, so that Carlo could come to my rescue and increase my faith in him. Also, there was a time when he and I were almost run down by a wagon, but Carlo managed to see it in time and saved me again. Of course I was grateful. Carlo was the one man who knew what I was doing all the time. Although for some reason—maybe pure instinct—I began to keep my activities from him. It wasn't difficult since I saw him only at the salon. Yes, he must be the man."

"He is," Papa said. "We've suspected him for some time. He spent more money than he earned. He was in the habit of keeping secret rendezvous with men from the Mafia. When he rebelled—and I'm sure he did—they beat him almost to death. That kept him in line and also reduced any suspicion of him by you—and by us."

"What will happen now? I certainly can't permit him to work for me."

"You must, for the time being. If they discover you know he is a traitor, they'll also know you have been in contact with us, or those close to us."

Mama spoke in her brother's defense. "He was likely forced to do these things, Angela. He had to obey or he'd be killed."

"Papa, don't you have any way of ending this? Must you and Mama keep hidden the rest of your lives?"

"Perhaps not. Thanks to you, we have finally gained on them. We have someone definite to strike against, someone we can hold as hostage."

I was again confused. "Why are you thanking me?"

Papa rose, went to the sideboard, opened a drawer and removed a photograph. He placed it before me. I looked at Pietro Liggio's picture.

"He is an important man in the Mafia?" I asked.

"The most important in Louisiana and perhaps a dozen other states. He directs everything they do in the area he controls. Vito asked you to photograph him because it was possible I might be able to identify him. I knew all of the important men, Angela. By the time I revealed what I knew, many of them had been sent all over the world to set up branches of the organization, or take over those already established. So you obtained the photo and . . . I know him."

"Is he that evil? Could his wife know what he does?" I asked. "I always considered her a friend of mine."

"I doubt she knows. She may suspect some of his dealings are not exactly legal, but I don't think she realizes how powerful he is, or how dangerous those people he directs can be. Pietro himself is not a man of violence. He is an organizer. An executive who does what he is ordered to do. If not, he will be killed as ruthlessly as we will be if they catch up with us."

"But knowing his position in the Mafia, can't you do something about that and gain your own freedom?"

"That's what we're hoping to do. Plans are being made. It's a delicate situation and it may not work at all, but we're going to try something."

"I should hope so. How can I face him again? I'm sure you don't want me to let him know I'm aware of what he is."

"It would cost you your life," Papa said.

"Must I go back and act as if nothing has happened?"

"I'm afraid that's all you can do for the time being."

"Angela, we know how worried you were," Mama said. "How many years you've lived without knowing about us, or where we were. We decided neither you nor we could exist under those circumstances without our getting together for explanations and . . . to show you how much we love you. We had to find a safe way. And now we are together even if only for a few hours."

I went to her impulsively and I kissed and hugged her. I was happy one moment, frustrated the next because unless things changed, these might be the only moments I would have with them, perhaps for several years to come.

"What are the next steps I must take?" I asked.

"You will be brought to the railroad station in time to catch another train for New York. Go to your hotel where you will be already checked in. Visit your store, take up the problem your store manager thinks exists. Go to the bankers and straighten things out. Wear the ring. Everything will soon be in order. Return to New Orleans and your husband—and say nothing. Not even to him. We trust him, we love him, really, because he is so protective of you, but still. . . ."

"I know. I'll continue to treat Carlo as if nothing is wrong."

"Good. Now, let's forget all this for the moment and just talk. Get to know one another a little better. After all, we've seen you so few times . . . there is so much to say. . . ."

I was more than happy to throw aside this mantle of evil, suspicion, treason and violence. We talked far into the morning hours. They were happy hours, ones I would never forget, but there was going to be sadness in leaving them. For it might be forever. I couldn't bring myself to express this thought and neither could they, but the three of us knew it existed, unspoken as it was.

When we had exhausted our memories, Papa went back once more to those who had threatened us for so long, and who still did, now probably more than ever.

"We have set up this worldwide secret group to battle the Mafia," he explained. "Thus far we have had little success."

"They kept you and Mama alive," I said.

"Yes, that's true. But we've not succeeded in destroying the enemy as we had hoped and planned to do. They are too big, too powerful, and too numerous. We no longer hope to win the war, but we'll continue to hit them where and when we can. Perhaps, with Pietro Liggio, we'll have a tool that will open up some way to get at them."

"I only hope that I won't give it all away when I come face to face with him," I said.

"Avoid him, then, if possible. And be as friendly with his wife as you have been."

"I'm sure she knows nothing about what he is really like," Mama said. "He'd never confide in her if he was doing anything wrong. So I would say you could consider her innocent."

"I'm glad you said that, Mama. I do like her, and I'll hate to be a part of whatever brings her heartache. Though certainly we've had our share of it."

Papa snapped open the case of his pocket watch. "We've been chattering the night away. It's after two in the morning. Time you got some sleep, Angela."

"When will I have to leave?" I asked.

"Tomorrow evening. It will be just as if you left New Orleans one day later. In your New York hotel, someone is taking your place. Your husband has been sent a telegram saying all is well and the journey was a safe one. Go home when your business is finished and I dare anyone to find out you lost twenty-four hours somewhere."

"In the most wonderful way," I said. "And will I ever see you again?"

"We don't know. I think it possible. We shall have to be patient."

"I have been for more than twenty years," I said.

Mama put her arm around my waist and led me to the narrow stairway to the second floor of the farmhouse.

"That is why," she told me, "we decided you must be brought to us. So that you would fully understand."

"I'm thankful for that. I know you are both well and perhaps something will be done soon to bring us together again."

"I've neglected to tell you how much I liked the painting you did of me. At the showing you had in New Orleans."

"Mama, you fooled me there."

"Well, perhaps. Not entirely, I think. The man you talked to was one of those who belong to the organization your father has spoken of. He noticed that you saw my footprints. He sent me word about it."

"It proved something else," I said. "You can run faster than I."

Mama turned down my sheets while I made ready to retire, but we sat up for almost another hour. It seemed there were endless things to talk about. Little Alexa was the main topic most of the time, and I knew how Mama's heart ached to hold the baby in her arms.

In the morning we continued our talk during a long walk about the countryside. I discovered how isolated this farmhouse was. Nothing was closer than three miles. Extreme caution was used in bringing in food and supplies. I noticed also that wherever we went, two men followed at no more than a few hundred feet, each well armed.

When the time came to leave we fought valiantly to hold back the tears. I kissed Papa and Mama and I held our embrace until the woman who had brought me here reminded us the train would not wait.

In the carriage I was again blindfolded, but that didn't prevent my tears. The woman placed an arm around my shoulders.

"I understand how you feel," she said, "but this has to be and even though your father must remain in hiding, he is doing some wonderful work."

"He told me nothing about that," I said.

"He wouldn't, but the fact remains that he is. Oh, I can tell you who I am now. My name is Felicia Carlini. My husband is one of those who guard the farmhouse. We are supposed to be the tenants and we farm some of the land nearby, but we are here more to protect your father and mother."

"And I thank you for doing it so well," I said.

"All of us do our share in what has to be done. Your father, however, does the planning for the . . . you might call it the Society of the Ring. A term I know you invented yesterday. To him comes all news and whatever evidence we can gather against the Mafia. He decides what is to be done, so you can see he is not an idle man in his exile. I would say he has done more to hurt the Mafia than anyone."

"Do you think it will ever be over?" I asked. "So my father and mother can come home?"

"There is something being planned now that may allow them to return, but as to the fight ever being over, none

382

of us believes it will be. They are too strong, there are too many of them and they find willing disciples wherever they go. If there is a rebellion, those who rebel vanish and are never heard of again. They are as wealthy as a small nation and that wealth grows, for they take everything they can without paying for it. They pay no taxes, they look for every opportunity to enlarge their numbers and their bank accounts."

"I came to estimate their strength from what Papa told me. Thank you for enlightening me even more. Papa refrained from being as frank as you, because he thought I'd worry too much.".

"You are entitled to know the truth," Felicia told me. "I too—with my husband—we are afraid to go abroad. We were once among them, but when we joined in Italy —we were very young then. It sounded like an organization that was determined to do good. What naive idiots we were."

"I hope and trust then that you will also be set free, Felicia. In the meantime, take good care of Papa and Mama. Now that I've been with them, it will be harder than ever to have to live apart from them."

We talked more of the days back in Italy. I learned how Felicia and her husband risked their lives to spoil one deathly dangerous scheme of the Mafia. I heard about several of their defeats Papa had been responsible for, making his death more eagerly sought than ever.

"It may be they'll try something soon," Felicia warned. "We know that Mr. Liggio lives in constant fear because those above him are growing impatient. He will be a dangerous man because he is growing desperate."

"I'll be careful," I promised. "Papa must have known him years ago. He recognized him quickly."

"Your father knew them all. The big ones and the small ones. That's why he did so much damage when he denounced them. No matter what happens, you can be assured your father and mother are two people of great courage."

At the depot, my blindfold was removed and I saw there were other passengers, a dozen or more we saw at a glance, waiting on the platform for the train. Felicia warned me to remain in the carriage while she looked over the prospective passengers. When she returned, she thought everything was safe, but we waited until we heard the train coming in.

Once aboard, I shut myself in my drawing room. I slept well that night because I was exhausted.

I was sorely grieved about Carlo. It was like a death in the family, in a way—the uncle I had thought I knew was gone forever. It would be difficult to see him each day at the salon.

I reached New York, entered the hotel and asked for my room key. It was handed over without a question. In the suite I found my baggage unpacked and everything neatly put away. I used the room telephone to call Suzette, informing her I would see her within the hour.

I found her lovelier than ever and filled with a devotion to Vito that equaled mine for Stan.

"I felt that I would never marry," she confided over our dinner table. "Vito doesn't care a fig about my heritage. He will go back to Italy someday. I shall go with him, Angela. It will break my heart to leave you and the store, but my heartache would be even worse if I was parted from Vito."

"I'm glad," I said. "Nothing could please me more than to have two of the best friends I've ever had fall in love. I've known Vito a long time. He is a fine man with an excellent future. No one could possibly make you happier."

"It's so wonderful," she said, dreamy-eyed as she spoke, "that I will not have to endure living alone the rest of my life. And to have found such a man as Vito. He is teaching me Italian. I know a little already."

Then our conversation turned to business. Suzette was quite confused over this matter of finance which had been deliberately set up without her knowledge. But when we visited the bank that afternoon, everything was soon straightened out, much to her relief.

And so, after inspecting the store and workshop, talking fashions with the clerks and seamstresses, paying brief visits to wholesalers, I was ready to go home the following day. I sent Stan a telegram announcing the time of my arrival and once aboard the train heading South, I looked forward to the reunion with my husband and my daughter. My only regret was that my father and mother could not join us. Not now. Possibly not ever.

TWENTY-ONE

Both Stan and Carlo met me at the depot. When I turned from Stan's loving welcome to face Carlo and accept his kiss, I was quite sure I hadn't let my contempt for his treacherous actions show.

"It was certainly a short trip," Carlo commented.

"Too long for me," Stan said. "If I ever catch up with my work, I'll not let you go off alone again."

"May the day come soon," I said.

"You'll have to drop me off at the courthouse," Stan told me. "The trial is in recess and I do have to get back."

"I have work at the salon," I said. "We'll make up for it when we get home."

After Stan left the carriage at the courthouse, Carlo and I first rode to my home where I had the maid take charge of my luggage while I paid a hasty visit to the nursery, where my daughter slept blissfully. Then Carlo and I drove to the store.

All during the ride Carlo plied me with questions. If I'd not been aware of what a two-faced man he was, I might not have recognized the insinuations in some of his questions. I could see now how he was seeking information he could pass on.

"I can't understand what went wrong in New York that required your personal attention," he said. "Was it with the help, or the stock?"

"It was a banking affair," I explained. "Complicated . . ."

"How could it be complicated? I set up the bookkeeping system at the store so anyone could handle it. In what way was it not correct?"

"It had to do with a transaction between us and the Farris Company."

"Textiles? We've done business with them for years. They quote a price, we accept, they send a bill, we pay it. What's so complicated?"

"Carlo, there was an error. Not in our bookkeeping, but in the manufacturer's and this was compounded by another mistake at the bank. It's all straightened out now."

He shook his head in doubt. "I still don't see why you had to go."

"I'm tired of talking about it," I said. "I went, the affair is now closed, as I said, and that's all there is to it. I'm travel-weary, Uncle."

"Did you see much of Suzette?"

"We had supper one night and we talked business. Also, we were at the bank together."

"Just one night? You were there two."

I looked at him sharply. "Why do you ask so many questions about such an inconsequential thing as what I did with my time?"

"You needn't be so irritable," he replied indignantly. "I was just making talk. What you did was your business, of course. I was interested only because this was not handled in your usual expert manner. Besides, I don't see why I couldn't have been sent."

"Because the bank asked to see me and you know it. What kind of business did you do while I was away?"

"The usual. You weren't gone long enough to need a report on that. Five days."

"Four," I corrected him. It was becoming clear that my trip to New York was regarded with some suspicion by those Carlo reported to and he'd been asked to establish the reason fully. What worried me was that his report would be in the same suspicious vein as his questions, and they might decide to check up on everything I said. While my tracks were well covered, there was always the chance of a slipup and these people were well equipped to ferret it out.

That night I told Stan about the trip, but the details didn't interest him, making Carlo's interest stand out all the more. Stan and I talked until nearly midnight and a dozen times I almost gave away the real purpose of my trip. I wanted to, but I'd given my word to maintain silence.

I'd spent the late afternoon and early evening with Alexa who greeted my return with all the aplomb of her two months, and it was wonderful to find her thriving. Jennie Atkins was doing a marvelous job with the child.

For two or three days I lived in a mild state of apprehension, as if I felt something was going to happen, though nothing did. After a week I settled down to my old routine and I was once again working at my drawing board. Fashions were in a constant state of change. It had always been my ambition and policy to stay a step ahead of the current ones and I had derived a great deal of satisfaction from seeing so many of my creations being worn in New York.

Carlo reported to the store late each morning and remained most of the day. I could not fault him on the job he was doing, but I wasn't always successful at concealing my feelings toward him. I knew I was being curt with him and it might have been that he suspected something. Certainly he had nothing definite to base his suspicions on. During this entire week, except for the day of my arrival, he never came near the house. Prior to that, he seemed to have enjoyed visiting with Alexa, whom he doted on.

I ached to confide in Stan. It broke my heart not to tell him the truth, but there was so much at stake I didn't dare violate the instructions I'd received.

I was at my drawing board twelve days after my return from New York. It was my habit to telephone Jennie at least once every morning and again in the afternoon. I gave my house number to the operator and I heard her ring the phone. I waited a long time, growing nervous after the first two or three minutes. Jennie always expected my call and if she was otherwise occupied, the maid should have answered.

I hung up, thought about calling Stan, but decided I'd

make certain there was need for it first. I called a carriage and was driven directly home. The first thing amiss was the lack of the usual guard near the front door. He was under orders not to leave his post under any circumstances.

The front door was locked and I had to root out the key from the bottom of my handbag. My hands shook so much I had difficulty getting the key into the lock. I threw open the door.

"Jennie!" I called out. "Emily!"

I was greeted with a stunning silence. I felt prickles of fear crawling up my back. I ran into the drawing room. No one was there, and the dining room was similarly empty. So was the kitchen, but on the stove was Alexa's bottle warming in a pan of water. The water had almost all evaporated. I turned off the gas.

I was at the top of the stairs to the second floor when I detected a strange, sweetish odor which I was unable to identify. It grew stronger as I hurried down the hall, calling out to Jennie and Emily with every few steps.

I opened the door to the nursery. The crib was empty, the pink blanket was missing. Now the strange odor grew even more noticeable. By following its growing intensity, I was led to one of the bedrooms well down the hall. There I found Jennie on the floor and Emily thrown across the bed. Their hands were tied behind their backs, their ankles were bound with rope, gags were in place, but there seemed to be little need for them. Beside them lay two thick rags, each soaked in chloroform. I knew then that it was this drug I'd been trying to identify.

I knew what had happened. Alexa was gone. No doubt about that. Jennie and Emily needed my help now and I must notify Stan quickly.

I managed to sever the cords at their wrists and ankles with scissors I got from a bureau drawer. I ran to the bathroom, soaked a towel in cold water and returned to apply it to Jennie's face and then Emily's. They'd evidently been heavily drugged and were slow in recovering consciousness. So I ran downstairs and telephoned Stan's office. He was in court. I instructed his secretary to reach him no matter what she had to do and to tell him Alexa and I needed him desperately. I didn't want this kidnapping to be made public yet. Certainly not without Stan's approval.

Before I returned to Jennie and Emily, I opened the front door and left it that way to expedite Stan's arrival. Jennie was beginning to moan, but Emily's face was ghastly pale and her breathing didn't seem very good. I lifted her onto a chair and pushed this across the room to a window, which I opened wide. I fanned some of the cool air across her face.

After a few more minutes she opened her eyes, at first in terror from something she remembered. Then she recognized me and her body relaxed. Jennie too was waking up. Neither was yet able to talk or even to keep her eyes open for long. I used more cold towels, I brought Jennie close to the window as well, and the fresh air began to work its wonders.

I kept looking out to see if Stan was on his way along the street until I realized there'd not yet been time for him to have been driven all the way from the courthouse.

Jennie recovered her wits first. I gave her a glass of water which she drank with evident appreciation.

"Alexa is gone," I told her. "What happened?"

"I don't know, ma'am. I was sitting beside the crib. Alexa had just awakened. Emily had put her bottle on the stove to heat and I was about to fetch it. When I stepped out of the room, someone seized me. I couldn't see who it was. They pressed a cloth over my face and that's all I remember."

"You were chloroformed," I told her. She looked as if she was about to go into a state of panic. "You're all right now," I assured her. "There are no lasting effects. Can you get up and walk? Can you take care of Emily?"

"I'll try. I don't feel very good, but I'll try."

"Good," I said. "I have to go down to meet my husband. Give Emily some water, tell her she is in no danger."

I left the room and paused in front of the open door to the nursery. When I first entered the room I'd been too

390

excited and upset to look about, but now I did, and I saw the heavy piece of paper propped up against the bureau mirror. There was no message on it, only the imprint of a man's hand—in black ink. The Black Hand had my baby. I knew why. I knew what their demands would be.

I heard the carriage pull up and Stan's running steps ascend the porch stairs. I rushed up to him and he enveloped me in his arms.

"You're shaking," he said. "It happened?"

"She's gone, Stan. Jennie and Emily were chloroformed. The guard wasn't there when I returned. I called Jennie on the telephone and when I received no answer, I hurried home. Alexa is gone, darling. Upstairs is a paper with the imprint of the Black Hand."

Stan led me into the drawing room and helped me sit down on a sofa.

"Now just try to relax," he said. "They may have Alexa, but they won't harm her. That would not be in their interest. They want to exchange her for whatever they'll demand. She must be alive and well cared for, or they defeat their own purpose. Do you understand, darling?"

"I understand only that she is in their hands. They are cruel, inhuman people. You know what they'll demand—the lives of my father and mother. Even then we'd not be certain they'd return Alexa. If they hate me as much as they hate my parents, they'll never allow me the joy of having my baby in my arms again."

"They can't afford to harm her," he insisted.

"Not until after they have exacted their vengeance on my father and mother. After that they won't care about the baby—or me—or you or anyone else. Stan, we have to do something about these people. We can't sit here asking one another questions."

"I'm going to telephone the police station," Stan said. "You'd better see if Jennie and Emily are able to talk. Find out if they recognized anyone."

"Jennie didn't. I'll ask Emily."

I made my way upstairs, not hurriedly this time, but

more as if I carried a heavy weight on my shoulders. I could hear Stan on the phone, issuing orders. It was some small gratification to realize that he would be in charge of this case, trying to get his own daughter back. I had great faith in Stan, far less in myself, and none at all so far as these Black Handers were concerned.

Emily knew nothing. She'd been seized in the kitchen and remembered only being in an anesthesized daze as they carried her upstairs.

"Like I was a sack of potatoes, ma'am. I know there were two men, at least, but I didn't have a look at either one."

I tried to calm her. "I expect the police will be here soon, and they'll ask a great many questions. Don't keep anything back, no matter how trivial it may seem to you. Mr. Talbot is downstairs. I'm going to join him. Both of you had better rest a bit. You don't look very well, either of you."

Stan was finishing his calls when I joined him. I took his hand and led him back into the drawing room. What we'd feared had now taken place. There was no longer any need for secrets. I must have Stan's help and he would require mine. Any vows to maintain secrecy were overcome by the urgency of this situation.

"Darling, I think they took Alexa because they're aware that I have been with Mama and Papa. I swore not to tell anyone, but the time for that is past. I didn't go directly to New York. I was met by a woman who took me to a farmhouse. I don't know if I could find it again. I was blindfolded both coming and going. But . . . they were there. It was wonderful to see them, to know they were alive and well."

"You did actually go to New York though." Stan made it a statement.

"Yes—the following evening. Someone had changed places with me so it would seem that I hadn't left the train. Yes, I did go to New York. I was already checked into the hotel by the woman who took my place."

"I ask only to try and figure out how they knew you'd been with your parents."

"I think Carlo must have guessed. He's a traitor, Stan. When I returned, Carlo asked me many pointed questions. I suppose those who paid him suspected this trip was made too abruptly. Carlo seemed to have his suspicions about it too. When they heard from him, they must have made up their minds that I could, for the first time in my life, tell them where Mama and Papa are hiding.

"If your parents hear of this, they'll come forward. We can't have that, Angela."

"I know. I'll try my best to do what they demand, but take as much time as I can. Darling, is there anything you and the police can do?"

"I can't think of anything right now. Perhaps there are clues. Someone may have seen them. The guard might know something when we find him. But I say again, they'll not harm Alexa because if they do, they've nothing to bargain with.

Before we could talk further, the police arrived, a large number of them. Stan gave them all the information he could. Some of the men went upstairs to talk to Jennie and Emily and to inspect the nursery. Others were dispatched to hunt for the missing guard. A man in uniform with captain's bars on his shoulders was in command.

"I'm terribly sorry this happened," he told us. "We took precautions, but they were not enough. Can you give me any other facts?"

"What of Carlo?" Stan asked me.

"I'm too upset to think properly," I admitted. "Carlo Guillermo is my uncle. He works at my store. We believe he has been working for the Black Hand. Perhaps he could be induced to tell you something."

"Induced will be the word for it," the Captain said grimly.

"He's not to be hurt," Stan ordered. "Darling, this is Captain Burke. He was only letting off steam. Carlo will be arrested, but he won't be harmed. Though I'll put him in prison if we prove he has been a member of this Black Hand."

"He's my uncle," I said. "He's not a strong person in character. I think what he did was under the threat of

393

death if he refused to comply and you know how many times they beat him nearly to death."

"I'll see he's well cared for," Captain Burke assured me.

I said, "Captain, there are certain reasons why we don't want this made public yet."

"We want to hear from the kidnappers first," Stan added.

"The reporters are already at the police station. Someone told them. They'll be here any minute. It's hard to keep this kind of news out of the papers."

"Thank you," Stan said. "We'll do the best we can with them."

The Captain hurried away. Stan looked at me and gestured hopelessly. "They want it in the newspapers so your father and mother are bound to hear of it quickly."

"Stan, they'll come. I know them. They'll give themselves up to spare Alexa. What can we do? Where do we turn?"

"I have no answers yet," he said. "We've got to keep our heads. Remember, we've an entire police force working on this. Criminals leave clues."

"The Black Hand," I said, "leaves nothing. Have you ever convicted any member of that hellish crew?"

"No, I have not. Not directly. Many have gone to prison for some crime, though we couldn't connect it with the Black Hand or the Mafia. Whatever you want to call it."

"Meanwhile our baby is in their hands."

"Yes. When do you think your father will hear the news?"

"That's not easy to say. They live in a very isolated place and send to town for supplies, but not daily. Perhaps not even very often."

"Could you reach them?"

"When I was taken there I was blindfolded. When I left, I was again prevented from seeing the route over which I traveled. I know now how essential that was. If I returned to the town and the depot, I'd have no idea in which direction to turn."

Stan was holding his anger and frustration in check.

His immediate concern was for me. "Can you stand up to this, Angela? It may take some time, you understand."

"I know. I also know how helpless you are. It will be up to Papa and . . . the Black Hand."

"Perhaps we can get Carlo to help," Stan said. "After all, Alexa is the daughter of his niece."

"You'd be wasting your time. They will have told Carlo only what was absolutely necessary for him to know. Papa explained many of their tricks and procedures. They are extremely cautious people and the leaders are— Stan . . . there is one thing. In the excitement I forgot. It may be the very thing we need."

"What is it? Anything may help."

"The man who is in charge of all Black Hand activities in this state and perhaps others . . . is Pietro Liggio."

Stan didn't look surprised. "We've suspected that, but without a particle of proof."

"We haven't any now. If you arrest him, there won't be a single thing to connect him with the Black Hand. Except the evidence of my father."

"Then we'll use that."

"To do so you'd have to bring Papa into the open and they'll kill him before he could tell anything." I was frowning deeply and considering an idea that just come to me.

"We may have to take that chance," Stan said.

"Perhaps," I said slowly, "the stories in the newspapers may help us after all."

"What's on your mind?" he asked.

"I don't even dare express it. We have to wait, Stan. You said so yourself. There is nothing we can do at the moment, but I'm getting an idea. If it is to work, the beginning of it will have to generate somewhere else because I can't start it without arousing suspicion. Bear with me. It's so nebulous an idea I can't even express it yet. The moment I can, you'll know."

"If that's how you want it to be. I've every confidence in you, Angela. I only wish my hands were not so tied."

"If this is to happen, it will begin soon," I said.

He didn't press me for any more information. I must

have been much like Papa, because I didn't dare reveal what I had in mind to a living soul for fear there might be a slip. And my idea was so desperate a one Stan might not have approved. It wouldn't have taken much to make me abandon it.

TWENTY-TWO

It was a sleepless night. I spent some of the hours in the nursery where I could shed my tears in private. Stan respected my sorrow and made no futile attempts to cheer me up. Sitting alone by that empty crib, I studied the magic ring. Papa had said it was not magic, that it was possessed of no powers whatsoever. Yet I brought it to my lips as I prayed silently. I'd done this before. True, the way had been prepared for my prayers to be answered, not by magic or heavenly consideration, but by man-made devices put into motion when the ring was seen. And yet . . . I'd had confidence in it. Blind confidence, to be sure, but there were times when I thought it had brought about something of value which had not been prepared for me.

Whether it was by this unique magic I'd assigned to the ring, or the quiet of this room and the memory it contained for me, the plan I had in mind began to take shape.

I was able to go quietly to bed where Stan lay wide awake. The nearness of him gave me more confidence and I was without fear for the first time since I'd discovered Alexa had been kidnapped.

In the morning it all began again, this time with the arrival of reporters from the *Picayune*, which carried the story in scare headlines. Captain Burke came by to inform us that the missing guard had been found shot to death in a wooded area five miles from our house. His other news struck even closer to me.

"Your uncle," Captain Burke reported, "this man Carlo, he's gone. He lit out yesterday and he took with him as much as he could carry. Drew all his money out of the bank. He bought a railroad ticket for New York, but I

397

don't think he'll go there. Your uncle, Mrs. Talbot, will be running for the rest of his life, if I'm correct."

"Quite likely you are, Captain. Thank you."

"So that source of information is gone. We have notified police all along the route north to be on the lookout for him, but if I guess right, he'll get off that train where there isn't a depot for miles. Even if he breaks his fool neck doing it."

There was nothing else to report. A heavy guard had been placed around my store, every source of possible information was being used, but the results were not promising.

Stan, who'd explained the urgency of going to the office, was to question two men who'd been arrested in the forlorn hope they might know something about the Black Hand.

I kissed him and prepared to send him off. "Stan, one thing you must promise me not to do. Don't begin any action or any investigation against Pietro Liggio."

"I was thinking of asking him if he could help, hoping if he controlled the situation, he might relent."

"Darling, if he sent Alexa back to us just because we asked him to, he'd be dead by nightfall. Please, don't go near him or mention his name to anyone."

"If that is your wish. You've got something stirring in your mind."

"Yes. But don't ask me about it."

Stan's arms enclosed me and drew me close.

"Very well—for now I'll not press you to confide in me. But for God's sake be careful."

"I promise."

Moments after Stan's departure, his mother arrived, in tears.

I put my arm around her waist. "I'm sure you've not even eaten. Please have coffee and a croissant with me. We have to be calm. If we lose our heads, we may lose Alexa."

"Please don't say that, Angela. Is there anything I can do to help? Of course they'll want a great deal of money. They're welcome to all I have."

"It's not money they'll demand," I said, "but something of far graver importance. I hope I can explain everything soon."

"Why must you make it seem so mysterious, Angela? Don't you trust me? Isn't this a simple case of kidnapping for money?"

"No," I said. "More than that. I will need your help, I'm sure, so please plan to stay with me for some time."

"Angela, you know I'll stay here forever if that's necessary. Just tell me what to do."

"For now, have coffee and croissants with me," I said.

The morning went by somehow. I telephoned the salon and asked Alice Keane to take over the operation, explaining that Carlo had been called away and would likely not return to his job for some time.

Mrs. Talbot and I attempted to eat something early in the afternoon, but our nerves were too on edge. Nothing had happened. I didn't hear from Stan. I didn't hear from the police. No message came from the kidnappers.

I realized how confused Mrs. Talbot must have been. I talked of things not even remotely concerned with the kidnapping. Anything, everything, just to get through the endless hours until Mrs. Liggio arrived, as I hoped she would. Unless her husband forbade her to console me, and I doubted he'd find any reason that would satisfy her.

It was mid-afternoon when she was ushered into the drawing room by Emily, who withdrew promptly. Little Amorita was with her mother and Mrs. Liggio's tear-stained face showed me how great was her sorrow over what had happened. Amorita, of course, didn't know that anything was amiss.

"My heart is broken," Mrs. Liggio said. "That such an awful thing could happen to you. Such a nice person as you." And then she told me, indirectly, what I'd been hoping to learn. "I have often worried this might happen to me and . . . to her." She indicated Amorita who was quietly seated across the room.

I knew now, even more surely, that Mrs. Liggio had no knowledge of her husband's connection with the band of outlaws who had stolen my child. If she had known she'd not be here now, expressing her genuine sorrow.

399

"We are supposed to be a civilized society," Clare said. "That such a thing could happen is almost beyond my comprehension."

"It happens more often than you think," I said. "Isn't that so, Laurari?"

"*Si*—it happens," she nodded. "Oh yes, I have heard of this before, many times in Italy I heard of it as well."

I said, "Laurari, I'm glad you came."

"How could I stay away?" she asked. "At a time like this."

"Does your husband know you are visiting me?"

"What does he know? The last two days he has not been at home very much. I don't have to ask his permission to go and see my good friend who has suffered this tragedy."

"I appreciate your friendship," I began cautiously. "I intend to put it to a very severe test."

She looked at me inquisitively. "You know, Angela, I will do anything."

I glanced at Mrs. Talbot. "Would you feel insulted if Laurari and I spoke in Italian?"

"Certainly not." She was puzzled, though.

"It will be easier for me to say what I must say if I speak in our native tongue. Afterwards, I'll tell you what we talked about."

"That isn't necessary."

"It will be, for you will be very important in what I intend for you."

I turned back to Laurari. I thought I could possibly make myself better understood in Italian. Besides, Amorita wouldn't be able to follow the rapid conversation we'd have after Laurari grew as excited as I knew she would.

"I do not understand," she said to me. "Have I done something?"

"No indeed," I assured her. "But I am going to ask something of you that is going to break your heart. You know how dearly I love my baby."

"*Si*, of course I do. As dearly as I love mine."

"Laurari, it pains me to bring you into this, but there is no other way. You can help me save the life of Alexa."

Her chin jutted out. "You ask. I will do. Anything!"

400

"Your husband is responsible for Alexa being kidnapped."

The jutted chin dropped. "What is this?" she asked, her tone suddenly cold and indignant. "My husband? A kidnapper?"

"Not personally," I explained. "But he is head of the Black Hand."

"I cannot understand what you are saying, Angela. Pietro . . . what has he to do with the Black Hand? This I cannot believe. He loves me. Our daughter. He is good to us."

"Laurari, I know. But I speak the truth. My father recognized him from a photograph."

"A picture of Pietro? You must be mistaken. There are no pictures."

"I took it that day he opened the camera and ruined the film."

"You have just said he ruined the film. How could there be a picture?"

"I had two cameras. I had his photograph on the film in the second one. You see, Laurari, while you have been one of my best friends, I've been compelled to do these things behind your back, even though it was painful to me."

She had moved to the edge of her chair and sat stiffly, defiantly. "You will please explain this to me."

"The Mafia, the Black Hand, wish to kill my father and mother who have been in hiding for years. They have kidnapped Alexa to force my parents to surrender to them. It is a long story that began many years ago in Rome and Florence. There is no time to give you the details."

"You are telling me my Pietro is an evil man? Is that what you are trying to say?"

"I'm afraid it is."

"I say it cannot be."

"But it's true, Laurari. I can prove it if necessary. You see, I'm left with the choice of having my parents murdered or having my baby killed. And your husband, your Pietro, is the head of the Black Hand here in New Orleans and is behind all of it."

She said nothing for a long time, sitting there staring into space. Clare Talbot, completely mystified, remained silent. Amorita, with no understanding of what went on, was growing restless. She left her chair and ran over to her mother. That was what broke Laurari's silence.

"For a long time," Laurari said, "I have wondered about him. His excuses for being away were lies, but if they were, it was not for me to question him. I have asked him nothing. I have closed my eyes to whatever it is that keeps him busy and supplies him with much money. That sends men I do not care to be around to my home for long talks with Pietro. Oh yes, I have wondered, and now you tell me what he is. A monster!"

"I didn't say that," I said quickly. "He does what they require of him because if he doesn't, someone else will. And Pietro will die. I know this, for my father was once a part of them. Someday I will explain."

"And what has this to do with me? Are you telling me this because you hate Pietro so that you wish to make it known to me what he is?"

"No, Laurari. If my baby's life, if my parents' safety, were not at stake, I would never have mentioned this to you. How Pietro became associated with this band of murderers and kidnappers I don't know. But he is now a member and he is sworn to absolute silence. He cannot confide in you, though perhaps he wished to many times. I know how much he cares for you and how greatly he loves Amorita."

"What do you wish of me then?"

"As the most important man in this region, Pietro holds the lives of Alexa and my parents in his hands. I know if he betrays those above him, he will be in danger, as my father and mother have been for twenty years. Twenty years, Laurari! That's how long they have pursued them and even now, after all this time, they must kill them."

"It is hard for me to understand everything."

"It's a wonder you make any sense of it," I said. "This is a situation that seems impossible—that cannot happen —but it has. Pietro could set my baby free, but he will not unless . . ."

"Do you think he will listen to me? If he is what you say he is, how can I ask him to do this?"

Now was the moment I dreaded. She would either see the logic of what I was about to suggest or she would have nothing to do with it. Her sympathy for a baby had to be stronger than her love—and fear—of her husband. Had I been in her position, I didn't know what I would have done, but lives depended on which way she would turn.

I continued to press her. "Laurari, Pietro will listen to no one. He can't! He is under orders. But if he is responsible for the death of anyone, he will have to pay the penalty for it—and my husband will see that he does."

"You must not threaten me," she said. "It is not the way of friends."

"I am not threatening. What I have in mind may set your husband free. I want you to agree to be kidnapped, with Amorita. I want you to write a note to Pietro telling him if my baby is killed, if my parents are harmed, you and Amorita will vanish and never be heard of again."

She stared at me as if she couldn't believe the words I'd spoken. "You ask me to do this? I will betray my husband? Do you understand that I love him? He is the father of my child. I adore him as he adores me, and our daughter. You are a devil, Angela. A black devil. As black a devil as those who make up the Black Hand."

"Your husband is head of the Black Hand," I said. "When you speak of a devil, think of that. They gave me a choice between my parents and my daughter. Now I give you one—if your husband allows murder to be done, he will hang for it. That is a threat! I have to make it! Yet you are my friend and I wish no harm to come to you or your husband. This is the only way out he has left."

"You say if he does not obey these . . . these people . . . they will kill him? If he does obey, your husband will kill him. Do you call that a choice?"

"If I go to your husband—alone—and no one in this world will ever find out what we did—he will set Alexa free even if he has to disappear. As my father and mother did. For he is the kind of man who will come to realize what it is like when he is the father of a girl whose life

403

he can save. And the husband of a woman he loves and whose life he will believe depends on what he does. As a kidnapper, he will be caught in a web he has created, and this time it will close around him. If he is an evil man, then you would never go back to him. I know you too well for that. You would never allow him to see Amorita again. I know that too. But you can save his life if you have trust in his goodness."

"I will have nothing to do with this," she said brusquely. "I don't think you are telling me the truth."

"Laurari, my baby is in the hands of men who will kill her as casually as if she were . . . nothing. Do you think your husband will be part of that?"

"You say he is. What kind of crazy talk is that?"

"I say he is part of it because he can't help himself. He is in as much danger as my baby and my parents. Perhaps he doesn't know what is going on, but he is head of those who have stolen my daughter, those who threaten her life. I prefer to think he is over his head in this business and he cannot get out. I will give him an urgent incentive to get out. Don't you see? He cannot allow anything to happen to you or Amorita. As his punishment, he will have to hide—and so will you."

"Hide? Where could he hide if these people are as powerful as you say they are?"

"My father and mother did. We have means of concealing your whereabouts. We live in the hope this organization will be destroyed before long. Then you can be free again. But it is better to stay hidden than to be executed for murder."

"You wish me to pretend I am kidnapped, with Amorita. You ask this of me. Do you have no heart, Angela? Have I been mistaken in my great regard for you?"

"I am a mother, like you. My baby is in the hands of murderers. Yours is not. If your husband can do nothing to set Alexa free, do you think I will make you responsible for that? We are both mothers, each with a child we love. I will not let anything happen to Alexa without a fight, and I care little who will be destroyed because of what I do. Except you. We are friends. That is why I ask this of you. It is the only way for both of us."

"You must give me time to think . . ."

"There is no time. Every passing moment increases the danger to my baby. And when my parents hear what has happened, they will come out of hiding and they will be murdered."

"Pietro will look for me."

"He will, but he won't find you."

"With these men to hunt, you think he will not?"

"You and Amorita will be with Stan's mother. They will never guess that she is harboring you or being a party to what we must call another kidnapping. I will go to Pietro alone. I will tell him my offer. I will show him proof you are being held by us. If he loves you, he will see to it that you are set free by ordering Alexa returned to us."

"And then . . . we live in danger?"

"That's the penalty he will have to pay, and do not tell me it is too much. My father and mother endured it most of my lifetime. But they are alive and I am alive."

"You give me no choice, Angela. But I must be sure."

"He is the head of the Black Hand," I reiterated. "I can prove it, but there isn't time for that now. You must take my word."

"Will she agree?" Laurari gestured toward Stan's mother, who looked more puzzled than ever.

"If you say you will do this, she must. She is helping to save the life of her grandchild."

"If I go to Pietro, perhaps—"

"No! He won't listen. He will be too frightened to listen. But if he believes you and Amorita are in danger he will do as I say."

"Ask her," Laurari said.

I turned to Stan's mother and I spoke rapidly but quietly, and somewhat to my surprise she showed no tendency to hysterics. I thought that all of Stan's determination and courage didn't come from his father alone.

A carriage pulled up after dark. Laurari and Amorita, sleepy and bundled up, were hurried out of the house, entered the closed carriage, and drove away. Now it was up to me.

Stan telephoned that he'd be very late. They had

rounded up some men they suspected were part of the Black Hand and were questioning them intensely.

I cautioned Jennie and Emily not to open the door for anyone except Stan and if he returned, to tell him I would be home soon. Then I was driven to the Liggio estate.

I'd been there so many times the man guarding the gate knew me well. He passed me through without argument or even notifying the house I was on the way. However, I thought he'd do that before I reached the front door.

Apparently he did, for it was Pietro himself who greeted me and I could see how worried he was.

"Laurari and Amorita are not with you?" he asked. "I thought you were bringing them home."

"We will go inside and talk," I said.

"What is this? What do you mean? Talk about what?"

"About the Black Hand, about my baby—about your daughter and your wife."

"You must be crazy . . . you make no sense to me."

"Pietro," I said, "you were afraid to have your picture taken that day I was here. But I took it and my father recognized you. You know who my father is. Now my baby has been taken, a Black Hand symbol left behind. So if my parents hear of it they will give up—and be killed. Perhaps they will kill my baby too. If they do, you will never see Laurari or Amorita again."

He was ushering me into the drawing room as I talked. I sat down and opened my handbag. I took from it a scarf which Amorita had worn and a rosary of engraved beads, unusual and rare. I placed these on the table between us.

"You need evidence that I am telling you the truth. You and your entire organization will never find Laurari or Amorita. For one thing, they do not wish to be found. I have a note from Laurari. I'll read it to you."

He sat with his eyes closed, like a man who had lived in terror of this moment, and now that it was here, his life seemed to have all but stopped.

I read the contents of the note. "My dear and loving husband. What Angela tells you is the truth. I at last know what you are and what you have been. Yet I would spend the rest of my life with you, unless you murder Angela's

406

baby or her father and mother. If this happens, Amorita's life and mine will also be taken. This I know. Listen to Angela. Do as she says. Save my life. Save that of our daughter—and your own, if you believe it is worth saving. I swear that I love you still, and I will go away with you no matter what hardships we must endure."

He looked at me with the eyes of a doomed man.

I placed the note on the table. "She signs it 'Your loving wife.' What is it to be, Pietro?"

"You could not do this," he said. "It is not in you to do such a thing."

I said, "Pietro, surely you know that the Mafia—the Black Hand—has enemies dedicated to its destruction. It is they who have Amorita and Laurari. They have struck back at your kind before, an eye for an eye. I assure you they are very capable of this, though as you say, I might not be. They will not wait."

"How long?" he asked.

I almost cried out in relief, for he was convinced I told him the truth.

"Why do you ask?"

"I need time. A little time."

"If they kill . . ."

"They will not. I know how your father and mother have lived."

"For twenty years," I reminded him.

"Yes, for twenty years. Protected by this committee— that's what we call them—of influential men. Do I have that same protection?"

"You will have. I promise."

"For Laurari and Amorita as well?"

"For them too. Think well about this, Pietro. Laurari is my friend. I love your daughter, and I would hate myself to my dying day if anything happened to them. But my daughter's life is also in peril. My father and mother will be killed. I too have a hard choice, but my mind was made up before I came here."

"There are men in this house . . . on the estate . . . they must not know."

"I will do nothing to give them any cause to be sus-

407

picious. You might even leave with me. Tell them you are meeting Laurari at my store. Any excuse you like."

"I will go alone," he said. "You will please leave now. Be patient. I will do what I can."

"You will set my baby free and you will not destroy my parents," I said. "For if you do, there will be destruction on both sides."

I rose and walked with him to the door. As we neared it, the big man who was supposed to be Amorita's tutor came down the stairs, yawning and rubbing his eyes. Clearly he'd been asleep.

"I will see you then," Pietro said in a surprisingly firm voice. "Tell Laurari that I will join all of you at once. It is a terrrible thing, this kidnapping. Of course I will do whatever I can."

"I'll see you in about an hour?" I asked. He knew what I meant.

"Yes. I will be there."

I said, "Thank you."

The big man gave me a smile as he opened the door for me. Perhaps he was too sleepy to suspect anything, or he trusted me as a good friend of the family, asking for help. I reached my waiting carriage and my heart didn't beat normally until we were clear of the gate.

Stan was waiting for me, restless and beside himself with worry. I sat with him in our drawing room and told him exactly what I had done, while he listened in amazement.

"Did Pietro admit what you accused him of?"

"He didn't have to, darling. He knew I wasn't lying."

"Amorita and Laurari are hiding in my mother's house?"

"Well taken care of, I would say."

"You know he's bound to have a search made for them."

"No, he will not. Ever since Papa identified him as head of the Black Hand here, I have come to believe that if he had a strong reason for quitting the Black Hand, he'd take advantage of it. He is too devoted to his wife and daughter. He is convinced that if he sends Alexa back to us safely and my parents are not harmed, no danger will come to

408

those he loves. Otherwise Laurari and Amorita will die. It is a stalemate that he must break."

"I wish you'd come to me . . ."

"There wasn't time. This had to be done at once, so tomorrow's papers will carry the story that Alexa is free. Otherwise Papa and Mama may come straight here and Pietro may not be able to control those he leads and they will murder."

"At least you did something. I haven't been able to. There was not one thing we could do, with all the police and everyone else trying to help us. I admitted to defeat and I hated to have to tell you."

"We will sit here and wait. That's all we can do. It may take some time, but I don't think so. Pietro cannot afford to waste a moment. If he sets Alexa free, we will send Laurari to him, and Amorita. They will live as my father and mother had to live—and still do. But Pietro and Laurari will be together with their daughter, which is more than I was granted." I moved over to the sofa where he sat.

"Hold me, darling. Tightly, or I'll begin to shake. I'm afraid. I think everything will work, but I'm not sure and it does not . . ."

His arms tightened around me. "It will, Angela."

I raised my hand so I might brush my lips against the ring. It was the only thing I could do. Perhaps there was a kind of magic there. At this moment, I needed it.

Two hours went by and the tension grew more and more severe until I felt I could no longer stand it. Stan did his best to console me and lend what encouragement he could, but I knew he was as distraught as I.

"What's keeping him?" I asked. "He couldn't afford to waste any time."

Stan's trips to the window threatened to wear out the carpets. Upstairs Emily and Jennie waited and I could also imagine their impatience. Once I broke the monotony by going up to the nursery and standing at the crib to pray. And to doubt myself. To wonder if I'd done the proper thing. It was all dependent on my judgment of a man. If Pietro was as heartless as the men who worked under him, and more particularly those above him, then my plan would end in disaster.

I heard a carriage stop in front of the house and I rushed to the window to look out onto the street. A man—no, it looked more like a boy—was walking casually toward our door.

I went downstairs as quickly as I could to find Stan at the door taking a large, thick envelope from the young man, who was explaining that he had been paid to deliver the envelope and even been provided with a hired carriage.

Stan asked the obvious question. "Where did this man meet you and what did he look like?"

"On Rampart Street," the boy replied. "I couldn't see him very well. It was awful dark there. He said I should hurry."

Stan gave him money and shut the door on the boy's thanks. He turned around, holding the envelope.

"It's addressed to you," he said. He handed it to me.

I hurried into the drawing room where the light was better. I pulled apart the envelope flap. Inside was another sealed envelope with a note inside. It was brief and to the point.

"I am to deliver the envelope to Laurari after I am satisfied Pietro has met his end of the bargain. He tells me the sealed envelope for his wife contains money and directions as to how to meet him. I must not invade the privacy of the message to her because, from now on, Pietro will have to live in the same exile as Mama and Papa, and even I must not know where Laurari will go to meet him."

"That means Alexa is free," Stan said with an enthusiasm I shared, though so far we'd had no idea whether Pietro had kept his word.

Our rapture over my success quickly dulled—until Stan went to answer the telephone. He spoke briefly, hung up and returned to me. He took me in his arms.

"That was Police Headquarters. Alexa was delivered to the police station a few minutes ago, left on the steps by an unidentified man who escaped. They are bringing our baby here now."

I went straight to the front door, threw it wide and

410

stepped onto the porch to await the return of my baby. There were no tears, there was no satisfaction in what I had done, only the knowledge that I had succeeded. Stan quietly joined me.

A late-working vendor wheeled his handcart by, looked up and cried out his wares.

I said, "Stan, get some berries for tomorrow."

Stan called down to the vendor and hurried to the side of the cart. Things were back to normal. Some distance down the street I saw a carriage approaching at top speed. Someone in that carriage would be cradling Alexa in his strong arms and soon now she'd be in mine.

As directed, I personally delivered Pietro's sealed envelope to Laurari.

She read the instructions and then asked permission to burn them in the kitchen stove. She said good-bye to me, formally and without shedding a tear. Amorita slept soundly as Laurari went down to the waiting carriage. Only she knew her destination and how she would eventually join her husband.

"I feel sorry for her," Clare Talbot said. "She talked to me about Pietro and about you. She bears you no hatred, Angela. She knows what you did was best for her and for Pietro. She asked me to tell you this. I don't think she could have told you herself."

"Thank you," I said.

"Alexa is well, not harmed?"

"She was taken care of properly. She was not injured in any way. I'll go back to her now." I impulsively embraced Clare. "Thank you. I couldn't have accomplished this without your help. I'll never forget."

"Thank you, darling daughter, for accepting me when I acted so rudely at our first meeting. I'll be around tomorrow to see Alexa."

I had the pleasure of watching Alexa fall asleep in her own crib, safe once more. Then I went downstairs to join Stan, who had two glasses of brandy waiting.

"Tomorrow," he said, "the *Picayune* will have headlines about Alexa being returned by persons unknown. The papers will be sent into the countryside as early as possible

411

so your father and mother may read of Alexa's kidnapping and the happy outcome at the same time. What will happen to them now?"

"They will stay where they are. It must be considered a safe place. I don't know when they'll be able to come home."

"It won't be too long," Stan promised. "We've been making some headway in identifying members of the Black Hand, and with Pietro no longer here to lead them, I'm sure they'll be broken up and we'll keep them that way. I predict your father and mother will be able to return and live openly before very long."

"At least," I said, "they're safe and we have our daughter back. I'm sorry for Laurari. I wish it hadn't had to happen that way."

"For Pietro it isn't too harsh a punishment," Stan said. "Not for what he did. Now it's up to us to try and forget this and learn how to live normally again."

I nodded happily. "It's almost time for the season to change and I've some fine ideas for women's clothing that are going to shock a few people. You see, darling, I am back to normal."

Stan's prediction was too optimistic, it turned out. Mama and Papa did not come to us and live openly. The Black Hand was demoralized as an organization, wrecked beyond repair, thanks to Stan's unflagging work in bringing its members to justice. But the Mafia only retreated—and waited. We still fought them and always would, but they were dangerous enough that Papa and Mama had to live apart from the rest of the world.

So did Laurari and Pietro. We never heard from them again. Vito and Suzette were married and went off to Italy. I receive letters from her. She is learning Italian, is going to have a baby and she is happier than she has ever been.

Carlo was traced as far as Philadelphia, but there he vanished. I often wonder if he is still alive in some remote place in the world. Or did those murderers who compelled him to do their bidding finally catch up with him? I hope he lives, though I can never forgive him for his treachery.

Now I could dream the designs I meant to share with

412

women all over the world, watch my creations take shape and either fall by the wayside or become popular. It was an exciting gamble. The female mind was unpredictable.

Most of all, I could watch my daughter grow into a young woman, without fear, without undergoing any of the terrors I'd had to endure. And there was Stan, to make my happiness complete.

THE BEST OF THE BESTSELLERS
FROM WARNER BOOKS!

DAUGHTERS OF THE WILD COUNTRY   (82-583, $2.25)
by Aola Vandergriff
THE DAUGHTERS OF THE SOUTHWIND travel northward to the wild country of Russian Alaska, where nature is raw, men are rough, and love, when it comes, shines like a gold nugget in the cold Alaskan waters. A lusty sequel to a giant bestseller.

THE FRENCH ATLANTIC AFFAIR   (81-562, $2.50)
by Ernest Lehman
In mid-ocean, the S.S. Marseille is taken over! The conspirators —174 of them—are unidentifiable among the other passengers. Unless a ransom of 35 million dollars in gold is paid within 48 hours, the ship and everyone on it will be blown skyhigh!

DARE TO LOVE by Jennifer Wilde   (81-826, $2.50)
Who dared to love Elena Lopez? Who was willing to risk reputation and wealth to win the Spanish dancer who was the scandal of Europe? Kings, princes, great composers and writers . . . the famous and wealthy men of the 19th century vied for her affection, fought duels for her.

THE OTHER SIDE OF THE MOUNTAIN:
PART 2 by E.G. Valens   (82-463, $2.25)
Part 2 of the inspirational story of a young Olympic contender's courageous climb from paralysis and total helplessness to a useful life and meaningful marriage. An NBC-TV movie and serialized in **Family Circle** magazine.

THE KINGDOM by Ronald Joseph   (81-467, $2.25)
The saga of a passionate and powerful family who carves out of the wilderness the largest cattle ranch in the world. Filled with both adventure and romance, hard-bitten empire building and tender moments of intimate love, **The Kingdom** is a book for all readers.

THE GREEK TYCOON by Eileen Lottman   (82-712, $2.25)
The story of a romance that fascinated the world—between the mightiest magnate on earth and the woman he loved . . . the woman who would become the widow of the President of the United States.

THE BEST OF THE BESTSELLERS FROM WARNER BOOKS!

FISHBAIT: MEMOIRS OF THE CONGRESSIONAL DOORKEEPER by William "Fishbait" Miller   (81-637, $2.25)
Fishbait rattles every skeleton in Washington's closets. Non-stop stories, scandal, and gossip from Capitol Hill, with 32 pages of photographs.

THE WINTER HEART by Frances Casey Kerns   (81-431, $2.50)
Like "The Thorn Birds," THE WINTER HEART is centered upon a forbidden love. It is the saga of two Colorado families—of the men who must answer the conflicting claims of ambition and love and of the women who must show them the way.

THE TUESDAY BLADE by Bob Ottum   (81-362, $2.50)
Gloria-Ann Cooper, fresh from Greer County, Oklahoma, hits the streets of New York City and discovers a world of pain and madness where she is picked up, drugged, raped, and passed around for sex like a rag doll. Then Gloria-Ann gets even.

SAVAGE IN SILK by Donna Comeaux Zide   (82-702, $2.25)
Born of violence, surrendered to the lust of evil men, forced to travel and suffer the world over, Mariah's only sanctuary lay in the love of one man. And nothing—neither distance nor war nor the danger of a wild continent—would keep her from him!

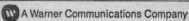 A Warner Communications Company

Please send me the books I have selected.

Enclose check or money order only, no cash please. Plus 50¢ per copy to cover postage and handling. N.Y. State residents add applicable sales tax.

Please allow 2 weeks for delivery.

WARNER BOOKS
P.O. Box 690
New York, N.Y. 10019

Name ....
Address ....
City .... State .... Zip ....
_____ Please send me your free mail order catalog